THE INVENTOR'S TOMB

A SEAN WYATT ARCHAEOLOGICAL THRILLER

ERNEST DEMPSEY

PROLOGUE

ALEXANDRIA, EGYPT | 43 BC

"Where do you think you're going?" A guard in shining Greek armor scowled with the question. He held a bronze spear in one hand, gripping it with a powerful fist. The base rested on the ground, keeping the weapon upright and ready.

Not that she was afraid he'd use it, though given the circumstances and her position, she probably should have always been wary of a potential assassination attempt.

"Wherever I want," she answered. She faced forward toward the gaping doorway, only slightly twisting her head toward the muscular warrior. She allowed a hint of playfulness to soften the stern expression written in stone on her face. "I am queen, after all. Am I not?"

The guard had been her protector long enough to know that she was toying with him. Even he could take a joke.

"If you would like to go with me, Theon, you may. But only you."

He frowned at the request. Normally, she wasn't allowed outside her own bedroom without two guards with her.

Her statement caused Theon to look across the palace corridor at his partner for the night.

The other guard shrugged, as if unsure what to say or do.

"You two can decide what you want to do. But I am leaving."

She started walking again. Her unusual drab, olive green robes flowed behind her, the bottom of the tail dragging along on the stone tile floor. She looked as though dressed as a commoner.

Theon shrugged at the other guy, motioned for him to stay there, and hurried after her.

"My queen, you—"

"I know, Theon," she drawled, cutting him off. "I am not supposed to be out at night. It isn't safe. We've been over this a hundred times. This is an urgent matter."

"Urgent?" Theon said. He looked around through the openings in the walls that allowed air to pass through, creating pleasant drafts in what would otherwise be a hot palace.

She took a breath and sighed, shaking her head.

"What could be so urgent that you risk your life to—"

"We are in my palace. Are we not?"

"Yes, but—"

"We have an entire garrison here protecting the fortress. Yes?"

"Yes, my queen."

He saw her point. But the instincts of a soldier, forged first by habits, then by training, and eventually the crucible of combat, were nearly impossible to break.

It didn't help that these were uncertain times, though she had no misgivings about any point in her life having a high degree of certainty. Sure, she had reign over a vast and still-powerful kingdom, but her own power and standing were far from secure.

Roman politics and military interest heavily influenced her kingdom. While not purely a vassal state to Rome, Egypt was heavily entwined with their politics, and it felt more and more as though they were subservient to the growing empire.

When she became co-regent with her brother, Rome was already deeply involved with Egyptian affairs. Egypt owed significant debts to the Roman Empire, which had a vested interest in ensuring the stability and the cooperation of her dynasty due to Egypt's role as a major grain supplier.

Things got even more complicated when she'd become romantically involved with one of Rome's most powerful figures—Julius Caesar.

The relationship had—conveniently at the time—bolstered her own position and power but had further entangled Egypt in Roman politics and conflicts.

Her latest affair hadn't changed that much, though she hoped if her lover's side came out the victor in all this, her kingdom would not only be restored to its former glory, but she would become queen of the Roman Empire.

She wasn't simply using Mark for his potential political gain, she genuinely cared for him and hoped on a very personal level that he came out on top. She believed that he was the best man to lead Rome into the future, and if there was anything she could do to help, she would.

That was the primary reason behind her late-night errand.

"I apologize, my queen," Theon offered as they proceeded between two guards standing under blazing braziers, one on either side. When they were out of earshot, he continued. "But where are we going at this hour?"

She knew how it probably looked to him. He must have figured she was sneaking out of her palace to meet a lover, but Mark wasn't in Alexandria at the moment, and he would have come here, anyway.

Theon had seen the Roman general many times, even broken bread with him on a few occasions.

Mark Antony had been kind, but there was an intensity to the man that was undeniable. He bore a charisma unlike anything Theon had ever encountered. It was easy to understand why so many people rallied to his cause, and why Queen Cleopatra loved him.

Even so, her relationship and alliance with him was viewed as a threat by Octavian, the man bent on total control of the empire, and the destruction of Antony.

She continued walking in silence for several strides before answering. "We are meeting one of the most important people in the world, Theon."

The answer silenced the guard, tripping him over any questions that may have fluttered into his mind.

Cleopatra knew her statement must have sounded like embellishment. But it was the truth. And the man meeting them this evening could not only turn the tide of the war in Rome but could alter the fate of the entire planet.

Theon realized she wasn't going to give him more than the curt answer he'd received, and so he followed alongside her through the palace corridor.

They reached an intersection where the only options were to go right or left. She veered to the right, her stride purposeful. Based on her body language and her gait, Theon realized this was not some whimsical, random meeting she was going to. She'd planned this, and knew exactly where she was going.

They wound their way through the palace until they arrived at the royal stables. The paddock was an impressive building, built from the same stone blocks as the rest of the palace. Each stall was built with high, swooping arches, and blocked with heavy wooden doors.

These animals had it better than many people around the known world.

A stable boy stood near the outer gate. He held the reins to a majestic white-and-brown horse.

"Are you going for a ride?" Theon asked. He was beginning to like this whole idea less and less. On top of that discomfort was the fact he didn't have a horse waiting for him.

She stopped next to her steed and took the reins from the young man. She thanked him, and he bowed low before stepping aside.

Cleopatra looked up at Theon with a mischievous grin spread across her lips. "It's the fastest way to get to the library. You are, of course, welcome to walk."

She climbed up onto the saddle without assistance and waited, staring down at him. "Are you coming, or have you decided to let your queen risk a ride through the city at night without an escort?"

He grunted a sigh and shook his head. "I'll get my horse."

Cleopatra pulled a scarf over her face. That combined with the ordinary clothing made her look even more like an average citizen. An average citizen with a fancy, expensive horse.

Within a few minutes, Theon sat atop his horse and trotted the animal over to the gate where two guards stood, one on either side, each holding a long spear.

"If we're going to the library," Theon said in a conspiratorial voice, "then you should let me lead the way."

"Very well," she said, bowing her head in playful mockery. "Lead the way."

The two rode out through the gate and into the night.

Stars glimmered in the sky like diamonds from the fabled mines of the ancient King Solomon. A crescent moon hung high among them, casting its comforting yet eerie glow down upon the city.

Theon kept his horse moving at a steady pace. Galloping through the crowded streets would be too dangerous. But he could tell the queen wanted to get to the library as fast as possible from the tone of her voice and the way she'd marched so quickly to the stables.

He glanced back at her often to make sure she was still close behind, even though he could hear the clopping of her steed's hooves in steady rhythm echoing off the houses around them.

Theon knew the city well. He'd spent his entire life here, other than when he was on assignment with the army. His familiarity with every street and alley wasn't only useful in a scenario like this. It could also come in handy if the queen needed to make an abrupt escape in the case of an enemy invasion.

He prayed to the gods that never happened, but as tensions with Rome continued to swell, he knew there were only two outcomes. Either Mark Anthony would win, or Octavian would. Neither would settle for a peaceful end to the conflict, satisfied with simply staying put in their respective homes to sit back and spend the rest of their days soaking up the sun.

Theon turned his horse to the left at a particularly wide intersection. The southeastern tower of the library appeared in front of him. He saw the torches burning atop the parapet, and in the windows along the façade near the gate.

He stole another glance back at his queen, again making sure she was safe. It was a habit he doubted would ever go away. Being the head of her royal guard for so long had embedded an almost fatherly nature in him. Being ten years older than her probably also had something to do with those instincts.

They slowed as they approached the huge wooden doors of the library. Theon stopped his horse near a hitching post to the right of the entrance, lashed his reigns over the wooden crossbar and then quickly turned to help Cleopatra dismount.

She was already halfway off the horse by the time he got to her and was only able to offer a hand.

She took it, nodded gratefully, and then proceeded toward the enormous doors.

An old man stood in the center of the entrance. He had a long white beard and wore the scholarly robes so many of his kind donned in this and other places of learning.

He smiled warmly at her as she approached and then bowed low.

Cleopatra shook her head, removing her scarf and the covering over her head to reveal her long, curly black hair—a trademark of her Greek ancestry that contrasted with the creamy skin of her face and neck.

"My queen," the librarian said, opening his hands out wide as he bowed.

"A man such as you who endeavors to preserve our way of life and the history of the world should never bow to me, Callisthenes. It is I who should bow to you."

"And yet I do anyway," the old man replied in a cracked, aged tone.

He was known to most as Callisthenes the Keeper and had been the head librarian of the Great Library for many years. Under his watch, the center had continued to collect and safeguard some of the world's most priceless artifacts and documents. After the fire that had spread as a result of Julius Caesar's reckless gamble, a portion of the library had suffered significant damage.

Callisthenes and his team had managed to salvage some of the scrolls from the burning wing, but many more had been lost.

Fortunately, the majority of the library was spared from the fire, and its contents remained intact.

"I hope you have good news for me, my friend," Cleopatra said. She stopped just in front of the man.

He stood up straight and exhaled. From the drawn expression on his face, and the exasperated sigh, she knew the news wasn't good.

"Unfortunately, it appears the document you seek was, in fact, destroyed in the fire all those years ago. I, and my apprentice, have scoured the shelves in every possible wing where it could have been located. Based on our catalogs, it was located in the wing that burned, and our records do not indicate it was reentered when we salvaged what we could. I still have two men searching, but I am afraid the scroll you are looking for is most likely gone."

The queen's shoulders slumped visibly. She turned away and looked off toward the sea. Only a small part of it was visible through the narrow causeway between the library and a row of homes lining the street. But the salty air funneled through the corridor and filled her nostrils.

Theon and the librarian watched as she took a few steps away from them, her head hung low.

She took a deep breath and stiffened, still looking out toward the sea. The wind bristled her hair and tickled her ears. She raised her right hand and rubbed the bridge of her nose.

"I really thought this was the answer," she whispered so low the men could barely hear her. "This could have solved everything."

Theon took a step toward her. "What is it you're looking for, my queen? Perhaps I can—"

"I'm sorry, Theon. There's nothing you can do. It's gone." A deep sadness filled her voice, causing it to crack. She spun slowly and faced the two men. "That scroll was our best chance at ending this war once and for all. Now, it is left to the gods to decide."

Callisthenes stepped forward. "That is not entirely true, my queen."

"What do you mean?"

"Perhaps I should have said this sooner. Please, forgive me."

She stepped closer to him and stopped a few feet away. Her eyes burned with the intensity of the sun. "What is it? What should you have told me?"

He smiled at her. It was a comforting expression, one he might have given his grandchildren when they'd hurt themselves playing.

"That is not the only scroll containing the information you seek, my queen."

Hope teased at her heart, like a carrot in front of a mule. "What do you mean?"

His smile broadened. "Every volume contained within these walls has a copy. It is a safeguard against catastrophes such as the fire. That scroll also has a copy."

"Where? Where is it?" Urgency forced her words.

"In our sister library."

1

JORDAN | PRESENT DAY

Sean Wyatt leaned timidly into the crowbar. If he and the others had misjudged the tool's positioning and load bearing of the slab blocking the passage, the entire corridor could come crashing down on all of them.

Their best guess was that the heavy rectangular stone was merely a barrier, not a support. But a lot could change in an ancient place like this. Two thousand years of earthquakes, temperature shifts, and even the rare desert flood could have altered the structural integrity of the subterranean passage.

"You're sure about this, right, Sean?" Craig asked.

Dr. Craig Freeman stood just behind Sean and next to Tommy Schultz, Sean's best friend and the founder of the International Archaeological Agency.

Craig was an archaeologist of a more traditional kind compared to the two IAA agents. His work was typically boring, with days spent filling out paperwork or shaking sifters in pits of dig sites while inhaling dust under the scorching sun.

"Based on the map," Tommy answered, "this has to be the right corridor."

Sean hesitated, only keeping enough force on the crowbar to make sure the wedge didn't fall out of the tight seam he'd worked it into. "This place hasn't been opened for two millennia, Craig," Sean added. "The only way to know what's on the other side is to pry open this door. Could it kill us? Sure. You're welcome to go back up and wait topside if you like."

Craig forced an uneasy laugh. "And let you two knuckleheads get all the credit? Not to mention you'd be the first to lay eyes on this thing in two thousand years. I don't think so."

He winked to emphasize he was joking, but something in his voice also seemed serious.

Craig's two assistants remained just behind him—two hulking men that looked more like bodyguards than archaeologists. One was a tank with short brown hair cut in a military style. His white, dirt-stained T-shirt stretched across his muscular chest, pushing the threads to their breaking point. The other guy was slimmer but still extremely fit, and taller with a hawkish nose and sharp jaw. His brown eyes looked black in the dim light of the tunnel, and his perpetual silence made him seem all the more like a predator waiting to pick off its prey. He could have passed for a serial killer. The man bun holding up his dark blond hair, however, blunted his intimidating appearance.

To date, only 5 percent of the ancient city of Petra had been discovered or excavated by archaeologists through the years. It was an astonishingly low number for a place of such historical significance, and that brimmed with mystery.

This passage was part of the 95 percent that had yet to be explored, until now.

Two months prior, Tommy received a text message from Craig with an unusual request to meet up and discuss something he'd been working on.

Tommy had known Craig for years, even spent some time on a few recovery missions with him—both in the Middle East. Surprisingly, both of those had gone relatively easily compared to some of Tommy and Sean's more complicated entanglements.

The Middle East was Craig's area of expertise, and he rarely operated outside of it. Sean and Tommy had joked only a few hours before when they were out in the blistering sun that Craig had become so acclimatized to the heat of the desert, he might feel cold were he to crawl into an oven.

The man didn't even seem to break a sweat, though with the air being so dry any perspiration they gave up evaporated almost instantly.

"With your permission, your highness," Sean said, almost as dryly as the westerly winds blew across the barren city.

"Do it," Craig said, releasing all doubts. "We didn't come this far to stop just because of a little stone block."

"I'd... hardly...call it...little," Sean grunted as he leaned into the metal bar. The stone began to shift. The movement was subtle at first.

Craig watched from what he considered a safe distance—about six feet behind Sean and Tommy. He clutched a stone disc in his left hand, his thumb rubbing across the eight prongs jutting out from one side.

Sean pushed into the bar. Tommy did the same, and the heavy stone blocking the corridor slid to the left. The sound of stone grinding on stone filled the passage.

Craig gritted his teeth and covered one ear with the back of his hand while keeping the lamp at waist level with his other. The sound was like fingernails on a chalk board—a one-ton chalkboard.

Sean grunted as he pushed the lever. He hadn't actually expected the enormous block to budge, much less slide as easily as it had. Sure, it took nearly every ounce of strength he could muster, but with Tommy's help the task was slightly easier.

As the slab shifted, it seemed to gain a little momentum. Sean wasn't going to let that make him ease up. When the gap was wide enough, he adjusted the bar to get a few more inches of leverage.

"Okay, stop right there," he said to Tommy, who stood uncomfortably close. "Craig, give us a couple those blocks."

Craig turned to his assistant, Brent. The man produced two six-inch-by-six-inch wooden blocks from a bag and handed one to Sean.

"Thank you," Sean said in deep staccato even as he turned and positioned the block on the wall side of the crowbar. "Ready, Schultzie?"

"Let's do it."

They pushed against the bar again, expecting the slab to move the corresponding distance to the block. Instead, the heavy stone slid easily away from the ancient frame, rolling across the threshold as if on unseen wheels.

It moved so suddenly that Sean and Tommy both lost their balance and fell backward, with Sean hitting the wall behind them, then catching Tommy in his arms. The metal bar clattered on the floor, ringing loudly for a second before coming to silent rest on the stone.

"Easy, big guy," Sean said. "I'm not the cuddling type."

Tommy chuckled and regained his balance. "That's not what I heard."

"Do you two need some time alone?" Craig asked. "Or do you want to look in there?" He pointed the light into the opening. The darkness beyond the threshold retreated, revealing a chamber beyond.

"Boys," Sean breathed as he stood up straight, "human eyes haven't seen this place for a very long time."

He took a step forward, scooping up his lamp and flashlight from the floor where he'd left it. He held the lamp up high as he took a wary step across the threshold, sweeping it to his left to illuminate the walls.

Tommy and the others followed closely behind, their eyes and mouths wide upon seeing the spacious, ornate room before them. The acoustics were so perfect within the cubed chamber that even their quiet footsteps echoed off the walls.

"Look at this place," Tommy whispered, his voice reverent. He split off in the other direction, holding a light close to the wall. Koine Greek letters covered huge sections of the smooth stone, inscribed thousands of years before and highlighted with a black ink that had faded to a dim gray through the millennia.

Reliefs depicting battles, ceremonies, and other events adorned the wall above the writing, the scenes protruding out as if an ancient 3-D story.

"This looks like Egyptian Coptic," Sean said, studying the wall closer.

"I have Koine Greek over here," Tommy replied. "Those were two of the languages she spoke."

Craig walked between the two of them, heading straight to the center of the room where a raised dais made of white marble sat upon the floor.

Tommy continued around to his left and discovered more writings in a third language. "This is Latin," he exclaimed. "Sean, you know what this means, yeah?"

Sean shifted to the last section of wall and inspected the characters engraved on it. "Aramaic," he whispered. "Four of the languages Cleopatra spoke."

"Yes," Tommy agreed. "We found it. We found the lost scriptorium of Cleopatra."

"Beautiful," Craig said, running his fingers along the surface of the platform in the middle of the room. Brent looked around with wide eyes, not exactly sure what he was looking at, or how he should feel.

Sean and Tommy had only met Brent just prior to leaving for Jordan. Craig had introduced him as an assistant who would be helping with the investigation, but the guy smacked of former military, or at the very least some kind of upper-echelon private security. Maybe he was former law enforcement.

It never hurt to have a little extra muscle on your side, especially when dealing with antiquities. The world was full of those who would happily let others do the more difficult, complicated tasks and then swoop in and steal the bounty for themselves.

Sean had worked on group projects with those types when he was in college. Now, however, the consequences were far more dramatic. In this game, priceless pieces of lost history could be damaged or taken, and more than once the others trying for the same goal were ready to kill to win.

"Tommy?" Craig said with an over-the-shoulder look. "What do you make of this?"

Tommy tore himself away from the intricate messages carved in stone and walked over to the center of the room where Craig stood next to the dais.

The solid marble pedestal stood nearly five feet high, and equally as long. At first glance, there didn't appear to be anything else unusual about the cube.

"What are we supposed to do?" Craig asked. His admiration of the immaculately preserved marble dimmed with frustration. "And if this is the scriptorium, where are the scripts? Shouldn't there be scrolls or something lying around in here?"

Tommy nodded. "Yes. There would be unless the place was robbed right after it was built."

"What?"

Sean shook his head. "It's possible, but unlikely. That stone hadn't budged, probably since this room was sealed. There's something here," he said, turning his head around to take in the chamber in all its splendor.

"What do the walls say?" Craig asked.

"It's an accounting of the scriptorium's construction," Tommy explained. "It's a vault more than a scriptorium or library. Something very powerful was stored here."

Craig nodded. "Yes. That's why we're here. But where is it?"

Sean moved over to the white block, and silently studied the surface of the marble cube, running his fingers along the top, and then down the backside facing the chamber's rear wall.

"You still have that stone?" Sean asked.

Craig nodded, holding out his palm with the round disc in the center, its eight raised cylindrical prongs sticking up.

"I think it goes back here," Sean said, taking the disc from Craig.

The other three maneuvered around the marble block to where

Sean stood and looked down at what he'd discovered—a circle set within the stone's back, with eight holes that appeared to match the pattern on the disc.

"Where'd you say you found this thing, Craig?" Sean asked as he fit the prongs into the corresponding holes.

"A tomb near Giza. We were excavating a new area—basically uncovered an entire village. The bodies we found buried there weren't done in the usual way for commoners, particularly the one who was holding that."

Sean pressed the disc into the side of the marble until it was flush. He looked up for a second at Craig. "You took this off a dead body?" He wiped his hands on his pants.

His counterpart chuckled. "I doubt it has any germs on it."

"Need me to get you some hand sanitizer?" Tommy joked.

"You guys are hilarious," Sean chirped. "You know that?"

He gripped the disc along its edge, and turned it clockwise.

"How do you know what direction to twist that?" Craig asked, trepidation littering his words.

"I don't," Sean admitted. "But I figure we have a fifty-fifty shot."

"What happens if you turn it the wrong way?" Brent asked, chiming in for the first time since they'd entered the passage. The man had been as quiet as a statue.

"Well," Sean said, still turning the dial carefully, "we could die a painful death via some ancient booby trap."

Brent snickered uneasily. "Seriously?" He took an involuntary step back toward the doorway.

"It's almost happened before. The people who go to such great lengths to hide these kinds of things didn't stop at just blocking them with a heavy stone slab. They wanted to make sure anyone coming in here was someone who should be here, not just some treasure hunters or thieves. This stuff was sacred, and in the case of what we're looking for, extremely powerful."

"Theoretically," Tommy added.

"Right."

The dial stopped turning with a click. The sound reverberated around the room. Several thuds followed it. Then, the marble cube started descending into the floor. Sean and the others took a step back as they watched the impressive dais sink inch by inch.

The seam had been so perfectly tight between the marble sides and the sandstone tiles of the floor that none of the men had even noticed.

"What's happening?" Craig asked. A hint of panic trailed along in his voice.

"Just relax," Tommy cautioned.

"Have you two seen anything like this before?"

"Never with a block of marble," Sean answered.

"Wow. I have got to get out of the trenches more often."

The cube sank beneath the floor surface and into the darkness below.

The four men pointed their flashlights into the underground cavity but could only see the immediate area around the dais.

The cube stopped with a bump, and something that sounded like the click of a lock.

Sean peered into the hole. The marble top was four feet down, more than enough for him to fit through.

"I'll check it out," he said, fixing the flashlight to his belt with a blue clip. He adjusted the headlamp on his forehead and eased down onto the cavity's lip, lowered his feet through, and then eased himself down until his boots touched the top of the cube.

He bent his knees, turned, and repeated the process until his feet hit the floor of the chamber below.

Sean looked around while the other three peered down from above, their lights casting a bright glare across his vision.

"Do you guys mind pointing those away from my face?" he chided.

"Sorry," Tommy apologized.

He and the other two adjusted their beams.

"What do you see?" Craig pressed.

Sean didn't answer immediately. It was one of the rare moments he found the words difficult to come by, and his response caught in his throat.

He twisted his head around, pointing the headlamp's beam along the walls surrounding him. Sean's eyes were wide like a child staring at the bounty beneath the tree on Christmas morning.

"You guys have to see this."

2

Craig's feet hit the floor next to the marble cube with a thud. Brent and Tommy followed.

Sean had stepped away from the plinth, wandering over to one of the four walls. Brilliantly colored hieroglyphs adorned every inch of the surface of ancient stone surrounding them. Tommy and the other two scanned the room, each inspecting a different part of the enclosure.

On the floor, four golden discs glimmered in the darkness, the lights dancing off the metallic circles. The discs were equidistant in space from the marble altar, each placed from a corner of the cube. The plates were three feet in diameter, each engraved with faces.

As Sean circled the room, shining his light on each disc, he saw that they were created in a Hellenistic design. Greek letters were engraved beneath the faces.

"Soter," Sean said, deciphering the ancient script.

Tommy joined him, nodding his agreement. "Ptolemy the First," he added. "Close friend and general of Alexander the Great. He became the ruler of Egypt after Alexander's death, and established Alexandria as a major cultural and economic hub."

Craig and Brent joined the two as they moved on to the next disc. Brent nearly stepped on the first as he followed.

"Don't... step on that," Sean said with urgency. Brent's foot hovered over the golden circle.

"Why?" Brent asked, obliviousness drooping his eyelids.

"Because we don't know what those are. They could be some kind of safety measure."

"As in a booby trap?" Craig asked. He sounded dubious.

"This isn't a dig site, Craig. There are real dangers in places like this. Trust me, we've seen stuff that you wouldn't believe."

"He's right," Tommy said. "There's a lot the textbooks and post-graduate courses don't teach you about the lost history of the world. Best to avoid those plates for now. Could be weight triggered."

Brent lowered his foot back to the floor, his ego blunted like a chastised child. He walked around the disc and followed the others to the next.

"Soter's son, Philadelphus—Ptolemy the Second." Tommy announced. "Expanded the cultural and scientific advancements in Alexandria. Under his reign, the library became a renowned center of learning."

Sean led the way round to the third golden plate. "This must be Euergetes, Ptolemy the Third. Powerful military leader. Known for his conquest and the significant expansion of the empire's territory."

"And he continued the tradition of patronage to the arts and sciences," Craig quickly added.

"Yes."

"Let me guess," Brent said, making his way to the fourth disc. "Ptolemy the Fourth." He pointed his beam down at the golden circle. "Looks like a woman, though."

The others sidled up next to him.

"That's because it is a woman," Tommy said with a degree of annoyance. "And it's not Ptolemy the Fourth. That is Cleopatra. The last of the Ptolemaic line. Extremely smart, and politically savvy. Her relationships with Julius Caesar and Mark Antony helped play a major role in the Roman political battles of her time."

"The reign of the Ptolemaic Dynasty ended with her," Sean said, his voice reverent.

"It must be some kind of homage to them," Craig guessed. "A sort of shrine to the greatest of the dynasty."

"Could be," Sean half agreed. "But still best to not step on them."

Tommy held his lantern high and turned toward the wall nearest him. He stared at the colorful hieroglyphs painted on the smooth stone surface.

"This is fascinating," he breathed.

"What does it say?" Brent asked.

Tommy wasn't surprised that the man couldn't decipher the hieroglyphs. As far as the population of humanity was concerned, very few could. Sure, there were archaeologists, Egyptologists, and historians all over the world who knew how. But per capita, it was a fraction of a percent.

Even Craig, as expert as he was in the field of archaeology, only had a minimal grasp on the ancient form of writing. Sean spoke multiple languages fluently, but also only understood a small portion of how to read hieroglyphs.

"It's a story," Tommy said. He pored over the lines, going back and forth along the wall until he reached the bottom.

"What kind of story?"

Brent really was the muscle of the group. Both Tommy and Sean had surmised as much within minutes of meeting the guy. His strengths were focused mainly on his physicality, though Sean knew the man probably had a few pieces of tactical intelligence built into that muscular frame.

"It's about the war against Rome," Tommy said. "During the time of Cleopatra."

Craig frowned at the answer. "Then it should be written in the Coptic language, or perhaps Greek."

Tommy nodded. "Yes, that's true. It could have been. But hieroglyphics were still used until the fifth century AD. Perhaps it was done this way as a part of that tradition."

"I suppose." He sounded frustrated at not being able to read everything on the walls.

Sean stood next to his friend with his hands on his hips while Tommy continued to translate.

"Strange," Tommy said.

"What is?" Sean asked.

"I've never heard this part of the story before."

"What part?" Craig wondered, pointing his headlamp beam along the same wall.

"This seems to suggest that Cleopatra was trying to find something—a weapon, I think. It says that a messenger went out from the palace to find an object. It's difficult to say, but if I had to guess I would venture that this was a powerful item, something that could harness the power of Ra himself."

"You mean the sun," Sean clarified.

"Correct."

"The Archimedes Scroll," Craig whispered with reverence.

Tommy nodded. "So it would seem."

"So, the rumors were true. The scroll is real."

There was no hiding the simmering excitement in Craig's voice. It brimmed with hope, and the sense of finally finding something that had been lost for two millennia.

"Well, I would hope so," Sean quipped. "Otherwise, what are we all doing here?"

"Yeah," Tommy agreed. "It's not like we go out looking for stuff unless we think it actually exists."

"Okay. Okay. I get it," Craig resigned. "Jeez. I'm just saying, even though you believe it's out there, you still gotta have doubts. Right?"

"Always," Sean said. "We're just busting your chops, man. You never really know until you see it."

"Let's not get ahead of ourselves," Tommy cautioned. "All we have is ancient writing on the walls. In case you haven't noticed, there isn't a scroll sitting out in the open in here."

The others panned the room, his words reminding them that the mission was far from complete.

"Okay," Brent chimed in. "So, where is it?"

Tommy remained focused on the hieroglyphs along the wall. "I'm working on that." The others remained silent as he deciphered the images one by one. He shifted his feet to the right as he read, and then back to the left. When he was done with that wall, he moved to the next until he completed the circuit.

"Well?" Craig asked when Tommy was done. "Where is it?"

"I don't know," Tommy admitted.

"What? What do you mean, you don't know? Can't you read this stuff?"

"Yes. And by the way, I'm not sure why you're not helping. I know you can decipher some of it. Second, this story is fascinating. It talks about the conflict with Rome leading up to the Battle of Actium."

"Actium?" Sean wondered. "That was basically the deciding battle in the war."

"Right. According to this story"—Tommy pointed at the wall as he continued—"Cleopatra was trying to find Archimedes' fabled death ray, a weapon that could harness the power of the sun and destroy enemy ships, siege weapons, vast numbers of troops. Sort of like a Death Star-type deal from the description."

"You sort of mentioned that before," Craig said, impatience tipping him up onto his toes.

"Yeah, but it gets better. Apparently, the Library of Alexandria had the original scroll. The library was a prominent place during the Ptolemaic Dynasty. That must be why those discs are here."

For a few seconds, no one said a word. Tommy's statement seemed to suck the stale air out of the sandstone room.

"*The* Library of Alexandria?" Craig clarified.

"Unless you've heard of another."

"So, the scroll was at the library," Sean said. "The library was lost thousands of years ago."

Every man in the room, perhaps except for Brent, knew the true story of how the Great Library had been lost.

Books, movies, and legend told dramatic tales of how the library was destroyed by a fire, looted by barbarians, or torn down stone by stone with the hands of demented, power-hungry rulers—the truth was far less enthralling.

It was true that a portion of the library was burned during a battle involving Julius Caesar, but only one wing was damaged during the inferno, and it was largely believed that many of the records and scrolls contained within the building's walls were saved.

Beyond that, the real story of the library was one of decline and neglect.

At its height, rulers and scholars placed a great deal of importance on the contents of the library, creating a place that would contain ancient knowledge of the entire world for generations to come. But over time, people lost interest. Those in power no longer saw the benefit nor the need to sustain the Great Library. Little by little, it fell into disrepair, and through the centuries as the building wore down, its priceless contents slowly dripped away from its hallowed halls like a leaky faucet until the well ran dry.

Over the years, countless treasure hunters, looters, historians, and archaeologists had searched for the remains of the once-proud museum. But not a single stone of it had ever been found.

Many believed that the ruins lay somewhere along the coast, under the modern city of Alexandria, but those who've searched were only rewarded with more speculation.

"You don't mean to tell me that the scroll we're looking for was lost along with everything else in the library," Craig clarified.

"I wasn't finished," Tommy said, doing his best to stay patient. "According to this"—he pointed at the wall—"the original scroll was either destroyed or lost from the library's museum. But it had a twin."

"A twin?" Brent asked.

"A copy. Just like with modern documents and how we make backups or copies of things, they did the same back then. Everything that was contained in the Library of Alexandria had a duplicate."

"And where were all these copies kept? Craig wondered. "Certainly not on site, I would hope."

"No. The Library of Alexandria had a sister, Pergamum. It was in Turkey, and contained copies of all the scrolls, documents, maps, and other records that were kept in Egypt. The keepers of the library knew that it wasn't safe to only have one of each item, so they spent an enormous amount of time and resources to make sure everything was duplicated."

"So, we have to go to Pergamum?" Craig asked.

"Doubtful," Tommy said, stepping closer to the wall and inspecting the imagery. "There's nothing but ruins there now. More likely, the contents of that museum were taken to various parts of the world for safekeeping."

"Or stolen by looters."

"True. Although, educational materials weren't usually targets for thieves. They were more interested in valuables—gold, jewelry, that sort of thing. Academic treasures were rarely of interest to those types. There wasn't a market for that sort of stuff."

"Well, that's good. But what happened to all of it?"

"That's the hundred-million-dollar question," Tommy mused. "But right now we don't have to figure out where all of it went. Just one piece."

He stared at the wall for another minute, and then shifted to his right, running his fingers along about an inch above the surface. "This," he said.

"The Eye of Horus?" Sean asked.

"It is in a similar location on each of these walls." He raised his light closer to it. Tommy twisted his head and looked down at the golden disc with the face of Soter engraved on it. I wonder... if those plates are the key."

"Like a button."

"Right."

"Okay," Craig said. "Let's step on one and find out." He moved toward the disc with Soter's likeness on it and raised his foot.

"No," Tommy said, grabbing him by the wrist. "Not so fast. There's a warning here too that goes along with the story. It says that those who seek the power of Ra—death awaits those who don't follow his path."

3

Craig took a step back, his face paling in the light. "Oh. Well, what does that mean? Follow his path? I'm not a particularly religious guy, Schultzie. But I'm definitely not ancient-Egyptian religious."

Sean studied the Eye of Horus, then shifted his attention to the images around it. "Hold on," he said, and stepped away to the wall to his left. "Did you notice one of those eyes over here as well?"

"Yeah," Tommy said. "Why?"

Sean didn't answer immediately. Instead, he swept his gaze across the surface, holding his lantern up to assist until he located the same symbol. The emblem to the left was of the sun hanging in the sky over a field of grain.

He pivoted toward the wall to his left and hurried over to it while the others watched.

"What are you looking for, man?" Craig asked. His patience was at the tipping point.

Sean ignored him and repeated the same search as before until he located the next Eye of Horus. To the left of this one, the image of the sun was only halfway up over the horizon.

"Morning," Sean said.

He moved to the last wall and quickly found the fourth eye. The sun next to it was barely visible. A pointed star occupied the top left corner of that section of the picture.

"What about morning?" Craig asked. "What are you doing?"

Sean returned to the original wall where Tommy and the others stood and checked the image of the sun next to the eye. This one was similar to the one on the opposite wall, hanging about the same distance above the horizon and the field of grain.

"Follow Ra's path," Sean said, finally offering a redundant and vague answer to Craig's question. "If these are buttons, they have to be pressed in sequence," he explained. "They follow the path of the sun across the sky. Dawn, morning, afternoon, and evening. The path of Ra."

Tommy's eyes widened. He offered a proud grin to his friend. "I knew there was a reason I kept you on with the agency."

Sean chuckled. "Yeah, that's the reason."

"Genius," Craig said, pointing his headlamp around the room at the different walls.

"Thanks."

"I was talking about the people who built this place."

The men laughed at the barb.

"Okay," Tommy said. "So, you said that one over there is morning?" He pointed at the prescribed wall.

"Yeah. The one with evening has a star in the corner, so we do that one last."

"Good enough. Brent, you want to do the honors? The rest of us each take a disc, and wait until it's your turn."

"Okay," Brent said, sounding a little uncertain. He lumbered over to his position and waited. "Do I have to stay on it or what?"

"I doubt the people who designed this place planned on exactly four explorers discovering it. So, I would say no."

"You're sure?"

Tommy saw the concern in the man's eyes, fear glowing in the light of the lanterns. "Yeah—90 percent."

"Wait. That leaves 10 percent. I don't like that."

"Oh, would you shut it? You've never been afraid of anything. Why would you be now?"

The comment shut Brent up, and the others took their positions.

"I'll take this one," Craig said, pointing to the wall adjacent to where Brent stood.

Tommy and Sean divided up the last two, with Sean taking the wall with the final piece.

"You guys ready?" Tommy asked.

"Ready," the others echoed. "Okay, Brent. Go ahead. Step on it."

"If I fall into some kind of bottomless pit, I swear—"

"Just do it already," Craig barked.

"Fine." Brent raised his foot over the disc, held it there hesitantly, and then lowered it gently onto the metallic surface. He breathed uneasily, doubt racking his body.

"You have to put your weight on it," Sean sighed.

"Okay. Okay. Jeez."

Brent lifted his back foot and stepped fully onto the disc. It immediately shifted, descending into the floor.

"What's happening?"

"Exactly what we thought," Tommy said. "Just relax. It shouldn't drop far."

"What is your definition of far?"

Sean knew Brent had some kind of a dark past, something military or maybe private security. Craig had brought him along for just that, a little added protection in case they ran into trouble out in the desert. Sean wasn't fooled by the man's behavior here in the chamber. Everyone had their kryptonite, that thing that could unhinge the sturdiest oak door.

For Sean, it was his crippling fear of heights. He'd been afraid of high places since childhood. The phobia wasn't just personal. It transferred over to other people, those he knew, and even complete strangers. If anyone was standing close to a precipice or a big drop-off, he felt a tightness in his gut and a gripping paranoia that the person was going to fall—even if they were simply blown off balance by the slightest breeze.

He recalled going to the Grand Canyon once and seeing children playing next to a ledge. Sean wanted to grab the parents by the shoulders and shake them into reality. He didn't, of course, but the desire to do it was nearly overwhelming. All he could do was turn away and walk the other direction.

Sean and Tommy both knew Brent was right to be worried, but they didn't encourage that fear. The two of them had seen dozens of ancient devices and traps that had nearly cut their lives short. It was the sort of thing men like Craig believed only happened in the movies. They'd heard it said in lectures at renowned universities.

For the most part, it was true. The majority of ancient ruins around the world where archaeologists and anthropologists toiled away their days had never once presented them with any sort of real danger.

But Sean and Tommy weren't like them. They were a different breed, venturing down paths that others couldn't even see.

The disc stopped moving, and the grinding sound that had accompanied it ceased.

Relief washed over Brent's face as the plate stabilized. "It stopped," he announced.

"Thanks, Captain Obvious," Sean quipped, much to Brent's obvious displeasure.

"You next, Craig," Tommy said.

Craig nodded. Unlike his bodyguard, he stepped bravely out onto the disc, and it immediately began to descend. He looked weary as it dropped inch by inch into the floor, but when it stopped, he nodded in pride. "That wasn't so bad."

"Famous last words," Sean warned. "Schultzie?"

"On it."

Tommy moved onto his disc, and the same process repeated, along with the grinding noise from somewhere under the floor.

Once Tommy's circle stopped, Sean shuffled forward. "I guess we find out if we're right," he said, and stepped onto the disc with the face of Cleopatra carved into it.

Sean descended until his shins disappeared under the floor. Then the mechanism came to a halt.

"Now what?" Craig asked.

Something deep within the floor clicked, and suddenly the discs dropped out from under their feet.

The four men slid down through the holes in the floor and into the darkness. They landed on a hard surface with a thud, their lanterns and gear clattering around them. The drop was short, and more frightening than a real threat of injury.

Each of them scrambled to their feet, pointing their headlamps around the new room, lanterns swinging wildly as if they expected some unseen enemy to attack at any moment.

Instead, what they found was another chamber. This one, however, shimmered in the lamplight.

"Is that..." Craig started but tripped over his words.

"Sure looks like it," Sean said.

The walls surrounding them were adorned with reliefs of the four great members of the Ptolemaic Dynasty, each displaying various stages of their lives and reigns in Egypt. Some portrayed great battles. Others portrayed the sharing of knowledge, culture, and expansion.

A dark doorway was cut into the center of Soter's wall, providing the visitors with the only way out of the chamber.

While the gilded walls were spectacular, and unlike anything they'd ever seen before, something else sucked in Tommy's attention and didn't let it go.

He shuffled across the smooth sandstone floor as if in a trance.

A second later, everyone else saw what had grabbed him.

"A sarcophagus," Craig realized.

Tommy stopped next to the head of the stone container and stared down at the face painted on the surface. Its curved, painted features were shaped and colored to mirror the image of how the person within may have looked when they walked this earth thousands of years ago.

The sarcophagus rested atop a golden altar with the head a few feet from the wall. The corresponding reliefs along the wall depicted a face similar to the one on the chest.

"This isn't just any sarcophagus," Tommy whispered, his breath seemingly removed from his chest. "This is *the* sarcophagus."

Craig and Sean both knew exactly what Tommy meant. More importantly, they understood his reference to who was buried within the chest. It was a funerary box that had been sought by treasure hunters and archaeologists for centuries but had always eluded every one of them. Legends had been forged around it—stories of its supposed location, or what secrets it could hold.

One of those legends had brought the four men to this place, one that had been an unlikely keeper of this incredible piece of history.

"What do you mean, *the* sarcophagus?" Brent asked. His ignorance was unsurprising, even though the answer was beyond obvious for the other three.

Sean nodded as he stared with wide eyes at the sarcophagus. "This is the final resting place of Queen Cleopatra."

4

The answer didn't seem possible.

They'd come to Petra seeking the fabled Scroll of Archimedes, a blueprint for a device some believed was a superweapon designed to obliterate enemy vessels approaching coastal fortifications and cities.

Sean and Tommy weren't under any delusions in that regard. They didn't believe that Archimedes had figured out how to construct some kind of death ray, despite all the fantastical things they'd witnessed over the years.

To them, the scroll represented a priceless piece of history, a gap to be filled for the world in order to give a better understanding of a man regarded as an ancient genius of math and science.

"You mean Cleopatra is inside this thing?" Brent asked. He seemed more curious than awestruck. That was to be expected given his blatant lack of historical knowledge.

"Yeah," Craig said. "That's exactly what he means."

"Well, what are we waiting for? Let's open it and see what's inside."

"Hold on," Tommy ordered. "We need to make sure it's safe."

"You mean make sure it isn't another trap?"

"It's probably fine, but we've come this far. I don't want to rush into this and catch some kind of ancient acid to the face."

Brent took a step back. "Seriously?"

"No," Tommy chuckled. "Not about the acid, anyway. How would it be preserved for over two thousand years?"

"I don't know."

"That doesn't mean there isn't something in there that could be dangerous. We need to be careful. That's all. And we don't want to damage anything."

Sean bent down and inspected the thin seam separating the lid from the main container. There were no cracks, no jagged areas. The stone had been cut with such incredible precision a business card would barely fit into the gap.

He removed his headlamp and pointed it into the seam, then moved along the side until he reached the end. He repeated the process around the entire sarcophagus, stopping when he'd completed the loop.

Sean stood and fixed the light to his forehead once more.

"Well?" Craig asked.

"I couldn't see anything."

"Well that's a relief," Brent said.

"No, I mean it's so tight I couldn't tell if the thing is rigged or not. We're just going to have to pull it off and see."

The relief on Brent's face vanished.

"We didn't come this far to just have a look," Tommy said with a sigh. "Sean and I can do it."

"Are you sure?" Craig asked. His concern sounded almost genuine.

"Sure. Wouldn't be the first time we went into something like this without knowing what would happen."

Sean moved back to the other side of the chest and gripped the head of the lid. Tommy did the same, and when the two were in position, Sean nodded to his friend.

The two grunted as they pushed on the heavy stone piece. The grinding sound echoed loudly off the metallic yellow walls around them and rang in their ears.

"Heck of a warning system," Sean commented in a strained voice. His forearms rippled with veins as he kept pushing.

Tommy's thick muscles bulged, too, but their effort didn't go unrewarded. The lid continued sliding toward the feet until they saw wrappings inside the coffer.

"That's good," Tommy said. "Stop here for a second."

The two ceased their push and took a moment to catch their breath. They stared into the sarcophagus at the shape of a human head wrapped in bandages. The figure was slender, somewhat smallish.

For a minute, no one said a word. They merely stared into the chest at a golden face designed to resemble the real face of one of the most fascinating people in all of history.

"I don't believe it," Craig said, inching closer to the chest.

"That... is why you fail," Tommy quipped.

"What?"

"*Empire Strikes Back*," Sean said. "Yoda said that, too—you know what, never mind. Not sure it really fits in this situation anyway, Schultzie."

"Star Wars always fits," Tommy countered.

Craig did his best to ignore them, leaning over to have a closer look. "Should we pull the lid the rest of the way off?"

"Sure, but we'll need you two to help with that. This thing is really heavy, and I would prefer not to break it."

"Definitely," Craig agreed. "Brent, take the other end with Sean. I'll help Tommy."

The four men positioned themselves on the ends of the sarcophagus, each gripping an edge.

They slid it to the side this time, with Sean and Tommy taking the brunt of the weight first until all four of them held it over the floor.

"Now, ease it down," Tommy ordered. "Lean it against the main box."

He and Sean lowered their edge to the floor while the other two gently tilted the lid against the container.

They breathed a collective sigh when the lid rested safely on the floor. Then, their eyes all went to the interior of the sarcophagus.

The inner coffin was made of pure gold, with highlights painted in black to accentuate the famous queen's figure and features. The head and face were adorned with the traditional garb of the pharaohs. And as with those kings of old, her arms were crossed over her chest, with a striped scepter carved into the right. The left clutched what appeared to be a scroll.

"Incredible," Craig breathed, virtually salivating over the find.

"This, along with the room, would be worth hundreds of millions if not more," Brent said.

Tommy rolled his eyes. "That's not why we're here, man. Come on. Stay focused."

"See the scroll?" Sean asked, the question rhetorical. "That must be it."

"You think it's inside the coffin?" Craig asked.

"I know how we can find out."

Sean slipped the pack off his shoulders and unzipped the main compartment. He removed a small iron chisel and fit the sharp end into the seam along the side of the golden coffin.

"Careful," Tommy insisted.

Sean gave him a sidelong glance as if to say, "No kidding." Then he gently wiggled the tool until he had it wedged tightly in the crease. "Help me lift this once we have a gap," he said.

Tommy nodded and placed his fingers near the chisel.

Sean carefully pushed down on the iron, and the lid raised a centimeter above the base. Tommy quickly stuck his fingers inside. Sean did the same with his free hand, then once he had a good grip, pulled the chisel out and dropped it on top of his bag.

The two friends lifted the lid and pulled it back.

A strange combination of odors wafted out from the chest—bitter and dusty, with faint traces of spice.

Sean's nose tingled, but the urge to sneeze that built up just as quickly went away.

"Help us slide this off," he said to Craig and Brent.

The other two men gripped the edge on the other side, and the four moved the lid toward the foot of the coffin.

"Good grief, this is heavy," Brent complained.

"It's pure gold," Sean grunted.

"That's far enough," Tommy said when the lid hung nearly halfway over the end.

As the men caught their breath, they stared into the golden container at the mummified figure. The wrappings were tattered and discolored, ravaged by time. But they remained mostly intact, tightly pressed against the queen's slender remains.

"Do you guys realize we are seeing the remains of one of the most storied figures in all of history?" Tommy muttered reverently.

"Yeah," Craig said.

His eyes fell to something clutched in the fabric covering the mummy's right hand.

It was a golden scepter. The shaft ran just over a foot in length, with a sapphire fixed to the base. At the top, a fierce head of a golden cobra stared back at them with two rubies for eyes. The mouth was open wide with two fangs jutting out from the roof within.

"Bloody thing almost looks like it's alive," Brent said.

"Yeah," Tommy agreed, leaning in for a closer examination. He trained his head at an angle, and peered at the scepter's shaft and the Greek lettering carved into the golden cylinder.

Craig looked deeply concerned, and it wasn't because of some unseen traps. His face had turned grave, and his jaw firm. "That is an impressive scepter, but where is the scroll? The lid showed a scepter and a scroll."

"That's a good question," Tommy said as he carefully reached into the sarcophagus, running his finger along the scepter's shaft.

"What are you doing?" Craig asked. Concern and confusion mingling in his words.

"Getting a closer look at this thing. See those hieroglyphs around the shaft? I want to know what they mean. It could be another clue. You wanted to know where the scroll is. This might help us find it."

"Besides," Sean interrupted, "based on the preliminary evidence, it looks like we just discovered one of the greatest archaeological finds in all of history. You should be smiling, Craig. This is the achievement of ten lifetimes, man."

He turned and faced the golden wall behind the funerary chest's head. The raised profile of Cleopatra was carved in intricate detail, surrounded by hieroglyphic reliefs.

Craig allowed an uneasy grin to stretch across his lips, but it was an insincere gesture, and Sean wasn't quite sure why.

The room alone was worth a sizable fortune and, more importantly, would represent the single most extraordinary discovery since King Tut's tomb. And their reward for the find would also be substantial.

Tommy and Sean weren't in it for the money, and they figured Craig wasn't, either. Brent seemed to be of a different mindset, but he'd get over it and would be well compensated for his time.

Sean turned to his friend, who was still studying the scepter. "Schultzie, what does all this say? I can only get a few pieces of it."

Tommy stood up straight and stretched his back, the muscles tightening from bending over the sarcophagus at an awkward angle.

He peered at the wall and stepped away from the chest, eyes poring over the ancient artwork.

"This can't be right," Tommy said after analyzing the images cut in gold.

"What can't?" Craig asked, suddenly acutely more interested in the hieroglyphs. He walked around the coffer and over to where the others stood. Brent joined them, just behind his employer.

"This is the clue to the location of the scroll," Tommy explained.

"So, it isn't here," Craig realized.

"No." Tommy echoed his frustration. "But this doesn't make sense."

"Enlighten us, Schultzie," Sean said. "What doesn't make sense about it?"

Tommy turned and faced the others, extending his right hand toward the wall. "Up there is an aerial map of Giza. See the three pyramids?"

"Incredible. How in the world did they create an overhead view of the area like that in such detail."

"That's not all," Tommy continued. "The hieroglyphs speak of a place hidden under the watchful gaze of Her-em-akhet."

Sean clenched his jaw, trying to recall the name. Nothing came to mind.

"That translates to Horus of the Horizon," Tommy said.

"Another reference to the sun," Craig guessed.

"Yes and no. In the New Kingdom, that was what they called the Sphinx. And this says that the hall protects the secret of the great sesh. Sesh was their term for scribe."

"Archimedes," Sean realized.

"Yes," Tommy agreed.

"So, we are supposed to find the scroll inside the Sphinx of Giza?" Craig asked, dejection filling his lungs.

"No. Inside the Hall of Records."

5

C raig shook his head. "The Hall of Records doesn't exist, Schultzie. You know that as well as I do. That place has been excavated more than a playground sandbox. There's nothing else to find."

Tommy didn't answer immediately. He rubbed the stubble on his chin and turned away from the group. Deep in thought, he paced silently over to the adjacent wall and inspected the images.

They offered stories about Ptolemy III, but nothing regarding the Sphinx or the Hall of Records.

"What is the Hall of Records?" Brent asked. "Am I the only one in the room that doesn't know what that is?"

Craig sighed. "The Hall of Records was supposedly seen in a vision in the 1930s by a supposed American clairvoyant named Edgar Cayce. He claimed that while he was in a trance, he visited the Hall and that it was located underneath the Sphinx. Cayce died in the 1940s. As I said, the Sphinx has been studied and excavated many times, before and after Cayce's astral visit. No one ever found anything."

"That's mostly true," Tommy said.

"What do you mean, mostly?"

"The structure was investigated, and the area around it was cleared out. Some tunnels were found, but this could be a reference to something deeper beneath the Sphinx. What if the archaeologists didn't go far enough underground?"

"Surely with modern technology, someone has run scans that would tell us if there were hidden chambers or passages under the Sphinx."

"I'm not so sure," Tommy countered. "You have to go through a ton of red tape to get permission to move a single piece of sand in that area. I know some of the folks who've worked extensively there. A few of them on the Sphinx. Most of the time, they're retracing steps."

"So, you're saying you believe the Hall of Records really exists?" Hope flittered through Craig's words.

"Sure. Sean and I have seen stranger things."

"He ain't lying," Sean added.

"But it's like I said, if we were to try to do anything there, getting the permits could take months, or more. On top of that, there are already archaeologists on site trying to find her." He extended a finger toward the sarcophagus behind Craig.

"So, we come forward with this find, and they'll clear out."

"It's not that simple, man. I mean, yeah, we will have to report this through the appropriate channels. But then there will be press conferences, teams that have to be brought in to handle everything the right way. When it's all said and done, it could be a few years before we get a chance to investigate the Sphinx."

"Seems like you're finding all the blockades and not any ways around them, Schultzie. I thought you were the guy who gets things done."

Tommy ignored the venom in the statement, at least outwardly. "Look, Craig, I want to find the scroll as much as you, but this..." He kept his arm out, pointing at the chest. "This is everything we could have ever hoped for. More, actually."

He walked over to the sarcophagus and looked inside at the

mummy of Cleopatra. "If it's recognition you're after, brother, you're about to get it."

Craig nodded, as if surrendering the entire argument. He turned away from Tommy and Sean and looked at Brent.

The other two didn't see the unspoken exchange between them before Craig spun back around slowly on his heels.

"While I appreciate the sentiment about the recognition," he said, steepling his fingers toward his chin, "and the gravity of this discovery, it isn't recognition I'm after. Or even the financial reward this find will bring me."

Sean shifted his stance. He wasn't sure where this was going, but he didn't like the tone in Craig's voice.

He hadn't been able to interpret much from the writing on the wall, save for one part—a warning to thieves who would try to steal the scepter from the dead queen. Sean shuffled closer to the sarcophagus, letting his hand drift over the edge and hover above the mummy.

Craig was so caught up in his argument with Tommy, he didn't pay any mind to Sean's movement.

"Then what do you want out of all this?" Tommy asked. "I thought we were searching for the Scroll of Archimedes. That bit of papyrus pales in comparison to finding the tomb of Cleopatra."

"You're not seeing the bigger picture, Schultzie," Craig mused. "Sure, we'll get featured in some magazines, maybe get a few documentaries. And we'd get, what, a few mil as a reward for finding all this?" He waved his hands around like a drunk preaching on the street. "You still don't know what the scroll is. Do you?"

"It was a weapon," Tommy said, though now he didn't sound so sure. "Archimedes designed it to defend—"

"Sure," Craig cut him off. "That's what he thought he'd created. But what he really made was something far more powerful. A machine that can harness and distribute the power of the sun. Energy, Schultzie. Power. Archimedes, probably unwittingly, built a device that could power entire cities indefinitely. But even he didn't understand the implications. How could he? They didn't have electricity back then."

Craig took a breath and glanced around the room as if it were made of cardboard. "None of this can compare to the trillions we'll make. Control the power, and you control the world."

"You can't be serious. Craig, you're kidding. Right?" Tommy peered into his colleague's dark eyes. He searched for a sign that the joke was about to end, but he saw nothing of the sort. "You're not joking. Are you?"

Craig took a step toward Tommy. His expression softened. He reached out his hand and placed his palm on Tommy's left shoulder.

"The world has an energy crisis, Schultzie. Governments are pushing for green energy they can't supply. Do you have any idea the amount of electricity they'll have to generate for all those electric cars they're pushing? All the factories they're forcing to go electric? And the gap between the First World and the Third is only going to grow. We can end that. We can provide clean, cheap energy to everyone. All we have to do is find Archimedes' Scroll."

Tommy frowned as he held Craig's stare. The man he thought he knew was no longer there. Instead, he saw the look of a fanatic, of a madman, of someone who was so drunk on the idea of wealth and power they'd forgotten their life's calling. He'd seen it before—too many times. But he usually hadn't known those people, the villains he and Sean had been forced to combat with wit and strength. Those had been strangers, randoms. It was easier to accept that there were some bad and some good people in the world, and most of the time the bad ones were hell-bent on getting a leg up on the rest—even if that meant chasing down mythical artifacts they believed would grant them fortune or power.

But not Craig.

Craig had been someone Tommy and Sean both trusted, someone they had collaborated with on various projects. He'd dedicated his life to discovering the truth about the past, to uncovering history long lost to humanity.

Now, standing here in this shimmering golden chamber, Tommy

realized he didn't know the man at all. And that betrayal stabbed through his chest like a spear.

"What about preserving history, Craig? Isn't that the job? That's why we're here? Not for glory or power. We're here because we're the only ones who believe we can share these incredible things with the world."

"You know what? I did all that. I spent decades doing it. Toiling in the hot sun in the middle of barren wastelands. But no more. It's time for me to finally get mine. It's easy for you to say you do it for the love of history and discovery when you're sitting there in your ivory IAA tower in Atlanta. What's your net worth now, Schultzie? Did you hit a hundred million yet?"

"That is not fair, Craig." Tommy felt his muscles tighten.

Sean listened quietly from just behind him, his hand still hanging over the sarcophagus lip.

"On that, we agree, my old friend."

Tommy shook his head. "The reward we will get for finding this is not insignificant. From there, you can build up the same way I did. It just takes—"

"Time?" Craig interrupted. "I'm tired of waiting. And like I said, what this will fetch us is a pittance compared to what the scroll will bring. If you don't want to help us get into the Hall of Records to find it, fine by me. I'd rather split the empire two ways than four." He nodded at the golden wall. "It didn't work out so well for Alexander's generals to do it like that anyway."

He stepped to the side, removing his hand from Tommy's shoulder to reveal Brent holding a pistol at waist level, aimed straight at Tommy's chest.

"You can't do this, Craig. You don't know where to look for the hall. No one does."

"I'm sure I'll figure something out," Craig countered. "It's a shame you didn't want to join us, Schultzie. We could have done amazing things together. But it's just as well." He moved back to Brent's side. "Kill them both."

Brent raised the pistol higher, steadying his aim toward Tommy's nose. At such close range, less than twenty feet away, it would be like shooting fish in a coffee mug.

"Come on, Brent. You don't want to do this."

Brent shrugged and bobbed his head. "Actually, I really do. Like he said, bigger slice of the pie." His finger tensed on the trigger.

"I wouldn't do that if I were you, Brent," Sean cautioned.

He hadn't been able to retrieve the pistol in his bag. The move would have been too obvious. He'd already seen what Brent was doing, and his only play was a semi-bluff.

Sean had spent more time than he cared to admit at Texas Hold 'Em poker tables, and he'd used the semi-bluff to his advantage in countless situations. He'd make a bet in hopes of taking down the pot even when he didn't have a hand, but still had a decent statistical chance of winning depending on what cards came out on the turn and river.

In this situation, he didn't like the odds, but he had to try.

"And why is that?" Brent asked, hesitating for a moment.

"Because if I pull this scepter, this entire place comes down on top of us. We all die."

Sean's fingers gripped the serpent's head on the scepter.

Brent snickered at the hollow gesture. "You're bluffing, Sean. Go ahead, pull it out. I'll wait. You two aren't going anywhere, anyway."

Tommy's eyes shifted to his left, but he couldn't see what his friend was doing behind him.

"I'd prefer none of us die here," Sean said. "Put the gun down. Let's talk about this."

"What are you waiting for?" Craig spat. "Kill them."

"You pull that trigger, and you die here," Sean warned. "Both of you."

What Craig, Brent, and even Tommy didn't know was that Sean had seen something in the hieroglyphs on the wall—a warning concerning the scepter, for whoever tried to take it from the queen.

He hoped his remedial understanding of the ancient language was correct, but for all he knew, he might have misinterpreted it.

"What are you waiting for, Sean?" Brent coaxed. "Take it."

Sean took a breath and exhaled. It seemed like a lose-lose situation. If he was right, and removing the scepter actually did trigger some ancient trap, he and Tommy would die right alongside the other two. But at this point, it was his only play.

With no other option, Sean pulled the cobra's head—and jerked the scepter from the mummy's embrace.

6

Brent's lips creased for a second when nothing happened. It was a smug expression, one that Sean wished he could head-butt right off the guy's face. But it didn't last long.

A mechanism clicked from within the sarcophagus. More sounds echoed from the ancient stone box, rippling through the floor underneath the men.

Brent's eyes widened. He looked down around at his feet, then back toward Craig, who had stopped near the door.

A winding sound echoed through the chamber, like a cable being pulled through pulleys and hoops.

"Get out!" Craig shouted at Brent and sprinted for the doorway.

Brent flashed a furious look, and fired his pistol.

But his aim had been thrown off by the distraction, and the round missed Tommy's head by mere inches. The bullet ricocheted dangerously off the wall, causing Brent to duck lest it randomly hit him instead of his intended target.

Sean snatched his friend by the shoulder and yanked him down behind the sarcophagus for cover. It wouldn't be enough if Brent shifted even a step or two to one side, but Sean was betting on the ancient trap taking care of that problem.

His gut proved true, and Brent darted for the door behind Craig.

The chamber rumbled its warning to the remaining occupants.

"What did you do?" Tommy asked.

Sean peered around the side of the coffer and saw the other two were gone.

He grabbed his bag, stuffed the scepter inside, and pulled the pistol out of the main compartment, ready to pursue their erstwhile partners.

"I'll tell you after we take them down. We have to move."

Tommy stood and picked up his bag. Sean was already three steps toward the door when suddenly a massive stone slab fell into the doorway, blocking their only way out.

Sean didn't stop. He ran to the door and pushed on the heavy stone with both hands, praying he could somehow get the thing to move.

But it wouldn't budge.

Tommy caught up two seconds later and likewise leaned into the slab with his friend.

They grunted, pushing with every muscle they could summon, but it was no use.

"It's... too heavy," Sean said between breaths. "This thing weighs a ton."

"At least," Tommy panted. He looked back into the chamber and around at the golden walls. "To be honest, I think I would have preferred the bullet to staying down here and starving to death."

Sean sighed and stepped away from the blocked door. "Well, bullets we have," Sean said, brandishing his pistol. "But you'd die from dehydration before you starved."

"Did anyone ever tell you you're the comforting type? Because they lied."

Sean chuckled and walked back over to the sarcophagus. He peered inside the coffer, leaning over it to see if there was something inside that might help them escape.

"How did you know about the scepter?" Tommy asked.

Sean reached into his rucksack and removed the scepter. He held it aloft and stared at it. The light from the lanterns and his headlamp gleamed off the gold, and shimmered through the precious gems.

"Lucky guess," Sean half lied. He handed the object to Tommy. "You saw it, right?"

"Yeah, but I didn't want to spook them. Well, not until they pulled a gun on us." Tommy sounded dejected, betrayed, lost. "I can't believe Craig was just using us to get to the scroll. But his reasoning... It's disturbing. He really believes whatever Archimedes designed can create more energy than any of our current technologies."

"Strange? Yes. Possible? Also yes." Sean thought back to some of the incredible, ancient structures they'd seen. From underground pyramids to enormous hidden cities, high-tech energy had been at the core of all of them.

Sean went on. "We've always known the ancients had access to technology that's been kept from us, or was lost eons ago. We're only now scratching the surface. Think about Shangri-la, and what we found there. Or in Alaska. Never would have dreamed it."

"You're right," Tommy said. "And those things have been under investigation for years now." He held up quotes as he said the word.

Sean knew what that meant. Once governments stepped in, those who made the decisions for humanity would put things under wraps forever if they could, or at least until they could figure out how to best use it to secure their control of the commoners—also known as voters.

"Look at these markings on the side of that," Sean said, switching subjects to the present. "It's Greek. I thought maybe you could figure it out."

Tommy rolled the scepter in his palm and nodded. "Yeah. I can read it." He studied it for a couple of minutes while Sean searched the room for a way out. The only thing he could find were the four trap doors overhead. They were more than ten feet high, which hadn't felt good on the unexpected drop to the hard floor below. He felt lucky none of them had broken any bones or sprained something.

He also felt unlucky Craig and Brent hadn't broken their necks. Sean found his dark side hoping for the chance to do it himself.

Vengeance wasn't a helpful sentiment at the moment. They needed to get out of here.

He noticed the discs that made up the trap doors were hanging on bronze hinges, and still open. But there was no way he could jump up through the openings. It was too high. In his high school and college years, the best he'd ever done was dunking a tennis ball through a basketball hoop, but could never leap high enough to get the actual basketball through the rim.

"This is a map," Tommy said, breaking the silence.

Sean turned and saw him holding up the scepter. "What?"

"This describes the distance from the Sphinx to the entrance into the Hall of Records."

"Seriously?" Sean hurried back to where his friend stood and looked closely at the scepter's shaft.

"Yeah, seriously. Only problem is, I don't know if it is from the face of the Sphinx or from its backside."

"The clue said under the gaze of the Sphinx, right? Or whatever you called it."

"Har-em-akhet," Tommy said. "And yes, it did. So, I guess from its face. Not that it does us any good, unless you happen to have some explosives in your pack that can blow through that rock blocking the exit."

"I don't. Even if I did, I wouldn't use it in here unless I absolutely had to. Could bring down the whole place on top of us."

"Might be worth the gamble at this point."

Tommy walked over to the nearest wall and ran his fingers along the golden surface. He read the ancient messages carved into the metal as he moved right to left but couldn't find a clue to another exit, or a seam that might present some other unseen door.

"Find anything?" Sean asked, guessing what his friend was doing.

"No. Check the other walls. Maybe there's another way out of here."

Sean took the opposite wall and started tracing his fingers along the surface. "This really is impressive," he said as he shuffled sideways. "I wonder how they got all of this down here."

"I know. It really is amazing how much we don't know about the ancients, how they accomplished so many of the feats we marvel at today."

"Sucks we're basically buried alive in one of those feats."

Tommy forced an uneasy laugh. "Yeah."

After searching the room, the two met in a corner.

"Nothing?" Sean asked.

"No." Tommy's stomach grumbled.

"Don't start, Schultzie. We've only been down here for a few minutes, man."

"I had a light lunch."

Sean shook his head and walked back to the center of the room. He felt a draft of air tickle his skin. He tilted his head up, eyes drifting to one of the four holes above him and the golden trap door still hanging there on its hinge.

"What are you thinking?" Tommy asked, walking over to where his friend stood. "No way we can reach that."

Sean bit his lip. *He's never going to let me hear the end of this.*

"So, you don't happen to have that rope you're always carrying in your bag, do you?"

"No. I left it at home."

"Seriously?" Sean looked at him in surprise.

Tommy cracked a smile. "Of course I have it. I always bring a rope. You never—"

"Know when you're going to need one," Sean finished. "I'm aware."

"That rope bailed us out of a few sticky situations in the past."

Sean let out a long, slow exhale. "Well, I think it might be able to get us out of this one, too."

Tommy followed Sean's gaze up to the hole above. "That might be true if I had a way to anchor it in the room above. But that's not possible. Maybe if I had a grappling hook I could attach to the end."

Sean glanced over at him. "Maybe put that on the list for the next trip."

He returned his focus to the trap door hanging above them. "Still, I think we can make it work. Grab the rope, and let me try something."

"So, you're saying that you want me to get my rope? The rope that can possibly get us out of this mess?"

"Yes," Sean drawled.

"The rope that you have given me crap about so many times in the past, despite the fact that it's saved your neck on multiple occasions?"

"Yes. And for the record, I haven't complained about it recently. Or even in a few years."

"I'm just making sure."

"You're an idiot," Sean said and stalked toward Tommy's bag lying on the floor near his own.

"Hey, stay out of my stuff," Tommy warned, walking after him.

Sean ignored the order, unzipped the bag, and pulled out the black climbing rope.

He looped it over his forearm and walked back to where he'd stood before, passing Tommy in the process and leaving him with an annoyed expression like a child who didn't want to share his toys.

"I already told you, there's no way to hook that to anything up in that other chamber," Tommy said.

"I'm not trying to anchor it in the chamber," Sean said, tying the rope into a sort of lasso with a slip knot.

He held most of the rope in a loop in his left hand, while allowing a little slack for the other end. Then, standing underneath the trap door, he tossed the lasso up toward the metal disc.

The cord looped around the base of the door near the hinge, and Sean quickly snapped the rope so it would close around the clasps, then pulled it until it was taut. He leaned back, gripping the rope with both hands to test the strength of the hinge until it bore all of his weight.

"Why didn't I think of that?" Tommy muttered, staring up at the door. "Still, how are you going to get up through the hole?"

"Watch and learn, Schultzie."

Sean slipped a loop of the cord around his right forearm, and then slid his hand upward, gripped a higher point, and then pulled again. Fortunately, Tommy's rope wasn't a pure climbing and rappelling type. Those were made with a certain amount of stretch and flexibility. If a rock climber fell using one of those, it would offer a certain amount of give to keep from jarring the user.

This rope was slightly more dense and offered less stretch.

Sean raised his left hand above the right and pulled himself higher.

"I sucked at this in high school gym class," Tommy admitted.

Sean chuckled as he continued upward. "I know," he grunted. "I was there."

"I hate you."

"Stop making me laugh. I don't want to have to do this again."

Sean kept going until he reached the metal disc. Then he reached up with his left hand and grabbed onto the top edge of it.

"Now what's your plan?" Tommy wondered.

Instead of answering, Sean loosened the loop around his right forearm and then stuck his right foot through it, wrapped it until it was tight, and then pressed down to test its strength. The cord held firm, and he quickly lifted his left foot up to the top of the disc while boosting his torso into the open shaft.

Once he was into the hole, Sean pulled his right foot up and pushed his boot into the base of the shaft wall to keep his back against the opposite side.

"Wow," Tommy gasped from below. "Genius."

"Not there yet."

Now with his entire body wedged into the cylindrical hole, Sean reached down and loosened the rope around his foot and hooked it through a carabiner on a belt loop. It wouldn't give him any security for the rest of the climb, but that wasn't the plan.

Sean shimmied his way up the shaft, keeping his upper back and shoulders pressed firmly against the side. It took patience, and at one point he felt the tip of his boot slip, nearly causing him to lose his balance and fall back down.

The drop from the disc to the floor wasn't comfortable, but from where he was above the opening, Sean doubted he'd escape a fall without a broken bone at the very least.

He dug the balls of his feet in harder against the side of the wall and pushed again. His back and shoulders scraped along the surface until he felt a sudden absence of support. His spine straightened as his head and shoulders reached the surface of the next room, and he quickly ran his feet up the shaft until he could roll out and away from the opening.

Sean looked around the chamber he'd been in before, shining the headlamp in every direction.

The place was eerily dark compared to before when he and the other three illuminated it with their lanterns. At the moment, he welcomed the darkness. Had there been other lights, it would have meant Craig and Brent were there, somehow connected by the passage below to this chamber.

Sean realized that was irrational. There'd been no other way in or out of this room. Only the passage they'd come through before. He appreciated that Tommy hadn't said anything yet, probably being careful for the same reason Sean had been on alert at first.

"It's clear up here!" he shouted down to Tommy. "Hook the two bags onto the rope, and I'll pull them up first."

"Copy that," Tommy replied.

After a minute, Tommy let Sean know the bags were on the line.

Sean pulled the bags up through the shaft and into the upper chamber, unhooked them, and lowered the rope back down through the opening.

It took Tommy a little longer to get up into the shaft. While he was stronger than Sean, he also had more bulk, like a pro football linebacker, so the challenge was formidable. Sean had an athletic figure, strong in his own right, but leaner.

Tommy gasped when he finally reached the top of the shaft and rolled out onto the floor. "I... don't... want to do that again," he said between breaths.

Sean grinned at him. "You did good, kid. Way better than back in high school."

"Thanks," Tommy said, only half serious. "No sign of the others?"

"No," Sean said, shaking his head. "I don't think that tunnel connects to this one. It must lead to another exit somewhere. Still, we should be careful on the way out. It's possible we could run into them."

"I would love that, actually."

Sean agreed. "Yeah. I would, too."

"Do you think they're really going to try to find the Hall of Records?"

"Sure sounds like it. But like you said, no one has been able to locate it yet."

Tommy nodded, then stood and walked over to the two bags. He reached into Sean's rucksack and pulled out the scepter. "Yeah. But none of them had this."

7

CAIRO

The dim rays of first light pierced the slit between the curtains and stretched across the pillow next to Sean's head.

He'd already been awake for an hour, as it seemed he was every day before dawn. Sometimes it was more than an hour.

In his youth, sleeping had never been a problem. He could go to bed at ten at night and sleep until seven the next morning. And hitting the hay later, say around one in the morning, didn't have any impact on his quality of sleep. He'd just sleep later into the morning —unless it was a school night.

But as he'd gotten older, that superpower had faded. Now, it seemed more nights than not he roused from his slumber for no reason at all—sometimes after only sleeping for three or four hours. And he almost never found the ability to return to the dreams from which he'd awakened.

Insomnia was a vicious criminal, stealing from him the thing he probably needed most. He ate well and exercised. Stress or worry about finances, marriage, and other problems so many people faced didn't darken Sean's bedroom door.

He joked that if he could get that last of the four pillars of health —that being sleep—he might find immortality.

As yet he hadn't been able to unwrap the secret, and no amount of sleep medications seemed to do the trick, either.

Tonight hadn't been bad. He'd gotten six hours before his mind shook him free of the darkness behind his eyes. It was fine.

He spent forty-five minutes meditating, focusing on calming his mind. His favorite visualization was walking on the beach along the Emerald Coast of the Florida Panhandle—also known as 30A, named after the famous road that snaked its way along the gulf.

As he lay there, eyes closed and headphones sending binaural beats into his mind, he felt the warm, white sand between his toes. He heard the ocean waves crashing along the shore. The salty breeze blew through his hair and filled his nostrils.

But those moments were fleeting, constantly bombarded by the distraction of the task at hand—locating the entrance to the mythical Hall of Records.

He opened his eyes and swung his legs over the edge of the bed— planting his feet flat on the dense carpet.

Sean sat there for a few seconds, still listening to the drone of the frequency radiating through his ears and into his brain. Then, he removed the AirPods and placed them back in their charging case on the nightstand.

He stood and walked over to the window, pulled back the curtains, and looked out through the glass. The orange-yellow sun peeked over the horizon to the east, rippling through the haze. Across the street below, the ancient Nile ran slowly through the city—the artery that had brought life through this valley for millennia.

He stared at the scene for a minute, then another. Somewhere out there, his wife, Adriana, was on a hunt of her own, searching for another of the seemingly endless trove of masterpieces that had been pilfered by the Nazis more than eighty years ago.

They'd spoken two days ago, when she was in Salzburg, one of his favorite European cities. He'd wished he could be there with her, but he had a treasure hunt of his own to manage—one that had turned south in a most unexpected way.

He could only hope her luck was better than his, though Sean knew that with her unusual skill set, fortune needed her more than the other way around.

He walked back over to the nightstand and checked the time, then his text messages. He hadn't received anything from her or anyone else, which didn't surprise him. Sean didn't have many friends outside the scope of his career. He kept in touch with his parents back in Chattanooga and a few friends from high school he rarely saw, but other than that his life revolved around Adriana, Tommy, and their work recovering artifacts and securing them for study and analysis.

The clock on his phone told him he still had thirty minutes before he had to meet Tommy downstairs.

So, he did four sets of push-ups with his rucksack strapped to his shoulders and four sets of squats before hopping into a cold shower.

After drying off, he got dressed, collected his belongings into his backpack and a messenger bag, and made his way out into the hall toward the elevator.

Even something as mundane as leaving a hotel room was never something Sean took for granted. Not in decades.

With every step he sensed the air around him, listened for sounds of change in pressure or of movement. Most of the time all of this happened unconsciously. It was deeply ingrained in him, and had been for years. Most people would think him crazy if he told them any of that, but it was part of surviving in a world full of bad people with worse intentions.

Perfect case in point was what happened to them the day before in Jordan.

Sean was still kicking himself over not seeing that one coming from Craig. Sean had always prided himself on his ability to read people. It was one of those skills that had kept him alive through the years, or won him some big pots at a poker table. But Craig's serpentine move had evaded detection. And that needled at Sean's mind, scratching it and poking it like a mosquito that would never die.

He pressed the elevator button and waited for it to arrive, then stepped on when the doors opened and pressed the button for the lobby.

When the doors separated again, he was greeted by the smell of fresh coffee and pastries. The sounds of people conversing filled his ears, along with the espresso machine hissing and gurgling out the orders of people in line at the coffee bar across from the elevator atrium.

Sean looked around for Tommy but didn't spot him. That wasn't surprising. Sean was usually the first one to arrive at pretty much everything.

He made his way across the room and stood in line, eyeing the menu in hopes of spotting a cortado. There wasn't one, though that didn't surprise him. Most chain coffee shops and bars didn't offer them, although there were some he'd visited that said they could make them.

He decided on a black coffee and after paying the barista took his cup over to a corner near the back of the coffee bar, where he could keep an eye on both the front entrance and the elevators.

Tommy appeared four minutes later, and Sean gave him a single upward nod to acknowledge he'd seen him.

Tommy brought his things over and set them on the floor next to the little table.

"Nice of you to join me," Sean joked.

"Nice of you to get me a coffee," Tommy returned.

Sean shrugged as he sipped his brew with an overtly satisfied look on his face. "I wasn't sure when you would get here. It could have been cold."

Tommy merely shook his head and joined the short line at the bar, got his coffee, and returned.

Sean enjoyed the moment. Mornings like this, he knew, could be few and far between. And they were about to dive face-first into a busy and challenging day.

"The meeting is still on, right?" Sean asked when Tommy returned with his brew.

"Yeah." Tommy stirred the cup with a wooden stick and sat down across from Sean. "Why wouldn't it be?"

"You never know. Something may have come up."

"Dr. Amid isn't flaky like that. If he couldn't meet with us, he wouldn't have set aside the time. He's a busy guy. Honestly, I'm surprised he could work us in on such short notice."

"How come I've never met him before?" Sean raised the cup to his lips, and raised a curious right eyebrow with it.

"I don't know. Guess you weren't in the right place at the right time. Like I said, he's a busy man. He's one of the leading Egyptologists in the world."

"Oh," Sean said in a lengthy tone. "I know who he is. He's that guy I've seen on television on some of the history shows about the pyramids and the Valley of the Kings, right?"

"Probably. He's been on several of those."

"Yeah. Okay, I knew I recognized the name. Wow, you do have connections, Schultzie. I'm impressed." Sean raised the cup to his friend in salute.

Tommy snorted. "I've definitely made some interesting connections over the years doing this kind of work."

"You think he can help us?"

"I wouldn't have called him if I didn't."

"Fair point."

"But he's mapped a lot of the ancient tunnels in this area, taken old records from previous excavations, and created a massive database with the schematics. It's not something you'll find with a Google search."

Sean watched a man in a dark blue business suit walk by with his coffee in one hand and a briefcase in the other. He continued walking until he found an empty seat on a couch at the end of the dining area and sat down, then immediately began looking at his phone and unconsciously sipping the coffee.

"Why all the secrecy?"

"Isn't it obvious?" Tommy snipped.

Sean cocked his head to the side. "No. Not really. I mean, I guess maybe they don't want stuff like that out there for the public, or they would get a never-ending line of curious tourists in places they ought not be."

"Bingo. And there are definitely some places in that database that are off-limits to the public. I would say there are several that have been intentionally kept under wraps for reasons even I don't know."

Sean held his question for a second before asking, "How do you know what's in that database?"

Tommy raised his coffee to his lips, and smirked. "Because I've seen it."

8

The Garden City of Cairo offered splendors and wonders both of the natural world and the retail variety.

Its wide streets were lined and shaded with lush trees, shrubs, and flowers in planters. The plant life stood as a sort of silent, vibrant tribute to the power of the Nile and what it had done for this valley since the first inhabitants began to dwell here. The river gave life to this narrow strip of land, producing a green splinter in an otherwise barren land. Many thousands of years ago, this entire area had been covered in lush grasslands, lakes, and rivers. This modern strip was most of what was left.

High-end clothiers hid behind burgeoning tree branches that hung out over the sidewalks and streets. Of course, there were several American fast-food chains located on the strip as well—a blight that seemed to be spreading around the world, infecting places of unique culture and culinary distinction.

Sean recalled a trip to Berlin with a high school group when he was younger, and how with all the delicacies on offer, many of his friends opted to hit up KFC. Not that he hated the place, but he didn't travel halfway around the world for the same "eleven herbs and spices" he could get within five minutes of anywhere back home.

Dr. Amid's home was just over a mile from the hotel, which was a good thing since the morning traffic was thick with commuters in cars, motorcycles, and scooters—none of whom seemed to have any regard for the laws of the road, and all of whom seemed to have one hand surgically attached to their horns.

Sean recalled talking to a Greek cab driver once on his way from Athens to the port in Piraeus. The driver was a tall guy and had played professional basketball in Greece in his younger days.

"The only worse drivers in the world than the Greeks are the Egyptians," he boomed, laughing heartily at the statement as if coming in second place in that competition was something to be proud of.

This wasn't Sean's first visit to Cairo, but he was reminded of who came in first as their driver weaved in and out of the jagged lines of vehicles. At one point, he saw a guy on a moped clip a parked car's mirror with his right handlebar. The mirror exploded into a plume of glass and plastic. To the rider's credit, the moped only wobbled for a second before the man steadied it. But instead of stopping to leave a note or see if he could wait for the car's owner to explain what happened, he simply kept driving.

Sean merely shook his head. That kind of thing would get someone's butt kicked back in the States. Here, it seemed to be the norm.

Their driver turned off the main drag and into a quieter neighborhood. Palatial mansions stood along the tree-lined sidewalks, with lush vegetation growing out through iron fences and over the tops of perimeter walls.

The car stopped outside a two-story, yellow home with white trim around the windows and balcony doors. It stood behind a brick wall and an iron gate that curled up from both doors to meet in the center.

"Looks like the professor is doing pretty well for himself," Sean mused.

"Yeah. He definitely does. A string of best-selling books, documentaries, and television appearances will do that. Plus he's kind of considered an international treasure by many of our peers."

The two thanked the driver for the ride, and walked up to the gate, where a keypad stood to the left of the paved driveway.

Tommy stepped up to it and pressed the call button.

The sound of a phone rang loudly from the speaker. It stopped suddenly on the fourth ring, and the gate began to part in the middle.

"So, I guess we just walk in?" Sean asked.

"Vokum always had a flair for the dramatic."

"His first name is Vokum? That's a new one. And I've met a lot of people."

"Yeah, but to be fair, you were shooting at a lot of those."

"Hey, they were shooting at me, too."

They walked through the opening of the gate. Sean glanced back at the street, just to make sure they weren't being followed.

He got that weird feeling someone was watching them, and he wouldn't put it beyond Craig to have come to the same place.

"Just curious," Sean said. "Does Craig happen to know Vokum, too?"

"Probably," Tommy answered.

Sean watched the gate close behind them, though it didn't fill him with a ton of reassurance.

"I mean, we know a lot of the same folks in the historical community. If Craig doesn't know him personally, he certainly knows who Vokum is." Tommy glanced over at his friend as they approached the mansion. "You didn't see anything suspicious, did you?"

"No," Sean said with a shake of the head. "Just checking."

"You sure?" Tommy hesitated as they reached the steps leading up to the entrance. He looked back at the gate, suddenly feeling trepidation snake its way through his gut.

"I'll keep a lookout," Sean said. "Let's just see what your friend can do for us."

They ascended the steps to the front door, and as Tommy was about to ring the doorbell, the huge white door swung open, revealing a man with dark brown skin tanned from years spent on archaeological digs, and fluffy white hair bleached by the same. His eyebrows were thick, matched by his broad nose and jaw.

He wore a black, short-sleeve button-up and gray slacks. It was an ensemble Sean had seen many times when hanging out with cigar dons at events held at a local billiard club near his previous home in Chattanooga. The style apparently translated well to this country and its culture. Vokum looked relaxed but sharp.

"Tommy Schultz," Vokum boomed with a broad smile. He extended his arms out wide and wrapped them around Tommy, bracing him in a bear hug.

"Vokum," Tommy answered. "Been too long, my friend."

"Yes, it has." He slapped Tommy on the back and then let him go. "It's definitely been a while."

He turned his attention to Sean. "And you must be Sean Wyatt. Tommy has told me much about you."

Sean offered his hand, but the man grabbed it and pulled him in for a hug.

After he let go, Sean grinned. "I hope he edited some of those stories."

Vokum wagged a meaty finger in the air and laughed. "Oh, I'm sure he did. But he's told me about some of your more thrilling adventures. I have to say, better you than me. I prefer to keep the excitement in my life more localized to the golf course. That's more than enough for me."

"Tommy didn't tell me you're a golfer."

"It didn't come up," Tommy defended.

"That's probably because I took a few hundred dollars off your friend here the last time we played Dreamland."

Sean turned his head slowly toward his friend with eyebrows raised in surprise. "He definitely didn't tell me about that, or that you were a member at the Dreamland Club. That's one of the best courses in the region."

He wasn't wrong. Dreamland Golf Resort was like an oasis within an oasis, offering spectacular fairways, greens, and a challenging layout worthy of some of the top players in the world.

"Ah, so you know a bit about golf, too?" Vokum asked.

"It's the perfect game," Sean said. "My mom always said that heaven is a golf course because you can spend eternity playing it and never perfect it."

Vokum's eyelids widened, showing off the whites of his eyes. "I like that. And you know, I think your mother might be right. What's your handicap?"

"Our friend Dr. Amid's is like a 3," Tommy said before Sean could answer.

"Three? Very strong. Last I checked I was in the 10–12 range."

"That's better than 85 percent of the golfers in the world," Vokum said. He turned sideways. "Please, you two didn't come here to stand out in the heat and talk about golf. Come in. I have coffee and some semolina sweet cakes for you in the kitchen."

The two Americans stepped inside, and their host followed, closing the door behind.

The foyer shot up high to the ceiling more than twenty feet above where a black chandelier shaped like a wire metal box hung. Ahead, to the left, a staircase went up to a landing, turned, and continued to the second story above.

They passed through a hall that branched to the left and into a grand living room with coffered ceilings, a gas fireplace surrounded by black granite, and a sitting area with luxurious black sofas and chairs.

Vokum led them into the kitchen, which was equally as impressive as the small glimpse of the rest of the interior they'd managed to catch.

"Wow," Sean exclaimed. "Now this is a kitchen."

White cabinets with brushed accents hung over white marble countertops. A steel gas stove with a professional kitchen vent stretched along the far wall, and matched the Sub-Zero refrigerator to Sean's left.

The smell of strong Egyptian coffee filled the room. As promised, on the counter to the left of an island sink, three plates with semolina sweet cakes—a unique Egyptian dessert—sat on the surface.

"Please, have a seat over there," their host said, pointing to a small wooden table in a breakfast nook across from the island. Four seats were positioned around it. The tall, wide windows offered a view out into a vast garden where flowers spilled out of planters, and hung from shepherd's hooks around a stone patio.

Sean and Tommy took a seat and waited as Vokum poured the coffee into three white mugs and then brought them over to the table. Then he returned to the island, collected the treats, and placed them next to the mugs.

"Been a while since I've had these," Tommy said. "Thanks, my old friend. You didn't have to go through the trouble."

"No trouble at all, Tommy. I can't have one of my favorite archaeology friends eating ordinary commercial cakes. You have to have the real thing while you're here. And same with the coffee."

Sean peered into the near black liquid, raised it, and took a sip. He nodded appreciatively.

"Good, huh?" Vokum said with pride.

"Yes," Sean said. "I like my coffee strong."

"Like your women, yeah?"

"Only one woman, but yes. She's the strongest I've met."

Their host laughed. "I hear Tommy's wife is quite the same. Shame I have never had the chance to meet her."

"I don't get to see her as often as I would like, either," Tommy confessed. "But I have a feeling that's going to change soon."

Sean flicked a questioning glance at his friend as if to ask what that was supposed to mean but said nothing and redirected his focus back to the dessert on the table.

He picked up the cake and took a bite. The sweet, syrupy richness spilled over the lingering taste of the bold coffee, combining for an incredible flavor.

"You like it?" Vokum asked, as if desperate for a compliment.

"Very much," Sean said with a nod. "It's spectacular. Did you make it?"

Vokum nodded, his secret revealed. "Yes, just this morning. They're fresh. That's when they taste the best."

"No doubt," Tommy agreed, taking a bite for himself.

After Vokum took a sip of coffee, he looked across at his two guests, his expression turning more serious. "So, you said you were wanting to take a look at some of the maps in my database. Anything in particular?"

Tommy chewed on another piece of cake, washed it down with a bit of coffee, then nodded. "Yeah." He hesitated, cast a sidelong look at Sean, then refocused on their host. "But you have to swear you won't tell anyone about this."

Sean stopped eating and waited to hear what his friend was going to say. They'd already agreed on how to approach this, what to tell Dr. Amid, and what to keep. There was no way they could simply blurt out what they had found deep within the underground passages of Petra. Vokum would probably laugh at first, and then when he saw they were serious, would question their sanity.

They would need to ease him into the truth.

Dr. Amid's face darkened. It was the first time Sean had seen him look serious since they'd met at the door. The guy was like an Egyptian Santa Claus up until then. Except the cookies were semolina cakes.

"Don't tell anyone what?" Vokum asked.

Sean and Tommy exchanged another look, then Tommy reached into the bag he'd set down by his chair. He pulled out the golden scepter they'd found in Jordan and extended it across the table toward their host.

"What is this?" Vokum's eyes were full of wonder and curiosity.

"Uh, well, it's a scepter," Tommy managed.

He set it down gently on the table in front of Vokum's plate. The Egyptian stared at it, unwilling to touch the golden shaft with its jeweled eyes and base. "Where did you get this?"

"Before we get to that, do you see the writings engraved on the handle?" Tommy pointed at the object so that his finger nearly touched it.

"May I?" Vokum asked.

"Obviously." Tommy leaned back, picked up the cake again, and popped the rest of it in his mouth.

Vokum picked up the scepter and inspected the shaft. "This is

Greek. Old Greek, too. The craftsmanship is incredible." He turned it and studied the snake's head. "The cobra looks so real. I'll have nightmares about this for sure."

Tommy bit his lip while their host translated the encryption. Sean took a drink of the coffee, holding the mug close to his face as he watched.

Vokum's expression changed to one of confusion. He looked up and met Tommy's gaze. "Are these directions?"

"Sort of."

"What do you mean, sort of? They either are or they aren't. Where did you find this?"

"We think," Sean said, "they're directions for a passage somewhere here in Cairo. Under the gaze of the Sphinx."

"Yes. I see that. It includes dimensions that haven't been used in thousands of years." He rolled the scepter over to look at the inscriptions one more time.

"We believe there is a secret passage somewhere to the east of the Sphinx. One that may lead..." Tommy hesitated to say it. He didn't want his friend to think him a quack. But there was no other way.

"Lead to what?" Vokum pressed.

"Underneath the Sphinx to the Hall of Records." Tommy winced as he said it, bracing himself for the verbal lashing he was about to receive from one of the most decorated archaeologists of all time.

"Well, I must say I didn't expect that." Vokum stared across the table at Tommy, but there was no disappointment in his eyes, no judgment. Instead, he nodded, and placed the scepter back on the table. "So, you're hoping that you can find the Hall of Records in my underground maps?"

"No," Tommy said, maybe a little too quickly. "You'd have already found it."

"We know that the area has been searched and excavated many times," Sean added. "And we also understand the context of the story behind this supposed repository. More than likely, it doesn't exist. And yet—"

"You have a scepter that suggests it could."

"Yeah," Tommy said.

"So," Vokum said with an exhale. "Are you going to tell me where you got this?"

Tommy looked over at Sean as if for permission, then back across the table at their host. "We found it in Jordan, at Petra."

Vokum's eyebrows shot up. "I didn't expect that. Now I'm even more curious. Why would something connected to the Sphinx be buried there? Were you doing a recovery for your agency? I have so many questions."

"We were there investigating a lead," Tommy said.

"A lead? What kind of lead? Was this one of those... You know what, maybe I don't want to know."

"We're looking for the Archimedes Scroll," Sean confessed.

"The Archimedes Scroll?" It sounded like it didn't ring a bell.

"Yeah," Tommy confirmed. "You know. *The* Archimedes Scroll."

"Oh. But why would it be in Jordan?"

"We found evidence that suggested it might be there. So, we brought Dr. Craig Freeman on board to help us."

"Freeman? What were you doing working with him?" Distrust sharpened his words like blades.

Tommy felt a little uncomfortable but kept going. "He brought information to us, Vokum. I had no reason not to trust him. We've worked on projects before."

"Pfft. Well, what happened? Where is he now? If this is a joint effort, he should be here."

"He tried to kill us," Sean said. "He and his assistant left us for dead in an underground chamber at Petra. We were barely able to escape."

"Well," Vokum tried to sound empathetic, "I'm glad you're alive. But I never trusted Freeman. Which I believe you were aware of, Tommy."

"Wait," Sean interrupted. "You knew this guy was shady?"

"No. Not really," Tommy said, doing his best to retreat. "Craig had a decent reputation until yesterday."

Vokum scoffed and threw up one hand. "He spent most of his

time doing nothing. I'm sure he would have snapped at the chance to work on a project with you."

"Well, in my defense, he brought the clue to us."

"I suppose you don't have that clue now? And what are we talking about here? What is all this? You really are trying to find the Archimedes Scroll? It was lost thousands of years ago when the contents of the Library at Alexandria drifted into obscurity."

"No," Tommy countered. "There was a copy. At Pergamum." He let the answer sink in, and watched as Vokum settled back into his seat.

"Pergamum? But those records vanished, too. They're lost just like everything else from Alexandria."

"Not everything," Tommy insisted.

Their host studied Tommy's face for a minute, gauging the meaning of his statement. "What else did you find in Jordan?"

Tommy drew a breath. "You won't believe me if I told you."

"Try me."

9

E ven with Sean and Tommy left for dead and having no way out of the chamber in Jordan, Craig felt an impending sense that time wasn't on his side.

Maybe he was just being paranoid. It certainly wasn't guilt. It was true Tommy had been a loyal advocate and friend over the years. But it wasn't like they went out for beers together on Thursday nights. They were distant coworkers. Besides, none of this would have happened if he and Wyatt had agreed to his proposition. They would all still be working together, trying to find a piece of papyrus that would solve the world's swelling energy crisis and make them the wealthiest people on the planet.

They'd been shortsighted, though, and there was nothing Craig could do about that. Tommy and Sean could have solved homelessness, world hunger, education, and other societal issues with that kind of money. They could have been the biggest do-gooders in the world.

But they had to let their immediate morals get in the way of long-term gains.

In the end, they got what they deserved.

Still, Craig knew he'd feel a lot better when the scroll was in his hands.

He peered out the window of the sedan at the people on the sidewalk. They passed shops and cafés, restaurants, and everything else the strip along the Nile offered to the Garden City district of Cairo.

Some were tourists, some locals. It made no difference to Craig. They were all pawns.

He'd been a pawn his entire life. Growing up in a middle-class suburban home in Oklahoma, Craig had watched his family work away their lives, paying more than their fair share in taxes but receiving little compensation in return from both their jobs and the government.

His parents died within four months of each other—a common thing the world over, but they were penniless when it happened, and there was little Craig could do to help them.

That part of him resented Tommy Schultz, even though he'd pushed beyond the useless sentiment and tried to work with the man on this mission. Tommy's financial standing had been a cold reminder to Craig that while the two men essentially did the same job in title, they were very different when it came to the rewards.

Then again, Schultz wasn't in the pits of dig sites in the scorching sun for days on end in hopes of finding a two-thousand-year-old spoon fragment. He was pulling treasures out of jungles or seas that others had already found, and getting paid handsomely for his efforts.

It was a good racket. Craig had to give him that.

Sure, Tommy and Sean had found a few things here and there thanks to their own efforts, but people like Craig did the real archaeological work.

And Tommy had had the gall to insinuate that Craig had no integrity because he wanted to use one artifact to enrich himself and solve a global problem at the same time. He was half-surprised Schultz hadn't wanted to give the thing to some government for free. Or all the world governments.

Brent hadn't said much since they left the airport, and neither had Craig other than suggesting they stop and get a cup of coffee.

After they'd fueled up on caffeine, they got back in their rental car and drove toward the Garden City district, where Dr. Vokum Amid resided.

Craig knew about Amid's database and the vast digital stores of underground maps he'd compiled for the area in and around Cairo, as well as an extensive set of schematics for Alexandria.

The man was one of the preeminent archaeologists searching for the Library of Alexandria and had more than once been convinced he'd found pieces of it—only to be disappointed.

While the fabled museum's contents had been lost or dispersed throughout the world over centuries of decline, finding the exact location of the ruins would be one of the greatest discoveries in history.

Craig felt certain the man was a fame-seeker. While he was a credible archaeologist, and historian, his books and appearances on documentaries smacked of a man trying to stuff his pockets.

Again, Craig thought, *why should I be any different?*

He sipped his coffee while they sat at a red light. Brent checked the GPS on his phone propped in one of the spare cup holders.

"This traffic sucks," he said, cutting through the silence.

"Welcome to Cairo," Craig said, also annoyed at the gridlock. "You ever been here before?"

Brent shook his head. "No. My team was in Iraq for a while. Then we were sent to Mexico to handle some things with the cartels down there. But I missed out on Egypt. Worked with a few guys who were here, though."

"Sounds like the private war sector is all over the place."

"Huh," Brent snorted. "You could say that. Private security teams, mercenaries, you name it. We're in virtually every theater you can imagine."

He sounded proud of the fact, as if it made him more manly. Craig also noted how he used the present tense.

"That doesn't even take into account all the underground stuff that goes on. Mercs who can't get work with agencies and legit companies will sell out to the highest bidders."

"You mean hit men, assassins," Craig guessed.

"Sometimes. If that's what's needed. People with money don't like to get their hands dirty. Mobs don't mind so much, but they have their own people. It's pretty rare for those types to hire out."

He spoke about the sinister underworld of hired guns so casually it was disturbing. Craig probably would have slept better without knowing all that. He'd found Brent almost by accident, through a friend of a friend who ran a private security agency similar to what Brent referred to moments ago. That friend primarily operated in the Middle East and parts of Central Africa.

Craig knew that this mission could be fraught with danger, and with the stakes being stratospherically high, he could take no chances. His friend had recommended Brent, saying that he'd just come back from a mission in the Congo and was looking to make some extra cash off the books. Not only that; Brent was amenable to the idea of getting paid later, and once Craig teased him with the mission and its potential rewards, he was in.

Brent had wanted more money up front than Craig could offer. He managed to sell a few pieces he'd failed to document from sites he'd been working, and collected enough money to convince Brent to join him with the promise of significantly greater riches when the job was done.

"Life-changing money" was how he'd described it at first before laying out the plan.

Brent knew it was a gamble of sorts, and he'd made that clear before reluctantly accepting the gig. Craig had also told him there was little to no chance of needing to use his combat skills since they'd be working with a former government agent, and because no one else knew what they were working on.

That had been true until Brent pulled the gun on Sean and Tommy in the chamber at Petra. Even then, Brent had only fired a single shot.

Craig felt relieved at the discovery of the next clue, but he could also sense that Brent's patience was already running thin. There were only so many places he could be dragged with only the payout of another clue, another riddle, before he would bail on the mission and leave Craig to fend for himself.

There were certainly worse consequences Craig could face, and he felt somewhat confident that he could complete this quest on his own. But he had no idea where this might lead. He could end up in a violent country somewhere, or being pursued by dangerous people.

He'd never done anything like this before, unlike Sean and Tommy, whose experience with these kinds of missions was beyond extensive.

So far, Brent hadn't let on that he was considering bailing. In fact, being surrounded by all that gold down in the chamber had been proof enough that this was going to be a lucrative proposal.

During their escape through the underground tunnels of Petra, he'd complained about leaving all that gold behind, but Craig quickly alleviated those questions by telling him that was just a taste of what was to come.

"It's coming up at the next intersection," Craig said, noticing the directions on the phone. A second later, the voice confirmed his statement by ordering the driver to make a right turn at the next light.

"Yes, sir," Brent said.

He slowed down before reaching the light and flipped on the turn signal. The next street came into view as he spun the wheel to the right. While there were still trees lining the sidewalks, the buildings beyond the concrete pathways were different than the many businesses and apartments along the main strip.

Here, luxurious mansions sat behind high walls and iron gates.

"Your destination is ahead on the right," the GPS navigation said in its robotic voice.

As they neared the entrance to the property, Brent feathered the brakes.

"Let's go by slowly," Craig said. "Get a quick look, then park up the street, and we'll come back on foot."

"Understood," Brent confirmed.

The car rolled slowly by the driveway. Craig peered through the gate and into a large bay window in a room jutting out of the right side of the home. For a second, he couldn't believe what he was seeing. It had to be the way the sunlight reflected off the glass, or perhaps it was merely his imagination running wild with paranoid-fueled guilt, like Edgar Poe's telltale heart beating over his head.

"That's impossible," Craig muttered, leaning closer to the window.

"What?" Brent asked, slowing the car to a near-stop.

"Keep going," Craig ordered quickly.

"Okay, but what's the problem?" He stepped on the gas pedal, and the car accelerated out of the mansion's view.

Craig looked straight ahead and motioned to an empty parking spot along the curb on the other side of the street.

"Park on that side. We'll wait there."

"Wait? Wait for what?"

Craig glanced in the rearview mirror on his side, then turned his head and looked again. His nervous tension pulsed through the vehicle.

"What is going on, Craig? Something spook you back there?"

"Yeah," Craig said. "I can't be sure, but I thought I just saw Sean."

10

"Sean?" Brent asked. "As in Sean Wyatt? The same Sean we left buried alive in an ancient crypt back in Jordan? That Sean?"

"Yes," Craig replied. "I didn't believe it, either."

"So, what's the plan? We're going to sit here and wait until they leave?"

"We can't very well barge in there. The place is surrounded by a wall, blocked by an iron gate, and there are security cameras everywhere."

Brent said nothing. He merely stared at the driveway like a cop on a sting.

"How in the world did they get out of that chamber?" Craig went on. "There's no way they could have gotten through that stone slab. It must have weighed two tons."

"Maybe they blew it with explosives," Brent offered. "Although the risk of something like that would have been insanely high. The kind of energy required to blow out a stone that big is immense. The concussion could be lethal in close quarters like that. Not to mention the potential for a cave-in. That ceiling might have collapsed on them. More likely they found another way out. If that really was him you saw back there."

"I can't be sure," Craig said after a moment of contemplation. "There was some glare on the window, and it was probably seventy yards away."

"Maybe you were just imagining things. You're not feeling guilty, are you?"

Craig didn't like Brent's accusatory tone. It carried a threat with it, a warning that if he went soft, the mercenary would cut his losses—and that cutting could also mean loose ends.

"No," Craig said. "I don't feel guilty about it. Those idiots had every chance to keep going with us on this. They dug their own graves."

"Okay."

Brent seemed to accept the answer, but it was difficult to tell. The man had the emotional range of a mosquito, which was exactly what you wanted in a bodyguard. But that coin had two sides, and Craig knew it.

"So," Brent said after a minute of silence, "just for argument's sake, let's say that is Wyatt you saw back there. And assuming Tommy made it out, too, what are they doing here?"

"Same thing as us." Craig rolled his shoulders as if the answer should have been obvious. "I guess Tommy must know about Dr. Amid's map database and came here to have a look at it."

"If that is them, what's your plan now? Sit here and wait until they come out? Kill 'em for real this time?"

He sounded as if he wanted that to happen. The man's bloodlust had been suppressed for most of their time together, but now the real killer was apparently coming out. And Craig didn't like it.

He'd spent his entire adult life around passive types, betas who toiled in the dirt, never giving a second thought to ending a human life—because their emotions couldn't handle something so dark. Craig tried to recall any moment in his younger days when he'd been around anyone so callous with regard to human life, but that, too, failed to register a memory. Brent was, in his estimation, a pure, unadulterated killer.

"No," Craig answered, doing his best not to sound disturbed by the man's eagerness to squeeze the trigger again. "This is a quiet area of Cairo. That sort of thing doesn't happen here."

"I'll use a suppressor. It'll be quiet." He smirked with the statement.

"They may still be of some use to us. If Sean and Tommy really are in there with the professor, they'll figure out the location of the entrance to the hall. So, we wait here until they come out, and then follow them to wherever they're going."

He peered through the glass as he laid his head back against the headrest. It had been a long twenty-four hours, and he needed to rest.

No chance of that now. There was no telling how long they'd have to sit here and wait for Sean and Tommy to emerge, if that was indeed them he'd seen in the house.

If it wasn't, Dr. Amid would leave sooner or later. That would give Craig confirmation as to whether his former friends were still alive and in the area, and it would potentially delay him getting the information he wanted... unless.

"If that isn't Wyatt," Craig said, "and by all counts it shouldn't be, Dr. Amid will probably go out for lunch, or to a meeting within the next hour or so."

"How do you know that?" Brent wondered.

"The man likes to eat, and he's also usually in various meetings for any number of things. The guy's calendar is packed. I doubt he's ever home for long."

"How did you know he'd be home now?"

It was a valid question, and one that Craig hadn't adequately answered before even traveling to Cairo. They'd taken the risk based on the assumption, with a lot of potential wasted time on the line if the man wasn't here. The odds that Amid was home were actually pretty low.

That didn't matter.

"You said you could bypass the security system," Craig said.

"Yeah. That shouldn't be a problem. I doubt this guy has anything too high end. Probably got sold some cheaply made, glammed-up system from China. I've worked with those before."

"So, if Amid leaves, we break into his house, find the database, and download it to my computer."

"You know how to do all that?" Brent looked surprised.

"I have a few tech skills I picked up along the way. The problem will be if his stuff is password protected, which it probably is. That could take time."

"And if you can't hack it?"

Craig's expression darkened. "Then we wait for Amid to get home, and we make him give us access."

It was a long shot, and Craig knew it. He had no idea if he could access the database without the password, but there was no way he'd let Brent know that. The psychopath might just kill him right there.

The best chance for this to work was if Amid's guests—whoever they were—left within the next hour or so. Then Craig could simply walk up to the gate, call in, and request to see the professor.

They'd met before, and it would be easy enough for Craig to lie and say he was in Cairo for work and decided to stop by and say hello, and maybe get a look at the database.

It was a stretch, but it would work. Craig could explain he'd been working on a project on the Sphinx and was curious to see if there were any yet-undiscovered, outlying tunnels that could have been missed during previous excavations.

And if that didn't work, Brent could always use his own brand of persuasion.

11

After finishing the bold coffee and sweet treats, Dr. Amid and his two guests abandoned the kitchen and went upstairs to one of the most spectacular studies Sean had ever seen.

The man had good taste. Sean had to give him that.

The room was a rectangle encased in ebony wood paneling, and shelves stocked with tomes ranging from very old to some that looked as if they'd been purchased yesterday. There wasn't much fiction from what Sean could tell—mostly biographies, history books, and volumes containing information about ancient cultures and religions practices.

A few pictures of Egyptian ruins, the pyramids, and temples adorned the black-painted walls between the shelves. Two pedestals stood on either side of a wide oak desk on the left side of the room, their glass cases containing ceremonial bowls from one of the long-lost kingdoms of Egypt. Three wide-screen computer monitors stood atop the desk behind a keyboard.

"I love this room," Sean said. "I'm going to have to do some redecorating when I get home."

"Thank you," Vokum said. "I do love it in here. This place is my sanctuary. I find that the dark colors, the wood, being surrounded by all this, helps me focus on my research." He extended his right hand and swept it around the room.

Then he moved behind the desk and eased into his chair, beckoning his two guests to stand behind him and look over his shoulder.

Vokum clicked the mouse, and the screens blinked to life.

"Three monitors," Tommy said. "You day-trading or something in your spare time?"

"No," Vokum replied with a husky laugh. "What spare time?" He maneuvered the arrow on the center screen to a folder in the bottom right corner marked Tunnel Maps Cairo.

Not exactly trying to hide it, Sean thought. Then again, Amid probably figured that the gate at the front and the wall around it were sufficient. And he doubted if there were a break-in that the burglars would be interested in the contents of his computer—particularly the one tabbed as containing tunnel maps of Cairo. Amid's slack view of security was emphasized by the fact he didn't password-protect the computer, which was pretty much the minimum a person could do.

Vokum clicked on the folder, and a new window with a list of places popped up in the center.

He scrolled down until he found one marked Sphinx and clicked it.

A new window replaced the previous one, displaying locations indicating the directions and locations of the maps—east, west, north, south, and more that related to prior excavations and the dates the passages were mapped.

"Here are all the schematics I've compiled over the years for the area surrounding the Sphinx. You said you're interested in checking anything that might be to the east of it, yes?"

Tommy nodded. "Yeah. The Sphinx faces to the east. That's where we should start."

"Very well."

Their host moved the arrow down the screen. The files rolled upward until he found the one he was looking for. He opened it, and the schematic filled the screen.

"Wow," Sean gasped. "You did all this?"

"Yes. And it wasn't easy. It's not like I'm an engineer or a cartographer, though this kind of mapping isn't necessarily what they do. I had to figure it out on the fly. But I caught on pretty quick."

"So, what are we looking at here?" Tommy asked, pointing at the screen and a series of above-view tunnels.

"This is what we have found so far in the area. Beyond this line over here," Vokum said, pointing at a dashed line to the right, "is where the road goes by the protected historical property. On the other side is where the city begins. Not much there to be honest. Some run-down buildings. A parking garage is there." He tapped the screen to indicate where the imagined structure would sit.

"What's that there?" Sean asked, pointing to a tunnel on the other side of the road that seemed to stop abruptly before reaching the boundary of the area.

"Dead end," Vokum said. "I remember because I was the one who discovered it. Strange, that one. It's underneath that parking garage. Blocked off now. No one is permitted down there. We didn't find anything except the passage."

"Why would anyone create a tunnel like that and just stop building it?" Tommy wondered.

"Ever been to the Road to Nowhere near Bryson City, North Carolina?" Sean asked, half joking.

"Actually, I haven't. But I hear it's weird."

"What is that?" Vokum asked, now curious about the unusual turn in the conversation.

"It's a road in the hills of North Carolina that just stops for no reason in the middle of nowhere. You're driving along, and then there's just no more road."

"There isn't a cliff or anything dangerous, is there?"

"No, nothing like that," Tommy clarified. "It just ends in the forest."

"Strange," Vokum said, turning back to the screen. "Anyway, with this dead end, we left it because getting the permits to excavate farther was difficult, and didn't seem worth the effort."

Tommy considered the statement for a minute. He thumbed his chin while he stared at the screen.

"What was the dead end?" he asked. "Like, was it just uncut rock?"

"Yes." The Egyptian bobbed his head to go with the matter-of-fact answer. "It was as if they had begun construction of the tunnel, then decided to stop right there. Very bizarre."

Sean stared at the screen as he listened. Dr. Amid had missed something. He was sure of it, but what it was he didn't know.

He looked back toward the outline of the Sphinx to the west. A thought bubbled to the surface of his mind. He doubted it was the answer. Vokum was an extremely smart, meticulous archaeologist. He wouldn't have missed something so simple.

Then again, Vokum had said getting permits wasn't worth the trouble. He'd given up on the passage as just one of many he must have come across where ancient people had decided to build in other places after beginning a project.

"What was the floor made of?" Sean blurted.

The other two turned and looked at him, both with curiosity filling their eyes.

"It was soil," Vokum said. "Just dirt."

"Did you use any ground-penetrating radar to see if there was anything underneath it?"

"Yes. We conducted a few sweeps of the passage, but it produced nothing of interest. No artifacts were detected."

"Did you go all the way to the end of the corridor? To where the passage stopped?"

"Sure." Vokum sounded anything but.

"How sure?" Sean pressed.

The man shrugged. "I don't know. We are usually very thorough with such things. What are you thinking?"

"I remember seeing a documentary on the Sphinx. It was about the excavation there. You were featured in it, Doctor," he added with a nod in Vokum's direction. "You and some of the other experts talked about how flooding and erosion had filled some of the passages around the Sphinx, and buried some of the structure that is now above ground."

"Yes, that's true. Those kinds of floods don't really happen anymore. It was long ago, most definitely."

"Right. What if the passage you found didn't stop at the wall? What if it descended down farther into the earth, but the way was blocked by soil brought in by one of those floods?"

Sean could see the gears turning in the man's eyes.

"Yes. I suppose that is possible. I suppose the radar we used was designed to detect solid anomalies. We are capable of finding openings, but in this instance, I would guess if there was one under the dirt, it would be surrounded by the same walls as above, making it more difficult to differentiate."

"Just do be clear," Tommy cut in, "you didn't do any digging down there?"

"No. We didn't see a reason to. Not that it matters. It would take months to get a permit to do any excavations there. Maybe longer than that."

Sean paced away from the desk, running his fingers through his short blond hair. He stopped over by the wall in front of a bookshelf filled with the history of Egypt, Sumer, Babylon, and Israel. It was a fascinating collection of books, each thick with hundreds of pages of what Sean was certain were pictures from sites to go along with the trove of information.

He spun around and faced the other two, who he was surprised to find still looking at him.

"So, could you tell us how to get to the entrance of this tunnel?" He locked eyes with Vokum, unwilling to break.

"Yes. Of course. But it wouldn't do any good because—"

"It's blocked. I know. I'm not worried about that. I'll assume a chain, metal gate, maybe a padlock or two with a bunch of warning signs?"

"Probably. But like I said, you don't have the permits."

Sean lifted his shoulders. "So, I'm thinking of doing this off the books."

12

Fear darkened Vokum's face. "You can't just go digging around in Cairo, Sean. First of all, that is private property, just beyond the government owned-restricted area. It's trespassing. Not to mention all the other laws that you'd be breaking."

"Relax, Doc," Sean said. "You're not going to go in there with us. We just need to know where it is."

"We?" Tommy cowed. "Maybe you didn't hear him, but I can't just go onto someone's property and start digging around. We need to get permits."

Sean inclined his head, looking down at both of them from across the room. "Do you think Craig is going to wait for a permit?"

"Craig?" Vokum faltered. "Here? In Cairo? But you said he left you for dead in Petra."

"He did."

Vokum stood and looked around the room. Panic washed over him. "Do you think he would come here looking for me?"

"I doubt it," Tommy said. "Didn't seem like you two got along based on what you said about him."

"We didn't. But if he knows about this database, it's possible he would come here anyway. And I doubt it would be a friendly encounter."

Sean walked over to their host and grabbed him by the shoulders to calm him down. "Dr. Amid. Relax. Nothing is going to happen to you. Okay? I'll handle Craig. But we need to get to that entrance before he can."

"Without the maps," Tommy said, "he won't know where to look." He faced Vokum. "Come with us, and we'll make sure you're safe. Is there a friend you can stay with? Someone you trust here in the city?"

Vokum shook his head, putting his palms to his face. "No. No, this is insane. Why did you two bring this kind of trouble to my door?"

"We didn't," Sean defended. "It's possible Craig is already out there looking for the entrance to the hall. If you two weren't friends, you might well be the last person he would want help from."

The reasoning seemed to calm Vokum down a little. "Fine. I'm sorry I overreacted." He raised a finger in warning. "But you cannot simply go around Cairo digging holes wherever you want. There are protocols in place, rules that must be followed. It's one of the few things the government here does right. At least most of the time."

Tommy knew what he meant. The restrictions on conducting excavations were stringent.

For nearly a minute, no one said anything until their host let out an audible sigh.

"Look, maybe if you could tell me a bit more. What is all this really about, Tommy? Downstairs, in the kitchen, it seemed like you were holding something back. Are you being completely honest with me?"

"I am. And I was holding something back. A lot, actually. Not that I wasn't going to tell you. I was just waiting for the right moment."

Vokum stood there, not sure what to anticipate next. But it was clear he was tired of being strung along.

"What I'm about to tell you is nothing less than the most ground-breaking find in the last thousand years. You cannot say a word about it to anyone. Do you understand?"

"Groundbreaking find? What are you talking about? You mean the Archimedes Scroll? I thought you didn't recover that."

"We didn't."

"Yet," Sean added with confidence.

Vokum looked at one then the other like he was watching a tennis match. "Then what is this find you're talking about? Was there something else in Jordan?"

Tommy hesitated. Not because he wasn't planning on telling his friend. That was always part of the deal. But it wasn't an easy confession to make. And he knew there would be a ton of questions to follow, chief among them, where exactly this secret chamber was located.

"So, you know that female archaeologist who's been getting a lot of attention lately for her excavations in this area, the one hunting for the lost tomb of Cleopatra?"

"Of course. I've assisted her with some of her research. She believes she's getting very close, actually."

Sean and Tommy shared a knowing glance, like two fourth graders sitting in the back of the classroom after dropping a whoopee cushion in the teacher's chair.

"She isn't," Tommy said.

"What? What are you talking about?" More questions dripped from their host's eyes. "She's the foremost expert in the world on Cleopatra, and all the research points to—"

"Not where she's digging" Tommy finished.

"But... you can't mean..." Vokum scoffed at the insinuation. He waved a dismissive hand and turned away from the two Americans. "If you don't want to tell me what you found out there, if there is anything at all, fine. But if you get arrested trying to break into that tunnel, I wash my hands of it."

"Vokum," Tommy said, sincerity smothering his words. "We found it. We found the tomb of Queen Cleopatra, the last of the Ptolemaic rulers of Egypt. You don't have to believe us if you don't want to. But we can take you there, just as soon as we're done with this mission."

"That's... not possible."

"It is, my old friend. It's where we found this scepter," Tommy said, holding up the golden object.

Vokum turned and looked at the artifact. It gleamed in the dim light of the study. The gems in the eyes and on the base sparkled.

He shook his head, still not believing the story. "She killed herself with an asp. Not a cobra. Why would that be in her tomb? And why would it be in Jordan, in Petra of all places?"

"We wondered the same thing," Tommy admitted. "It was a surprise to say the least. We went there trying to find the scroll, and discovered her sarcophagus."

Vokum swallowed back his disbelief. He licked his lips, thirsty for more, as much as he could take. He was ready to drink from a fire hose.

"You're not joking. Are you?" he asked.

Sean and Tommy shook their heads.

"I wouldn't joke with something as important as this."

Their host shuffled over to the far wall. He stopped there, looking down at the shelf of books near his waist. He shook his head and rubbed the base of his skull with his thumb and forefinger before turning around.

"What did it look like?" Vokum wondered. "The tomb. The sarcophagus. All of it."

Tommy guessed he might go there and was ready to answer. "It was unlike anything I've ever seen. The tomb was a room encased in walls made of pure gold, each engraved with hieroglyphs featuring the four great Ptolemies."

Vokum's lips quivered as he listened. Sean wasn't sure, but he thought he saw the man's eyes welling with tears.

"And the sarcophagus?" Vokum pleaded for more.

"Ornate. Beautiful. Done in the style of some of the greatest pharaohs. Worthy of a place in the Valley of the Kings."

"We'll tell you how to get there," Sean said, trying to hurry things along without coming off as a jerk. "Take a team to the site and do your thing. I'm sure Tommy would be happy for the IAA to lend a hand however we can."

"Absolutely," Tommy agreed. "And you'll find the story about the scroll there, on the walls. At least part of it. We believe that Cleopatra was searching for the Archimedes Scroll as well. Legend suggests it was a powerful weapon capable of destroying enemy ships, or wiping out swaths of troops."

The Egyptian nodded absently. "I know the stories. I've heard them all. No one knows if it was real or not. Or if such a weapon could even work. Archimedes' heat ray was supposedly an array of mirrors—paraboloids that could focus immense light on an enemy ship until it burst into flames. It was purported to be used against attacking Roman ships during the Siege of Syracuse in 213 and 212 BC. The second-century AD author Lucian suggested that during the siege, Archimedes destroyed the enemy ships with fire. Years later, Anthemius of Tralles spoke of burning-glasses being used as the weapon."

Vokum shook his head. "There have, of course, been experiments throughout the centuries to attempt to recreate the weapon, and its effects on wood. Some of the results that came from the research confirmed that the array really could do what the historians said. Others debunked it, often basing their rationale on the mirrors needing perfect weather and a stationary target to work effectively. Most conclude that the reflectors were used to blind or distract enemies so they could be attacked by more conventional means such as flaming arrows or siege weapons."

Despite the expert's response, Sean couldn't help but wonder if every possible angle had been investigated.

"Dr. Amid," Sean began, "Tommy and I have seen things in the last decade and a half that I would have never believed possible. Technology no one thought the ancient world capable of. They were far ahead of even our modern tech in so many ways, yet we act like they built all of these marvels, all the wonders of the world with stone wheels, hand tools, and slave labor. What if Archimedes was one of those, a part of that group who understood far more than anyone else from his time? Throughout history, there have been tales of hidden knowledge and the masters who wielded it. Look at Nikola Tesla. We're only just now beginning to fathom the things that he understood more than a century ago."

Tommy stepped closer to their host. "Craig mentioned the possibility of the heat ray being used as a way to create energy more efficiently, and cheaply. Basically like solar power on steroids from the sound of it. What if he's right?"

Vokum shrugged. "Paraboloids are already used to amplify solar power in some places. This isn't a new thing."

"Right. But solar still is nowhere near as efficient as it could be. Everyone knows that. What if the Archimedes Scroll contains the secret to that?"

"Clean, cheap energy for the entire world," Sean added.

"Craig doesn't seem the benevolent type," Vokum suggested with a scowl.

"He isn't. He plans on making an unimaginable fortune off it. At least, that's what he told us."

"That... I believe." Vokum shook his head dismissively and threw up his hands in frustration. "But this is madness. We don't even know if that scroll is real."

"You'd heard about it," Tommy reminded.

"Of course I've heard of it. I've heard of Thor's Hammer and a hundred other mythical objects. That doesn't mean they're real. Let Craig waste his time hunting for something that doesn't exist. It doesn't mean you two have to. And it certainly doesn't mean I have to help you break the law."

Sean nodded as if surrendering the argument. He took a deep breath, looking over at Tommy as he did. They both wondered what would sway their host's mind.

"Dr. Amid," Sean said, "Tommy and I have traveled all over the world and found artifacts and treasures none of the experts believed were real. If the Archimedes Scroll truly is out there, we can't let it fall into the hands of someone like Craig. Whatever technology Archimedes tapped into should be shared with the world."

Sean's face hardened with determination as he continued. "We found Cleopatra's tomb in a place no one would have ever guessed. Many have suggested there isn't a tomb, that her body was disposed of unceremoniously in an anonymous place that would never be identified. All we're asking, Professor, is that you take a leap of faith with us. You don't have to come with us. But we need you to tell us where that entrance is."

Tommy took a step forward toward Vokum. "We would never suggest you come along. You can't risk your reputation. And if we get caught, no one will know you told us about this place. We'll take the rap."

Vokum snorted a quiet laugh. "And you don't have a reputation to consider, Thomas? Your agency has done so much good to preserve forgotten history. Everyone in our community knows who you are. You could be ruined."

"It's worth the risk. If I hadn't been willing to take some chances, much of that history our agency has preserved would still be forgotten."

His words struck Vokum in the chest. There was no disguising that they'd convinced him. A fire flickered in the Egyptian's dark eyes.

"Very well," he surrendered. "There are a pair of green metal doors in the basement level of the parking garage. These lead into a concrete corridor where you'll find another few doors on either side. Don't worry about those. They're just closets or maintenance rooms. The doors you're looking for are at the end of that hallway. You can't miss them. They're chained and locked and plastered with warnings to keep out under the penalty of prosecution. You'll need something to cut the chains or break the locks."

"I can handle that," Sean said, remembering the lockpicking tool stowed in his rucksack.

"A man of many talents," Vokum mused. "Once you're through those doors, that's it. You'll find yourself in a very different sort of passage. We believe it was created during the Old Kingdom, probably while Kafre was pharaoh."

"Same as the Sphinx—if you hold the mainstream view," Tommy realized.

"Yes. The corridor runs fifty meters before it ends."

"That's not very long," Sean noted.

"It isn't. Again, more proof in our minds that it was a project that they began but never finished."

Vokum walked back over behind his desk. He entered a few commands and the screen changed to a modern Google Earth view of the area in question. "That is the parking deck," he said, pointing at the screen.

Sean and Tommy sidled up next to him on either side and studied the monitor. The top of the parking garage looked like basically every one they'd ever seen. It was an unremarkable, light gray structure with an asphalt surface. The lines that had been painted for the individual parking spots were either not visible from the high-altitude camera or had faded over time in the blazing Egyptian sun.

"This is the best I can do for you, my friends," Vokum said. "I hope you understand."

"Thank you, Professor," Sean offered.

"I'm still concerned about your safety," Tommy said. "You do have someone you can stay with, right? Someone you trust?"

"Of course. But are you really sure that is necessary? I doubt Craig will show up here. And if he does, I'll simply turn him away and call the police. I'll be fine."

Sean turned his head. "These guys left us for dead. Craig isn't the benign archaeologist we thought. And the dude working for him is definitely a killer. You need to be somewhere safe. Somewhere they can't find you."

All three of them noticed movement on the screen to the left. That monitor displayed six camera views of the property's exterior.

The panel in the top right showed the front gate and the access keypad—and a familiar face standing next to it.

"You have to be kidding me," Tommy grumbled.

"He certainly didn't waste any time getting here," Sean said.

They watched Craig reach out and press the call button on the keypad. A second later, the phone started ringing on the left side of the desk near the monitor.

Craig turned and walked toward the camera, staring into it with eyes none of the men in the study recognized.

They were hollow; full of malice and evil. "I know you're in there, Professor. I just want to come in and talk."

"Where's Brent?" Sean wondered between the phone rings.

He looked at the other camera angles but didn't see Craig's bodyguard.

"Those cameras have every potential entry point covered on the property," Vokum said.

"He must be in their car, waiting in case we try to get away."

"What should we do?" Tommy asked, facing Sean.

Sean, in turn, looked to their host. "You wouldn't happen to have a car, would you?"

13

C raig stared into the camera until the phone stopped ringing through the speaker on the keypad. He shook his head in disdain.

"I just want to come in and talk, Dr. Amid. You remember me, don't you? Craig Freeman? It hasn't been that long. I was hoping to take a look at your database of maps." He held his hands out wide as if to show he meant no harm or ill will.

He waited for a few seconds and then shook his head. "I know you're in there, Professor. I saw you a few minutes ago when I drove by." It was nearly an hour, but that didn't matter.

Craig had sat in the car, initially prepared to wait all day if necessary. But he'd grown impatient. Beyond that, concerns started to filter into his mind, teasing him with visions of Dr. Amid sneaking out a back entrance, or climbing over the wall into a neighbor's yard before making a dramatic escape.

So far, he'd detected no signs of such a getaway, but maybe that was because it had already happened.

After sitting in the car for forty minutes, he decided something wasn't right.

The more Craig thought about it, the more his imagination toyed with him, taunting him with the visage of the person he swore was Sean Wyatt in the window of Amid's home.

He tried to remind himself that it wasn't possible, that Sean and Tommy were still deep underground in a hidden chamber in Petra. No one would find them until it was too late.

That much Craig was sure of.

An hour after emerging from the other tunnel, he and Brent were able to circle back to the entrance of the initial passage, and they had closed it off with an improvised ordnance Brent put together. No one would ever be able to get in there again without some heavy equipment.

Of course, Craig planned on returning to the fabled tomb of Queen Cleopatra. He wasn't going to let that little gem slip from his grasp.

Once he'd recovered the scroll, he would return to the site with a team and excavate the crypt, along with all of its treasures.

He would be hailed as a hero in the historical community. After a lifetime of toiling in the field, doing the hard work without ever truly getting the credit he deserved, his day would finally come.

Then he would start rolling out the patents for his new energy technology. *Lowly archaeologist turns hero, then saves the planet from the looming energy crisis.* The headlines played on a loop in his mind.

Was it grandiose? Over the top? The biggest pipe dream of all time?

Sure. But he'd earned it.

And nothing was going to stand in his way—certainly not an old Egyptian historian selling out to the media and the publishing houses for thirty pieces of silver.

Craig didn't want his thirty pieces. He wanted the entire mine.

"Come on, Dr. Amid," he urged into the camera. "I have some really important stuff to share with you. But if you're not home, I can come back later. I would have called, but I don't have your number."

He hoped the ploy would urge the professor to open the gate, but the motors didn't whine, and the iron bars remained in place.

Frustrated, Craig stepped back over to the keypad and hit the call button again.

Doubt wormed through his mind. He wondered if he should have just stayed in the car, waiting it out with Brent until Dr. Amid left his home, which would happen eventually.

Brent seemed perfectly content to sit there all day if necessary, which had been Craig's intention, too, until the heat of the day began to bake them into their leather car seats. They couldn't run the vehicle's engine indefinitely simply to keep the air conditioning on.

The phone rang again through the speaker holes on the keypad.

Craig tried to remain calm. With the camera on him, the last thing he wanted to appear was desperate or angry. But those were the emotions coursing through his veins. And with every unanswered, obnoxious ring of the phone they only grew stronger.

He forced a smile across his lips, putting on the most patient expression he could muster.

He knew there was *someone* home. Perhaps it was the maid. A house worker such as that could have been instructed not to answer any calls from the gate while the professor was out.

But the person he'd seen inside the window was a man. Craig knew it. Unless his brain was playing tricks on him.

He shook it off internally and kept waiting as the phone continued to ring.

Just as before, the ringing stopped.

Regret swelled inside Craig's chest over the decision to leave the car and approach the gate. With each passing second it seemed like a terrible idea, and regret tugged on him like a rope.

He'd acted like an impatient child on Christmas Eve, desperate to sneak downstairs and see what presents his parents were wrapping before the big morning.

I'm not cut out for this. What was I thinking? I should have stayed in the car. Or figured out some other way to access the tunnel maps.

The thoughts echoed in his head, battering against the sides of his skull like tormenting demons trying to smash their way out.

He turned away from the camera and squeezed his eyes, grappling with his will to calm down and think.

"Stop being irrational. He's not home. That's the only reasonable answer. I'll just go back to the car and wait. Or we can return later when I know he'll be home."

More doubts sprang up, though, and he began to wonder if Amid had left the city, or even the country, to go work on a project far away from here.

If that were the case, he and Brent would have to break into the house. That part was easy enough. Bypassing the alarm would take some skill, but Brent seemed to have that under control, which left the entire mission hinging on Craig's ability to get into the professor's computer—an act he claimed he could pull off, but in truth had no idea how to.

He had to tell Brent something.

Reluctantly, Craig decided to give up and go back to the car. There was no point in standing here. But now he was in a pickle.

If someone was indeed inside the house, breaking in might prove problematic—whether it was Amid or someone else. Craig just wanted things to be simple.

He turned away from the gate and started back toward the car, his brain already trying to come up with another way to access Amid's database.

Suddenly, the motors on the gate began to whir. Hinges creaked.

Craig spun around and saw the iron bars parting in the center, slowly swinging in toward the house.

A mixture of relief and confusion spilled over Craig as he stepped warily toward the opening.

"I guess Amid was on the toilet or something," he muttered to himself.

He passed through the columns housing the gate hinges and continued forward another ten steps before he heard a new sound.

This wasn't the gentle grind of electric motors pulling open the gate. It was throaty, aggressive, racy. In only two more seconds, Craig saw the source of the noise.

A black Maserati Ghibli GT whipped around from the back of the mansion and sped toward him. The engine growled angrily as it bore down on him.

Craig squinted against the glare of the sunlight, half in shock that the car appeared to be on a collision course with him, and half-curious as to who was behind the wheel.

He quickly realized the vehicle wasn't slowing down, and didn't seem to be inclined to. At the last second, with eyes still focused on the windshield, Craig dove clear of the car and rolled into the thick grass to the side of the driveway.

He scrambled to his feet as the sedan slowed for a second at the street before veering to the left and speeding toward the main drag.

Craig sprinted after the car as the gates slowly began closing again, the hinges once more squeaking in protest.

"No. No. No. No!" he shouted. The iron bars met in the middle, hemming him in.

He hurried over to a panel on the column to his right and found a button to manually open the gates. But it wouldn't matter. The Maserati would be gone by the time Craig made it in the car with Brent.

Craig pressed the button, and the gates began opening again.

He returned to the center of the driveway, and the instant the two doors were far enough apart, he sprinted through and down to the edge of the street.

Another engine revved to his right, and Craig stopped short to allow Brent to pull up close to the curb before running around to the passenger's side and hopping in.

"What happened?" Brent demanded, stepping on the gas pedal.

Ahead at the end of the street, the Maserati's taillights flashed red before it turned right and disappeared around the building at the corner.

Craig swore, both at himself and the situation.

"I went to the gate, hit the call button, and waited."

"And?"

The car sped past the opulent mansions. The trees along the sidewalk whooshed by until they reached the first apartment building on the right.

"Amid didn't answer."

"I told you this was a bad idea. The plan was to wait in the car."

Craig didn't appreciate being chastised even if his assistant was right. He was the one in charge here, not Brent.

Brent stopped the car at the red light. The two looked to the right, but the Maserati was already gone, either concealed by the endless stream of traffic or having turned down another street in that direction.

"That's not the only bad news," Craig said, thinking diverting to a bigger issue would take the heat off his reckless play.

"We lost him. So what? He has to come home sometime." Brent merged into traffic and accelerated ahead. "We can go back and wait for him. But I do wonder, why was he in such a hurry?"

"The bad news I'm talking about isn't the fact Amid got away. It's who was driving his car."

Brent took his eyes off the road for a second, sensing the concern in Craig's voice. "Who was driving?"

Craig swallowed. It was a pill of frustration and disbelief. "I only got a clear look through the windshield for a second before I had to dive out of the way. They almost hit me."

"Who was it, Craig?" Brent demanded.

Craig hesitated for another breath before he answered. "It was Sean Wyatt."

14

Sean sped down the street, knifing in and out between the tightly packed cars like an asphalt surgeon.

He glanced back in the rearview mirror every few seconds to make sure Craig and Brent weren't behind them. By now he figured there was no way they could have caught up, but Sean preferred not to make such assumptions. That kind of thinking could get him killed. And he hadn't died yet.

He noticed the terrified look on Vokum's face, his white knuckles and fingers gripping the edge of his seat.

"We're good," Sean said, hoping the words would console the man into some semblance of calm.

Tommy had been keeping watch behind them as well and agreed. "No sign of them. That was close back there. Almost seemed like you were trying to hit Craig."

"I wasn't." The grim answer didn't carry an ounce of humor with it, and neither of the other two men could figure if Sean was joking or not.

He waited a few seconds before saying, "I'm kidding, guys." After the other two let out a tentative chuckle, Sean added, "If I was trying to hit him, I wouldn't have missed."

"I wouldn't have blamed you," Tommy said. "Honestly, I might have hit him. He tried to kill us. You know what kind of long, slow death that would have been down in that chamber?"

"Someone would have found us eventually. I mean, sure, weeks or months, maybe years later. But at some point, you know Craig would have returned to the scene of the crime. He wouldn't let a discovery like that simply be lost again."

"True." Tommy tried to avoid visions of his and Sean's decomposing bodies lying on the hard floor of the tomb. They'd avoided that future. "It does make me wonder, though."

"Wonder what?"

"Someone could stumble on the entrance. I mean, it wasn't easy to get to, and I didn't notice anyone else in that area, but still. It's kind of wide open now if they can get through to the passage."

"I would guess our old friends back there probably sealed it off somehow," Sean said, jerking his thumb toward wherever Craig and Brent were behind them.

Sean noticed Dr. Amid still didn't look comfortable. "You okay back there, Professor? I didn't mean to scare you with my driving."

"Does he always drive like this?" Vokum asked, directing his question to Tommy.

"No. Sometimes he drives fast."

"This isn't fast?" The Egyptian tightened the seatbelt around his shoulder and lap, checking to make sure it was working.

Sean cracked a smile as he swerved around a delivery truck to the left, and then back into the middle lane ahead of it. He slowed down a little, easing his foot off the gas pedal. No need to frighten Amid if there was no immediate danger.

He flipped on the turn signal, merged right, and then turned down the next street.

"Where are you going?" Vokum asked.

"Just taking a less direct route," Sean answered. "Don't want to make it too easy on them."

The street was lined with apartment buildings. Most of them looked like newer construction, built in the last decade or so. The architecture was modern and clean, with sharp lines and distinct contrasts of dark and light colors on the exteriors. Young trees lined the sidewalks where young people jogged or walked dogs. Some drank cups of coffee as they strolled, listening to music through wireless headphones.

"Nice area," Sean commented, noting the restaurants and bars at the ground floor of some of the apartments. "If I was single and living in Cairo, this is where I would want to be."

"Reminds me of Inman Park near Atlanta," Tommy added.

"It is a newer area," Vokum said. "They renovated this entire neighborhood. It was old buildings before. Many of them were in terrible shape. It's nice to see it flourishing. If we could get some consistent leadership here in my country, more of Cairo would look like this."

"Consistent leadership isn't really a thing governments are good at," Sean said.

Tommy laughed at the snark. "No kidding."

"How far is your friend's house from here?" Sean asked.

"Fifteen minutes with the traffic. I'll tell you how to get there."

"Fifteen doesn't sound like a lot of distance to put between yourself and Craig," Tommy warned.

"It's a big city. Millions of people. Easy to get lost here. He won't find me."

Sean liked the confidence in the man. The fear of crashing the car had disappeared, and now he was back to acting more like himself.

"I do have one more question," Sean said as he turned left onto an adjacent street.

"Another favor? Seems like I've done a few of those for you today."

"I know. But I was wondering if we could borrow your car."

Vokum frowned at the thought. "This car is my baby. I can't—"

"Craig and Brent will be looking for it. Leaving it parked outside your friend's place is probably not a good idea, however unlikely it might be that they happen to stumble across it. We need transportation, and getting a rental or taking cabs isn't going to cut it. We need to work fast. And with Craig still out there, it's better for us to get the heat than you, Professor."

Understanding sketched across Vokum's face, and Sean could see the man knew he was right.

"Very well," he sighed. "But please, be careful with it. I'd prefer to get it back in one piece."

"Good luck with that," Tommy muttered.

"What?"

"Nothing. I said, he'll be sure of that."

Amid seemed to accept the answer, albeit with suspicion in his eyes.

The rest of the drive was spent with him giving Sean directions to get to the friend's house, a woman he claimed was a colleague. But the way Vokum said her name, described her work, and talked about her personality, it was obvious he had more than just professional admiration of her.

Neither Sean nor Tommy pressed him further about his feelings for her. But both were thinking the same thing as they dropped Vokum off at the door of her beige two-story home on one of the quiet streets near the Garden City.

They both watched as the professor stepped inside with the beautiful woman. She had to be at least ten years younger than him and wore a white blouse with khaki trousers. The ensemble looked stereotypical for her profession, but worn in a way that told the world she meant business. Her curly, dark brown hair hung down to her shoulders, hinting at a playful side perhaps she only let a few select friends see.

"He has good taste," Tommy said as the door closed behind the two.

"Sounds like she's a brilliant anthropologist," Sean noted as he shifted the car into drive and accelerated away from the house.

As habit dictated, he looked back in the rearview mirror to see if there was any sign of Craig and Brent, but the street was empty save for the cars parked along the curb and a few pedestrians walking on the sidewalk.

"You sure he'll be safe there?" Tommy wondered.

"No. But it's the only option right now. I doubt Craig knows her, or that they're connected in any way. Besides, he'll be looking for this car."

"Yeah, but come on. There's no way they'll find it. Like Vokum said, it's a huge city."

"How many Maseratis are here, though? It's not Dubai, where you see them like you see Hondas or Toyotas back home."

"I've seen a few," Tommy defended.

"Sure," Sean half agreed. "But they aren't exactly common, either."

"Even so, it would be like finding a blueberry in a cranberry bog."

Sean glanced over at him as he slowed to a stop at an intersection. His eyebrows lowered in disdain. "That's what you're going with?"

Sean looked both ways and accelerated through the crossing.

"What? I figured needle in a haystack is way overused. Thought I would try something different."

"Maybe you should just stick with the clichés, Schultzie," Sean laughed.

"Have you ever seen a cranberry bog? It would be impossible to find a single blueberry in one of those."

"Okay. Okay," Sean surrendered. "Point taken. Maybe it's not such a reach after all."

"Thank you."

Neither of them said a word for a few minutes. Sean checked the GPS on the navigation screen in the console, making sure they were on the right route to the location Vokum had given them.

"Now I'm thirsty for cranberry juice," Tommy confessed.

Sean merely shook his head in derision. "You can get something to drink when we pick up the tools we need. Keep an eye out for a hardware store or any place that might sell gardening tools."

"Sounds like we're going to be in for a long afternoon and night of digging."

"Yeah. And hopefully the manual labor is all we have to deal with."

15

"You're absolutely sure it was him?" Brent asked for what must have been the hundredth time.

"Yes. I'm sure. And Tommy was in the front passenger seat."

Brent continued watching through the windshield for any sign of the black Maserati while Craig's head swiveled back and forth as he looked both directions down side streets.

They'd turned off the main drag at the next intersection to search the next street up from Amid's home but found no sign of the car or its occupants.

"How did they get out of that tomb?" Brent wondered. He sounded angry and frustrated. His tone was dark, like a storm raging over the sea.

"How should I know?" Craig answered with his own question. "There's no way they could have gotten through that rock blocking the exit. And that passage was the only way out."

Brent didn't respond to the statement. Instead, he stewed in the driver's seat with his hands gripping the steering wheel so tight his forearms bulged with muscles and veins.

He kept driving until they reached the end of the street, where an intersection offered them multiple directions.

"Which way?" Brent asked, almost as if it were rhetorical.

"Does it make a difference? I doubt they would have gone back the way they came."

When the light turned green, Brent veered to the left. Craig looked down the streets to the right while Brent checked the ones to the left that ran all the way back to the main strip where they'd been earlier.

They spent fifteen minutes driving back and forth, looking in driveways, down alleys and side streets, and everywhere between but found no sign of their quarry.

"This is a waste of time," Craig realized. "We're never going to find them in this huge city. And they'll be miles away by now."

"Agreed," Brent grumbled. "So, what do you want to do?"

Craig thought for a minute as they sat at a red light.

"They left Amid's house in a hurry," he noted. He lowered his voice a little. "And I'm pretty sure Sean was trying to hit me back there with that car."

"Can't say I blame him," Brent said with a sidelong glance. "We did leave them for dead in an ancient tomb. Once the batteries in their lights burned out, that would be an awful way to go, if you think about it. Not that I care. Just saying."

Craig wished the meathead behind the wheel would shut up. He wasn't helping.

Instead, Brent kept talking. "I do still wonder how they got out. If it wasn't through the tunnel we took, how did they do it?"

Theorizing about Sean and Tommy's miraculous escape wasn't helping the here and now, but it did give Craig a break for a second.

"I don't know. Maybe they found some other mechanism that opened a door we didn't know about. Anything's possible."

"Could be. Unless they just climbed back up through one of those holes we came through. You know, the ones that dropped us into the crypt?"

"Those were too high. You'd need a ladder to reach them, and even then, without something to hold onto it would be nearly impossible to climb out."

Brent's logic didn't give Craig a satisfactory answer to that problem, but it did get him thinking back to the other.

"They left in a hurry," he breathed.

"The tomb?" Brent asked.

The light turned green, and he steered the car onto the adjacent street to his left, basically circling back in the direction they'd come before.

"No. I mean back at the house."

"You said that before."

"Yes, I realize that. But they didn't take the time to lock any doors or set alarms. I wonder if when they saw me at the gate that spooked them."

"Probably," Brent said. "I told you not to go over there."

Craig didn't let him see his eyes roll. *Everyone loves to hear I told you so.*

"If they didn't lock up, odds are they might have left Amid's computer on, too, if that was what they were doing before we showed up."

"Could be. Worth a shot."

"Yeah, definitely worth a shot. Let's head back there and see what we can find."

16

B rent parked the car along the curb a few yards beyond Amid's driveway. He and Craig climbed out and approached the wall that ran along the sidewalk until it stopped at the next property, where it cut sharply toward the rear and where the neighbor's wall began.

They both looked around, checking both directions as they stopped near the wall. This street wasn't busy like many of the others. It was quieter here, with only the sounds of the main drag filtering over to disturb the peace.

Here, no one was out walking their dogs or exercising. Only the trees and a few cars parked on the street bore witness to the two interlopers.

"We'll have to go over the wall," Brent said, sizing up the jump. "I'll give you a boost. Then you can go in and open the gate from the inside."

"Good idea," Craig agreed.

Brent knelt down and cupped his hands together. Craig was about to step up when the sound of a car engine and tires on asphalt froze him in place with his foot in midair. He quickly lowered it back down while Brent remained in a kneeling position.

A white Mercedes coupe cruised by heading down the street away from them. It turned into a driveway a few hundred yards from Amid's, and when it was gone, Craig lifted his foot again.

"Let's do this. I don't want to risk one of the neighbors seeing us."

Brent lifted Craig up until he could reach the bars atop the wall. Craig grabbed onto the black metal and pulled himself up, using his feet to boost him over the top.

Once there, he stepped over the iron bars then used them again—this time to lower himself down into the grass on the other side.

Craig's shoes hit the turf with a thud, and he immediately crouched down as if that would keep him from being spotted by unseen eyes. He looked around the yard, noting the trees and the house beyond. There were no signs of life, as he suspected. They would still have to deal with security cameras. That much he knew, but that was a problem for another time.

He scurried along the wall and over to the nearest column with the gate button he'd used earlier to get out. He pressed the button again and stepped back to wait as the gates slowly parted, allowing Brent to enter.

Brent took a few quick looks down the street again and then trotted through the opening.

"Which way should we go?" Brent asked. "You're the one who knows this guy."

"They came out the back," Craig said. "So that entrance is the one that's most likely unlocked, but we can try both. Since he had visitors, it's doubtful the front was locked. Maybe we just try the front door first."

"Fine. Doesn't matter to me. So long as we get inside. You're sure you saw all three of them?"

"Yeah," Craig lied. "I'm sure." He'd seen Tommy and Sean in the front seat of the car and a figure in the back through the tinted windows, but he couldn't tell for certain if it had been Amid or someone else. Even so, if the Egyptian was the only one left in the house, Craig doubted he'd be much of a threat. The man was an academic, not a killer. He also wasn't in the best shape, and based on his physical appearance, he didn't spend much time if any in the gym or working on self-defense. The only threat he could pose was calling the police.

Still, Craig was convinced that everyone had left. The way Sean had sped off suggested that they were trying to get out, probably to take Amid somewhere safe.

The two jogged up the driveway and to the front steps. Craig looked into the window again where he'd first seen Sean. He remembered thinking it was Sean and talking himself out of that truth with logic and reasoning that had, eventually, proved incorrect.

It *had* been Wyatt after all. Craig realized Sean was just as good as his reputation.

The two men ascended the steps, and when they reached the door, Craig grasped the latch and pressed the button down.

The door cracked open without resistance.

"Good call," Craig said.

He pushed the door open so they could pass through and then closed it quietly once they were both inside.

The two looked around the foyer, up the stairs to the landing, and then ahead through the halls.

Brent produced a pistol from inside his jacket and held it at the ready.

The sight of the weapon unnerved Craig for a split second, but he didn't let it show. He'd never really been around firearms much, both growing up and during his adulthood. Unlike with Tommy's agency, Craig and his teams used the more conventional tools of the trade when conducting excavations. There'd never been a need for guns in all his years in the field.

Then again, given the stories he'd heard about Tommy and Sean's operations, Craig was starting to rethink that logic.

Brent had insisted that he carry a weapon—even if he didn't want to, just in case. He felt the sidearm against his hip, tucked into a concealed holster. The pistol was compact, and with a single stack magazine, even his thin, short fingers wrapped around the grip easily. Of course Brent had recommended something with a little more stopping power. But Brent was content with the 9mm. And anything larger would have felt even more uncomfortable.

The two men stood there for ten seconds, listening for any sounds of life that would tell them someone might still be at home. They didn't hear a single noise, save for the gentle sound of air blowing through a vent in the floor to the right.

Brent crept forward, keeping his pistol in front of him with elbows bent, the weapon high.

They passed into the kitchen, where the lingering smell of strong coffee still filled the room. Craig veered behind the island and over to the sink where he found three dessert plates and three empty cups of coffee sitting in the bottom. Across from him sat a bistro table surrounded by windows—one of which Craig had spotted Sean through when they'd first arrived at the home.

Brent pressed on through the kitchen and into the next room, sweeping the area as he'd probably done on multiple missions with his private security agency.

Craig followed him, thinking that splitting up could result in him catching a bullet by accident.

The two made their way through a sitting room with luxurious couches and a heavy oak coffee table stained a dark reddish brown. The high, coffered ceilings made the room feel even larger than it was. The windows on the back wall offered views of the huge yard in the back, filled with flowers, shrubs, and ornamental trees.

Brent turned to Craig. "Where would he keep his computer with the database?" he whispered.

"Probably in a study or home office," Craig breathed. "We should check upstairs."

Brent nodded. "Wait here. I'm going to make sure the rest of the main floor is clear."

He didn't wait for a protest from Craig. Instead, he moved ahead through the room and into the next, where a television hung over a mantel with more couches and chairs positioned around it. Then he disappeared to the left.

Anxiety gripped Craig as he stood alone in the big room. It didn't help that he couldn't even hear Brent moving through the house as he waited.

His hand involuntarily drifted to his hip. He'd practiced drawing the weapon a few times to get the feel of it, and to test his reflexes. He didn't feel comfortable with it, and his movements were clumsy. He'd nearly dropped the thing once and remembered being terrified it might go off despite the safety mechanism.

Brent had asked him if he was comfortable with a firearm, and Craig lied and said he was. He hoped the mercenary believed him, and it seemed like he did. But Craig knew if it came down to any sort of gunfight, his true colors would more than likely come through.

"Downstairs is clear," Brent whispered from behind.

Craig nearly jumped out of his shoes as he spun around, instinctively reaching for the pistol at his side.

"You scared the crap out of me," Craig hissed. "How do you move like that?"

"Years of practice," Brent said with a wry grin. "Let's move up to the second floor."

Craig nodded and followed him back through the kitchen to the stairwell in the foyer.

They ascended quietly, making sure to use the sides of each step to avoid any creaks the boards could make if they'd put all their weight in the center. The only sound they made was the occasional swish of their clothing, but even that was almost inaudible.

When the two men reached the top of the stairs, Brent remained on point and checked the first room straight ahead—a guest bedroom with a queen-size bed surrounded by pale green walls.

Craig moved down the hall and looked into a bathroom on the left. Brent reemerged and pushed through to the next bedroom on the right, cleared it, and continued forward with Craig until they reached an open door at the end.

The two stepped through the doorway and into a vast study. The room ran left to right, covering at least half the width of the house.

Craig scanned the room, noting the artifacts, the bookshelves, the furniture, and finally the desk off to one side.

A dim light glowed from the computer monitor and reflected off the surface of the desk and the chair behind it.

"Looks like they left the computer on," Craig said. "Watch the hallway."

He left Brent by the door and walked over to the desk. He moved the chair out of the way and stood over the keyboard. The monitor was still on, but a screen saver of a bamboo forest on a mountain slope occupied the screen. It faded away and changed to a scene of a desert somewhere in the American Southwest.

"What is it?" Brent asked. He sounded impatient. Not that Craig blamed him. He felt like any second Amid and Wyatt might barge in and catch them in the act. Even with Brent guarding the door, Craig feared a sound from downstairs signaling the others' return.

"Just a screen saver," Craig answered.

He rested his hand over the mouse and nudged it to the right. The screen saver blinked out of view, and Amid's desktop bloomed before him.

"I hope you can find more than just a screen saver. Or this entire play will be one big waste of time."

Craig held back the urge to roll his eyes. "I'm already in," he said, maintaining composure.

Wyatt and the others had left the screen open to the last thing they'd been looking at, and Craig instantly knew what it was.

"There's an aerial map here," he announced. "It's of the area around the Sphinx."

"So, that's where they're headed?"

"Yes, Brent. That's where they're headed. As I'm sure you'll recall was the plan all along."

"Right. I'm just making sure, Craig. You don't have to get all high and mighty about it."

Craig ignored him and continued to study the map. He squinted his eyes, staring at the screen. "Why were they looking at this spot?" he muttered to himself. "It's just a parking garage."

"What's that?" Brent asked.

"The map they were looking at. It's a current one. And it seems like they were focused on the area just east of the Sphinx, beyond the road and the barriers that separate the protected historic area from the city.

"Maybe they left that open to throw you off. Or maybe it's a trap."

"No, I don't think so." Craig shook off the notion. "They left here in a hurry. Their only thought was to leave as soon as possible. The only problem is, what is so special about this area?"

Craig moved the mouse around, dragging the view to the left until he could see the entire body of the Sphinx. "There you are. But why did they leave this over here?"

He dragged the image back to the right at what looked like a derelict area just outside the parking garage and the businesses surrounding it. One building looked like an abandoned shed, another an old garage.

Unable to figure out what the meaning of this image could be, Craig minimized the window, determined to locate the database with the maps in it. Instead of finding the desktop with several folder icons, he was greeted by another map.

This one was different than the first. It displayed a series of passages, complete with notations and specific locations in relation to the Sphinx. Craig's eyes widened as he realized what he saw.

"This is it," he whispered only loud enough for himself to hear. He zoomed out to analyze the entire document.

Again, he noted the Sphinx, poring over the various tunnels and chambers in and around the ancient structure. "This must be the known passages they found during various excavations." There were dates noted along the tunnels, which Craig took to indicate the years of the discoveries.

"Finding anything useful?" Brent asked.

"Yeah. I found the map to the tunnels they were looking at."

"Great. So you know where to go?"

"Not yet," Craig said, sounding annoyed. "There are a ton of these passages around the Sphinx. If we just show up over there, Sean and Tommy will spot us."

Brent thought for a second then shrugged. "Unless we wear

disguises. Lot of people in this region cover their faces and heads all the time. Wouldn't be out of the ordinary."

"Good idea. But I still need to zero in on which exact spot they're thinking of looking."

Something still bothered Craig. The first image he'd seen on the monitor was the one Amid and his two guests had left on before they hurried out of the house. It couldn't be a coincidence.

He dragged the map to the right and looked in the area where the road cut past the protected historical land. On the other side, the city buildings weren't visible, but Craig could roughly estimate.

"Hold on," he said, this time louder than intended. "What's this?"

"What's what?" Brent asked.

He left his post and walked over to the desk, taking up a position behind Craig to look over his shoulder.

"Over here," Craig said, pointing at the screen and a corridor drawn on the schematic.

"Says it's a dead end," Brent noticed.

"Yeah. Which is odd. If this is a tunnel like all the others, it should go somewhere. I don't think the builders in Ancient Egypt spent a lot of time making passages that didn't go anywhere. There must be an explanation." He pointed to the screen and ran his finger along the corridor in question. "See how long this is compared to some of the others over by the Sphinx? There's no way they would build something of that length and just decide to stop."

"Maybe they ran into a spot they couldn't dig through."

Craig shook his head. "The Egyptians could cut through rock. That's not the problem."

"Then what is the problem?"

"I'm not sure. And it's entirely possible that there really is nothing there. Except, why would Amid and the others leave this window up, as well as this one?" He clicked on the minimized window on the bottom bar, and the Google Earth view popped up to fill the monitor once more.

"What's that?" Brent wondered. "Overhead view of the Sphinx?"

"Yes. And if we scroll over to here, we can see that this area where the parking garage sits is in the same spot as that dead-end tunnel. The only question is, what's so special about that parking deck?"

Brent didn't utter anything other than a low, unintelligible grumble. Craig was thankful for the quiet. He needed to think.

Obviously, Sean and Tommy must have figured there was something about that parking garage, some clue there. But the garage would be built into the ground, with a basement level down below the upper decks. If there'd been some kind of an Ancient Egyptian tunnel there, it was unlikely anyone would have been able to build the place. Craig knew the Egyptian government was highly protective of anything remotely related to historical significance.

He moved the mouse again, bringing the schematics from Amid's database to the screen's forefront. He wanted to overlay the tunnel but didn't have a good way to do that. Still, clicking back and forth gave him a close enough idea.

Craig switched to the view from the internet, then back to the blueprints, then back to the modern image again, adjusting both until he had them somewhat closely aligned.

"That's as good as I can get it," he said after a few minutes of working with the images. "From the looks of it, that passage begins somewhere just outside the northwest wall of the parking garage. If that's the case, the construction company wouldn't have disturbed the ruins, or whatever that passage contains. Still, it's pretty close. I wonder how they were able to pull that off."

"Bribery goes a long way," Brent chuffed.

"Yeah, that's true. Maybe that is how they did it. Either way, I think this corridor is what Tommy and Sean are looking for. It's the only thing that makes sense. They left here quickly, and this spot was what was on the screen when we got here." Craig tapped the monitor and stood up straight. He felt confident and a little proud of himself for figuring it out, even if it hadn't been proved yet.

"So, we go to that parking deck and take them out?" Brent clarified.

"Yes. And if they are there, we make sure Sean and Tommy don't survive this time."

17

Sean took the parking ticket from the automated dispenser and waited for the bar blocking the way to lift and let him through.

A second after he took the ticket, the gate raised, and he drove through, careful not to get too close to the concrete edges of the driveway leading into the garage.

"This car really is something," Tommy said, rubbing his hand along the black-stitched leather along the door.

"Why don't you buy one?" Sean asked as he steered the vehicle around to the right. He noted the arrows pointing to the upper parking decks, and one that aimed the other direction toward a down ramp.

"Meh. My car is fine. Nothing wrong with it."

Tommy was much like Sean in that regard. Neither of them had expensive tastes, save for the private jet the IAA owned and the modest motorcycle collection Sean kept in his garage.

They stayed at nice places when they traveled, but neither was much into supercars or multimillion dollar yachts, or anything else that screamed opulence. Their homes weren't small, and were decorated with good taste, but both of them lived below their means—a seemingly lost art to so many Americans.

Sean guided the Maserati down and to the left, following the signs leading to the basement level.

Sterile, pale lights glowed from fixtures along the concrete supports overhead. The garage looked old, perhaps built in the 1970s or '80s. It showed signs of cracks along some of the supports, though that kind of wear and tear was to be expected over time. The engineers would have planned for that—Sean hoped.

His biggest fear had always been heights, but he was not a big fan of being underground, especially in old structures like this one. Ironically, he and Tommy often found themselves in subterranean places such as caves or underground chambers, or as the case was probably going to be here—an ancient tunnel.

"Where is this green door Vokum was talking about?" Tommy asked.

It was a rhetorical question, but Sean answered anyway. "I was just wondering the same thing."

"Drive over there to that wall. That should be it if that's the northwest-facing one."

"Ten-four." Sean steered the Maserati in that direction, passing dozens of empty parking spaces. Only a few were occupied, and Sean wondered why even those were taken. They'd passed some businesses, along with the ticket office for the Sphinx and the Pyramids up the street, but at this late hour of the afternoon, he doubted any new tours were starting. Most of the visitors would either be on their way back or would have already left. He guessed these remaining vehicles belonged to workers or the last straggling tourists of the day.

Thankfully, no one was around at the moment, not that he could see. If they were going to break into a restricted area, having no witnesses around was paramount.

They'd stopped at a hardware store on the way here and picked up some tools—a bolt cutter, a couple of shovels and mattocks, and some flashlights and lamps. The Maserati wasn't exactly a vehicle built to carry such tools, which made Sean and Tommy both feel more than a little awkward as they left the shop and placed the equipment in the trunk.

Both agreed that they would not be stowing the tools in Vokum's luxury car after they'd been used and dirtied. If Brent or Craig didn't kill them, Vokum would for such an offense.

"There," Tommy said, pointing at a door in the back-left corner next to a wall that jutted out from the main one.

"I see it."

Sean drove to the other side of the basement and eased the car into an empty spot at an angle from the green door.

"Doesn't look so bad," Tommy said, unfastening his seatbelt.

"That's not the one we have to worry about," Sean reminded. "It's the one at the end of that corridor we'll need to break through."

"Shouldn't be too much of a problem. Unless we don't have the right tools for the job."

"That's what concerns me."

Sean opened the door and climbed out, popped the trunk with the button on the key fob, and walked back to collect the tools.

He and Tommy split the load and then looked around the garage to make sure no one was watching from one of the few cars.

"No cameras down here," Sean said. "Though I'm not surprised. I've seen parking decks way newer than this one that don't have them."

"With all the crime that happens in these kinds of places, you'd think the owners would spring for a few cameras."

"Yeah. No kidding."

Sean closed the trunk, slung his rucksack over his shoulders, and carried the tools over to the green double doors.

He pulled on the right one and found it unlocked, which could have been a problem. They'd just assumed that getting through would be simple enough, but now he realized that making assumptions was foolhardy.

He held the door open and let Tommy enter first, then followed behind into a concrete-block hallway.

Just as Amid had described, there were doors on the right and on both sides up ahead. The corridor's fluorescent lights cast a dim, eerie light on the walls and floor.

"It's like an old hospital hallway," Tommy said, keeping his voice down.

They stepped forward, wary that someone might pop out from one of the other rooms and ask them what they were doing down here.

"Or an asylum," Sean suggested.

"And great. Now I'm thinking asylum. It wasn't creepy enough in here already."

"At least we don't hear the sounds of people screaming."

"You just don't know when to stop, do you?"

"It's one of the things you love about me," Sean said with a devilish grin.

They passed a couple of doors, one on either side.

"Can you just focus?" Tommy hissed. He looked back over his shoulder, worried someone might have followed them in. Or perhaps a maintenance worker emerging from one of the rooms they passed and spotted them in what was probably a restricted area.

"Oh, I'm focused."

They reached the end of the hall and the pair of doors Amid had described. Two heavy chains blocked the entry, along with two padlocks. Multiple signs were fixed to the surface—warnings in both English and Arabic that entry was forbidden, and trespassers would be prosecuted.

Sean set his bag down, along with the tools he'd carried in. Tommy did the same and looked to his friend as he held the bolt cutters.

"You want to do the honors, or should I?" Tommy asked.

"I'll do it. Just in case someone does come in here, I don't want you to be the one holding the evidence."

"You really think it matters, Eddie?"

"Always a great reference," Sean said. "Even if it isn't Christmas."

"The quotes from that movie work in all seasons," Tommy said. "But here, you do it." He held out the bolt cutters.

Sean took them and faced the door. "Keep a lookout," he said and opened the mouth of the tool.

He fit the first padlock's bolt into the cutter, then clamped the handles together. Sean grimaced as he squeezed. Even with the leverage the tool provided, it wasn't an easy task. After a few seconds of effort, he felt the jaws of the bolt cutter shut. The padlock fell toward the ground, and Sean instinctively kicked out his right foot and caught the heavy lock on the top of his boot like a soccer player would a ball.

He cradled it carefully to the ground and then reached down and picked it up off his foot before setting it on the floor to the left.

"Nice reflexes," Tommy said. "Maybe I should hold on to the other one so we don't risk making a noise if it hits the concrete."

"Yeah, we probably should have thought of that the first time."

Tommy got down on one knee and held the base of the second lock.

"I'm already married," Sean joked, mocking the compromising position his friend was in.

"You're an idiot. Just cut the thing already."

"All right. And you watch the door."

Sean fitted the tool into place again and repeated the process. When the bolt was cut, the chains fell loose to the side, clattering against the metal doors. Tommy set the lock down on the floor to the right of the doors.

"Guess we didn't think of the noise those chains would make," Sean muttered. He looked back at the other end of the corridor, concerned any second someone might burst through and demand to know what they were doing.

But no one appeared.

Tommy pulled on the latch and opened the right-side door. A dusty odor plumed from beyond the threshold. It smelled like other passages he'd been in before. There was something in the scent that hinted at ancient things and at the people who had made this place so long ago.

The pair fixed headlamps onto their heads and switched on the lamps clipped to their rucksacks. Then they picked up their tools and bags and slipped into the black corridor.

18

Sean closed the door until the bolt clicked into place. There was nothing they could do about making the chains look undisturbed. Not from the inside. But that was the risk they had to take—and hope that no one ventured down far enough to notice.

It was unlikely the doors into this passage were ever really checked. Sean and Tommy were betting on the fact that the blocked doorway had probably become a blind spot to anyone working there.

Inside the corridor, only a sliver of light penetrated the crack between the doors. The two turned and faced the other direction, both feeling the sense that they were on the clock.

"We'd better move," Sean echoed Tommy's thoughts. "No telling how much we might have to dig."

"If at all," Tommy kicked the hard dirt under his feet. "This seems pretty dense. It's probably just silt from floods long ago. I bet underneath here we got nothing but more rock."

"Probably. But we're not leaving until we try. Come on. Let's see what's at the end of this passage."

The two moved quietly through the corridor. The walls offered no answers as to who had built this or why. Sean noticed the tunnel had been cut flawlessly, with smooth sides and ceiling, all perfectly symmetrical.

"Incredible how they were able to cut this so accurately," Tommy whispered.

"Yeah," Sean agreed from just in front of his friend. "Pretty amazing, and we need expensive tools and tech to reproduce anything close to this."

"Right."

As they kept moving forward, the thin strip of light from the door seemed much more distant than in reality. It looked smaller, too. On top of that, as Tommy stole occasional glances back to the doors, the realization that they were trapped in here with only one way out sank deep into his gut. It twisted his stomach into knots. All he could do was try to focus on why they were here.

It only took a few minutes of walking before they saw the end of the passage up ahead. Their lights touched the rock wall before they were close.

"Looks like this is it," Sean said, slowing to a stop.

Just as Amid had described, the path ended abruptly in a smoothly cut wall. The corners were just as perfect as the rest of the work, which told Sean and Tommy it wasn't just because they were told to stop. This showed no signs of a sudden halt with the work.

"Whoever built this went to the trouble of cleanly cutting the end here," Sean noted.

"I was just thinking the same thing," Tommy said. "Sure doesn't look like they abandoned the project."

Sean jammed his heel into the dirt beneath them. It didn't make much of a sound except for the little dust that scraped from his boot.

"If there's something down there," he said, "it could take a while to get to it."

"Strange they didn't detect any anomalies."

"Like Vokum said, if there was anything down there, their scans would have picked up the objects. But if this whole thing is just filled with dirt, and there was nothing unusual on the scans, why bother digging?"

"I suppose so." Sean picked up a mattock and flipped it around so the wide blade faced away from him. "Shall we?"

Tommy picked up a similar tool and nodded. "Yeah, let's see how hard this really is."

Sean whipped the mattock down hard. The blade made a clinking sound as it dug into the dirt. The shaft of the tool vibrated in Sean's hand, but as he pulled it back, a chunk of the floor came loose and flopped onto the surface.

"Not too bad," Sean said. "Wish it was quieter, but we don't have much of a choice."

Tommy twisted his tool around so the pick was facing out, and slammed it into the surface. The sound it made was quieter than the blade, and it dug deeper.

The two of them toiled for half an hour, working away the silt near the end of the corridor.

Sweating, and tired, they stood knee deep in the hole. They'd scraped away a significant portion from the end of the corridor in case there was something underground, perhaps a clue engraved into the stone, or undiscovered hieroglyphs.

"So far, so good," Sean said. He wiped his forehead with the tail of his shirt and grabbed a half-empty bottle of water next to his bag.

"I wouldn't call this kind of work good," Tommy countered as he scraped away another layer of dirt from the wall. The soil at this level broke away easily, crumbling into the hole to be shoveled out with the rest.

"Well, back when I used to work in landscaping, the dirt was worse than this. Clay filled with tons of rocks, roots, you name it. Don't have to deal with any of that here."

"Yeah," Tommy grunted as he scored out another layer. "I will say, I am starting to believe there is more to this passage than I initially thought."

"You mean we've been trespassing and disturbing a historical site while you were iffy on all this?"

Tommy rolled his shoulders and kept digging. "Oh, I believed it was possible. But it's always the same with me. I prefer to stay pragmatic until I see evidence. Right now, I'm seeing some fascinating evidence that this corridor was originally much lower."

Sean twisted the cap back on the bottle and set it by his bag. Then he took the shovel and scooped out two more heaps of dirt, tossing them onto the pile behind the pit.

Tommy dragged the pike end of the mattock across the dirt again, but this time the point sank deeper.

"Whoa," he gasped.

Sean was in the middle of tossing another shovelful of dirt back when Tommy made the sound.

"What?" Sean got his answer as soon as the question left his lips.

"If this is a solid wall, it shouldn't sink that far in," Tommy said. "I think I just broke through."

He pulled back on the handle, and a large chunk of packed dirt stripped away from the wall to reveal a dark hole. With the opening revealed, Tommy worked faster, hurriedly picking away at the layers of dirt until they could see a sharp edge, carved perfectly flat, and a black space beyond.

"This is another doorway," Tommy realized. "This isn't just some random passage. It leads to something else."

Sean said what both of them were thinking. "The Hall of Records."

19

B rent stopped at the ticket dispenser at the entrance to the parking garage. "I guess I have to get a ticket," he complained.

"So? Get a ticket," Craig ordered.

"I hope it's free for the first two hours."

"Seriously?"

Brent shook his head. "No, I'm kidding."

Wow, thought Craig, *he does have a personality. Twisted, sure, but there's clearly more to this stoic psychopath.*

He reached out the window and pressed the button. A second later, the machine printed him a parking ticket, and the blocking bar lifted up to allow them through.

Brent drove past the gate and into the garage, where he stopped and looked in both directions.

"Where should I go?"

"Let's drive around this area first," Craig said. "See if we can spot their car."

"You think they would still be driving that Maserati?" Brent wondered.

"Maybe. That would be a stupid thing to do, but if they're in a hurry, and I think they are, I doubt they took the time to swap out the vehicle for a rental."

"All about giving up one thing for another."

Brent steered the car to the left and drove slowly toward the end of the deck. They looked at each car as they passed, but there was no sign of the Maserati. At the end of the rows, another row of cars lined the outer wall, with several empty spaces offering a place to park for new visitors.

When they reached the corner, Brent turned the wheel to the right, following the green sign hanging from the ceiling with a white arrow on it.

He and Craig searched the outer row, then turned and continued back in the other direction.

"It's not on this deck," Craig said. "Why would it be? If there is some kind of secret tunnel, it would be down on the basement level. That's where we should go."

"Good thinking."

Brent guided the vehicle around the next bend and then followed the signs to the lower deck. He turned onto the down ramp and kept going until it leveled out at the bottom, where he spun the wheel again and steered into the aisle.

"There," Craig said, raising a finger toward the black Maserati parked in a spot near the far wall.

"I see it." Brent slowed down, peering out through the window to his left and then to the right. "Keep your eyes peeled. This smells like a trap."

Craig didn't protest. Instead, the warning set him on edge, and he swept the dimly lit garage deck from left to right and back again, checking under and behind the few cars parked in the basement level.

"No sign of them, other than the car," Brent said. "You see anything?"

"No. Nothing."

"I'll drive around this level one time then park over there." He indicated one of the several empty spots near the Maserati.

After a slow loop around, they still didn't see any sign of Wyatt and Shultz and returned back to the Maserati. Brent stopped the car behind the other and peered through the tinted windows.

"Well, they're not out here," he surmised. "Unless they're hiding in the car."

"I guess we should check and see?" Craig didn't sound so sure that he wanted to be the one to do it, but wasn't about to come off as weak.

"Yeah. I'm going to leave the car here for a second. If they're not in there, I'll park a few spots over. But if they are, we wouldn't want them getting away." He looked down at Craig's side. "Time to pull out that piece in case this is a setup."

Craig nodded that he understood, but that didn't make him feel more comfortable about the gun situation.

He opened the door and stepped out, pulling the pistol from its concealed holster. The grip felt too thin in his hand, and he started regretting going with the single stack model. It almost seemed like a toy or a replica, even though he knew the rounds in the magazine and the one in the chamber were definitely real.

Brent slid out of the seat and drew his pistol. He held it out away from him as he approached the Maserati. Craig copied his movements even though he didn't really know what he was doing. He did his best to add in what little he'd gleaned from cop shows or military movies, but all of it felt unnatural.

They stopped at the rear doors and looked inside, but no one was in the back seat, and a quick sidestep to the front doors revealed the same.

Brent made a motion that they should return to the sedan.

Back in the vehicle, the two men eased the doors shut so that they barely made a sound.

"Maybe we should leave our car behind theirs while we look around," Craig suggested. "That way, if they come back before us, they'll have no way to get out."

"I was thinking the same thing," Brent agreed. "Any guesses where they might be?"

Craig stared at the green doors set in the wall beyond the Maserati. "I know the first place we should check."

Brent turned and looked that direction. "As good a place as any." He spoke in a low, conspiratorial tone. "But I'll go in first. They might be waiting on the other side, ready to ambush us."

"Fair enough. I'll cover you." Craig surprised himself with how confident he sounded.

"Okay, let's do it."

Brent killed the engine, opened the door, and stepped out onto the smooth concrete surface. He glanced around, surveying the immediate area to make sure nothing had changed in the last minute since they got in their vehicle.

They skirted around the Maserati once more. Brent ran his fingers along the hood. "Cold," he mouthed.

Craig knew what that meant. If the hood was cold, the engine hadn't run in a while, maybe an hour. It had been well over an hour since they last saw the Maserati leaving Amid's home.

The two men stopped in front of the green metal doors. There were no windows to allow a view inside to whatever lay beyond the doorway, which made this a particularly tricky scenario.

As Craig stood to the right of the right-hand door, he held his pistol up at the ready, the same way he'd seen Brent do before.

Brent looked over at him, put his hand on the door handle, and nodded. Craig returned the gesture, and Brent pulled open the door.

He stepped back for a second in case Wyatt and Schultz were inside waiting with weapons drawn to fire on the first person to come through.

No gunshots erupted from within the doorway. There were no sounds of movement either. Only the monotonous drone of an obscure machine running somewhere in the building.

Brent hung back behind the door for a second, then spun around and pointed his pistol into the opening.

He stepped through, clearing the area to the right behind the other door, then looked down the long hall.

"Clear," he said quietly, retreating back a step so Craig could see him. "Nothing in here. Just a corridor, some doors on the sides, and doors at the end. It's possible they're hiding in one of those."

"I doubt they'd be hiding," Craig countered. "They're here to find something, and I don't think they'll waste any time."

"Still, we'll need to check each room, just in case."

There was another factor Craig considered: the doors along the walls.

Behind one of them might wait the entrance to the Hall of Records.

Even thinking about it sent a tingle across his skin but also filled his gut with doubt. He knew all about what the experts said regarding the Hall of Records, and he'd joined in with that skepticism. Now, here he was, in the basement of a parking garage, hoping to somehow find the hall's entrance.

One thing he knew: If it was down here, Sean and Tommy might have already discovered it. They were annoyingly good at such things, and the accolades proclaiming that fact were numerous.

"Are we in the right place?" Brent whispered. "Doesn't seem like the sort of spot you'd find ancient stuff. I mean, other than the proximity of Giza and all that."

"According to the map, that corridor we noticed on the map at Amid's should be here somewhere. If I recall correctly." He pointed at the end of the hall illuminated by pale fluorescent light. The glow caused his pale skin to take on a deathly cold color. "That should be the northwest end of the building, and the tunnel plans we saw ran out from that area."

"Unless we didn't assess it correctly."

"No," Craig said. "We did. Notice all the warning signs on those doors at the end? I bet this place has been excavated before, but when they didn't find anything, they closed it off."

"You ever heard of it?" Brent wondered. He was getting antsy standing there at the doorway. They were exposed, and effectively in a shooting gallery were Wyatt or Schultz to emerge from one of the doors on the side.

"Not until today. But I also don't spend much time in this part of the world. I only know what I read or watch, or hear on occasion."

Brent accepted the explanation and moved ahead. He pointed at the first set of doors on the right and stopped in front of them. He listened carefully, but all he could hear was the sound of a machine running on the other side.

He pointed down toward the end of the hall, motioning for Craig to cover him. Craig nodded and aimed his weapon toward the barricaded doorway.

Brent jerked the door on the right open and jammed his pistol through the opening, quickly clearing the room from left to right.

Inside, he found several pumps, air conditioning units, a few tools lying around, and a small metal desk with a rolling swivel chair that looked like it came out of a 1970s office cubicle.

"Nothing," he said, turning back to Craig and reentering the hall. "Let's check these last two. Be careful. If it was me, I would split up and have one of us on either side to create a crossfire."

"Okay. I'll follow your lead."

They made their way down to the next set of doors on the right, ignoring the ones opposite for the moment, and took positions on either side just as they'd done before.

The entire process was tedious, and a test of patience, but Brent knew what he was doing, and Craig had to trust that. Even if it meant they were losing ground on Sean and Tommy with every second that passed.

Brent reached out and grasped the handle, nodded at Craig to cover him again, and then pulled the door open.

He repeated the process from before, stepping into the room, checking from left to right. This was a small bathroom with a sink and a single stall with a toilet inside. He looked up to make sure no one was hanging overhead and then looked in the stall before finally returning to the corridor.

Brent stepped across the hall, yanked open the door, and methodically checked the last room, which turned out to be a storage closet with a few old maintenance uniforms, a mop and bucket, a broom, some cleaning supplies, and a single gray locker.

"Nothing here," he said as he reemerged into the corridor.

"Which means they went through there," Craig added, pointing to the doors at the end.

Brent looked at the doors with the warning signs on them. He stalked the thirty feet over to them and inspected the chains dangling on either side. Then he bent down and picked up a padlock with the bolt severed in half.

"Looks like they cut these off," Brent noted. "Must have some bolt cutters."

"Why would they have those unless—"

"They knew they'd need them."

"Right. Amid must have told them about this door being blocked off."

"Let's see what's behind door number five," Brent said and pulled it open. As before, he pointed his pistol through the opening. This time, instead of an empty room, he found an exceedingly different kind of corridor than the one where they stood.

It was cut from rock, hewn to a smooth finish. The passage was dark, with no identifying markings or hieroglyphs to indicate who'd built it, or why.

"Fascinating," Craig said, peering into the darkness. "We're going to need lights."

"You want to go back and get them, or you want me to?"

"I'll do it. You stay here and keep watch in case Sean or Tommy come back this way."

Brent agreed, handed Craig the keys, and continued watching the tunnel from a position close to the corner of the doorframe. If Sean and Tommy were to return this direction, they'd likely have lights and be easy to spot. Still, if they were careful, they'd dim the lights or turn them off entirely, which would make Brent a silhouetted target bathed in light.

Even though it was doubtful their former partners would fire a shot at a man whose face they couldn't identify, Brent wasn't about to take that chance.

Craig took off back down the hall at a steady trot, careful not to let his footfalls make too much noise with every step.

He reached the end of the corridor and cautiously opened the door, fully aware that everything up to that point could have been a ruse by Tommy and Sean to lure them into a dead-end tunnel, and take off without them knowing.

A trickle of relief fluttered through Craig's chest when he saw both the Maserati and their rental sedan still where they had left them.

He pressed the button on the key fob to open the trunk. The latch popped, and the lid opened automatically, slowly rising to its stopping point.

Craig retrieved both the backpacks containing their gear and then closed the trunk. He turned back toward the doors and was about to open them when a man's voice stopped him in his tracks.

"What are you doing?"

20

Tommy set the mattock down and peered into the darkness beyond the gaping cavity. His headlamp illuminated a round area on the other side, giving a glimpse of a stone pillar to the left and another to the right.

He and Sean had dug out a berth wide enough for both of them to fit through, yet still low enough to the floor on the other side that they could easily climb out.

"What are you waiting for?" Sean asked.

"Nothing. Just taking it all in."

"Well, can you take it in a little faster. Those guys might still be behind us."

"Right." Tommy let his legs hang over the short two-foot drop to the floor and lowered himself down.

He stepped away from the door so Sean could get through, holding out his lantern toward the nearest pillar.

Egyptian hieroglyphs covered the entire surface all the way around.

Sean joined his friend by the column. He held out his lantern and cast the light around the rest of the room.

The floor was covered in enormous mosaic tiles. The colors were still as vibrant as they would have been thousands of years ago—seemingly untouched by time.

More pillars lined the aisle in the center, each raised in perfect rows that stretched up near the ceiling. Rectangular capstones rested on top of them, connecting the columns in the same fashion as Egyptian temples along the Nile.

Tommy aimed his light toward the nearest wall and discovered stone shelves carved into the rock that went twenty feet up.

"Incredible," Tommy murmured. "I never thought this place was real. And yet here we are."

"Yeah. Too bad it looks like the place was cleared out a long time ago. This floor is next level, though. I can't imagine how much time it must have taken to bring all these tiles in here. And there's no telling where they came from."

Tommy walked over to one of the shelves and ran his finger along the smooth surface. "There's nothing left," he realized. Dejection smothered his words.

"I wonder if it was looted before the flooding brought all that silt in, or if all the stuff in here was moved before that happened."

"Maybe there's a clue inscribed on the pillars."

Tommy moved back over to the column from before and pored over the images. Sean made his way farther down the wall. He stopped and looked across the aisle into the darkness. The place seemed to go on forever. He shined his light back toward the way he'd been walking and saw the far wall was at least another fifty yards away.

"This place is enormous," Sean said.

"What's that?" Tommy asked, still staring at the column as he sidestepped his way around it.

"I said this place is enormous," Sean raised his voice.

"Oh, yeah. So, I'm not seeing much about why everything was removed. This pillar contains religious ceremonial stuff. Nothing really helpful for us."

"Keep moving then. If there is something here, it would be nice to find it sooner rather than later."

"Copy that."

Tommy moved away from the pillar and on to the next in the row. He analyzed it for a couple of minutes and kept going.

"Most of this seems to either be historical records or religious rites. It's fascinating, though."

"What is?" Sean kept moving slowly along the wall as he listened.

"The Sphinx was built during the Old Kingdom," Tommy explained. "These hieroglyphs are from that time. Nothing was changed from the original work."

"Cleopatra was wise, from what I understand. She doesn't seem the type to go into a sacred place of records like this and start redecorating. And I'm guessing it wasn't open to the public. Possibly it was a secret repository for some of the more valuable, or even dangerous, items from the Great Library."

Tommy shrugged. "I didn't think about that."

Sean kept going until he stopped at the end of the room in a corner where the shelves met. He looked down at the bare space and imagined what must have been here thousands of years before.

He turned and pointed his lights toward the center of the aisle. The circular glow illuminated something sticking out from the wall. It looked like a stone counter, or maybe an altar.

"Tommy?"

"Yeah."

"Meet me down here in the middle."

"You got something?"

"I don't know."

Sean picked up his pace, moving quickly across the floor until he reached the center. Now he could see there were two counters. The space between them was empty, but on the wall in the middle, a huge disc was carved into the rock.

Tommy stopped next to Sean and stared at the relief. "Okay, so that's obviously Ra," he said. "And under it is the Sphinx." He pointed to the image resembling the great structure to the west. "But what is that hole in the center of the disc? That's an unusual shape. And look at that seam straight down the middle. This is two huge sections of stone."

Sean had been wondering about the same things and had already moved close to the wall to get a better look at the tightly sealed gap between the massive pieces.

The hole was widest in the center, where two ear-like shapes expanded out before narrowing again on the bottom.

He removed his headlamp and shined the light inside. "It's some kind of mechanism," he said.

"Hold on a second," Tommy said.

He set his bag down and unzipped the top, then reached in and removed the golden cobra head scepter.

Then he held it out horizontally and looked down the end of it as he would a board to see if it was flat.

"I think this goes in there," he realized.

He stepped forward and past Sean, then carefully interred the cobra's head into the hole. Nothing happened.

"Maybe a little deeper," Sean suggested.

Tommy glanced over at him with a wary expression, then pushed the scepter farther into the cavity.

He met resistance; then a click echoed from the wall as he eased it forward. A loud clack sounded from inside the hole. Something inside the wall started moving. It was impossible to tell what made the racket.

"Step back," Sean said.

Tommy did, taking a step back as he pulled the scepter out of the opening.

The seam in the center began to part, splitting like two huge sliding doors. The entire hall filled with the deep rumbling sound of stone grinding on stone.

Sean and Tommy stood in disbelief as the massive gate parted. Their lights gradually broke through into the darkness and sprayed into another chamber. Neither of them took a breath, unable to fully grasp what they were seeing.

"This is unreal," Tommy gasped.

Sean risked a step forward, inspecting the locking mechanism on the edge of the foot-thick door before it stopped flush with the wall.

Beyond the threshold, two golden arks sat on the mosaic floor in front of what appeared to be a giant map.

"Are those..." Sean faltered. "Arks? As in like the Ark of the Covenant?"

"Yeah, but instead of angels, these have cats on top of them. Something similar was found in Tut's tomb, if you recall."

"Oh, I remember all that. Including research on ark technology. Egyptians used them for electrical displays during religious ceremonies. Having grown up in the Egyptian schools and religion, Moses knew all about them. So when he was instructed to build one, he knew exactly what to do. Only recently did new research reveal he'd created the ultimate superweapon of the time."

"Right. You didn't have to give me the whole recap, but yes. You clearly remember."

Sean fired his friend a snarky glower. "You asked. And I do have a really good memory."

"Also don't need to be reminded of that, but thanks."

Tommy moved forward into the chamber. "I wonder what's inside these." He looked ahead at a sandstone coffer sitting atop a plinth just in front of the map. It was sealed with a matching lid and measured two feet long and half as high.

He stopped next to the ark on the right and peered down at it, daring to touch one of the cats' ears with his index finger. The gold was cold. The detail immaculate. Right down to the whiskers.

"Persian cats if I'm not mistaken," Sean said.

"You *would* know that, crazy cat lady."

"Hey, I'm a cat person."

"I'm well aware," Tommy said, moving forward toward the wall-size map.

The surface spanned twenty feet across and ten feet high. A single line of hieroglyphs lined the map's top edge.

Sean passed the ark on the left and looked up at the colorful message from the past.

"The power of Ra awaits those who take the right path," Tommy said, reading the ancient language out loud.

"Another clue," Sean realized. He neared the map and looked over it, spotting the pyramids and the Sphinx. "This is an ancient map of Cairo," he said, his heart quickening.

"Indeed it is." Tommy moved closer, inspecting the astonishing detail. "This is amazing. There's the Nile, the city as it was thousands of years ago, and…" He paused, his words catching in his throat.

"What?" Sean wondered. "Cat got your—"

"Please, don't. I know you have a thing with cats."

"It's not like you're a dog person."

Tommy let out an exasperated sigh. "Look. Up there. Near the top of the map where the Nile ends."

"Okay. I see a red dot there. Is that what I'm supposed to be looking at?"

"Yes."

"And that is…?"

Tommy looked over at his friend in disbelief. "Seriously? I finally know something the great Sean Wyatt doesn't know?"

"Uh, there are a ton of things you know that I don't. Like a thousand and one uses for rope. What are we looking at here, Schultzie? Or are you going to waste time gloating while a couple of guys who tried to kill us catch up?"

"No. You're right," Tommy said with a nod. "I just need a second to breathe it in." He sucked in a long breath through his nose. "You really don't know what that—"

"Just tell me already," Sean ordered, tired of the charade.

"That is Heracleion."

"I thought that was a city on the island of Crete."

"No, it is. This one is also known as Thonis or Thonis-Heracleion. It's been in the news a ton lately."

The light went on in Sean's eyes. "Oh right. The underwater city. Ton of artifacts being pulled up from there over the last few years. One of our teams went there to take care of a few heavy items."

"Yes. Exactly. You know, I'm still surprised you didn't remember it or recognize it. Weren't you the one who handled the logistics and security for it?"

Sean beamed over at his friend, and Tommy knew he'd been had.

"You knew this whole time, didn't you?"

"Yeah. But I wanted you to have some fun for a minute."

Tommy shook his head. "You're an idiot."

"I know." Sean focused on the map again. "So, this map must have been created before all the earthquakes and tsunamis took out the port."

"Yes. Precisely. And see, over here is Canopus to the east."

"Canopus. Is that where the name for canopic jars comes from?"

"Not the time, Sean. Focus." Tommy studied the map another five seconds. "But no. That name comes from a mix-up with historians and archaeologists a long time ago. Nothing to do with this area."

Sean held back laughing. "So, this red dot must mean something. But what?"

Their eyes fell to the stone box between them. Then they looked at each other.

"I wonder if that answer is in here," Tommy said.

"Could be. Or it could be a mummy curse. You never know."

"This is too small to be a sarcophagus, although it's possible someone's remains were condensed into something that could fit in here."

"Condensed? That's a weird, and potentially disgusting, thought."

"Forget it. The answer we're looking for must be in here." Tommy ran his hand over the top of it. "I know you want to say it."

"Say what?" Sean wondered.

"There's only one way to find out?"

"There you go! That's how you use a cliché."

21

Craig turned the direction he'd heard the voice and met the gaze of an older Egyptian man in a security uniform.

The whites of the man's eyes glowed in the garage lights. He looked surprised and angry all at once, and full of purpose he'd not felt in a long time.

"Hey," Craig said, fumbling for an answer. "Sorry, you startled me. I didn't see you there."

The security guard raised a flashlight in his right hand and aimed it straight into Craig's eyes. The blinding light seared his vision for a second, and he had to drop the gear in his left hand and raise it to shield himself.

"I asked you what you are doing," the night guard said.

"Oh yeah. I was just... um, switching some—"

"You are not permitted back there," the guard stated with a nod toward the green doors. "What were you doing back there?"

"I'm... here to fix an electrical problem." It was the best lie Craig could think of. Normally, he fancied himself a pretty good liar, but in this instance, he had to come up with something faster than he could have anticipated. "That's what all this stuff is in these bags. Just tools and such."

"I don't know anything about that," the guard said in a thick accent. "I will need to see a work order or some documentation."

The guy wasn't a fool. Unfortunately for Craig. The old guard must have seen him come out of the corridor, or perhaps seen him and Brent go in. He wondered if there were cameras hidden that they might have missed, but so far, the man hadn't mentioned his partner.

"Could you at least put the light down?" Craig asked. "It's hurting my eyes."

The guard acquiesced and lowered the light but kept it aimed in Craig's direction, the bright white circle covering his feet and the concrete around it.

"You're not supposed to be in there without a work order," the guard continued. "And you don't look like you're here to work on any electrical issues." He raised his radio from his right hip and held it close to his mouth.

"No, wait," Craig said. "I can show you. There are lots of tools in here. And I have the work order somewhere in this bag. Just give me a second, and I'll fish it out for you."

The man hesitated, and Craig bent down and opened his sack. He knew good and well there was nothing in the bag that could convince the man he was an electrician there to perform some kind of maintenance. It was a feeble lie at best—a house of sticks built on a stormy shore in the sand.

But he needed to buy some time, a few seconds to think of something, anything that could get him out of this mess. If the guy called in a trespasser, more guards would show up. Worse than that, the cops would arrive, and that would pose an entirely new problem.

"It's in here somewhere," Craig lied. "Sorry about all this. I have a bunch of stuff in this bag. I need to be better organized."

The man waited, but the expression on his face turned more suspicious by the second. Craig was running out of options.

One idea emerged from the dark recesses of his mind. It wasn't the first time he'd gone there, to a place where most people feared to go. He'd been willing to let his former friends and colleagues perish in an ancient tomb. This was child's play compared to that. At least, that's what he told himself.

"I'm going to call it in," the guard said.

"No. Wait," Craig protested. "I have it right here."

He stood up and spun around to face the uniformed man again. As he did so, Craig whipped the pistol around and pointed it at the guard's chest. "Put the radio down," he ordered. "Slowly."

His voice remained calm, steady, fully in control of the situation. He felt empowered with the gun in his hand. With it, he controlled whether or not this man lived or died, and that sent a rush through his mind and body unlike any he'd ever felt before.

And to Craig's surprise, he liked it.

"Who are you?" the guard asked, ignoring the order.

"I don't want any trouble," Craig said. "I am just here to investigate something. That's what I do. Okay? But I can't let you call for backup. I would rather you just go on your way, but you messed that up. So, now I'm going to have to take that radio from you, your phone too, and put you in my trunk until I'm done. When I finish what I'm doing, I'll let you go. All you have to do is put down the radio, and no one gets hurt."

The man merely stared back at Craig with his wide, vapid eyes.

"Don't make me say it again," Craig warned. "I don't want to kill you."

That much was true. He didn't want to kill the man. He probably had a family, friends, maybe a dog. But he'd gotten in the way, and that wasn't Craig's fault. And he wasn't going to allow this peon to stand in his way.

There was another reason Craig didn't want to shoot the guy, although it was far less benevolent than the other. Firing the weapon would be extremely loud and could be heard by others. That would draw unwanted attention, and throw the entire operation into chaos.

"Last chance," Craig threatened. "Put it down. And you live. It's that simple. Please." He tried to sound kind with the last word, but his pleading seemed to fall on deaf ears.

The resolve on the man's face told Craig he had no intention of lowering the radio. And if he pressed the button before Craig fired, whoever was on the other end would hear the gunshot, if they weren't already close enough to hear it by proximity.

The guard's finger tensed on the button, nudging Craig to the edge of a huge decision. He could kill the guy. The guard was nobody to him. People die every day. What's one more, especially when he'd been given every opportunity to walk free once they were done here?

And for what? His minimum-wage job as a security guard? Craig wondered why the man had such a deranged sense of duty to such a thankless gig.

"I'm going to count to three," Craig said. The counting was more to muster his own determination to take care of this problem by any means necessary.

"One."

The man didn't budge.

"Two."

The right side of the guard's head erupted in a plume of pink mist. A muted pop sounded from near the doorway nearly at the same time.

The guard's hand fell to his side—the radio dropping to the pavement with a clatter.

Craig couldn't move as he watched the man twist and collapse to the ground. Once the guard was down, Craig turned and looked toward the doors.

Brent stood there with his pistol extended, a trickle of gray smoke rising from the suppressor barrel.

"Never count," Brent said. "You're not doing it for them. You're doing it for you."

His assessment was as cold as is it was correct.

"I was trying to avoid firing my gun because of the sound," Craig half lied. "Someone could have heard. Fortunately, yours is equipped for that kind of problem."

Brent lowered the weapon and moved rapidly over to the body. "Come on. We need to get him out of view."

"Where do you want to put him?" Craig tried to sound callous, but he'd never handled a dead body before.

"In the pump room we checked first. We can hide it in the back behind the machinery. No one will find him there for a while."

Craig nodded and joined his partner.

"Get the legs," Brent ordered.

Craig bent down and grabbed the dead man's ankles while Brent lifted the man up by the armpits.

Brent turned and started walking backward toward the metal doors. It was all Craig could do not to look into the guard's hollow, lifeless eyes. He'd wished he'd closed them before picking the guy up, but it was too late for that.

The head lolled over to the right and hung low near Brent's wrist. Drops of blood fell onto the ground, leaving a trail as they carried the body over to the doors.

Brent stopped and in a quick move, flung open the door while holding up his end of their burden with one hand. Then he grasped under the guard's armpit again and continued backing up into the corridor.

"What about the blood trail," Craig asked. "Someone could see it."

"Yeah, but we gotta prioritize right now. No one saw what just happened. In a few minutes, that blood will just look like an ordinary chemical leaked out of a bucket or a piece of machinery. We need to keep moving."

Craig knew he was right. And he cursed himself for not being more of a headstrong leader at the moment.

This was all new to him. Sure, he'd imagined himself as a tough, powerful person many times. He'd stared in the mirror over and over reciting mantras to the same effect, that he'd finally gotten his due and was on top of the world.

He'd steeled his nerves and his consciousness in preparation for this mission. He also knew Tommy and Sean would most likely be irrationally stubborn.

Craig wanted them to join him. He didn't care if he had to split some of the profits. And he'd meant what he said about all the good they could do in the world, all the people they could help. They were Boy Scouts, after all, always trying to help those in need when they weren't off hogging glory for themselves.

That last piece dug deep into Craig's craw. It was all a show. There was no way two people were so good, so unselfish, so generous. They claimed to do everything to preserve history, and for charity. Meanwhile, neither of them lived in squalor. They had nice homes in Atlanta, and in Chattanooga. Tommy's agency owned a private jet.

No, they'd made a deal with the devil, and disguised themselves as angels.

The door closed shut behind Craig as he entered the corridor behind Brent. The door on the right was just ahead.

He couldn't get his hands off this body soon enough.

"You look concerned," Brent grunted.

"No. I'm fine," Craig said, letting the thoughts of Tommy and Sean drift away like clouds on a spring breeze. "He's just heavy, that's all."

"Yeah. That's why they call it dead weight."

Brent stopped at the next door and did the same trick as before, leaning the body over onto the right arm while he pulled on the latch with the other hand.

The metal door slammed into the wall behind him a little louder than planned, but at this point it was clear the body's weight was straining his muscles. Veins popped out on his neck and rippled across his forearms. His face was red from the effort, which was saying something since Brent looked like he hit the gym every day of the week.

They moved quickly through the doors and into the back of the room behind one of the pump machines in the corner. Brent shuffled into the space behind it and then lowered his end to the floor. Craig dropped the guy's feet with a thud and dusted his hands off as if that would cleanse them of the crime.

Brent breathed hard for a few seconds, stepped over the body, and looked back at it to make sure it was far enough out of sight. Then he returned to the door and checked again. If anyone was going to find the dead guard, they'd have to go to the rear of the room to see it.

"I think we're good," Brent said, ignoring the droplets of blood on the floor that led straight to the body.

"Agreed," Craig said, taking charge again. "Let's collect our things and get back to the tunnel. We've lost enough time already."

22

Sean and Tommy stood on either end of the stone box, their hands resting on the lid. The container reminded Sean of the hardest day of work he'd ever done in his life, some twenty-one years ago.

He'd been working for a friend for the summer, laying brick pavers for driveways, building retaining walls, and in one instance schlepping 200 pound sandstone blocks down to a homeowner's pool to be used as new coping.

He and his coworkers had toiled all day in the Tennessee July heat, working on the driveway. Twelve hours they'd worked, carrying and setting the pavers until the sun dipped low on the horizon. He'd felt relieved to be done for the day. His T-shirt that started the day as a medium had stretched with sweat until it was a large.

Then his friend, their foreman, announced that the truck with the coping had arrived and they needed it unloaded.

Sean and the crew sucked it up, after a few pizzas, and unloaded over two tons of the blocks.

Standing over this one brought all that back to his mind in such vivid detail he could feel his forearms burning from the work, and even smell the sauce and cheese from the pizza.

Once the pool job was finished a few weeks later and the crew was cleaning up the site, Sean found a chunk of the sandstone that had been discarded. He took it, and kept it in his home as a reminder that no matter how hard things get, nothing would likely ever top the amount of labor he'd done that day.

"You okay there, buddy?" Tommy asked. "You seem lost in thought."

"Yeah. I'm fine. Just thinking. Let's get this lid off and see what's inside."

They gripped the top on both edges and slowly slid it to one side. It was much heavier than even Sean had anticipated. The bottom of the lid ground against the lips of the container until it was halfway off. Then the two grabbed the edge and lowered the lid to the floor.

Both of them stood and peered into the box with unbelieving eyes.

"Is that..." Sean faltered.

"It can't be."

Resting in the center of the box, on a golden podium, was a piece of papyrus encased in a thin layer of golden resin.

"Are you sure that isn't the Archimedes Scroll?" Sean asked.

Tommy nodded. "Pretty sure."

They shifted around to the front of the box and studied the document.

"Whoever left this here was smart to cover it in that resin," Tommy said. "Otherwise, it could have disintegrated long ago."

"Notice how it's resting on that gilded stand? Kind of peculiar, like what a musician would use to hold their music."

"Yes." Tommy reached out to touch it, but Sean grabbed his wrist.

"Don't," Sean warned.

"I wasn't going to take it."

"See that little gap around the bottom of the stand?"

Tommy looked into the bottom. "It's a counterweight trap."

Sean nodded. "Looks like it."

"Good eye." Tommy leaned closer, shining his flashlight onto the script written on the papyrus. "I know this isn't the Archimedes Scroll because that isn't Greek. It's Coptic. And second, there are no drawings, no schematics. His designs are what Craig is after. Not just a text description of it."

Sean studied the flattened scroll but couldn't read it. "What does it say?"

Tommy read it silently for a moment, looking over the lines one by one to make sure he didn't miss any important details.

"It's a message from the queen," he said. "It sounds as if she knew the end was coming and there was no hope for her to stave off the Romans. She left these clues so that someone could come after her, find the scroll, and build the weapon that could rid her kingdom of the Romans once and for all."

That added serious context to this entire quest, but it still didn't answer the question of where they could find the scroll.

Tommy answered that in his next translation. "She said that to harness the power of Ra, those who seek it must find Cicero, and the Eye of Horus."

"Eye of Horus? Cicero?" Sean turned away from the document and rubbed his chin as he pondered the riddle.

"Great orator and politician in Ancient Rome," Tommy said. "But what does he have to do with this?"

"He lived near the end of the Old Republic in Rome," Sean said, working his way through history he'd packed away in his memory.

"Correct."

"And if I remember correctly, he documented much of Archimedes' life, his inventions, philosophies, basically everything about the guy."

"Yes. We owe pretty much all we know about Archimedes to Cicero. But he died before Cleopatra."

Sean paced toward the exit and then spun around, wagging his finger in the air. "Of course. She says that to harness the power of Ra, we have to find Cicero. She must be talking about his grave or tomb."

"But that tomb has never been found," Tommy countered. "He was assassinated, and probably buried as a commoner."

"And Archimedes' grave?"

"That's never been found, either."

Sean hummed. "Seems like maybe we've been slacking on the job."

Tommy chuckled. "There are more important graves out there that remain undiscovered than the other way around, I'm afraid."

"True."

Sean walked back to the box and glanced at the papyrus again, not that it would help. He couldn't read it. But he hoped the text or the material might lend some other clue.

"The Eye of Horus is another problem," Tommy said. "Why would that have anything to do with Cicero? There are no records of him practicing any of the ancient Egyptian religions. And it's unlikely he spent much time here."

"No. You're right. It's something else. But what?"

The two stood there in silence for two minutes, both spinning the gears in their minds to find the answer.

Sean took a step around the box toward the map and stared at it. His gaze swept over the hieroglyphs at the top, but that didn't reveal anything.

Then he looked at the red dot again, this time more closely than before. "Look at that," he said, pointing to the spot on the map.

"What? I saw it before."

"No, look. There's a faint outline within the red paint. It's the Eye of Horus," Sean said, his voice just above a whisper.

"Oh, okay. I see it now. The dark ink must have faded."

"Or it was done deliberately that way."

Tommy faced his friend. "But that doesn't make any sense. Cicero would have been buried in Rome. Not here, and certainly not at Thonis-Heracleion. I'm not sure he visited this area, though it could be possible."

Sean turned and paced to his left away from the papyrus. "There must be something we're not thinking of," he said. "Some piece we're missing."

"To be fair, we've only been trying to figure this out for a few minutes."

Sean ignored the statement and ran his fingers through his hair. He took a few quick, deep breaths to increase the blood circulation through his body. He found the practice to be helpful when he was feeling fatigued or when his brain wasn't giving him the solutions he needed.

"Eye of Horus," he muttered to himself. He rounded and faced Tommy. "Is there a famous artifact of that?"

"Of the eye?" Tommy shrugged. "Sure. I mean, many have been found. I'm not sure any of them are more famous than another. You thinking maybe we're meant to find an artifact shaped like the Eye of Horus?"

"Maybe." The more Sean thought about it, though, the more he doubted that was the answer. Tommy was right. There were all kinds of renderings of the eye: physical objects like talismans and baubles for tourists, paintings, markings on walls of temples and tombs.

Sean stepped back toward the box and stared up at the dot on the wall. "Do you know if they've found one in that location?"

"I honestly can't recall, man. They've retrieved a lot of things from there. I mean, it's an entire sunken city. It will probably take decades to excavate it all."

That wasn't helpful.

Another thought percolated in Sean's mind. It was off the beaten path, different than the line of thinking he'd been on.

"Do you know if they've found a statue or bust of Cicero there?"

He knew it was a random question given the context of the underwater city, its location, and culture. The befuddled expression on Tommy's face echoed that sentiment.

"I don't think so?" he said, questioning Sean's logic.

"We need to find out."

"Why? I mean, I understand trying to find out if an artifact related to the eye was found there, but Cicero? Like I said, I doubt he spent time in Egypt. Why would they keep a monument to him anywhere in the region?"

Sean smirked. "Why would Cleopatra leave us a reference to him if that were the case?"

Tommy hummed in agreement. "Point taken. Are you thinking if someone found a monument to Cicero that the Eye of Horus would be with it?"

A mischievous glint twinkled in Sean's eyes. "Maybe. But what if it's something else? Something on a more spiritual level?"

Tommy raised a curious eyebrow. "Go on."

"In many spiritual circles, the Eye of Horus is the gateway to higher understanding, or enlightenment. Some teachings call it the third eye." He touched his forehead above his nose with his index finger. "Many meditative practices work toward opening this part of the mind because directly behind it is the pineal gland. That gland is calcified for most people, so it appears to be dormant, or basically pointless."

"Like an appendix."

"Not sure that's the same, but anyway, when the pineal gland is activated or decalcified, it can actually produce dimethyltryptamine."

"DMT? As in ayahuasca?"

"Yes."

"How have I not heard about this?" Tommy wondered, scratching his head.

"Maybe you're not reading the same stuff. My point is, many spiritual teachings, including in Ancient Egypt, suggest that the path to wisdom and enlightenment is through opening the pineal gland. People who use ayahuasca report seeing all kinds of things, including angelic beings, spirit guides, and different realities."

"Hence the psychedelic part." Tommy sounded skeptical.

"Yes. But what if the psychedelic component wasn't, or isn't, the evil that the media and governments of the world want you to believe? What if it was used as a key to unlock greater spiritual awareness, and a way to change your reality for the better?"

Tommy stared at Sean for a long minute, confused as to where Sean was going with this. "Have... you done ayahuasca?"

"No. I don't want to puke and crap myself for an hour. Sounds awful. Although I have tried some of the pineal gland meditations. Haven't met any angels yet that I know of."

"Okay..."

"Look, a lot of this is also congruent with gnostic teachings of Jesus. He said it would be difficult for a rich person to enter the kingdom of heaven, more difficult than passing through the eye of a needle."

"That was a gate in Jerusalem."

"Sure. But what if it also meant the third eye? Those who are bent on materialism don't think much on spiritual things. They're consumed by the 3-D around them. He also taught that to enter the kingdom of heaven, one must become like a child, forgetting everything you've learned."

"The talk with Nicodemus."

"Yes. And discussions with the disciples. The gnostics believed that the kingdom of heaven was twofold: both the afterlife and the human imagination."

"Dual teaching," Tommy realized. "His ministry was full of that. A message for the here and now, and for eternity."

"Correct."

"But what does any of this have to do with Cicero and the scroll?"

"I'm getting to that." Sean pointed to his forehead again. "The third eye, the Eye of Horus, is here. The imagination takes place here. Cicero imagined a better world, a better Rome. He was a visionary, and was assassinated because of it. What if Cleopatra knew all of this? What if she knew the potential for the Archimedes Scroll, and as a way to pay tribute to Cicero, hid it through the third eye—in his head?"

Tommy stared blankly for fifteen seconds. "You're saying that she found Cicero's grave, dug it up, and hid the scroll in his skull?"

Sean shook his head vehemently. "No. And based on the size of a human head, it's unlikely the next thing we're looking for is the actual scroll. More likely, a clue. What if that clue is hidden in, say, a bust of Cicero?"

Tommy blinked several times before responding. "Whoa. Okay. That's a big leap." He turned and walked over to the wall, pivoted, and walked back as he processed everything he'd just heard.

"I know. But this clue is telling us to find Cicero, and the eye. And that map insinuates we're supposed to be looking there."

"Okay, so what if no one has pulled up a statue or a bust of Cicero from Thonis-Heracleion? Are we supposed to go through the process of getting permits and dive down to explore it ourselves?"

"If that's what it takes, Schultzie," Sean said.

"That could be months, Sean. And in case you hadn't noticed, there's a psychopath out there trying to find the scroll, too."

"Now that isn't a nice thing to say about your old friend, Tommy." The familiar voice came from the chamber's entrance.

Sean instinctively reached for his pistol as he turned, but it was too late. Both Brent and Craig blocked the exit with weapons raised.

"Don't," Craig ordered.

23

Sean could only guess as to why the two men hadn't shot him and Tommy the second they saw them.

They were thirty feet away, which wasn't long range but for sidearms would require excellent marksmanship, especially for the pistol Craig held in his hand—a slender single stack 9mm.

If they were to fire and miss, the rounds could ricochet and hit them instead of the targets.

The other reason for their hesitance was directly behind Sean—the encased papyrus. Sean couldn't be sure how much of his conversation with Tommy the two gunmen heard, but he guessed it was only the last few bits. Rather, he hoped it was.

"I didn't think you were the gun type, Craig," Sean said, immediately diving into trying to buy some time.

Craig ventured a step forward. "You know, I never really was. But it's growing on me. I can see why you like it."

"I never said I liked it. Firearms are tools. Not toys."

"I'm sure there are a lot of people in the States who would disagree with that. But we digress." He flicked the pistol barrel up. "What's in the box?"

"Reference," Tommy coughed.

"Shut up," Brent barked.

"What?" Sean asked. "He can't reference one of the all-time great movies just because you're pointing a gun at him?"

"He doesn't get it," Tommy piled on.

"Both of you shut up."

"You're not going to shoot," Sean said. "If you were, you'd have done it already. You can't risk it. You miss, and you might hit yourself. Which, Craig, I would say is the more likely scenario for you. And Brent, you might hit Tommy, but by the time you squeeze the trigger, I'll have a bead on you. Then you die. You know you can't beat me."

"Try me," Brent said.

"Everyone shut up!" Craig shouted. "I heard what you said about the bust of Cicero. You're trying to find something inside it. And you said it is, or was, located at Thonis-Heracleion. Very clever. I'll be sure to check there next and see if any of our colleagues have pulled up anything fitting that description."

"They're not your colleagues anymore, Craig," Tommy spat.

"We'll see. Now, Sean, move away from the box, or Brent here kills your friend."

Sean kept his stance at an angle, which put the pistol at his side in full view, but his left hand remained close to the corresponding pocket. Neither Craig nor Brent could see Sean ease his fingers into the pocket.

He felt the cool metal disc against his skin, and pinched it between his index finger and the middle one before slowly, cautiously retracting his hand along with the quarter-size piece.

"Go ahead," Tommy said. "Let them have it, Sean. It won't do them any good."

Sean fired a glare over at his friend but immediately caught the look in Tommy's eye. It was an unspoken signal to play along, one that they'd shared many times before.

"I can't do that, Schultzie. With that piece, we might as well just hand over the Archimedes Scroll to them too."

"What piece?" Craig asked, taking the bait.

"Nothing," Tommy insisted. "It's just an old sheet of papyrus encased in resin. Historical document. Nothing more. It's just a chronicle of the New Kingdom. A summary, really."

Emboldened by the forbidden fruit, Craig stepped forward. Sean held the disc in his left hand and let Tommy see it.

"Not another step," Sean warned. He held out the tiny, round piece of metal for Craig to see.

Craig laughed. "What are you going to do with that? Flick it at my head? Sean, I have a gun. And even if I'm not a great shot, I'm not going to miss from this range."

That statement was fifty-fifty, but Sean didn't want to risk it.

"You don't know what this is, do you?"

"Looks like one of those round, flat specialty batteries. Please, stop with the games. I don't want to shoot you."

"I'm sure you don't," Tommy blared. "You're completely fine leaving us to die in an underground chamber, though."

Craig bobbed his head. "Yes, well, that's true. But I won't make that mistake again. Now, get out of the way."

"Not another step, Craig," Sean warned. "Or I will use this, and I will take that papyrus off the stand."

"So?" Craig stopped a few steps into the chamber, just ahead of Brent. "Why would I care?"

"Because it's a counterweight trap. If I pull that off, this entire room will collapse down on us."

He had no way of knowing if that were true or not, but it felt like a plausible threat given what happened before in Jordan.

"He's bluffing," Brent guessed. "Kill him and let's be done with it."

"Not another step," Sean warned, gripping the disc with thumb and forefinger. "Last chance, Craig. Back out of here, tuck your tail between your legs, and leave. Or you'll regret it."

Sean saw the look in his enemy's eyes. Craig wasn't going to leave, not without the papyrus, and not without killing Sean and Tommy.

He squeezed the disc three times and waited.

"Enough of this," Craig said, his face darkening as his trigger finger tightened.

"Indeed." Sean tossed the disc at Craig's feet.

At first, Craig merely watched the impotent weapon land on the mosaic floor a foot away from him. He chuckled. Then he saw Sean and Tommy turn their heads an instant before the entire room filled with a blinding white light.

The mini flash-bang rocked the room with a thunderous pop.

Once it went off, Sean reached for his pistol and drew it.

He was about to aim and fire, but Craig panicked and fired three random shots, two that narrowly missed Sean's head.

He dove behind the box and the altar holding it.

Tommy took his cue and did the same, sliding in next to Sean. The plinth was just wide enough to give them both cover, though with Craig firing shots wildly into the room, they'd be lucky not to get hit by one of the bouncing rounds.

Sean pressed his back against the stone, waited until Craig stopped shooting, then risked a peek around the corner. He looked down his pistol sights for a half second just in time to see the assailants retreat behind the corners of the huge entrance.

Sean felt the temptation to fire a shot at Craig before he disappeared from sight, but at that range it would require extraordinary luck to hit the target—even for him.

He returned to his position behind the stone block and thought.

"What's the situation," Tommy whispered, catching his breath.

"They have the entrance blocked. And there's no other way out of here."

The answer wasn't exactly cheerful.

"Any other good news?" Tommy grinned.

"There is, actually." Sean looked around the corner again. This time, Brent was peeking from behind his position and fired a shot. It missed by several feet, and the bullet smashed into the wall. Dust and debris exploded from the spot where it struck, though where the round landed remained a mystery. The distance certainly made the shot more difficult, but Sean knew the gunman was still partially blinded from the extremely bright flash.

"Which is?"

"They think they need the papyrus. So, they're not going to leave here without it. Which means we're in a stalemate."

"That's the good news?" Tommy scowled. "Are you saying we're just going to sit here and wait it out until they break?"

Sean shook off the question. "No. They'll move in on us before that. My guess is they flank us from both sides. It's what I would do."

He'd barely finished the sentence when Craig's annoying voice cracked through the room. "That was a good trick, Sean. Very inventive. I wonder where an archaeologist gets those kinds of toys."

"Why don't you come over here and I'll tell you all about it?" Sean shouted back.

"You can't win, Sean. You're backed into a corner with no way out. You can do this the easy way, put down your weapons, and come out with your hands up, or you can die."

"You're going to kill us either way, Craig," Tommy answered. "We're not stupid."

"Come on, now, Schultzie. You both know there's no other way. Put down your guns, and hand over the papyrus."

Tommy and Sean listened intently. From the sound of Craig's voice, he hadn't moved away from his position near the entrance, but Brent had remained eerily quiet. If he was making a move toward them, the killer was doing it with remarkable stealth.

That was Sean's primary concern, that Craig was talking them up as a distraction while his partner approached from the side.

Sean gave a silent signal with his left hand for Tommy to check around the corner. Tommy acknowledged the order with a nod, and they both leaned out and checked the room.

Brent remained back at the entrance, still cautious. When Tommy emerged from hiding, he squeezed off another shot. This one cracked over Tommy's head and into the map in front of him. At this point, the gunfire was a warning to keep them in their place with the off chance one might get lucky and find its mark.

Sean and Tommy ducked for cover again, pinned down by the shooter.

"Nope," Tommy said in a volume only Sean could hear. "Still there."

"It would be risky to advance," Sean realized. "They could approach on the flanks, but they'd both be exposed. The only other cover in the room would be the two arks."

Sean frowned as though he'd just been smacked in the face with an epiphany.

"What?" Tommy wondered.

"The arks. We never figured out why those are in this room."

"Ceremonial, I guess. Why?"

"Those were used in ceremonies, yes, but they also served a purpose. You remember our conversation about them from before?"

Tommy nodded.

The two had been investigating the science behind the creation of arks, both in Ancient Egypt, and after Moses led the Children of Israel out of bondage.

There'd been remarkable new discoveries and research into the field of ark technology, and its capabilities both as a superconductor and potentially as a weapon.

Sean and Tommy had theorized that the Egyptians, while essentially inventors of the technology, never fully realized its potential as a superweapon. If they had, the course of history might have played out much differently.

Still, arks were extremely important in Ancient Egypt, and one of the most elevated roles of the container was to serve as a portable shrine that housed a deity's representation—not unlike how it was used by the high priest later on with Israel. And just like with Moses' ark, the ones used by the Egyptians contained statues or symbols of gods and were carried by the priests during festivals, allowing the deity to participate in the events or to visit other temples.

Arks were also integral for funerary practices and beliefs about the afterlife. They could transport mummified remains of the deceased to the tomb, with the procession emulating the journey of the sun god Ra across the sky.

"They're conveyances," Tommy said out loud as the realization hit him, recalling the conversation within a few seconds.

"Yes," Sean hissed. "And they traveled to Ra's solar boat, which would then travel across space and time to the afterlife."

"You can't hide there forever, boys," Craig interrupted. "You're going to have to come out sooner or later."

"Shut up," Sean snapped. "We're talking about it."

"Talk faster. I would prefer not to be here all night."

"I bet you wouldn't," Tommy answered.

He glanced around the corner of the plinth, just enough to make sure no one was coming but without allowing Brent to see him. Still nothing. He turned back to Sean. "Okay, so why does any of that matter with the arks? What are you thinking?"

"You said it," Sean replied. "They're conveyances."

"For the dead."

"Yes, but what if in this instance, they're our way out of this mess?"

"What? I'm not sure if you noticed, but those things don't exactly have wheels or motors."

Sean leaned out and looked down his side of the room. Neither Craig nor Brent approached.

"Notice the tiles where those things are sitting?" Sean asked.

"No."

"Don't look now, but both of those arks are resting on tiles with seams around them."

"So?"

"What if the papyrus triggers a trap that closes the entrance, but also opens another way out?"

"How much longer are you going to need to talk about this, Sean?" Craig shouted. "Would you mind hurrying up?"

"Yes, I would, Craig. I'm thinking."

"Don't hurt yourself."

Sean took a calming breath. "So unoriginal," he muttered. "Look, it's only a matter of time until one of them goes for reinforcements. There are killers for hire here in Egypt, and I'm guessing Brent knows where to find them. If they come back with more men, we're done. I don't like the idea of setting off that trap, but it might be our only way out."

Tommy's concern seemed to darken the entire section of the room. "Let me get this straight, you're actually going to set off a two-thousand-year-old booby trap? On purpose?"

"Unless you have another idea. My guess is if we take that papyrus off the stand, the doors at the entrance will shut again."

"And if your guess is wrong?"

"Then we're trapped in here forever. Or at least until we die of dehydration."

"Better than listening to Craig's voice for another ten minutes."

Tommy chuckled. "So true."

"So, you're good with it?" Sean asked.

"Not really." Tommy sounded resigned to their fate. "But what choice do we have?"

"None."

"Fine. Do it."

Sean gave a nod and then twisted around. "Craig? We're coming out. Don't shoot."

"You really think he's not going to?" Tommy asked.

"Smart choice, Sean," Craig answered. "We won't shoot. You have my word."

"Based on recent events, I'd say your word doesn't count for squat."

Sean remained low just in case they were going to lure him and Tommy out simply to get a clearer shot.

"That's too bad. You really don't have any other options."

"I can't let you have the papyrus, Craig," Sean said, playing up the artifact's importance.

In truth, he didn't want to give it to their betrayer. The ancient paper truly was a priceless piece of history that belonged in a lab, and eventually in a museum. Then again, Sean had no intention of handing over the papyrus. If he was right, and he prayed he was, it was going to unlock a chance for escape.

"Put down your guns and bring it over," Craig ordered. "And don't do anything stupid."

"They're going to shoot us," Tommy muttered. "You know that, right?"

"Not until we're close," Sean said out of the corner of his mouth. "They can't risk damaging the artifact. And we're not going to give them that chance."

Sean held up his gun hand and waved it back and forth. "We're coming out," he announced.

"Toss it to the side," Brent ordered, taking over negotiation. "And show us both hands. That goes for you, too, Tommy."

Tommy raised his pistol into the air and then tossed it aside. Sean threw his away as well, wincing as the weapon hit the hard tile floor with a clatter.

"Now, stand up. Nice and slow."

Sean turned and faced the entrance, then stood from his crouching position. Tommy did the same.

As they emerged from cover, both of them feared the worst—that the two gunmen would open fire and kill them right then. But that didn't happen.

They saw Brent and Craig standing on opposing sides of the entrance, both with guns trained on their respective targets.

"Well, well, well," Craig drawled. "This is twice I've gotten the drop on you, Sean. I'm starting to think you're not the big deal everyone makes you out to be."

"I didn't realize you were such a fan, Craig," Sean fired back.

"Your wit, however, does live up to the legend. Bring me that papyrus. And no sudden movements. Or Brent here will shoot Tommy."

"You're going to kill us anyway."

"Yes, but watching your friend die first must be an agonizing thing to endure, knowing that it was your fault. Bring me that artifact, and you both die at the same time."

"You suck at consolation prizes," Tommy complained.

"Okay, Craig," Sean said. "You win." He looked over at Tommy.

The lack of resolve on his friend's face was palpable, but Tommy also knew there was no other play. They wanted the papyrus, so taking it off the stand was part of the deal. They could only hope, ironically, that it really did trigger a counterweight trap, and that there was another way out of this chamber.

"I'm picking it up. Just like you said," Sean announced.

"That's a good boy."

Sean wanted to punch him. With his forehead. Over and over until Craig lost consciousness. Instead, he turned and reached down with both hands, one on each corner of the hardened resin.

He looked over at Tommy again, as if to ask if he was ready, then pinched the edges and lifted the papyrus off its stand.

Tommy grimaced, squinting his eyes as if afraid the ceiling might fall down upon them.

Sean caught himself wincing, too, thinking any number of harrowing things could be triggered by his actions.

As he picked up the artifact, the stand didn't budge. It remained in the same place, at the same height as it was before.

He and Tommy let out a collective sigh as they realized nothing happened, and that their fate was now sealed.

24

"Careful now, Sean," Craig said. "If you do something stupid like drop it on the floor, I'll make you both suffer before killing you."

Sean doubted Craig had it in him to do that, or any sort of killing, but he was sure looking and sounding the part.

A few witty barbs danced through Sean's mind. He'd just decided on a real doozy when all of a sudden the stand to his left clicked.

He caught the movement out of the corner of his eye and snapped his head around to see it rise a few inches.

A thunderous boom resonated from deep within the walls.

Panic and confusion streaked across Craig's face. He looked to Brent for answers but found only surprise in his wide eyes.

The doors that had blocked the way into the chamber before began to close, faster than they had opened.

Craig had to make a split-second decision. He could either run through, effectively trapping himself inside the room with Sean and Tommy, or remain safely outside—without the papyrus he believed he so desperately needed.

"Throw it to me!" he shouted.

Sean didn't acknowledge the order. Instead, he and Tommy slid back behind the altar as the other two opened fire. Bullets crashed into the map above. Chunks of the mural sprayed over them, but none of the rounds found their mark.

The grinding sound of the doors closing continued to roar for another few seconds before a loud thud ended it, as well as the gunfire.

The two friends waited, still uncertain if Craig and Brent had been stupid—or wise enough—to go through the doorway. Sean gave it five seconds, then peeked around the corner of the plinth.

Through the dust and gun smoke, he saw the doors were completely sealed again, and more importantly, there was no sign of Craig or Brent.

He also saw something else he didn't expect.

"Tommy?" he said. "You're going to want to see this."

"What is—" Tommy started to ask as he stood and looked back, but the words locked up in his throat.

They stared at the two arks. The objects were tilted at an angle, pointing into the floor, and the lids had slid off.

"They're empty," Tommy realized.

"Yeah," Sean said with a nod. "Just like we thought they might be."

He hurried around the stand to the one on his right and checked inside. "There's a lever in here," he said.

Tommy checked the other one. "Same." Then he peered into the black hole in the floor.

"These are like ancient bobsleds," Sean realized. "There's a groove just beneath this section of the floor.

"So, we each take one?"

Sean had initially thought the same thing, but now he wasn't so sure. "Hold on," he warned just as Tommy was lifting his leg over the side of the ark. "That's too simple. Why would there be two of them?"

"Why wouldn't there be?"

"Let's think about this." He looked to the map, and the hieroglyphs above it. "Didn't you say something about taking the right path?"

Tommy pulled his foot back down to the floor and joined Sean at the map. He looked up at the message written in pictures and read it again. "Yeah. That's what it says. But how do we know which one of these is the right path? It doesn't literally say the word *right*. The translation means upright, or righteous. As in the correct path."

Sean looked back at the two arks, stealing a look at the heavy doors blocking them from their pursuers.

He imagined the frustration burning inside Craig right about now, along with the utter disbelief that he'd lost any chance at finding the final piece to the puzzle that would lead to the Archimedes Scroll.

Sean also knew Craig wouldn't give up. He'd turned relentless, consumed by the idea of finding the scroll and turning its secrets into unimaginable wealth.

Craig heard the conversation between Sean and Tommy, and he certainly heard the part about Thonis-Heracleion and Cicero. With his extensive connections in the archaeological community, that would be Craig's next destination. The only thing he was truly missing was the exact point on the map that would provide a clue as to where the bust of Cicero either still remained hidden or had been discovered.

Initially, Sean had hoped the thing had already been found. Then it would simply be a matter of finding out where it was being kept. Of course, breaking the thing would prove problematic, if their assessment was correct in thinking the next clue was inside the bust.

But they'd cross that rickety bridge when the time came.

For the time being, there were more immediate issues to deal with.

"Let's take a step back and think about this," Sean suggested.

He walked toward the blocked entrance to the chamber, stopped just beyond the two arks, and pivoted around.

"Oh, you meant literally take a step back," Tommy said. "Okay, then." He joined Sean behind the two containers, and waited. "What are we looking at?"

"The whole thing," Sean said. "The map. The hieroglyphs. All of it. See anything different?"

Tommy paused for a few breaths, searching for something he may have missed before. After half a minute, he shook his head. "No. Not really. Nothing stands out."

"No. Not for me either."

"Maybe both arks go to the same place. What if we're over-thinking it?"

"Then why would the message say something about the right path? Is there something in Egyptian history or religion that could help us out here?"

"Like what?"

Sean knew the answer was right in front of them, but he couldn't figure it out. He wished he'd gone deeper into the study of Egyptology. The truth was, he probably knew more than most people, but most people weren't stuck in a subterranean ancient tunnel with a potential life-or-death decision to make.

"I don't know. Is there something they did in ancient times that had to do with left or right?"

Tommy thought about it, looking up to the ceiling overhead as he pondered the question. "Actually, there was." His eyes lit up. "The Egyptians did attribute specific significance to directions, including right and left. They were usually related to power, dominance, and protection rather than the simple binary of good versus evil. So, say someone was holding an object in the right hand—like a deity or king. That could symbolize power or action. The orientation of temples and pyramids, as well as symbols could carry special meaning, often connected to the..." Then it hit him.

"Connected to the what?" Sean pressed, ready to shake it out of his friend.

"To the path of the sun, or the flow of the Nile." Tommy looked at the ark on the right. "We take that one."

Sean grinned. "You're a genius, Schultzie. Don't let anyone tell you otherwise."

"You mean like when you call me an idiot?"

"No, that still counts." Sean moved over to the ark on the right. "Looks like there's just enough room for us both."

They gathered their bags and lanterns and stowed them at the front of the ark.

"You want to drive or you want me?" Sean asked.

"Sounds like a lose-lose proposition."

"You drive. It's your ark."

"Mine? Hey, I just connected the dots. If I'm wrong and we end up in a bottomless pit, I don't want you blaming me for it."

"Fine," Sean said, determined to get out of there. "Hop in."

He climbed into the bottom of the golden box and waited while Tommy sat behind him. There was just enough clearance at the end of the floor for their heads to go under if they ducked down. They secured their headlamps to their heads, tightening the straps in case the ride was rough.

Sean half looked over his shoulder. "Ready?"

Tommy pressed his knees against the sides of the ark to stabilize himself. "Ready when you are."

"Okay, duck your head. Let's see where this thing leads."

Sean gripped the golden lever in the bottom and shoved it forward.

The ark dropped into the darkness like a roller coaster. Everything around them was black except for the curved track in front of them.

"Where does this thing go?" Tommy shouted over the sound of the ark's bottom grinding on stone. He looked back, expecting to see sparks, but found none.

Sean noticed something black on the surface of the track. "Not sure. But I think whoever built this covered it with some kind of oil a long time ago."

The ark picked up speed as they continued the descent.

Sean turned to the left, looking back up at the entrance. He couldn't see it anymore, and wondered if there was another track for the other ark—or if the other container simply dropped off into the abyss.

As the sled continued to speed up, the scope of this entire construction overwhelmed the two men. It had been built in what appeared to be a vast underground cavern.

Turning left and right, the men saw the ancient stone walls forged by nature over eons. They didn't notice any of the usual cave formations from back home—stalactites and stalagmites—but whoever had designed this track had used the natural flow of the subterranean space.

Initially, the trough had been carved out of the wall, but after twenty seconds, the track veered to the left, and Sean realized they were sliding along what appeared to be something akin to a larger version of a Roman aqueduct.

Sean tried to swallow his fear, clenching his jaw tight. But it didn't help. Even though he couldn't see down into the blackness, he got the distinct and terrifying impression they were high up.

Thankfully, Tommy didn't say anything, though Sean could tell his friend was looking around from the movement of his light beam from left to right.

What had turned out to be their salvation had morphed into Sean's bane.

He did his best to focus on the track ahead, but that didn't help. His headlamp illuminated both the trough, and allowed him to see the gaping darkness around it.

His mind raced with questions, which helped distract him momentarily. *How far down does this go? Where is it taking us? How do we get out of this place once it stops? Or is it leading us to a gruesome death?*

A grim realization gripped him. If they died down here, wherever here was, no one would ever find them. Not for a long time, at least.

He'd faced death so many times, Sean had almost become numb to the notion. But this was something else. Knowing that his wife would never realize what happened, or where he was, shook him to his core. He never wanted her to feel that kind of pain.

With any of the other threats to his life, she'd have known what happened, and there would have been a body. She didn't even know where he was in the world at the moment other than the text he'd sent to tell her he'd landed in Cairo.

After that, he could be anywhere.

The ark turned slightly, tilting as it continued to speed along the track. Sean felt the g-force pushing him against the bottom. He had no idea how fast they were going, but it was enough to keep the ark on the track as it tilted at such a sharp angle that Talladega fans would have been jealous.

"Looks like we're heading into a loop!" Tommy shouted over the wind and the sound of the ark grinding on the track.

Sean nodded but didn't say anything. Despite his fear of heights, he'd always enjoyed roller coasters. They were a safely engineered way for him to conquer his nemesis. But this wasn't exactly like that. He didn't know who built it, or even if it was designed to help them or kill them. And he doubted the thing had ever been tested.

The g's increased as they descended, speeding along the coiled track.

Then, after three long loops, the track leveled out. The ark began to slow down, and Sean hoped the ride was finally at an end.

Up ahead, he saw what looked like the end of the track. A stone block lay across it twenty yards away. The grade of the trough tilted up slightly to further slow their speed.

"End of the line, Schultzie," Sean announced as the ark neared the barrier.

Tommy patted him on the back and shifted, preparing to disembark from the golden sled.

The ark ground to a halt a mere two feet from the stone block.

"I don't think I'm going to go on a roller coaster for a while," Tommy said as he gathered his gear and stood up.

Sean collected his bag and lantern and tried to stand. His legs felt heavy, and his mind twisted a little. He wobbled for a second before regaining his balance.

"You okay, man?" Tommy asked.

"Yeah," Sean said with a dismissive nod. "Just a little dizzy from the twisties back there. Maybe no coasters for me in the near future either."

Tommy looked up into the darkness, his headlamp barely

touching the lower part of the loop. "That is unreal," he said, pointing up at the labyrinthine structure.

Sean followed his gaze and saw what he was talking about.

The tracks had been built on towering columns eerily similar to the aqueducts in Rome. These builders had used sandstone blocks, and natural formations of the cavern, to support the ancient bobsled trough.

"The amount of manpower and resources used to construct that must have been staggering," Sean said, peering up at the mind-boggling structure.

"How did they even get all of the materials down here?" Tommy wondered.

Sean turned away and looked in the opposite direction. His light splashed over a staircase cut out of the side of the cavern. "Maybe they used those," he said.

25

"We have to find a way back in there," Brent said, running a knife blade along the seam between the giant stone doors. "They got in. We should be able to."

Craig merely stood behind him, staring at the barrier. The pistol still hung loosely in his right hand, and the smell of the spent powder lingered in his nostrils.

"It's no use," he said, his voice despondent.

"What?" Brent looked back at him in disbelief. "What do you mean it's no use?"

"See that hole in the center?" Craig motioned to the unusually shaped cavity. "That's what the scepter was for. The cobra was a key to unlock this. They still have it. Not that it would open it a second time anyway."

Brent studied him for a moment, allowing his irritation to fester. "So, you're just giving up? Is that it? Because you said we were going to be rich, Craig."

Craig saw the malice in his partner's eyes, the raging fury building like a wildfire in a field of hay.

"We will be," Craig reassured. "We just have to figure out what they were looking for, and where it is."

"How do you propose we do that?" Brent's temper had cooled slightly, but the smoldering embers could reignite any second.

Craig tucked his pistol back in its holster without bothering to check the magazine. He didn't remember how many shots he'd fired and figured it wasn't important at the time. There were no other threats at the moment, though concerns about the dead security guard in the pump room started to resurface.

"Didn't you hear? When we snuck up on them, they were talking about Cicero."

"So?" Brent holstered his weapon as well and tightened his rucksack over his shoulders.

"They were onto something. Cicero was a major political player just before the time of Cleopatra. Tommy and Sean seem to think there's an artifact that contains the next clue, and from what I heard them saying, it's inside a sculpture or a bust. They also mentioned Thonis-Heracleion."

Craig saw the blank expression on Brent's face, so he continued. "Thonis is an ancient city north of here. It disappeared underwater a long time ago, but excavations have been ongoing for a while now. I only heard bits and pieces of what they said, but I'm willing to bet that is where we will find the next clue. If not the scroll itself."

Brent stewed over the information. "I'm getting tired of chasing clues, Craig. And I'm starting to wonder if that's all we're ever going to find. When do we get the scroll? When do we get paid?"

Craig loathed his partner's one-track mind, but it was to be expected. The man was a mercenary, an employee. Like any employee, payment would come due sooner or later. And types like him always wanted it sooner.

"We're close," Craig said, without any way of knowing if he was telling the truth or not. "Cicero was the primary documentarian of Archimedes. Pretty much everything we know about him came from Cicero—his writings, inventions, theories, all of it. Tommy would definitely know all that. So, if he thinks the clue is or was located at Thonis-Heracleion, then that's where we should look."

"Okay. Fine. So what, we're supposed to go swimming around in an underwater city to try to find some statue?"

Craig hoped that wasn't the case. He wasn't scuba certified and had never even attempted diving.

"It's possible," he admitted. "But there's a chance, however slim, that the tribute to Cicero we're looking for has already been recovered."

"How slim?" Brent stared through him like a poker player with a royal flush.

"No way I could know that. But I have contacts, friends in the community who could tell me if anything like that has been found. And there's always the internet, too. We can double down the search. If anyone did pull up a bust or sculpture of Cicero, we'll know soon enough."

"And if they haven't?"

"Then I guess we're going to have to get a dive team together."

Craig turned away from the big doors, doing his best to stay positive. He wasn't about to tell Brent his real concern.

There wasn't any historical documentation regarding Cicero that would suggest he'd be honored anywhere in Egypt. It wasn't impossible, but it lacked any records. Maybe the politician had visited here once, maybe more than once, but Craig had never heard about it.

If Tommy and Sean were wrong, that made Craig wrong in Brent's eyes, and he knew the killer was quickly running out of patience.

In this dangerous game, Craig knew he was either going to be right, or be dead. Unless he took out Brent first.

They passed through the rows of pillars in the great hall in silence.

Craig wondered what Brent was thinking. He had no delusions that Brent was his friend, or even loyal as a business associate. Brent had a plan to kill Craig if things didn't work out the way he wanted. Of that he was certain.

Which meant Craig needed to plan for the same.

If they didn't find the bust of Cicero, or the scroll, Brent would have to die before he had the chance to strike first.

26

Terror gripped Sean. He clung to the wall with every ounce of his strength, pressing himself against it as he climbed the staircase one step at a time.

Tommy moved slowly so his friend didn't fall far behind.

He looked back for the umpteenth time at Sean, whose palms were flat against the wall, with fingernails dug into the rock.

The climb up the ancient stone stairs had started off easily enough. But after ascending twenty feet and seeing no end in sight, Tommy knew exactly what would follow.

Sean's fear of heights bordered on the irrational to someone who didn't suffer from the same malady. More than once, Sean had warned Tommy to get away from the edge, and to be more careful as if the slightest breeze could knock his friend over and to his doom.

Tommy remained patient, though it tested his will. He knew time was still against them. Craig and Brent were out there, probably heading back to the parking garage to regroup and muster their resources to locate the next clue.

There was no way to know exactly how much Craig had heard, but it was safe to assume he'd listened to enough to get a head start. That meant it would come down to who could dig up the answers faster. Except that Sean and Tommy were still deep underground with no way to know how much farther they had to go to escape.

On top of that, they had no reference as to where the wild bobsled ride had stopped. They could be a mile from where they began their journey in the garage earlier that evening.

"I'm sorry, Schultzie," Sean apologized. "I really am."

Tommy looked back at his friend as he took another sideways step up. "It's okay, man. Take your time. We'll get out of here."

Sean shook his head. "Yeah, but you go on ahead. See if you can find the way out of here. Maybe you can get a cell signal and reach out to the kids. Ask them to check if any artifacts honoring Cicero have been pulled out of the Med."

"I'm not leaving you, moron. That's not how this works."

Sean forced an uneasy laugh at the moniker. "Seriously. I'll be fine. I just have to go slow. That's all."

"Maybe if you got on your hands and knees," Tommy suggested. "Like that time in Bhutan at the Tiger Monastery."

"Don't remind me of that place."

"Sorry."

Sean shook his head. "No. It's okay. You obviously want me to propose."

It was Tommy's turn to chuckle. "We're both married, so no."

Sean decided to try his friend's suggestion and lowered himself down to his hands and knees. He felt a little more stable that way and continued climbing up the steps at a slightly faster clip.

"Seriously, Schultzie. Go on up ahead. I'll catch up. See if you can find the end of this blasted staircase."

"You sure?"

"Go. Before I throw you over the edge."

Tommy laughed again. "Okay. But just take it easy. I'll come back when I find the exit."

Sean nodded and waved his friend on, then quickly slapped his hand down onto the next step.

He felt better doing it this way. The lower center of gravity was more stable, and there was less chance of him losing his balance and tipping over the edge, which was a constant fear layered on top of everything else.

The light from Tommy's headlamp bobbed and weaved back and forth as he moved up the steps. The lantern in his left hand swung in tandem. The lights grew smaller with the distance Tommy put between himself and his friend.

Sean kept climbing, one step at a time until he'd gone another twenty. Then he paused to take a break for a second, catching his breath from the effort. Climbing steps the regular way was hard enough, but doing it like an animal worked the core, the legs, shoulders, arms, everything.

He'd done mountain climbers during his workouts for as long as he could remember, but never on steps. And certainly never with the threat of falling to his death.

After thirty seconds, he resumed the climb, one foot and one hand after another. He didn't dare look over, even though a morbid sense of curiosity beckoned him to do so. That was the last thing he needed. It was bad enough that he could see the black expanse to the left over the edge of the stairs ahead.

Sean suddenly realized he couldn't see Tommy's lights anymore. He wondered if his friend had reached the exit and gone through to check ahead. An irrational thought needled Sean as well. *Maybe Tommy fell off and I didn't hear him scream.*

"Stop it," Sean ordered himself. "He's fine. Keep going, man. You can do this."

He hated talking to himself, especially in situations like this where he was desperately trying to overcome his second-greatest fear.

The first was completely out of his hands. The thought of losing Adriana trumped everything else, way more than dying or fear of high places.

She could take care of herself. He knew that. But it didn't stop him from worrying whenever they were apart.

"Focus, Sean. Next step. Just keep going."

He pushed away the thoughts of his wife and continued ahead.

He wished he could go faster and get this over with. The climb seemed like it would never end.

"Where is Tommy?" he wondered out loud.

His right foot slipped on the edge of a step, and he scrambled to catch himself, lowering his weight down across the stairs as if to become one with the stone.

He trembled, unwilling to move again for nearly a minute.

Look at yourself, his ego teased. *You, the great Sean Wyatt. Highly trained government operative. Head of IAA Security and Recovery. Taken down by a few thousand-years-old set of stairs. Pathetic.*

Sean loathed that part of him. It was the part that judged him, the part that told him he wasn't worthy of anything great in life no matter how many goals or milestones he achieved.

His parents hadn't put that on him. They had always pushed him to be the best he could be in sports, academics, personal relationships. But they hadn't pressured him or made him feel weak, or some kind of loser, if he failed.

He wasn't sure where that self-loathing part had come from. It rarely reared its head. But in times like this, when he needed it the least, it usually popped up.

Sean looked up at the sight of lights moving above. Tommy's headlamp shone brightly down the stairs, moving back and forth with every step.

"Schultzie?" Sean said. "Did you find the way out?"

"You okay, man?" Tommy answered, seeing his friend lying flat on the stairs. "Did you fall?"

"I'm fine. Just slipped. Then freaked out."

"Aww, man. I'm sorry. I knew I shouldn't have left you."

There was no malice or taunting in Tommy's comment, only genuine concern for his friend. He and Sean had known each other since childhood. He'd given him a hard time about his fear every now and then, but right now Tommy knew wasn't the right moment for that kind of jeering.

"You want me to help you?"

"No, I'll be all right," Sean said, rising to his feet. "I just want to get out of here." He looked up the staircase. "Did you find the end?"

"Yeah. I found it."

"Where does it come out?"

"No idea. It's blocked."

"Blocked?" Sean felt a new wave of fear hit him, but Tommy didn't sound as concerned as he probably should have.

"There's a doorway at the top. It's filled in with sand. If I had to guess, that crazy bobsled ride dropped us off outside the city in the desert. We're going to have to dig our way out."

"Seriously? That could take forever."

"Maybe. But I don't think so. By my estimation, the stairs take us close to the level of the entrance from the garage. We'll only have to dig out a few feet to reach the surface."

"That won't be easy."

"No, but it's better than trying to dig through dirt or rock."

Sean agreed. "Okay. Lead the way. I'll try to keep up."

Tommy turned and began the ascent again, this time with Sean in tow—still navigating the stairs as if doing mountain climbers, but faster than before. The knowledge that there really was a way out of this place fueled his movements, and momentarily purged the fear of the drop-off a few feet to his left.

"I know you got rope in your bag," Sean said. "You wouldn't happen to have a shovel too, would you?"

27

Brent cracked open the door to the hallway in the garage. The sounds of the warning signs rustled in the air. The same drone of machinery filled the corridor.

"Looks clear," he stated and stepped out into the hall. He holstered the firearm he'd drawn in case there had been trouble.

Craig thought the notion of even brandishing it was stupid.

If someone had found the dead security guard in the maintenance room and the cops were swarming the place, their chances of shooting their way to freedom were slim to none—regardless of Brent's talents.

Craig followed him out into the hall. They walked quickly to the other end, ignoring the other doors until they made it to the last set leading to the parking deck beyond.

Again, Brent carefully nudged the left door open and peeked outside. "Clear," he said and moved through.

Back out in the garage, the dirty smells of the city returned and reminded Craig of the difference between the ancient, underground place he'd been in and modern civilization.

He'd have much preferred other scents the city provided—freshly baked baklava, strong coffee, onion bread, or spices. But for now, he'd take it.

He climbed into the passenger seat of the sedan and considered himself lucky. Brent got behind the wheel and quickly started the engine.

Craig looked out the window at the Maserati still sitting there.

"That's going to draw attention sooner or later," Brent commented as he shifted the vehicle into drive and pulled forward.

"What? The Maserati? Not the missing security guard?"

Brent chuffed a laugh. "That too."

Initially, it unsettled Craig that he could laugh about the dead man. Then again, earlier he'd been ready to kill Sean and Tommy. He'd even felt eager to do it. He'd crossed over to the dark side, and the only sense of right and wrong he felt now pertained to getting what he deserved.

Craig had heard about the sense of empowerment people felt with a gun in their hand, the ultimate control it wielded over life and death.

He'd never given much credence to it, or thought he would ever know what that meant. But he saw it now. He understood. And he liked it.

Perhaps that was why Brent did what he did before, and now. People always said, do what you love. Maybe Brent loved that sense of power.

Craig still knew he couldn't trust the man. Brent would shoot him in the back if things didn't go as planned. So far, that was—unfortunately—the trajectory. There'd been missteps, miscalculations, and unforeseen issues that were completely out of Craig's control.

Most of it was Sean and Tommy's fault.

He'd like to have believed that little thorn had been stripped from the branch and thrown in the fire, but those two had managed to escape what should have been a death trap in Jordan. Craig wasn't about to assume they were out of his hair.

"There aren't any cameras down here," Brent said, interrupting Craig's thoughts. "So, there is no way we can be connected to the body when they find it." He made a humming sound at an unvoiced thought.

"What?" Craig wondered. "What's funny?"

Brent guided the car into an empty spot at the end of the deck then backed out and turned toward the exit.

"Nothing. I was just thinking it would be interesting if, when they do find the body, the cops think it's suspicious that Amid's car is there. If it's a day or so, that'll look even more out of the ordinary. They'll start thinking maybe he had something to do with it, especially when they realize someone broke into those barricaded doors."

He steered the car around the corner and onto the ramp leading up to the main level.

"Yes," Craig said. An ember of hope warmed his chest. "Yes, of course. It's Vokum's car. Why would it be there, of all places? They'll think he was the one who broke into the passage. And those dots are easy to connect since he's an archaeologist. The cops will believe he went rogue, maybe went in there to investigate. When he came out, and the guard caught him, Vokum killed the guy and hid the body in that room behind the machinery."

"Bingo," Brent said, emphasizing the statements with a click.

He drove up to the gate and inserted the ticket into the payment tower then waited.

Craig took a few bills out of his pocket and passed them to Brent, who inserted the money into the machine. It dinged, and the bar impeding their path lifted. Brent eased the car forward and back out onto the street.

"The authorities will search the passage," Craig went on as he looked out the window. "They'll have to call in experts—archaeologists to study the great hall down there. Eventually, they'll figure out how to open those doors."

"The ones that sealed off Wyatt and Schultz?"

"Yeah."

"That won't be for a while, though, right? We have some time."

"Possibly. It's probably best that we assume we're still on the clock."

The mission was simple on the surface. They needed to learn if anyone had discovered an artifact pertaining to Cicero at Thonis-Heracleion, but it was getting late, and there was no way Craig would be able to call any of his contacts at this hour.

That would have to wait until the morning, which could prove problematic if Sean and Tommy somehow managed to escape again.

"What are you thinking?" Brent asked. He cast a sidelong glance over at Craig, whose gaze remained fixed out the window on some distant, non-specific thing.

"Trying to sort out what we do next. I can't exactly call on my contacts right now. Everyone will be in bed."

"Search the web. If someone found something to do with Cicero at that site, maybe there's an article about it."

Craig shook his head. "I doubt it. They've found so many things there. It's not like they have an online inventory of it all."

"Someone is cataloging it, though, right?"

"For sure."

As with any excavation, every artifact, every fragment that was unearthed, would be documented and analyzed.

"So, where can you find that information?" Brent asked.

"I don't know. Whoever is in charge of the site, I guess."

Saying it out loud turned on the light bulb in Craig's mind. "Of course," he said. "That will be easy enough to find out. The lead archaeologist will have access to the catalog."

Craig took out his phone and started searching the internet. He found articles about the incredible trove of historical treasures that had been discovered at Thonis-Heracleion, along with dozens of images. There were statues, coins, bowls, pillars, vases, discs, and more.

He tapped the screen to look at an article with a glamorous title about treasures of the Mediterranean being discovered in Egypt, and read until he found a name he recognized.

"Reyna Oluk," Craig said.

"What's that?" Brent turned the car to the right and onto another street.

"Not what. Who. She's the lead archaeologist at the site. She's in several of these pictures holding artifacts they've dredged up."

"She doesn't happen to be standing with a statue of Cicero, does she?"

"No. We're not that lucky."

He continued scrolling through the article, noting some of the details of the processes involved with extracting artifacts buried underwater for thousands of years.

He'd never been a part of a dig like that. But he understood the methods. Instead of brushes and trowels, archaeologists used more machinery to suck up silt and sediment, then filter everything through screens. The larger artifacts would remain on the seabed and be pulled out later.

Craig finished scanning the article and closed the app.

"So, we need to find this person and get her to tell us where the catalog is," Brent surmised.

"That or tell us if they found anything that looks like Cicero. If the teams there pulled up something like that, she'd know about it. That kind of find would be an anomaly, and she'd certainly be curious as to why it was there."

"You don't happen to know where this woman lives, do you?"

"No," Craig answered. "No clue. Could be here in Cairo, or farther north close to the port. I would think it's the latter. And there are no guarantees she's even here in Egypt right now."

"Didn't you say she's the one overseeing the dig?"

"Yeah, but maybe she went on vacation or something."

"No problem," Brent said. "We can find her."

"She'll be asleep now, or will be soon. And I'm exhausted. We need to get some rest. I say we locate her first thing in the morning, and go find out what we can. If she's around, of course."

Brent nodded. "I don't like slowing down when we've got some momentum. But you're right. We've been pushing hard. Let's get a place to stay for the night and figure out where she is, or where she's going to be tomorrow."

Craig looked back out the window again, resuming the blank

stare he had before. His thoughts now were more focused. They were getting close. Unless Reyna didn't know anything about a monument to Cicero. If not, things would be more difficult. They'd have to go underwater to look, and that could take forever. Craig knew he didn't have forever, not if Sean and Tommy managed to slip through death's fingers again.

His best hope was that Reyna's team had found the next clue—and didn't even know it.

28

E xhaustion tugged on Sean and Tommy like a one-ton yoke hanging from their necks.

They'd been digging for over an hour.

Their forearms burned from the long, exhausting effort. Sand filled their shoes and socks. But they didn't complain. Both of them knew how much good that would do. The more they focused on their misery, the harder the work would seem.

More than once, they'd wondered if they had really taken the correct ark from the chamber, and if the one on the left had led to some easy way out.

The initial digging had been the most dangerous. Pulling the sand out one scoop at a time posed the threat of a sort of avalanche from above. Such momentum and weight would crash into the two men and send them cascading over the edge of the landing and down to a sudden and deadly stop.

Once they were a few feet into the ancient doorway, though, that threat seemed less and less likely.

Still, the two remained careful, keeping their feet wedged against the inside of the door as they shoveled the sand out sideways.

Patches of the material were compacted by thousands of years of rain. The tools they'd brought with them helped with these sections, allowing them to break through and continue digging until they reached loose sand again.

After two hours of intense labor, Sean felt his foldable shovel jam into solid rock.

He looked back at Tommy, who'd been dragging the sand out of the cavity and kicking it out onto the landing.

"What?" Tommy asked.

"It's rock," Sean said between breaths. Sweat rolled down his forehead and over the tip of his nose.

"Dead end?"

"Not sure. Might be. Or it could be like what we encountered before. You know, with the drop-down into a passage?"

"Could be."

Tommy watched as Sean pulled away more sand from around the stone around knee high.

Sean took out his knife and scraped above the stone's edge. More packed sand broke away.

"It's a step," he realized.

Tommy looked up and exhaled. "Oh, thank goodness. For a second there, I thought we really did all this work for nothing."

Sean dug deeper into the sand wall, and suddenly felt it give way.

"Oh crap."

A wave of sand broke free and flowed out of the opening. The force of it knocked Sean back a few inches until he hit the doorframe.

Tommy, however, had lost his stance, and the sand pushed him back toward the landing and the precipice beyond.

Sean reacted instantly and threw out his left hand. Tommy grabbed it before he toppled backward.

The two held tight as the sand slowed its momentum, burying them both from the waist down. Then, as quickly as the disaster started, it was finished.

Tommy let go of Sean's hand and inspected the damage.

"Jeez. It's in my pants now, too."

"That's what—"

"Don't," Tommy said.

Sean laughed. Tommy resisted for a few seconds and then joined in.

"Thanks, by the way," Tommy added. "For a second there, I thought I was going over the edge. You haven't lost your reflexes with age."

"Yeah, well, sometimes it doesn't feel that way."

He turned his head and looked up as a wave of cool, dry air washed over him.

"You might want to start digging yourself out," Sean said, still staring up. "I think we just broke through."

Tommy leaned in as far as he could but was unable to see what Sean was looking at.

He dog-paddled into it, ripping away the sand around him until he could raise his knees and climb out. Sean also dug away the debris and climbed up onto the stair, then the next. Above that, sand still covered the upper steps, but that didn't matter now.

Above them, stars twinkled brightly in the night sky above, more dramatically so to the west. To the east, the glow of Cairo's lights radiated across the dark blanket overhead, dimming the sparkling heavens.

"Those stars have never looked as pretty as they do right now," Tommy said, joining his friend in the fresh air.

"No, they sure haven't."

They clambered up and out of the shaft until they were in the open between a pair of sand dunes.

The silhouette of the pyramids towered in the distance to the south. The outline of the city stood to the east, dotted with millions of lights.

Sean turned to the west and the vast, dark expanse of the desert beyond.

A cold wind rolled through, whipping up the sand around their legs.

They were at least a half mile away from the parking garage, based on Sean's estimation, and perhaps a little farther.

Beyond the border of the city, Craig and Brent would have no idea what happened to them.

But that didn't make Sean feel any better about the situation. They needed to find out whatever they could about the Cicero monument, if there was one. For all he knew, Craig was doing the exact same thing.

He fished the phone out of his pocket and shook some of the loose sand off it, then tapped the screen. He still had plenty of battery life, and was relieved to see he had service.

"Who you going to call?" Tommy asked.

"The kids. We need to find out if anyone pulled up a bust of Cicero from that underwater city. You got any other contacts in the city besides Dr. Amid? I don't want to bother him again if possible. We've caused that poor man enough trouble."

"True." Tommy thought about it for a minute. He knew several people in Cairo, including at the American University, and other institutions. The question wasn't whether or not he knew people. It was which one to call. "You thinking we need someone to come pick us up?"

"Maybe. We need a place to hole up for the night, and I don't think going to the hotel we booked would be a great idea right now."

"Why? Because Brent figured out where we were staying?"

"It's a reasonable assumption. We could just get another hotel. That might be better than involving another one of your colleagues in a potentially dangerous situation."

Tommy thought about it, but he didn't feel like putting any more colleagues in peril. He and Sean both had a bad track record when it came to that.

Dr. Frank Borringer had been the first casualty over a decade ago —a trusted friend who'd paid the ultimate price for helping Tommy.

"Let's just get another room," he said. "I don't want anyone else to get hurt because of us."

Sean understood, and nodded. "Okay. Fair enough." He held his phone, waiting to call the kids. "You want to call them? It's probably too late to check with any of your colleagues now anyway."

"Sure. I'll do it."

Tommy took his phone out of his pocket, dusted off the bits of sand around the case, and called the number.

Sean typed a text message to Adriana while the phone rang on speaker.

"Hey, Tommy," Alex answered. "How's your case going?"

"Full of wonders and mysteries," Tommy said. "How's Atlanta?"

"It's good to be back home. We're just working on that thing Helen and Mack brought in earlier in the week."

"The artifact from Alabama?"

"Yeah. It's really interesting. I—"

"Hey, Tommy," Tara interrupted.

"Hey, Tara. I hope you two have recovered from your trip to Peru."

"Yeah. We're good. Just hanging here at the lab again. Sean with you?"

"He's right in front of me."

Sean waved and finished sending his text.

"He says hi," Tommy added.

"Hi, Sean." She paused a second. "It sounds windy. Where are you guys?"

"Right now we're standing in the desert just outside of Cairo."

"The desert?" Alex asked. "Why are you out there?"

"It's a long story. I'll tell you all about it sometime."

"Do you two ever have any short stories?" Tara teased.

Tommy laughed with them. "Only a few. Hey, so the reason I called was, I wondered if you could help us out. We're on that case we discussed before we left, and I'm trying to get some information."

"What kind of information? And weren't you in Jordan with Craig Freeman?"

"He stabbed us in the back." Tommy stated it in a matter-of-fact tone.

"Stabbed you in the back?" Alex asked. "What happened? You guys okay?"

"We're fine. But now we're here wondering if a specific kind of artifact was found at the Thonis-Heracleion site."

"That's the underwater city thing, right?" Tara clarified.

"Yes. We have reason to believe there might be a statue or a bust of the Roman politician and historian Cicero there. Can you do some checking and find out if any of our colleagues have dragged up something like that?"

"Sure. Shouldn't take long. Malcom can dig that up in no time."

Sean cracked a smile. Even though Malcom was an AI assistant, they treated him like a person. The machine interacted in such human-like ways, there were moments when Sean wondered if Malcom had actually become self-aware, but not in a destroy-humanity sort of way.

"Thanks," Tommy said. "The app that connects to him still has some issues last I checked."

"Yeah, we're trying to work out the kinks," Alex replied. "No worries, boss. Anyway, if someone found anything at that site, we'll let you know."

"I appreciate it."

"Have you considered checking with Dr. Amid?" Tara suggested. "He would probably know about something like that. He's connected to everyone in that area."

Sean and Tommy exchanged a look, expressions that said they really hoped it didn't come down to that, but if there were no other options, they'd have to.

"Thanks, Tara," Tommy said. "We met with Dr. Amid earlier in the day, but we'll definitely call him if you guys aren't able to dig up anything. I'll talk with you soon. Sean and I are going to head back to the city."

"Okay, guys. We'll be in touch soon."

Tommy ended the call and shoved the phone back into his pocket. He looked off into the distance at the city lights, then to his friend.

"So, where to?"

29

"You're sure about that?" Tommy stood by the window in the hotel room. His phone sat on the desk nearby as he peered out through the glass at the buildings next door and across the street.

"Yes," Alex answered. "Nothing about a monument to Cicero at that site. If there was anything online about it, Malcom would know."

Tommy didn't doubt that. The powerful AI system was capable of locating anything that touched the internet in a matter of seconds.

If Malcom couldn't find it, it wasn't there to be found. Still, Tommy felt the need to double-check even if he knew better.

"Okay. So, you could have just texted me that. You must have found something. Right?"

Alex exhaled audibly. Tommy and Sean both caught his reluctance.

"What?" Sean asked. "What's the problem?"

"Nothing. It's just that... Reyna Oluk is the lead archaeologist at the site."

Sean frowned as he looked at Tommy, who in turn pivoted away from the window wearing a similar scowl.

"Who?" Sean asked.

"Seriously?" Tommy said, ignoring the question.

"Seems so," Alex confirmed. "She's been working on that site for over a year. Oversees everything that goes on there. It's a good bet she has the entire catalog of what's been discovered right down to fragments from plates."

"I'm sorry," Sean cut in again. "Who are we talking about?"

"Reyna Oluk has spent most of her life dedicated to finding the Library of Alexandria," Tommy explained. "It borders on obsession."

"I wouldn't say borders," Tara spoke up. "More like fully immersed in it."

"She also doesn't like Tommy," Alex added.

"Really?" Sean asked. "Why not?"

Tommy picked up a bottle of water from the desk and twisted the lid off. He stared at it for a few seconds. "Reyna doesn't like how we do things."

"So? There's a whole list of people who don't like how we do our jobs."

"I know. But she's particularly adamant about her feelings. If she had her way, she'd shut down the IAA permanently."

Sean's frown deepened. His eyebrows knit together, and his jaw bulged on both sides as he clenched it. "Well, it's a good thing she can't do that."

"No. She can't. But she's tried on multiple occasions to sway governments and other researchers not to call on us."

"So? We have multiple teams out in the field at any given moment, doing things the traditional way. Just like she does. She can deal with it."

"Yeah." Tommy took a drink of water, spun the cap back on the top, and set the bottle on the desk. "Unfortunately, if enough people start blocking us, getting permits could become problematic. All that fieldwork our other agents do will get shut down. Eventually, they'll have to go find work somewhere else. And the IAA will just be us."

A long pause followed his statement.

"You mean all of us, right?" Alex asked, as if reminding Tommy they were still on the line.

"Of course. Look, I'm not really worried about Reyna getting us blacklisted. If she had that kind of power, it would have already happened."

"So, what are you worried about?" Sean asked.

Tommy took a breath. "If she's the one in charge of cataloging all the artifacts found at Thonis-Heracleion, there's little to no chance she'll share any of that information with us. No, you know what? Scratch that. There is no chance."

Sean studied his friend as he would a child accused of stealing cookies. He searched Tommy's face for signs he was leaving something out. "Did you break her heart, Schultzie?"

Tommy looked up at him in surprise. "No. Of course not." He blinked rapidly. A little too rapidly. His eyes darted away to the left and then up to the ceiling.

"Wow," Sean said. "You really did, didn't you?"

"What? No. I didn't break Reyna's heart."

"He totally did," Tara said.

"You're a terrible liar, Schultzie," Sean added. "What in the world did you do?"

"Nothing," Tommy insisted. He stepped back over to the desk, removed the cap on the water bottle again, and chugged several gulps.

"Do you two know about this?" Sean asked the kids.

"I don't," Alex confessed.

"Me either," Tara said. "I was just going with how guilty he sounded."

"He did sound guilty."

Tommy set the bottle back down and shook his head vehemently. "Look, I didn't break her heart. At least, not on purpose."

"And there it is," Sean said. "Please, tell the jury what happened."

"It was nothing. Okay. We worked together like twenty years ago on a project. We were both brand new at the time. Here in Egypt, actually. South of Cairo. Dr. Amid was in charge of the dig. I guess spending so much time together, Reyna developed feelings for me.

One night, she came to my tent and told me how she felt. I guess her feelings had been pent up, and she couldn't take it anymore."

"Unreal," Sean blurted. "What happened?"

Tommy shrugged and looked out the window. "She told me she was in love with me. I...." He hesitated.

"What did you say?"

"I told her thank you."

"What?"

"Tommy!" Tara blurted. "You did not say that to that poor woman."

"Yeah. I kinda did," he admitted.

"Not good, man," Alex said. "She poured her heart out to you, and you gave her a consolation prize."

Sean chuckled. "Did you shake her hand too?"

"No." Tommy sounded defensive. "I told her thank you, and that I appreciated her honesty, but I thought it would be better if we kept our relationship professional and platonic. You know, work buddies."

"Ugh."

"Savage," Tara muttered.

"What?" Tommy asked. "I didn't have feelings for her. Okay? You can't just make that happen, you know. Honestly, I can't believe we're having this discussion."

"And I can't believe you broke the heart of the one person who can help us solve this mystery," Sean said. "Great going, Schultzie."

"Oh, come on. Seriously? Like you never rejected anyone before."

"Not that I recall."

"What was wrong with her, Tommy?" Alex asked.

"Nothing. She just wasn't my type. That's all. And I wasn't interested in a relationship. Okay? We were friends and coworkers."

"So, you put her in the friend zone," Sean realized.

"Yeah. I guess I did. There may have been a point when I thought maybe it would have been cool to see where things went with her, but that time passed. I moved on, focused on my work and seeing the world."

Sean chortled. "And now you need her more than she ever needed you."

"Well, I mean. Sure. Yeah."

Sean raised an eyebrow at that. "Oh, so you really think she needed you that badly?"

"I don't know. I mean, I am quite the catch."

"Someone sure sounds full of themselves."

"Look, can we please move on? We have a real issue here. Reyna is the only person who can help us. Unless any of you know someone else working under her who might be willing to give us information."

No one said anything.

"That's what I thought."

"Sounds like you're going to have to call your old friend, then," Sean said.

"Awkward," Tara added.

"Yes. It will be awkward," Tommy acknowledged. "Extremely awkward. We haven't really spoken since."

"Wait," Sean said with a frown. "You mean to tell me you didn't speak to her the rest of the time you were on that dig?"

Tommy raised his left shoulder innocently. "No. I left the site a week later. I've seen her a few times at different functions. But we've never spoken."

"Then how do you know she—"

"Hates me? Because she's been very vocal about how we do things, and how she disapproves."

"Maybe she's a purist?"

"No," Tommy said, dismissing it as he turned away. "I mean, yes. She is that, but this really is a problem. There's no way she'll let us see the Cicero monument, if there was one found to begin with."

"Well, we have to try. It isn't like we have much choice. We'll contact her in the morning."

Tommy groaned at the suggestion. "We don't even have her number."

"I just sent it to you," Alex said. "She'll most likely be at the port overseeing things. If I were you, I'd plan some sort of apology."

"A lot of good that will do. But yeah, you're right. We don't have a choice. Looks like I'm going to have to suck it up."

"That's the spirit," Sean said, rolling his eyes. "Tara, Alex, thanks so much for your help. We'll be in touch if we need anything else."

"No problem, guys," Tara said. "Y'all get some rest. Good luck."

The call ended, leaving Sean and Tommy standing in silence.

"I guess I'll head to my room," Sean said after a moment. "Need to get some shut-eye."

"Yeah, same. I'm wiped." Tommy ran both hands over his head, lacing his hair through his fingers. He stopped at the top of his scalp, and flapped his lips.

"You going to be okay?" Sean asked, stopping by the door.

"Yeah. It just sucks, man. I hope Reyna will help us. If not, I'm not sure what we're going to do."

"Hey, man. It's not that bad. Look, maybe they haven't found the thing we're looking for. If that's the case, there's a chance we can dig it up out of the sea."

"Yeah, right. To do that, we'd still have to go through her to get permission. It's a lose-lose scenario."

"Oh. That's true. Well, try to get some sleep. We'll reach out to her in the morning. Actually, maybe I should be the one to call. Might smooth things over before you speak to her."

"Good idea."

Sean opened the door and stepped out into the hall. As the door closed behind him, he couldn't help but feel like they were completely screwed.

30

Sean could feel the sense of dread seeping out of Tommy's soul. He felt it the entire journey from Cairo to Alexandria.

The two had woken early and gone to the train station to buy tickets for the first available train going north to the coastal city. And that was before they bothered contacting Reyna Oluk.

Sean felt guilty about leaving Vokum's Maserati at the parking garage, but they'd had no choice, and opted instead for a ride share to a new hotel.

Tommy reasoned it was too early in the morning to reach out to her, and that it would only make things worse if they woke her.

After 7 a.m. local time, however, he had no choice. If he waited too long to contact her, the opportunity could be lost to whatever busy plans her schedule laid out before her.

Unfortunately, Tommy could only locate her assistant and learn where she would be during the morning hours. The assistant, apparently, didn't know about the rift between them, or about Reyna's distaste for the way Tommy did things in the field.

His clout as a known archaeologist earned him enough trust with the assistant to get her itinerary for the day, which revealed she would be at the research center that had acted as the Thonis-Heracleion project headquarters for the last few years.

Tommy got the address and thanked the young woman for her help. He also added that he would prefer to surprise Dr. Oluk if that was okay. The assistant seemed to be amicable to the idea after Tommy explained they'd worked together years before and hadn't seen each other since.

After arriving at the train station in Alexandria, Sean hailed a cab, and Tommy gave the address to the driver.

The young Egyptian offered to stow their bags in the trunk, but both respectfully declined, opting to keep their belongings close by. They preferred not to risk the items in their bags being pilfered by a dishonest cabbie.

It had never happened to either of them, but they'd heard stories about tourists who'd lost valuables that way.

The cab was an old Honda Accord, with faded white paint that had chipped in several places. The interior smelled like a Middle Eastern restaurant was operating out of the back, with the scents of cumin, coriander, and harissa saturating the cabin air.

The driver was friendly enough, asking just the right number of questions without being too nosy. And after five minutes, he shut down and left the two Americans alone to their thoughts and own conversation.

"You going to be okay with all this?" Sean asked with a concerned glance at his friend.

Tommy was looking out the window at the clogged downtown full of tall apartment and hotel buildings. Cars packed the streets like salmon in a shallow ditch. Twice he saw cars bump into each other and keep going as if nothing happened.

"Little late to ask me that now, isn't it?" Tommy answered.

"Probably."

"Not that it matters anyway. Reyna is our only shot."

"Maybe not," Sean insisted. "There's always another way. It might be more difficult, but it's possible."

"I don't know. This feels pretty hard right now." He ended the sentence with a laugh. "I was never really good with women."

"You still aren't."

They shared a friendly laugh.

"That's true," Tommy agreed. "Luckily, I don't have to worry about my game anymore. June is amazing. I'm lucky to have her, even though I wish we could be together more."

"Any word on what she said about retiring?"

The conversation seemed to ease Tommy's nerves, if not for a few minutes. Focusing on his wife and things that were merely matter of fact took his mind off what he was certain would be a highly awkward reunion with Reyna.

"Still sorting out the details. She's been on several missions lately. Can't tell me where, or what she was doing. You know that drill."

Sean nodded that he did.

Having been involved in dozens of undercover, classified operations, he'd experienced, seen, and done things that he would carry with him for the rest of his life—unable to share them with anyone.

Sharing that stuff with someone else might help him feel like he'd lifted a weight off his shoulders, but at the same time he would be putting that burden on the listener. Most people weren't ready to hear those kinds of details. And so, Sean bore the burden alone, save for his former partner and current Axis director, Emily Starks. She was the only person in the world who knew what he'd done, and why.

They never spoke about those missions, and neither expressed a hint at needing to. Those events were buried deep in the past, and that is where they had to stay.

"Well, I hope it works out, man," Sean said, brushing aside the memories. "You two need to be together more."

Tommy chuffed. "You're one to talk. Your wife seems like she's always out having her own stand-alone adventures."

"We see each other plenty, but yeah, it would be good to be separated less."

"Well, if she ever decides to give up what she's doing with all the missing artwork from World War Two, the door to the IAA is wide open."

"I appreciate that, Schultzie. And she knows."

Adriana and Sean had discussed that very thing on numerous occasions, but she felt a sense of duty to recover as many of the lost masterpieces as she could.

He didn't let Tommy know it, but Sean had been considering doing the exact opposite of what his friend suggested. It wasn't that he'd grown tired of working with the IAA. He loved it, at least most of the time—when he wasn't being shot at. And he counted himself lucky to be able to work with his best friend, uncovering history that had been lost to the world.

But he missed Adriana.

As he grew older, every moment Sean was apart from her seemed to go by faster and faster. He couldn't help but feel as if his life with her was passing him by, and before he knew it, they would be too old to truly enjoy it anymore.

Sean wasn't sure if or how he would approach the subject with Tommy, but he'd been considering walking away for a while.

He'd done it once before to open a kayak and paddle board shop on the Emerald Coast of Florida's panhandle. But like with everything else, Sean had been sucked back into the life of intrigue and conspiracy he'd longed to leave behind.

That particular occasion had involved Secret Service agents showing up at his shop at the request of the president.

That had been a wild one, Sean recounted.

"You okay, man?" Tommy asked, breaking the contemplative silence in the car. "You seem like you're somewhere else."

"Yeah, sorry. Just thinking about Addy. She's looking into a painting that was taken from Poland in 1939."

"Anything I might have heard of?"

"Maybe. I hadn't heard of it. Anyway, I'm sure she's fine. I texted her yesterday. Haven't heard back so far today, but I will. She always gets back to me when she can."

"She got a timeline on when she'll be back in the States?"

"Nah," Sean said, shaking his head. He looked back out the window as the driver stopped at an intersection.

"Well, it's kind of nice being able to travel just the two of us, you know? Get some quality time together?"

The driver glanced back in the mirror at them when heard that last part, but the two occupants didn't notice.

"Listen, Schultzie," Sean said, his tone somber, full of sincerity. "I really appreciate last night. You were really understanding about my fears, and didn't pressure me."

The cabbie looked back again, a frown forming on his face as he listened.

"You're my guy, Sean. I'll never force you into doing anything you don't want to do. But if it makes you feel any better, I wouldn't want to be in a hole like that with anyone else."

Sean nodded. "Same, man. Same."

The driver cleared his throat and flipped on the blinker as they approached the research center ahead.

He pulled up to the curb in an empty spot between cars and slammed on the brakes.

Sean and Tommy rocked forward, then back, at the abrupt stop.

"Twenty-two," the cabbie said, his expression dark and full of disgust.

"Sure," Tommy said, fishing the bills out of his wallet. He paid the man and exited the back seat, following Sean onto the curb.

The second Sean shut the back door, the cab driver sped off, squealing his tires as he merged into traffic.

"What's with him?" Tommy asked.

Sean stared after the car, then it hit him. Laughter boomed from his throat, and he nearly doubled over.

"What?" Tommy insisted. "What is so funny?"

"Our conversation. I think the cab driver thought we were a couple of dudes cheating on their wives. With each other."

"Wait." Tommy turned around and looked in the direction the car had gone. It was out of sight now, blending with the rest of the traffic on the busy street. "He thought... you and I?" He pointed at himself, then Sean, then himself again.

"I think so."

Sean slung his backpack over one shoulder and patted Tommy on the back. Tommy jumped, unusually startled by the act.

"At least we shook off the jitters of talking to the woman whose heart you broke twenty years ago."

Sean walked away from his friend, leaving him there alone on the sidewalk to be abruptly submersed by the anxiety of the task ahead.

"Thanks for that," Tommy said.

"No problem!" Sean shouted without looking back.

31

Sean looked up at the gray building. Its black metal letters over the entrance declared it to be the Alexandria Historical Research Institute.

The two-story structure wasn't going to win any architectural accolades. Its boxy design was minimalist, at best, with narrow slits for windows on both floors. The entrance was a glass façade with steel frames supporting the doors and windows. A revolving door in the center of the entrance spun automatically in a slow, steady cadence.

"Impressive," Sean said, still staring up at the building.

"I guess." Tommy didn't echo the sentiment. "This was an office building before. I think a defunct oil company owned it."

"An oil company went out of business? That's a tough trick to pull off."

"No, I think they just got acquired. Rockefeller style."

"That makes more sense."

"Anyway, shall we?" Tommy motioned to the rotating door and stepped in.

Once in the lobby, they took a quick survey of their surroundings. The floor was covered in a short, charcoal-gray carpet. A reception desk stood straight across from them with a young Korean woman sitting behind it in a light blue business jacket and white shirt. Her smile was as bland as the building she worked in.

A few other people walked by, some coming from elevators off to the left, others to and from a hallway to the right of the desk. The corridor appeared to go straight back into the inner parts of the building.

Sean had expected there to be a few artifacts on display in the lobby, or perhaps pictures hanging from the walls, featuring prominent archaeologists or excavation sites. Instead, the lobby appeared to have been forgotten on the day the interior decorator showed up. It was clean to the point of sterile, right down to the LED strip lights hanging from the overhead ceiling.

He and Tommy walked over to the reception desk and waited until the young Korean woman looked up at them from her computer.

"How can I help you?" she asked in a British accent.

Tommy stepped up and cleared his throat. "I'm Tommy Schultz from the International Archaeological Agency. And this is Sean Wyatt, head of security and recovery. I don't have an appointment, but I was hoping I could speak to Reyna Oluk. Does she happen to be in the building today?"

The receptionist cocked her head to the side, causing the tight black ponytail to drop behind her shoulder.

"You're Tommy Schultz?" she asked.

Tommy held back the grimace his instincts nearly forced across his face. His hopes had been a mixed bag. On the one hand, using his clout as the founder of the IAA could gain him access into nearly every research center like this one the world over. On the other hand, if the receptionist shared Reyna's disdain for him, this could prove to be a short and unfruitful venture. If that were the case, he and Sean would have to find another way to get to Reyna, and none of those options appealed to him.

"Yes, ma'am. I realize she must be very busy, and probably gets lots of people coming in here to see her. But we have some questions about an artifact from the Thonis-Heracleion site."

"Wow," she exclaimed. "You're really Tommy Schultz?"

Sean pinched his lips together, teetering on the fence between laughing and praying she didn't make a big deal out of this. But he could already see it in the young woman's eyes—the admiration, the starstruck fangirl expression in her smile.

"Yes?" Tommy said, unsure where this was going.

"I can't believe it. You're one of the most well-known archaeologists in the world. I'm studying archaeology because of you." She looked down at her desk with a sheepish humility. "I'm doing this job to get my foot in the door once I'm done at university."

"Smart," Tommy said. "Sounds like you're well on your way."

"What you have done for the world of history is nothing short of heroic," she went on.

Now she's laying it on a little thick, Sean thought.

"Well, I appreciate that," Tommy said. "But I'm just doing my job like everyone else."

"Hardly. Your adventures are the stuff of legend."

Tommy blushed and managed a laugh.

She turned her attention to Sean. "And who is this?"

"This is my head of security and recovery, Sean Wyatt. You've probably heard of him too."

The blank stare in her eyes answered first. "Doesn't ring a bell," she said. "Nice to meet you, Sean. Do you get out in the field much?"

"A little," Sean said, holding back his laughter.

Tommy redirected the conversation back to the reason they were here. "Could you tell me how to find Reyna? It's kind of a surprise me showing up like this. I don't want to make a big deal out of it."

"Sure," the receptionist answered. "Just down that hall, last door on the right."

Sean and Tommy could tell she had one more thing to say. The woman brimmed with a request to the point she looked as though she might burst.

"Would it be okay if I took a selfie?" she asked.

Sean turned his head away to keep her from seeing him crack.

"Sure," Tommy said. "You want Sean in the pic, too, or just me?"

"Just you if that's okay. No offense to your friend."

"None taken," Sean mumbled.

"Would you mind taking it?" she asked, holding out her phone to Sean.

Tommy could barely contain his amusement.

"Not at all," Sean said.

The young woman stepped around her desk and stood in front of it, looping her arm around Tommy's waist. She smiled from ear to ear as Tommy wrapped his arm around her shoulder and offered his patented goofy grin.

"Say history," Sean said. He took three pictures and then returned the device to the receptionist.

"Thank you so much," she said.

"You're welcome."

"Oh, yeah. You too," she corrected.

Sean nearly erupted in laughter, but he managed to contain himself.

"Thanks for your help," Tommy said. "And if you ever think about moving to the States, we could always use a young go-getter like yourself."

Her eyes widened. "I will. Thank you!"

"Okay, big guy," Sean said. "We need to go." He pulled Tommy by the shoulder and started for the hallway.

Tommy waved at her as he disappeared around the corner. She waved back, still smiling like she'd just met Bono.

Once they were out of earshot, Sean looked at his friend. "Seems like you just found a new stalker."

Tommy blew it off with a dismissive scowl. "Nah. She's just a nice kid who seems to have her ducks all lined up."

"Go-getter?" Sean teased. "Seriously?"

"What? She is."

"I just didn't realize we were back in the 1960s again."

They passed open doors on either side, both leading into empty offices.

"She seems nice. And she knows what she wants."

"You can say that again."

"Someone sounds jealous," Tommy joked.

"Mm-hmm," Sean hummed. "That's what it is. Let's just hope Reyna is as big a fan of you as that receptionist back there."

The cheerful look on Tommy's face evaporated, sinking into a dark expression of impending doom.

"Ugh. Yeah. Probably not."

"You never know," Sean said, looking at the last door on the right thirty feet away. "Maybe she let bygones be bygones. It's been a long time, man."

"Yeah," Tommy managed. "Maybe." He said the words, but they lacked conviction.

The two slowed down as they neared the last door. A lump caught in Tommy's throat. Twenty feet from the door, they heard voices from inside. A woman's voice reached their ears.

Tommy stopped in his tracks and listened. Sean halted a half second after him.

"Sounds like she's talking to someone," Tommy whispered. "Maybe she's in a meeting."

"Or on the phone," Sean suggested.

They stood there listening for a moment as the woman continued speaking. Then she paused and made a few sounds as if agreeing with someone.

Must be on the phone, Sean guessed.

"Well, thank you so much for your help with all this," the woman said. "I look forward to meeting with you next week."

Tommy glanced over at Sean and shrugged, ready to move forward.

"So, what brings you two to Alexandria?" she said.

Sean and Tommy remained still and listened.

"Thanks so much for meeting with us on such short notice," a man said. "I know how busy you are with all the projects you have running. Honestly, I don't know how you manage it all."

Tommy inched forward to make sure he was hearing correctly.

"Well," Reyna said, "I've learned to hand off some of my responsibilities. I've taken on more of a managerial role with most of it, though I do still like to get out in the field whenever I can. There's nothing quite as invigorating as being on a site, seeing history pulled up right before your eyes, things that haven't been seen for hundreds, sometimes thousands of years."

"I know exactly what you mean. There's just something about being there when history comes alive, where you can feel the ghosts of those who walked before us. Never ceases to take my breath away."

Sean looked over at Tommy. Both men's eyes burgeoned with disbelief.

"How?" Tommy mouthed.

Sean only shook his head. He didn't know how, but Craig Freeman had beaten them here.

32

"You've done so much good work, Dr. Freeman. I have to say, it's an honor to have you here in Egypt. This is a little out of your area, though. What brings you to Alexandria?"

Craig cleared his throat. "Yes, Dr. Oluk. You're right. Egyptian history isn't my area of expertise. But I've been working on a project that brought me here."

"I'm intrigued. Go on."

"My colleague and I have been working on a new project to document the life of Cicero, his writings, and hopefully locate his grave. Of course, the last part is more of a pie-in-the-sky kind of thing. No one has been able to find it yet."

"Interesting," Reyna said. "But what does that have to do with me?"

Craig went on. "As you probably know, Cicero visited Egypt in the year 48 BC. Actually, he came here to Alexandria."

"That's true."

"That visit came during a time of significant political turmoil in the Roman Republic. Cicero came to Egypt after fleeing Rome due to the escalating conflict between Julius Caesar and Pompey. During his stay, he wanted to see and experience one of the most important cultural and intellectual centers of the time—Alexandria.

"This visit occurred after Pompey's assassination in Egypt and during the period when Julius Caesar was involved with Cleopatra the Seventh, aiming to stabilize Egypt as a dependable ally of Rome. Cicero's experiences and observations in Egypt, among other places, contributed to his broad knowledge of the political and cultural landscape of the Mediterranean world, which influenced his writings and political strategies upon his return to Rome. While he was here, however, he also shared his knowledge and ideas with the people, including the scholars at the Great Library."

"Ah," Reyna said. "You believe he spent time at the Library of Alexandria?"

"I do. But we need more evidence to support this hypothesis, which as you know, is difficult to come by." Craig paused for a second, as if reluctant to continue. "I know you've been heading up the excavation at Thonis-Heracleion, not far from here."

"Yes. It's been an all-consuming project. And we've still only scratched the surface with that lost city. I mean, we're talking about just that—an entire city that has been hidden underwater for thousands of years. What we've been able to find is nothing short of astounding, and an incredible glimpse into the ancient past."

"You've also been helping with the project in the city where it's believed Alexander the Great's tomb might be located, correct?"

"That is correct. Although I am not the lead on that one. We help process, catalog, and house most of the artifacts they find there. And their teams are able to use our facilities to conduct their research and analysis."

"Do you think they're going to find the tomb there?" Craig asked.

Sean listened intently. He didn't like the fact that Brent hadn't said anything yet, not that he should have been surprised by that fact. Brent wasn't in his element, and could add nothing to this conversation. Still, Sean would have preferred to know for certain that Craig's hired gun was in there with him.

He cast a glance back down the hall, but it was empty.

"I think they have as good a chance as any," Reyna answered. "They recently uncovered a series of blocks they believe could be the foundation of a massive structure. The tomb of Alexander would not have been modest. He was revered here in Egypt as a visionary, a leader, a warrior, and above all... a living god. His tomb would have been remarkable to say the least, a true monument to the man's life and accomplishments, both as an individual and for the people of Egypt. He honored their traditions and respected their culture in ways no other conquerors of his time, or before, ever had."

"I remember learning that about him," Craig added. "That was part of his reason for establishing the Great Library here, in the city he designed and built. Egypt was to be the cultural crossroads of the world, with Alexandria at its center."

"You know your history, Dr. Freeman."

"Please, call me Craig."

Tommy clenched his jaw at the man's easy candor, the way he acted like an innocent lamb, simply there to do nothing more than catch up with a colleague and maybe find out what he could about a long-dead Roman politician.

"Very well, Craig. So, how can I help you with your project?"

"I don't want to be a bother," he said. "I know how limited your time is."

"Actually, my schedule is clear today. I was just catching up on some emails, answering requests for speaking engagements and looking over permits. What is it you need from me?"

"So, back to the subject of Cicero, the whole reason we're here. I was wondering if—in your excavations or studies—you might have come across anything related to Cicero and his visit here to Alexandria. Some documents, perhaps? Or maybe something that memorialized his time here? I know, based on limited information, that he might have had a positive influence on some of the leaders here, or perhaps been honored by the librarians of the time. I realize we still don't know the library's exact location, but is it possible you've found something, anything, that might pay homage to his time here? Or perhaps, at least some kind of documentation? It would really help us put together a more complete picture of the man's life, and the scope of his influence throughout the world at the time."

Another pause dulled the conversation.

Sean wished he could see Reyna's expression. Was she suspicious, perhaps sizing up Craig to grasp if he was telling the truth? Or was she simply getting a drink of water before answering his question?

"You ask an interesting question," she said. "And a timely one."

"Timely?"

"Yes. Just over a month ago, we pulled an unusual item from the seabed."

The sound of fingers tapping on a keyboard cut in for a moment. "Right here," she continued.

Sean realized Reyna must have been showing them a map and the area where the artifact in question had been found.

Tommy looked over at him, astonishment drawing his mouth open. "They found it," he mouthed.

Sean shook his head, sternly warning his friend to keep quiet. Not that he needed to. Tommy hadn't said anything out loud, but the surprise on his face was as loud as a drum.

"Wow," Craig gasped. "That is extraordinary. Right there off the coast."

"Well, it wasn't close to shore if that's what you mean. But yes, it was in the underwater city. Remarkable, really. We were, of course, initially curious as to why the bust would be there. It was surprisingly well preserved, too, including the name inscribed on the pedestal."

"Fascinating."

"Indeed. Cicero must have had a much bigger impact on Alexandria than initially thought, though to what extent we cannot say. Perhaps that's where your study comes in, Craig."

"Perhaps."

Sean noted the subtle, sinister tone in the word. *There's the real Craig,* he thought. It was doubtful Reyna picked up on it. Why would she? At this point, she had no reason to distrust him. He was just another archaeologist showing up at her door to ask a question. His well-rehearsed story would sound completely legitimate as well.

Heck, Sean thought, he would have believed it if he didn't know the truth.

The question he and Tommy had to answer at the moment was how to break up this little charade.

If they marched in right now and interrupted, they'd look crazy. Especially given Tommy's history with Reyna. She'd be more inclined to believe Craig, no matter what Tommy told her, and from there it would be an uncomfortable escort out of the building by security, perhaps followed by an arrest if they resisted.

It wasn't in Sean's nature to hesitate with a crucial decision, but here, he decided to wait and keep listening to see where this conversation was going.

"I don't mean to be indelicate," Craig said, "but where is the bust now? Is it here in this facility?"

"Nothing indelicate about that question. But no, it's not here. We have a facility about ten minutes from here that houses most of the finds from the area. They are kept there to be cleaned and cataloged. It's highly secure, as you would expect. Once an artifact has been documented and prepped, it is brought here for deeper analysis."

"So, you haven't conducted much research on the bust yet?"

"No," she said. "Not yet, although we were planning to soon, if I remember correctly. I have a whole list of artifacts to study and analyze." She stopped for a moment. "Would you like to see it?"

The abrupt invitation sent a tingle of worry through Sean's chest. He saw the same anxiety written on Tommy's face.

If Craig and Brent got to the bust first, they would have access to the map hidden within. And if they got away with that, there'd be no chance of catching them before they found the scroll—or at least the location of Archimedes' tomb.

"I don't want to impose," Craig responded. "I know how busy you are and—"

"You are a good archaeologist, Craig. But apparently a bad listener. I already told you I don't have much on my plate today. I would be honored to take you over to the facility where the bust is being kept. If anyone should get a look at it before the public, it's you.

Especially considering the work you're doing to highlight the life and contributions of Cicero."

Sean wanted to puke, and from the nauseated look in Tommy's eyes, he did, too.

"Excellent. Do you have a car here? You could ride with me if you like."

"We do, but if it's just the same, I'd prefer to follow. We have a few other places to visit while we're here, and it might be best if we go straightaway from your facility."

Yeah, Sean thought. *Like the airport.*

"No problem at all," Reyna said. "I do think you'll appreciate our facility. We have quite the collection there. It will be nice, though, to get those artifacts out of storage and into museums for the world to appreciate."

"That's why we do this, after all."

"Indeed."

Sean heard them shuffling around. A chair scraped on carpet. Another one's wheels rolled, which he took to be Reyna's desk chair. The sounds of clothing swishing reached his ears.

They needed to get out of the hall.

Tommy saw the urgency on his face and visibly wondered what they should do.

Sean nodded toward an open door fifteen feet back. He turned and hurried toward it on his tiptoes, careful not to make a sound.

He ducked into the office with Tommy close on his tail, and slunk around the desk before crouching down behind it.

"I have to say," Craig said, his voice nearing the open door, "I really do appreciate this, Dr. Oluk. It's an honor just to speak with you. And now we're getting a personal tour of your discoveries. I really can't thank you enough."

"Please," she replied. "Call me Reyna. And it's no problem. All in the name of history, yes?"

"Definitely."

Sean looked under the front façade of the desk and saw three sets of shoes pass by.

"Your friend doesn't say much," Reyna noticed. Sean figured she must have been talking about Brent.

"Sorry, I'm new to all this," Brent said, his voice growing distant.

"He's a quick learner, though," Craig added.

Sean and Tommy waited behind the desk for ten more seconds before hurrying out to the door and peeking around it.

"We can't lose them," Sean said.

He saw the three reach the end of the corridor with Brent in the back. Sean was about to step out when Brent turned and looked back down the hall.

Sean caught the movement in the nick of time, and pulled back out of sight before he could be spotted—at least he hoped.

He waited by the corner with Tommy just behind him.

"What?" Tommy whispered.

"They stopped at the far end," Sean breathed. "Brent turned around."

"Did he see you?"

"I don't think so."

Sean waited a few more seconds and then peeked around the corner again. If Brent had been there looking his way, chaos could ensue. But when he looked down the hall, all he saw was an empty entrance.

"He's gone," Sean announced.

"Great. How are we going to follow them now? It's going to look suspicious if we're sneaking through the building after them."

Sean grinned. It was a devilish look, like a kid who had a sneaky, bad idea.

"What?" Tommy wondered, asking the question in an elongated syllable. "What are you thinking?"

"There's another way we can find out where they're going. We just have to ask your superfan up front."

"I had a bad feeling you were going to say that."

Sean snuck out the door and hurried up the hall to the next office. He slowed down there, waiting in case he needed to duck inside, but after a couple of seconds, he pushed ahead to the door leading back out to the lobby.

Again, he checked around the corner and this time spotted Reyna and the two men walking toward the exit.

Tommy sidled up next to him and looked out, also seeing the three just before they walked through the revolving door.

"Those two better not hurt her," Tommy said through clenched teeth.

"If I didn't know any better, I'd say you actually cared about her," Sean said.

"I do. She was my friend. I never wanted that to change just because I wasn't interested romantically. I never stopped caring about her, though."

Sean smirked. "You're a good man, Tommy Schultz."

He stepped out from behind the corner and walked over to the reception desk, where the young woman was still sitting at the computer.

She noticed them approaching, and her face lit up. "Did you get a chance to talk with her?" the young woman asked.

"She had a few other people with her," Tommy answered. "But we're supposed to meet her over at the other facility. You don't happen to have the address for that building, do you? I didn't get it from her."

He hoped the play worked. The receptionist could wonder, reasonably so, why Reyna hadn't just asked him to follow her, or given him her number, or why she'd simply forgotten or not thought to give the address to him.

It was a bet on her being unable to see through the Tommy-colored glasses.

"Of course," she said, all too happy to help out her hero. "I'll write it down for you."

She bent down, pulled open a drawer, and removed a notepad, then picked up a pen and scribbled the address on the paper. She added another part at the end and then handed the address to Tommy.

"I wrote my name on there since I think I forgot to introduce myself before. Just in case you need further assistance in the future."

"Thanks so much," Tommy said. "I really appreciate it. You're a lifesaver."

"No problem. And if you need anything, anything at all, you know where to find me."

He passed her a thankful smile and nod and turned toward the door. When he and Sean were six steps away from the desk, Sean leaned in close. "You still got it, Schultzie."

"Yeah," he said, glancing back over his shoulder. The young woman was still looking at him, and waved goodbye. "I guess I do."

33

B rent stopped the car in a parking space in front of the building, next to Reyna's Mercedes sedan. The warehouse looked like most of the other buildings in Alexandria, painted with a light beige and accents of white. The biggest difference between it and most of the other structures was that this one had no windows opening into a second story. It was, for all intents, a once-regular warehouse converted into a place where priceless artifacts from antiquity were kept and cataloged before being sent off to museums, or to the research headquarters they'd left twelve minutes before.

"Doesn't seem that secure for a high-security facility," Brent commented, shifting the gear into park.

They'd turned off the road and straight into the lot. No security gates. No guards. Just an open car park with plenty of empty spaces.

"I'm sure there's more inside the building," Craig suggested. "Or maybe the security lies in its obscurity." He panned the front façade. "They sure made it look like every other structure I've seen around here."

For all its splendor, history, and wonder, that was the one complaint Craig had about the city, and indeed many similar to it in the region. The similarity, or lack of innovation with the architecture reminded him of the tens of thousands of crowded buildings in Athens that stretched across the hills of Southern Greece.

They stepped out of the car and into the warm, dry morning air. A subtle breeze tickled their skin as they breathed in the smells around them. Here, in this part of the city, the air lacked the pleasant odors of exotic local foods from restaurants and cafés. Instead, it was laden with hints of exhaust from the passing traffic and an arid, dusty scent that Craig could only describe as the smell of the desert.

Reyna re-greeted them with a smile and walked toward a set of four glass doors set in aluminum frames.

Craig and Brent joined her, and both noted the lack of a security keypad or card reader.

Craig held the door for her and Brent, then followed them into the lobby. Unlike the atrium at the research headquarters building, this offered no reception desk, or even signs of life, save for the young man in a security guard uniform standing to the right of the doors. To his right, an RFID panel hung from the wall. A security camera hung over the doors at an angle, capturing whoever entered the building.

The interior was nothing more than a mix of concrete and steel, giving little away about the treasures within. The design struck a balance between utilitarian function and subtle reverence for the historical significance of the contents protected within. The polished concrete floors reflected the soft, diffused lighting overhead designed to mimic natural light.

"Good morning, Hanif," Reyna said as she approached the guard.

"Good morning, Dr. Oluk. Bringing a few guests to see the facility?"

"Yes. I'm showing them a piece we pulled out of the sea. They're working on a project that relates to it." She lifted the RFID card hanging from a lanyard around her neck and swiped it across the panel. The red light disappeared, and a green light blinked on. A click from within the door signaled it was unlocked.

"Sounds interesting." The guard grinned politely and opened the door for her and her guests.

"Thank you, Hanif. We'll see you on our way out."

He tipped his hat to the visitors and allowed the door to close behind them.

Craig and Brent followed Reyna into the corridor—a long, sterile hallway with reinforced doors leading to various rooms. Craig figured they concealed research labs, restoration workshops, and storage areas.

The floors were marked with colored lines to guide staff and authorized visitors to different sections. Calming earth tones covered the walls. Surveillance cameras dotted the ceiling at regular intervals, and motion sensors ensured any unauthorized movement after hours would trigger an alarm.

Clearly, these corridors were designed with efficiency and security in mind.

Craig noted the placards next to the doors as they passed, each designating the areas beyond to guide staff and visitors.

Halfway down the hall, the wall ended in enormous glass panels that offered views into some of the active workspaces. A pair of archaeologists—a middle-aged man and a woman in her thirties—worked meticulously on a bronze helmet. Craig guessed it was from the third century BC based on the design. The object was in immaculate condition for something so old, and he marveled at how the helmet had been so well preserved for so long.

As the group continued down the corridor, the windows opened into conservation labs and scanning rooms where technicians worked with various artifacts. Craig was familiar with many of the instruments and techniques they used, all relatively new to the world of archaeology.

"It's just ahead," Reyna said as they neared the doors on the left toward the end of the hall.

An RFID panel exactly like the one at the front hung to the left of the twin metal doors. She stopped in front of it and swiped her card. This panel made a buzzing sound before the red light turned green. The lock clicked.

Reyna grabbed the handle and opened the door, holding it so her two guests could enter the room beyond.

She followed them in and let it close behind. Two seconds after it shut, the lock clicked again.

Craig and Brent looked around, turning their heads 180 degrees to take in the vast, open space. It was quiet, with an air of reverence to it, a place where history was both safeguarded and studied. The design was a blend of modern, clean function and technology, crafted to protect and preserve the priceless history within its walls.

The room was segmented into different areas for various artifact categories. White LED lights hung in fixtures from a high ceiling where visible HVAC systems ran along the surface. Craig knew the ductwork and the central machinery of the system ensured precise climate control to protect the delicate items within from deterioration.

"Each zone," Reyna said, pointing to a partitioned area containing several pieces on long, metal tables, "is illuminated by LED lights that automatically adjust in brightness and temperature based on the time of day and the specific needs of the items stored there."

"High tech," Craig mused. "Incredible setup you have here. You really have it dialed in, Dr. Oluk."

"Reyna. Call me Reyna. And yes, we've received strong investment and grants through the years that allowed us to create all this." She motioned to a section where several display cases contained various Egyptian artifacts. "Those displays are made of anti-reflective glass, allowing unobstructed views of the artifacts while protecting them from UV light and external contaminants. The cases are fitted with state-of-the-art security sensors that are integrated seamlessly into the shelves and glass. They're almost invisible to the observer, maintaining aesthetic integrity of the space while providing unmatched protection."

"Sounds like those are about to go on display somewhere," Brent guessed.

"Correct," she confirmed. "Those will be taken to museums so the world can learn from them."

She turned toward the back right of the room and indicated that direction with a nod. "The Cicero piece is back there if you'd like to see it."

Craig responded with an easy grin. "Definitely. That's why we're here."

"Follow me, then."

Reyna walked along the near wall on a path laid out by blue-painted lines on the floor, then turned right at a row of tables containing fragments of artifacts, some laid out as if they were being prepared to reconstruct their original forms.

She passed the tables, more display cases, and a computer station with high-tech equipment connected to it.

Craig saw the bust when they were halfway to the back of the room. A laminated sign with the designation *Thonis-Heracleion Zone 4* on it hung from one of the tables in the center of the room to his left.

"These are all the artifacts we pulled from the zone where the Cicero sculpture was discovered," Reyna explained.

Craig understood what she meant by the term *zone*. He'd used the same methods in cordoning off areas of excavation sites to make sure everything was documented and organized in an efficient way. He wanted to know exactly where each item came from and when it was found. Zones could also be a helpful way to compare the ages of one area and its contents to another. As with modern construction, cities and villages weren't all built in a day. They were completed in stages, and using zones helped identify the various stages of both construction and the expansion of an area.

She led the two visitors to the bust tucked away in the back corner. It stood atop a metal table, secured by cloth-covered blocks on each side so it wouldn't tip over.

"Incredible," Craig breathed reverently. "Absolutely incredible."

"Yes. We have yet to fully analyze this one, but it certainly is a curiosity to say the least. But this shows that Cicero was much more important to Egypt than history gives credit. He must have had quite the impact here for this to have been created."

Craig leaned forward and inspected the inscription on the base of the sculpture. The engraving had blunted over time, worn down by water and weather, but it was still deeply cut enough for him to read the name of the Roman honored by its creation.

He admired the craftsmanship and the fact that this artifact had been buried for so long, unseen by human eyes until just recently. That part of him, he figured, would never go away—that piece of him that appreciated the history, the wonder weaved into archaeology. It would always be a big part of him, even after he achieved his goal.

Craig stood up straight, assessing the bust, still uncertain what their next move should be.

34

Sean and Tommy climbed out of the cab, thanked the driver after paying him, and stepped away from the curb toward the nondescript building.

"Not much in the way of security," Tommy noted.

"No. Not on the outside, at least. I'm sure there's more inside. Our building in Atlanta doesn't look very secure from the exterior either."

"True."

The two walked across the parking lot. The sun warmed their skin, and the dry air evaporated any traces of perspiration that might have glistened in the light.

Sean pointed at the two cars parked near the front entrance, a Mercedes sedan and a Honda with a rental sticker on the back window.

"I guess they're inside," Tommy said, echoing Sean's thoughts.

"Yeah. Hopefully, they're not standing just behind those doors," Sean added. "Better be ready in case they are."

"Right."

They both adjusted the holsters concealed under lightweight windbreakers.

Their rucksacks felt more cumbersome, a psychological weight that always seemed to hit at times such as these, when close quarters combat loomed. Being agile in any sort of fight was paramount, but in urban combat, where gunfire could be exchanged at point-blank range, reflex speed was even more crucial.

They reached the front doors and waited, staring at their reflections in the glass.

"Ready?" Sean asked.

"No time like the present."

Sean pulled open the door and held it for Tommy to pass then entered the building after him.

The cool lobby air draped over their skin.

They immediately noticed the single guard at the closed doors opposite them.

Sean assessed the situation within two seconds.

The guard was armed with a pistol on his right hip and had a radio attached to the black uniform shirt he wore, and most importantly, an RFID card dangling at his left side. Next to the doors, the panel for the security clearance card hung from the wall. Sean noticed the red light from the twenty-foot distance.

Neither of the men had any misgivings about being able to leverage their clout with the guard to gain entrance into the secure part of the building.

"Going to have to go with Plan C," Sean breathed so only Tommy could hear.

"Yep. Looks that way."

"Good morning," Tommy said, taking the lead. He walked toward the guard with a cheerful, goofy look on his face.

The man offered a nod. "Good morning."

The first sign was good. The guy didn't warn them that the building was restricted. That was encouraging. He probably figured they were just a couple of researchers here to work on a project.

"We're supposed to meet Dr. Oluk here," Tommy announced when he was fifteen feet from the guard. "Is she already here? That looked like her car outside."

He hoped they wouldn't have to use Plan C, and that the guard would take the hint that recognizing the archaeologist's car out front would be enough to label them a non-security threat.

"She is. Just inside. Do you have your security clearance card?"

And just like that, their hopes were dashed.

"Oh yeah. Of course. I have it in here somewhere." Tommy continued toward the doors while slumping the bag onto his right shoulder and then lowering it to knee level.

He stopped a few feet short of the doors at an angle to the guard.

Sean stayed at arm's length to Tommy's right, directly in front of the man in uniform. He noticed the name tag on the guy's shirt.

"How are you this morning, Hanif?" he asked. "Busy here?"

"No more than usual," the man answered. His eyes oozed with suspicion, either at the stranger's use of his name or at the fact he was trying to make small talk.

These types often took their jobs way too seriously, but here in this place Sean knew it was warranted. With a trove of priceless artifacts behind the walls to Hanif's back, caution had to be the modus operandi.

Tommy busied himself with unzipping the main compartment of his bag with his right hand while holding it with his left hand. "It's got to be in here somewhere," he said. "I know I put it in here."

"Please tell me you didn't forget it at headquarters," Sean begged. His voice carried disdain and a chiding tone like a father talking to their child who'd forgotten to put on socks before leaving the house.

"Hey, I don't see you swiping your card. Where's yours?"

"I left it at the office because you said you had yours."

"Why would you do that? Who does that?"

Hanif watched the two bickering like an old married couple. His suspicion teetered on the brink of amusement, but if he was going to laugh or even crack at the display, he didn't show it.

Sean saw him shift his right hand toward his hip, and for a moment thought the guard might be reaching for his gun. Instead, Hanif looped his thumb over his belt and let it hang there.

Tommy rummaged through the bag, his frustration visibly growing by the second.

"Seriously? Why wouldn't you just bring your badge too?" he asked. "What, is it too cumbersome? It's a badge on a lanyard."

"I didn't want to drop it. You know how clumsy I can be and how I lose things."

"Well, you're an adult. Maybe it's time you start being more responsible."

Hanif's gaze remained fixed on Tommy now as he continued to hunt for the missing card. Sean carefully reached into his pocket and produced a small knife, unsheathing it with his thumb as he pulled it from his pocket.

He took an innocuous sidestep toward the guard, the knife palmed in such a way that the blade ran up to his wrist, completely concealed from Hanif's view.

Sean steadied his breath. He knew what he had to do, even if he didn't want things to be this way. Hanif was just here doing his job. He'd probably woken up this morning, had some coffee and one of those sugar-laden syrup cakes before driving to work in his compact car to earn another honest day's wage.

His job wasn't difficult, at least not most of the time. He probably just stood here by these doors, floating around social media on his phone, greeting the people who came and went.

He didn't pay any attention to Sean drawing dangerously close, and he certainly had no idea of the weapon Sean held in his hand.

"Maybe it's in the front pouch," Sean suggested.

Hanif glanced at him, and Sean flashed an innocent, helpful smile.

"Maybe it's in the front pouch," Tommy repeated in a childish, condescending voice.

Suddenly, his bag slipped out of his right hand and onto the floor. His move was subtle, stripping the rope and a few tools out of it to make it look like the items fell on their own.

Part of the rope landed at Hanif's feet.

Moment of truth. If he stepped back, the plan would have to change again. But Sean was betting on the opposite.

"Why would you have a rope in your bag?" the guard asked, bending down to help Tommy collect his things.

"Everyone always asks me that. But you never know when you might need one."

Sean's move was quick, and completely undetected. He stepped forward as if to assist with the spilled items, and thrust the knife forward. He pinched the RFID card on the guard's waist, and deftly sliced through the cord with the knife, severing the tie.

In a single, swift motion, he slipped the knife back in his pocket and tucked the card in the back pocket of his jeans, then reached down as if to assist Tommy with his belongings.

A second before Tommy finished packing his things, Sean gasped and reached into his back pocket. "Oh, I am such an idiot," he said.

"You looking for an argument from me?" Tommy countered.

"Hilarious. If you're done picking up your rope, can we continue inside. I found my card in my back pocket. I guess it was there all along."

Tommy shook his head as he picked up his pack and slung it over his shoulder. "Seriously? It was in your pocket all along?"

"I forgot I put it there earlier when we were getting coffee."

"I can't take you anywhere." He looked to the guard. "Sorry about that."

"My bad, Hanif," Sean added. "Thanks for the help."

"Okay," the guard said. "No problem." He resumed his post while Sean swiped the card across the reader.

The light turned green, the door clicked, and Tommy pulled it open to allow Sean inside.

The two moved like they were in a hurry, but tried not to look like they were in a hurry.

When the door closed shut behind them, they both sucked in a relieved breath, then continued ahead.

"Which one of these doors is it?" Sean asked.

"Are we going to ignore the fact that our insane plan worked?

"Yeah, for now. If you feel like we need to debrief later, we can." He noted the signs next to the first door. "That's a lab."

"I think it would be in a room marked storage," Tommy thought out loud. "Based on what we heard Reyna say."

"Yeah, but maybe they moved it for analysis." They passed more doors on both sides and then reached the point where the wall ended and a long window began.

"Oh, well that's helpful," Tommy said. "Will be easy to see which one they're in from here."

"It'll also make us easy to spot," Sean argued.

"Right. That's not good."

"No sign of them yet, but maybe we should slow down at the next section."

"Good idea."

Sean held up at the next section of glass and peeked around the corner. He ducked back immediately, obviously spooked by what he'd seen.

"What?" Tommy wondered.

Sean breathed steadily before he answered in a hushed tone. "They're in there. And they're looking at the bust."

35

"What should we do?" Tommy asked.

Sean looked back down the corridor just to make sure Hanif hadn't gotten curious or noticed that his badge was missing. It was only a matter of time until that happened.

"When we open that door," Sean said, pointing toward the end of the long window, "they'll know someone's coming in."

"They'll think it's someone who works here. Right?"

"That would be optimal, but I don't think we can rely on that kind of luck. Best to assume the second we go through, Craig and Brent will be defensive."

"As far as they know, we're still stuck underground in an ancient chamber."

"Yeah, but they'll be on their toes. After all, they know we got out of a jam like that once."

Tommy looked toward the door leading into the storage room. "So, what? We burst in and start shooting? We could hit Reyna."

Sean knew that was no good and shook off the idea. Tommy was right. They couldn't go in with guns blazing. That narrowed their options considerably.

He glanced back down the hall, this time at one of the doors they'd passed on the way in. An idea simmered in his brain, and Tommy saw he was up to something.

"Follow me," Sean said.

They hurried back down the corridor and stopped at a door with a sign next to it marked Custodial Staff.

Sean checked the doorknob. It turned easily, and he pushed the door open.

"A janitor's locker room?" Tommy wondered.

"Yep. Quick. Get in here."

Sean stepped inside with Tommy right behind him. Sean closed the door, easing it shut so it wouldn't make a sound, then surveyed the little room. The wall to the left was lined with four tall gray lockers. To the right was a long wooden bench where Sean figured the staff could change shoes or put on their work clothes.

He opened the first locker and found it was empty. Then he tried the second and discovered dark blue coveralls and a matching baseball cap. He pulled out the uniform and held it up. It was too big for him, and the legs too short, but it might do for Tommy.

"Here, try this on."

"Seriously?"

"Yes, seriously. We need a disguise to at least get in the storage room without causing suspicion."

"Uh, unless there's a mask in there, I'm pretty sure they're going to recognize us."

Sean took the ball cap off the hanger and stuffed it into his chest along with the coveralls. "Put this on, and keep your head down. They won't see our faces that way."

He saw the light bulb go on in Tommy's eyes and left him to put on the outfit while he searched for his own. The third locker contained a hat but no coveralls. Luckily, the last one had a uniform that was roughly Sean's size.

He grabbed the clothes and hat and joined Tommy on the bench. He took off his shoes, slipped into the coveralls one leg at a time, then put the shoes back on before standing and zipping up the uniform.

It was a little tight, but not as tight as the one Tommy donned.

Sean snorted at his friend as he stood and tried to zip the front.

"Looks a little... snug on you," Sean joked.

"Ha-ha-ha. A little snug? The thing is practically painted on me."

"Ew. That's a visual I could go my entire life without."

"This was your idea, pal."

"I know. Come on, we need to move. Leave the zipper. It's not going to matter anyway. We just need to get in the room and close enough to get the drop on them."

"Get the drop on them? How you planning on doing that?"

Sean shrugged. A look of uncertainty sketched across his face. "Going to have to be quick, I guess." He motioned to a wide push broom leaning against the wall. "Grab that. I'll bring the mop."

He rolled the bucket and mop over to the door, opened it, and took a quick peek in both directions before stepping back out—this time with the mop bucket close behind.

Tommy walked beside him until they reached the window to the storage room again.

On Sean's signal, they ducked down below the windowsill, keeping the mop and the broomstick horizontal and out of view. They crawled over to the doors then stood again, both hiding behind the reinforced windows above the handles.

Sean nodded at his friend, a silent question if Tommy was ready or not. Tommy mirrored the gesture, indicating that he was, and Sean swiped the card across the reader.

The device buzzed loudly, and then the lock inside the door clicked.

Sean winced at the sound. It might as well have been a public address announcement that someone was entering the room. There was no going back now. Reyna was in there with a couple of guys who'd left Sean and Tommy for dead—twice. They wouldn't flinch to add one more name to the ledger.

Sean eased the door open, keeping his head down so the bill of the cap blocked his face from view of the men in the back. He thought they might not be able to see him anyway through various sections of artifacts that impeded the view to the front, but he wasn't taking any chances.

He rolled the mop bucket ahead, guiding it with the mop handle, and nudged it to the right until a section of wall completely blocked the three people in the back corner.

Tommy pretended to sweep the floor, also keeping his head down until he was out of sight.

"That's just the cleaning crew," Reyna explained. Her two inquisitors must have started at the sound of the door opening.

"What are your plans for the bust?" Craig asked, his voice distant and yet so close Sean could nearly squeeze the life out of it.

"Once we're done with the analysis," Reyna said, "we will take it to the museum here in the city. I think if Cicero had an important role to the people of Egypt, and of Alexandria, that should be honored and taught. Much like you're doing with your project."

Sean felt that wave of nausea again. That Craig had completely sold her on his lie—even the sound of his voice turned Sean's stomach. His imagination flashed a violent fantasy of bashing Craig's face to a pulp. *Soon, perhaps,* he thought, suppressing the vivid thought.

"What kind of analysis are you going to do?" Craig pressed.

Sean and Tommy both silently unzipped the front of their coveralls and drew their pistols, still hiding behind the partition. Then Sean took the mop handle and pushed the bucket toward the back wall, following along the blue lines painted on the floor. He kept his head down to buy as much time as possible.

Tommy split away and went the other direction around the partition, effectively cutting off the other way out for the enemy.

"I'm sure you're aware of the techniques we utilize, Craig. All the usual processes will be exhausted to determine the age of the piece, its origin if possible, that sort of thing. Though our initial estimates are that it was created sometime in the first century BC, probably after Cicero's death."

Sean moved ever closer, cautiously pushing toward the corner where the three stood by the bust.

"Oh," Reyna said. "Could you please wait to do this area until we leave?"

Sean bobbed his head but kept guiding the mop bucket ahead with one hand on the handle and the other concealing his pistol just behind his back.

To his left, Tommy nudged the broom forward with one hand, likewise hiding his firearm behind him.

"Shamir?" Reyna sounded more insistent. "Did you hear what I said? And why don't you have water in that bucket?"

The jig was up, and Sean knew he only had a split second to make his play.

He whipped the pistol around as he raised his head.

The ploy could have worked if Reyna hadn't been standing where she was. If she'd even been a foot or so to the right, Sean's sights would have immediately lined up on Craig's face, and the game would have ended.

But she wasn't standing off to the right. She stood squarely between Sean and Craig.

Sean's instincts kicked in. "Move out of the way, Dr. Oluk."

Fear struck her face. Her eyelids widened, and the color drained from her skin, turning to ash.

Before she could react, Craig grabbed her, wrapping his arm around her throat and pulling her close.

It was one of the worst-case scenarios Sean was trying to avoid.

"You know, Sean? You really are some kind of magician, aren't you? Why can't you just die?"

"I'm like a bad rash, Craig. I'm sure you probably know all about those."

Craig's brow furrowed at the insinuation. Then he realized it was just an insult. Craig might have been educated, but he wasn't the quickest.

Tommy held his ground on the other side of the room, his weapon pointed at Brent, whose hand was by his side, ready to draw his own.

Craig moved his free hand and produced a pistol, making a show of raising it and pressing it to the base of Reyna's skull.

To his credit, Craig was doing everything right in his role of taking a hostage. He used her as a human shield and gave almost no room for Sean to take the shot.

Sean had done this dance before, both before he worked for the IAA and since. Usually, he wouldn't have hesitated and would have eliminated the target with pinpoint accuracy. But the situation hadn't allowed for that, and now he was in a stalemate, waiting for an opening—however slim.

"Put the gun down, Sean," Craig ordered.

"You know I can't do that, Craig. Let her go. She doesn't have anything to do with this."

"Sean?" Reyna said. Her lips trembled. Terror filled her eyes with tears. She glanced over at the other side of the room. "Tommy?"

"Hey," Tommy managed. "Long time."

"Shut up!" Craig barked. "Both of you, put the guns down, or I kill her."

"We both know you're not a killer, Craig. You can act like one all you want, but deep down you know you're a coward. Look at you, hiding behind her. I can smell you sweating, Craig. I can hear your breath." Sean knew how to play this psychological game. He'd done it for decades now. "You also know there's only one way out of here, and if you kill her, you die. Is that how you want to go out?"

He saw the questions running through Craig's eyes: the doubt, the worries, the desperation.

Craig was an archaeologist not a tactician, a warrior, or even really a criminal for that matter. This was new to him, and Sean figured he was operating purely based on what he'd seen on television and in the movies.

Sean knew Tommy had a much better angle to take the shot from where he stood, but distance made it risky, and the second he squeezed the trigger, Brent would make his move.

"There's no way out of this for you, Craig," Sean insisted. "Except either dead or in handcuffs. I'd choose the latter if I were you. But seeing how you left me and Tommy in ancient underground chambers twice in the last few days, I'd be okay if you choose the first way."

"How did you get out of it this time, Sean? There was no other way. I saw you in there when the doors closed."

"There's always another way," Tommy answered for his friend. He saw Brent weighing the options, trying to determine if he could pull his pistol and take Tommy down, but at that range, whether Tommy was a good shot or not wouldn't matter. It was an easy kill from there.

"Let her go." Sean continued speaking to Craig. "She doesn't need to be involved with this. She's innocent. This is between you and me. Let her go," he repeated. Sean saw the indecision in his eyes and kept prodding, just as he'd been trained to do so long ago. "You made this choice, Craig. You knew the risk when you decided to take this path. There's no going back now. Give it up. I know you thought the rewards would be worth it. But it's over. Put the gun down, and let Dr. Oluk go."

Tears streamed down Reyna's face. The color had returned to her cheeks, but now they burned with fear.

"None of this would have happened if you weren't so stupid, Sean. You and Tommy sticking to your principles. Someone is going to find that scroll someday. And they're going to make more money than anyone on earth with it. But you had to be all high and mighty."

"We don't even know if the scroll is real, Craig," Tommy said. "Or if that contraption really works. People have tried to recreate it. None have really succeeded."

"But with the blueprints we will," Craig insisted. His voice carried the tone of insanity Sean had heard far too many times before. It was the sound of a man who'd gone over the edge, diving headfirst into total obsession.

"Sooner or later, Craig, the cops are going to show up. Then what are you going to do? You can't shoot your way out of this one. And you don't want to do this. You don't want anything to happen to her. Leave her out of this."

Sean thought, for a second, his words were getting through to Craig. Brent still looked like a coiled snake ready to strike. Burning embers of rage smoldered in his eyes, and his jaw remained tightly clenched.

"What's in the bust, Sean?" Craig asked. "What's in the bust?"

"*Seven,*" Tommy mused.

"What?" Craig asked.

"The movie. *Seven.* Final scene. This is the second time you've referenced it."

"Shut up, Tommy," Craig snapped.

"That one was a stretch, Schultzie," Sean said, his tone even and his eyes remaining locked on the target. "First one was spot on."

"You both came here for the bust. Go ahead. Tell her, Sean. Tell her you came here to break it open and find something inside. What is it? Huh?"

Disappointment displaced the look of fear in Reyna's eyes. "What is he talking about?" she asked.

Sean sighed. He started to speak, but Tommy beat him to it.

"We have reason to believe there is a map inside the bust, Reyna. A map that leads to the location of the Archimedes Scroll, an ancient papyrus that contain the schematics of his superweapon."

He realized the statement probably sounded insane to her, but at the same time he knew the longer he stalled, the better chance there would be of more help arriving. Then again, if the cops showed up, they were just as likely to think he and Sean were the bad guys.

"Tommy?" Reyna said, her voice cracking. "What do you mean, inside the bust?"

"They were going to steal it and destroy it," Craig answered. "They were going to break it open to find what was inside. I heard them talking about it before."

"Is that true?" she pressed.

"We came here to analyze the bust," Tommy said. "Actually, we came to ask your permission to analyze it."

Before she could respond, the door buzzed, and Hanif burst in.

"Drop your weapons!"

No one had seen him walk by the window. Sean guessed he must have ducked down the same way he and Tommy did before they entered. He would have only done it that way if he'd seen what was happening through the window.

The second Hanif spoke, Tommy made a critical error. For an instant, he twisted his head around to locate the new threat, and that's when the snake struck.

Brent drew his pistol in a flash, and fired a shot.

Forced to defend his friend, Sean turned his weapon at Brent before he could squeeze off another round, and fired. The round missed Brent by inches, burrowing into the wall behind him, and sending the man sprawling for cover.

Brent's shot missed Tommy, who dove to the floor behind a table. He looked back toward the door where Hanif had been standing and saw the man slumped against the wall, clutching his shoulder with blood oozing between his fingers.

He grimaced from the pain, and his chest rose and fell deeply. But he'd live.

After Brent dove out of view, Sean started to twist his pistol back toward Craig, but Craig leveled his weapon and fired. Sean ducked clear as the round cracked the air over his head and smashed into something behind him at the other end of the room.

"Give it up, Craig," Sean ordered. "There's no way out of this."

"Stand down, or we kill the guard!" Brent shouted back.

Sean looked over at Tommy crouching behind a table. He shook his head as if he didn't know whether or not Brent had the shot.

"I have him in my sights, and I will kill him," Brent added.

Tommy looked back at Hanif, who turned his head and looked toward the opposite end where Brent's voice came from. He offered a meager nod, as if to confirm Brent was telling the truth.

Sean waved at Tommy, motioning him to come over to his position.

While Tommy effectively had the exit blocked if Brent and Craig tried to go that route, the fact that Brent could shoot the innocent guard changed everything. At the same time, Sean wasn't about to put down his weapon. Then they'd all be dead.

Maybe Craig didn't have the guts to kill them all in cold blood, but Sean knew Brent did.

Tommy didn't understand the logic of Sean's request but shuffled across the floor until they were side by side.

"What are you doing?" Tommy mouthed.

Sean merely shook his head. Getting out of this jam wasn't going to be easy, and he had a bad feeling it was going to get worse.

36

"Leave Reyna here, and you can go," Sean said over the counter behind his head. "She isn't a part of this."

"Sure, Sean," Craig replied. "We let her go, and we'll just take your word that you'll let us walk out of here."

"You have my word. Unlike yours, it actually means something."

"Is that supposed to be a jab, Sean? One of your little insults to make me feel guilty?"

"Is it working?"

"You know, you really are pathetic," Craig said. "And so cliché. You have my word? Really?"

"One of us didn't stab the other in the back and leave them for dead in Cleopatra's tomb. And then again in the Hall of Records."

"What?" Reyna spat. "What did you just say?"

"That's right, Doc," Craig said. "We found the lost tomb of Cleopatra. And the fabled Hall of Records. Not a bad week's work, huh?"

"Technically," Tommy said, "Sean and I found the Hall of—"

"Shut up!" Craig barked.

"You're all the same," Reyna drawled. "Just a bunch of bloody treasure hunters looking for fame and fortune."

"Sounds like she knows you, Tommy."

"Reyna," Tommy said. "That isn't true. I know it seems like that sometimes, but that isn't who I am. I know you don't agree with how we do things. And I know I hurt you all those years ago."

"Whoa!" Craig interrupted. "What is going on here? Is this one of those daytime shows with all the shocking big reveals? Is Jerry hiding around here somewhere?"

"I'm sorry, Reyna. I really am. You were a good friend. I never wanted our friendship to end."

"Touching," Brent cut in. "But we need to get going."

"We're not putting our guns down, Craig," Sean said. "Your pet knows we can't do that. You'll kill all of us."

"Oh. Maybe if I gave you my word, Sean. Oh, right. I'm not an idiot. So, here's how this is going to go down. We're going to walk out of here. And Tommy, your friend is coming with us. So, don't do anything stupid. Again, anyway."

They heard shuffling from the direction where his voice had come from a moment before.

"You shoot at us," Brent warned, his voice now closer to the windows, "the guard dies. And so does your friend."

He appeared first at the end of the row and looked down at Sean and Tommy, both crouching behind a table with pistols pointed at him.

"That's a good place for you both," Brent snarled. "Couple of cowards."

He kept his pistol aimed at the guard on the floor. Hanif was beyond Sean's and Tommy's vision, and they hoped he was okay. Shock had probably set in, but there was little chance he'd bleed out from the wound.

Craig appeared next, still holding Reyna around the neck as they side stepped along the window.

The look of fear in Reyna's eyes ripped Tommy's heart out. He'd brought this to her doorstep—at least he felt like he did—and now all he wanted to do was make it right.

"There's nothing in the bust," she said as Craig ushered her out of view.

"Shut up," Craig ordered.

"But maybe you can come up with something off the top of your head."

"I said shut up."

Brent reached the wounded guard and kicked his pistol to the end of the room, where it clanked against the wall. Then he opened the door and held it for his partner and the hostage.

Sean and Tommy both stood slowly in time to see Craig jerk her toward the door, still forcing her between him and the two men pointing their weapons his direction.

"We'll get you out of this, Reyna," Tommy said. "I promise."

Craig dragged her out through the door, and once they were out in the hall, Brent allowed the door to close. Then he raised his pistol and fired a shot into the RFID scanner before following Craig down the corridor and out of sight beyond the windows.

Sean and Tommy quickly hurried over to the glass, catching view of them again as they pushed ahead. The villains weren't being stupid. Craig pulled Reyna backward toward the exit while Brent watched ahead in case anyone happened to walk in.

There were some lab techs working in one of the other rooms, but they might have been so engrossed in their work that they likely wouldn't even notice someone passing by. Maybe, Sean thought, it was better that way. If they did see the two gunmen and the hostage, they'd become loose ends. And loose ends met dead ends.

Sean rushed over to the guard and crouched down to check on him while Tommy pushed on the door handle. It didn't budge, and the door wouldn't open.

"You okay?" Sean asked the guard, inspecting the wound. His shirt was wet with dark, sticky blood.

Hanif nodded, but his ashen face told a different tale.

"You're going to be all right," Sean said. "I'll call an ambulance." He took out his phone and started to make the call.

"The door won't budge," Tommy announced.

Hanif shook his head. It was a feeble, almost uncontrolled motion. "It sounded like he... shot the security pad. The doors lock..." He took a few breaths before continuing. "If someone breaks the scanner. It's a counter... measure."

"Yes," Sean said into his phone to the dispatcher who answered. He gave the address, explained that there was a gunshot wound and to please send help immediately.

The dispatcher said they would send someone right away and asked Sean to remain on the line. Instead, he ended the call and turned his phone off before stuffing it into his pocket.

He looked down at the guard. "You said the door won't open?"

"Not... without the security override."

"Will the cops be able to do that?"

His head bobbed. "Yes."

"Next question. Are these windows bulletproof, or reinforced?"

Hanif frowned, confused by the query. Then he shook his head.

"Good."

Sean turned, picked up the nearest chair, and threw it into the glass eight feet from where Hanif sat on the floor.

The window shattered from the force as the chair flew through and out into the corridor.

Sean used his pistol grip to clear away jagged shards sticking up from the sill and to knock out the ones hanging from overhead.

"Schultzie, help me with this table," Sean ordered.

He moved to one side of a long, empty table and grabbed underneath it. Tommy took the other side, and the two lifted it then moved it over to the wall until it was flush under the broken window.

"Help is on the way," Sean said to the guard.

"I'll be fine," Hanif said, his voice scratchy and weak. "Help Reyna."

Tommy climbed onto the table and jumped through the opening, landing hard on his feet on the other side. He stumbled to the opposite wall and braced himself against it to stop his momentum.

Sean followed right behind him, twisting sideways as he ducked and jumped through the broken window.

He landed with near-perfect balance on the other side and immediately raised his weapon toward the far end where the exit was located.

But Craig and Brent were nowhere to be seen.

"Come on. We can't let them get away."

Sean sprinted toward the door, but Tommy hesitated, noticing something on the ground. He bent down and picked it up before barreling after his friend.

When Sean reached the doors to the lobby, he burst through them with a loud bang. He normally would have never done it that way. His typical strategy would be to push open one door, clear the right side, then the left before going through. But he didn't have time for strategy right now, or doing things the way the manual said. Reyna's life was in danger.

He rushed across the lobby to the front doors and barged into them, knocking the one on the left open.

Bright sunlight blinded him for a half second. He shielded his eyes from the sun with the back of his hand in time to see Brent level his pistol at him.

Sean ducked back as the gun popped. The round thumped into the metal part of the door six inches from Sean's shoulder. He heard the engine rev to life; then the tires squealed.

He ducked his head through the door again, aiming his pistol at the vehicle, but Brent whipped the car out of its spot then accelerated forward.

Sean never had a chance to take the shot. Even if he could have, the risk of hitting Reyna was too great. He saw her and Craig in the back seat, and his eyes met Craig's a second before the car turned out of the parking lot and onto the road.

Tommy ran loudly to the door and slowed to a stop next to Sean.

"What happened?" he asked, panting for breath.

"They got away," Sean said. "And we have no way of knowing where they'll go."

Tommy held up a black flash drive attached to a black Mercedes key fob. "Maybe not. We might be able to catch them in her car. I think Reyna dropped this for us as they were dragging her away. I found it in the hallway back there. And maybe she must have wanted us to see whatever is on there."

"We'll never catch them now," Sean said. "They'll have blended into traffic and disappeared on any number of side streets. But we will take the car. Can't risk waiting for a cab and then get nicked by the cops."

Sean grabbed the fob from his friend and marched over to the sedan. Tommy trotted over to the passenger side, and when Sean unlocked the doors climbed into the luxuriously stitched black leather seat.

Sean sat down, adjusted the seat position, and pressed the ignition button. The engine roared to life with a glorious growl.

"The last thing she said was maybe we could find something off the top of our heads," Sean recalled. "Did that mean anything to you?"

"No." Sirens whined in the distance. "But I think maybe we should try to figure that out somewhere else. Sticking around here till the cops arrive sounds like a bad idea."

"Yeah," Sean said. "Let's get somewhere safe and see what's on that thumb drive. Maybe we aren't dead in the water yet."

37

Sean eased into a chair in the back corner of the café and peered at the door while Tommy stirred milk and sugar into his coffee across the table. Ghostly tendrils of steam danced from the surface of Sean's white mug of black coffee.

"You done?" Sean asked as Tommy finished stirring in what must have been a gallon of milk. "Or did you want some coffee with that milk and sugar?"

"Hey, I don't tell you how to butter your biscuits."

"I don't butter my biscuits. If you make them properly, there's already butter in them. Now gravy on the other hand," he flashed his easy grin, "I'll put that on them. Sometimes I think maybe you've never even made your own biscuits."

Tommy stopped stirring his coffee and stared at Sean with refined disdain. "Of course I've made biscuits before. I'm Southern, ain't I?"

Sean held his gaze for a moment like a poker player trying to decide if the opponent was bluffing, then smiled, reached down to his bag by his side, and pulled out his laptop.

He set it on the table and flipped it open, careful not to spill the coffee next to it. "Yes, you are, my friend. Hand me the flash drive." He held out his palm.

"Would it kill you to say please?" Tommy complained.

"Are we really doing this?"

Tommy raised his eyebrows to emphasize his point.

"Fine. Please, hand me the flash drive."

"Was that so hard?" Tommy asked, passing him the storage device.

"Yes. Yes, it was."

Sean stuck the drive into his computer, and when it populated on the left-hand menu, clicked on it to open the files.

"I hate that they took her," Tommy said, his voice distant and full of regret. "I can't imagine how scared she must be right now, and how confused on top of it all. She trusted Craig."

"That's how he got to her," Sean said. "He used that trust to get what he wanted. Or close to it, anyway."

"I know. I just—"

"There's nothing we could have done to stop them, Schultzie," Sean interrupted. "We trusted Craig, too. Sure, in hindsight we were wrong. But you know what they say about hindsight."

"It's always twenty-twenty."

"Right. Craig left us for dead. Twice. We're lucky to even be here right now."

"Maybe it would have been better for Reyna if we weren't. She probably just would have helped them get what they want and been back in her office by now."

"You don't believe that any more than I do. More likely, they would have used her to get to the bust, then killed her. Maybe Craig wouldn't have pulled the trigger, but he would have let Brent do it."

Tommy nodded absently. "You're probably right."

"But we still have a chance to save her. They don't know where the scroll is."

"Neither do we."

"No, not yet. But maybe what's on this drive will." Sean scrolled through the list of things Reyna had saved on the device until he came to one that said Cicero. He clicked on it, and several more files opened in the next submenu.

"This is interesting," he mumbled.

"What?" Tommy stood, pulled his chair around so he could see the screen, and sat down. He sipped his coffee as he peered at the monitor and then the image files Sean had found.

Sean clicked on one, and the file opened, filling most of the screen. "These are scans of the bust." The image was of the left side of the bust's head.

He minimized that image and opened the next one in order. This one displayed a close-up of the bust's face. Sean repeated the process, finding the back of the head, the other side, and then finally clicked on the last image file.

It bloomed across the screen and gave a view of the top of the bust. Sean leaned closer, studying the detail of the hair on top of the head.

"Does that look strange to you?"

"The hair? I guess so. Amazing how well preserved it is. Especially considering what it must have gone through over the last few thousand years. I wonder—" Tommy stopped in mid-sentence. "Wait. That looks like—"

"Italy," Sean finished. "It looks like the boot of Italy."

"Yeah. But what's it doing there? Why would the sculptor do that?"

"Look here," Sean said, pointing below the sole of the boot.

"I guess that's Sicily?" Tommy guessed.

"Notice the black mark there?"

"Sure. Probably just some carbon scoring or something."

Sean slowly turned his head toward his friend, scowling at him. "Was that a *Star Wars* reference?"

Tommy brimmed with humor. "Why? Was it funny?"

"A little. Focus." Sean returned his attention back to the screen. "Notice the indentation on the surface of the island where that discoloration is? If I was betting, I'd say that was done deliberately."

They both gasped. The realization hit them like a tidal wave against the shore. The mark was in the shape of an eye.

"The Eye of Horus," Sean whispered. "That's where it must have been hidden."

"So, you're telling me that you think that's where we'll find the Archimedes Scroll?"

Sean opened the web browser and then typed in a search for Sicily. The island appeared on a map in the right-hand corner, and he clicked on it to enlarge it. Then he zoomed in until he saw the word *Syracuse*. He and Tommy stared at it for a minute before he clicked on the image of the bust's head again, then dragged it to the side so they could compare both pictures.

"You can't be serious," Tommy breathed. "That's incredible. The map was carved into the top of the bust."

"Archimedes was from Syracuse. He died there, too. That's where his supposed burial site is located."

"The lost tomb of Archimedes," Tommy said, his voice utterly reverent. "Wouldn't that be something? We find the tombs of Cleopatra and Archimedes on the same case?"

"And the Hall of Records. Heck of a haul."

Sean zoomed in closer on the map, then more on the sculpture. He repeated the process several times until the satellite view of Syracuse displayed buildings, streets, soccer fields, parks, and historical ruins.

He closed in on the sculpture again, and then adjusted the map—scrolling to match the locations.

"Hey, Schultzie, see if you can find anything about Cicero in Syracuse. Did he ever visit the town? Was there anything notable about it if he did?"

"I don't need to look that up. We know he went to Syracuse. He also documented the discovery of Archimedes' tomb. He claimed it had fallen into neglect and was covered with brush and bushes."

"Wait. If Cicero documented the location, what are we even doing? I thought this was some kind of hidden deal."

"It is," Tommy said. "After he found the tomb, Cicero cleaned it up, turned it into a place of honor. But over the years it fell into disrepair again. I believe Cicero may have moved the burial site to a more secure location, a place where it wouldn't be damaged or looted. Syracuse, and Sicily in general, had a history of being attacked, sieged, invaded, and plundered."

"Okay," Sean said, a little disappointed. "So, the search continues."

Tommy opened his laptop and set it on the table adjacent to Sean's. Once the screen flickered to life, he opened the web browser and performed a quick AI search with the chatbot. The answer began populating rapidly across the black box in the center of the screen. It finished within fifteen seconds, providing a two-paragraph answer to the query.

"Oh," Tommy gasped. "I guess I either didn't know, or forgot, about this. Syracuse is where Cicero gave the Verrine Orations."

"The what?" Sean looked across at his friend. "I've never heard of those."

"They were pretty famous, actually. Here, let me find more details." Tommy opened a new window and entered a new set of keywords. After the results popped up, he clicked the first one and read the information to Sean.

"The Verrine Orations were a series of speeches Cicero delivered in 70 BC. They are named after Gaius Verres, a former governor of Sicily, whom Cicero prosecuted for extortion and corruption."

"So, they had Mafia issues way back then," Sean said dryly.

"Apparently. The orations are a significant part of Cicero's legal and rhetorical legacy, showcasing his skills as a lawyer and orator, as well as providing insights into Roman law, politics, and society at the time.

"Cicero's prosecution of Verres was notable for several reasons. First, it was a considerable legal challenge because Verres had significant political connections and wealth—that does sound like Mafia—which he could use to influence the outcome of the trial. Second, Cicero strategically chose to speed up the trial process by focusing on the overwhelming evidence of Verres' misdeeds in Sicily, rather than following the usual lengthy procedure of Roman legal battles. This strategy forced Verres and his defense to confront the charges directly without extensive delays."

"Smart. Sounds like a system designed to protect those in power with miles of red tape."

"No kidding," Tommy agreed. He went on reading. "The Verrine Orations consist of seven speeches, although only the first two were actually delivered in court. The remaining five were prepared for subsequent stages of the trial but were never presented because Verres went into exile after realizing the likelihood of his conviction, given the strength of Cicero's evidence and arguments."

"Nothing like running away from your problems," Sean quipped. He said it in a lighthearted way, but the statement struck a chord with him. Again, he thought about the efforts he'd made in the past to get away from the hectic and often dangerous life he'd leaned into so long ago. He had faced those questions before, whether or not he should walk away or stay the course. Each time, he came to the conclusion that he was blessed with a set of skills that placed him in positions others shouldn't.

"The orations provide detailed accounts of Verres' abuses of power," Tommy said, "including extortion, theft, and the mistreatment of both Roman citizens and Sicilian locals. Cicero's arguments not only aimed to convict Verres but also to highlight broader issues of corruption and governance in the Roman Republic. The speeches are an excellent source for understanding Roman legal practices, provincial administration, and the intricacies of Republican politics.

"Beyond their historical and legal significance, the Verrine Orations are masterpieces of Latin rhetoric. Cicero's use of wit, moral indignation, detailed evidence, and appeals to the jurors' civic duty made these speeches a model of effective advocacy and a crucial part of Cicero's enduring legacy in Western literature and legal thought."

He scrolled a little farther, scanning the information until he found something that stuck out in the text.

"That's interesting," he said.

"What?"

"It says here that during the orations, he praised the beauty of the Latomia Quarries."

"Quarries?"

"Mmm-hmm. I've spent some time on Sicily, and been to Syracuse, but I don't recall seeing those." His fingers tapped along the keys, and then he entered a new search. More results populated the screen, and he selected the first one. A map of the city appeared on the right side of blocks of text, along with the location of the quarries highlighted by a purple flag.

"Apparently, there are three stone quarries located to the north of the city. The current name of Latomia is from the Greek *lithos* and *temnos*, which means cut stones. The first stone cutters were active in the sixth century BC. The most famous is the Ear of Dionysus. The Grotta dei Cordari—the Ropemaker's Grotto—is another. It's been closed since 1984."

"Why is it closed? Actually, why isn't the whole thing closed?"

"There's a third one that's open. That one and the first are parks that tourists can visit. The last one is called Latomia dei Cappuccini. It has something of a dark past. Seems the Syracusans forced seven thousand Athenians to work there after they were defeated."

"Ouch."

"Yeah, but look at this map," Tommy said, twisting his laptop so Sean could see the screen. "Compare that spot with what you're seeing on your monitor."

Sean edged his computer closer to Tommy's. Both pairs of eyes darted back and forth. The two friends reached the same conclusion almost simultaneously, but Sean spoke first.

"This solidifies the connection with Cicero and Archimedes," he said. "And the clue on the bust. All of it lines up. And why would he mention the quarries in a speech like that? Seems irrelevant."

"Sounds like Cicero was leaving a big, old Easter egg in that oration. Blatantly referencing what could have been one of the most important documents in history, right under the noses of the Syracusans."

"I wonder if he was flaunting it, teasing them with it."

"That one we may never know. But what we do know is that these quarries might be the location we're looking for."

"But how do we know which one?"

"That first one is interesting," Tommy said. "The Ear of Dionysus."

"God of wine," Sean said.

"And of ecstatic worship. His cult was one of the earliest examples of a Pentecostal-type church—albeit with a different belief system of course."

"That's interesting. Is there anything about Horus or Ra regarding those quarries?"

Tommy read through the text again and shook his head. Then he pulled up the search again and entered a new query.

"This one says that the Ropemaker's Grotto actually reopened in 2021 for visitors. I guess it closed for security reasons back in the eighties."

"You think that's where we'll find the tomb?"

"Maybe. But my money is on the last one."

"The one where the Athenians were forced to work?"

"Yeah. I'm not sure why. Call it a hunch." Tommy started doubting his logic but kept talking to work through it. "Archimedes spent most of his life in Syracuse. Sicily was part of Greece back then. Heck, it was colonized by the Greeks as far back as the seventh century BC. I don't know how much time he spent in Athens, though."

"But we do know he went to Alexandria."

"True. There's nothing else on this page about how the quarries might relate to his tomb, or to the Eye of Horus."

They both knew what had to be done, but it was going to be difficult, and the fact that Reyna was still being held hostage by Craig would only complicate things.

"We have to go to Syracuse," Sean stated. "Find the tomb. Get the scroll and deal with Craig."

"You make it sound so easy," Tommy joked.

The mood at the table dampened. Both of them thought of Reyna being held against her will by Craig and his lackey.

Tommy felt particularly guilty about her abduction due to his prior friendship with Reyna.

"For now," Sean said after a moment if silent contemplation, "we know we need to get to Sicily."

Tommy nodded. "I'll call the pilots and make sure the jet is ready to go ASAP."

"I suspect we might be getting a call pretty soon from Craig."

"Why wait?"

38

Brent shoved Reyna to the floor. Tears stained her eyes, streaking the mascara from her eyelashes down across her cheeks. She yelped when she hit the concrete, then cowered beneath the men who'd brought her here.

They'd found an abandoned home on the outskirts of the city and broken in through the back door after parking their rental car in the back where no one would see it from the road. The closest building was a thousand feet away, and it appeared no one was home there, either.

Here, they could regroup and figure out their next move.

Brent drew his pistol and pointed it down at the terrified woman. She curled up in the corner, covering part of her face with her forearms as if that would protect her.

"Tell us about the bust," Brent demanded.

"What? What do you want to know?" Her voice was full of desperate fear. She sounded like a child who'd just been punished for something she hadn't done.

"You ran the analysis on the sculpture," Craig said with menace. "Surely, you must have found something unusual about it, an anomaly of some kind. What was it?"

She shook her head vehemently in denial. "No. I didn't find anything. I swear it. One of our teams discovered the bust in the water at Thonis-Heracleion. We cleaned it up, scanned it, and prepared it to be put on display. That's all."

"You're lying!" Craig thundered.

"What are you talking about?" Reyna demanded, raising her voice. Fear and confusion fueled her righteous indignation. "What is all this about?"

"That bust contains a map. Something that points to the location of the Archimedes Scroll."

"What scroll?" she shouted through the tears. Her voice cracked, and she coughed.

Craig lowered his voice and held out his hand for Brent to lower the weapon. Maybe he'd gone too far pushing her this way. He'd allowed his own frustration and desperation to take control of his emotions, something that rarely happened. Then again, in his previous life he had been fairly docile—a beta by most accounts.

Now that he felt a sense of power and control for the first time in his life—other than being a supervisor over an excavation—he didn't want to lose that. Pressure was mounting, and the fact that Sean and Tommy were still out there hunting for the scroll didn't make things better.

But Craig knew he had leverage at this point.

He held no misgivings about Sean and Tommy somehow being arrested at the warehouse. It surprised Craig that the two hadn't followed them, though Brent had done a good job at making sure they had a head start. The suppressing fire he'd laid down before speeding out of the parking lot had given them enough time to disappear into traffic and then weave their way through the city streets until they were miles away from Wyatt and Tommy.

Craig had spent most of the drive here looking out the back window, only occasionally glancing over at his prisoner. He figured, correctly, that the pistol digging into her side would keep her quiet, or at least from doing anything stupid.

"Archimedes created a superweapon. You must have heard about it, or even studied it at some point."

Reyna looked confused for a moment, but her nerves settled down briefly as she tried to recall what she knew. She stared off at the wall to her left as she answered. "The weapon that could destroy enemy ships from the coast by harnessing the power of the sun?"

"Yes. The bust of Cicero points to the scroll, the blueprints that detail how to create that weapon. We need to know what you found, Reyna." He eased his voice to a more soothing, comforting tone. Anyone could have realized he was trying to manipulate her. But the forceful route had yielded nothing.

"What happened to you, Craig? You were a good archaeologist—respected by your peers. You've done such good work in your career. Now you want to be some kind of super arms dealer?" She scoffed. "No one knows if that sun ray even worked. I've heard of people building them based on the premise of the original but with minimal success. What makes you think you are any different?"

"I'm not trying to build a weapon, Reyna. I couldn't care less about the ridiculous wars countries wage. Most of them are proxy conflicts now anyway. My plan is to use those schematics to build a device that can harness the power of the sun and create cheap, readily available energy for all mankind. We will solve the world's power crisis. By doing that, we'll also eliminate poverty, hunger, and even wars. Don't you see? All you have to do is tell us what you found in that bust. There must have been something on one of your scans. An X-ray, perhaps."

Reyna's distant stare didn't waver. It remained fixed on some abstract point on the wall. She kept it there for nearly thirty seconds after Craig's plea. Then, she finally turned her head slowly upward and met his eyes.

"We didn't find anything," she said, her voice cold and resolute. "Whatever you're looking for isn't inside that sculpture. You were mistaken."

Craig blinked several times as he remained fixed on the woman. "I hope, for your sake, you're wrong. Because if that bust truly doesn't have anything to do with finding the Archimedes Scroll, then we have no further use of you."

He turned and walked over to the front door. It was barricaded from the outside with several boards across it. He moved to one of the windows that had likewise been boarded up and peeked through it. There wasn't much to see. The city wasn't visible from that vantage, only desert hills stretching for miles beyond the road.

Craig's mind drifted momentarily. He wondered who'd lived in the dilapidated building before leaving it to crumble.

The barren concrete floors were covered in a thin layer of dust and sand. Scattered fragments of broken tile lay around the room, evidence of what had been there before. He figured anything nice in the house had been stripped by either thieves or the homeowners upon their hurried exodus.

The only furnishings left in the kitchen were the sink, an old stove, and a wooden chair sitting in the corner near a window.

He wondered why the chair was still there but perished that curiosity by refocusing on his current problem.

Either Reyna knew something and wasn't telling them, or she was being honest. The latter could prove to be the end of the road for this entire operation.

He tried to think of another way to get her to talk, but he'd exhausted his options. Except for one.

Craig was willing to try anything at this point, but could he go that far? He'd loosened his morals to the point that they'd all but slipped away into a bottomless abyss. But there was one place he'd yet to go, one measure he would have never considered possible before. Now, though, it seemed he had no choice.

If Reyna did know something about the bust and refused to tell them, maybe she could be coerced through physical pain.

"Brent?" he said, cutting through the intense silence. The man twisted his head to face Craig. "Make her talk."

Brent nodded and took a step over to the woman huddled on the floor.

He holstered his pistol and drew a small knife from inside his belt, unsheathing it in one move. It was a short weapon, barely four inches long. The blade was designed as a personal defense weapon in extremely close-quarters-style combat. Now, however, it was a tool he could use to loosen the lips of a frightened, lying archaeologist.

Brent brandished the knife, allowing what little light that permeated the room to glint off the flat side of it.

She shook her head, and the tears started falling again. "No. Please. I swear. We didn't find anything in the bust. You have to believe me. It's just a sculpture, a tribute to a Roman politician. That's all."

He took another step toward her, letting her feel the threat of his encroachment, like dark clouds forming on the horizon.

"You're lying, Professor," Brent said with venom. "I know it. And you know it. Now, you can make this easy on yourself and tell the truth. Or you can make it hard. If you choose option number two, I'm going to make you hurt in ways you never imagined possible. And I'm going to enjoy it. Do you understand?"

Craig couldn't watch. He averted his eyes and looked back toward the window. He'd have had no problem with torturing Sean and Tommy. They'd been friends, but their senseless betrayal cut him in a way that stoked a fire in his belly. They'd been so foolish, so senselessly shortsighted. If given the opportunity, he thought he would enjoy beating the both of them to a pulp. But Reyna was innocent. She'd done nothing wrong, except for perhaps lying to him right now.

Not that he blamed her for that. He might have done the same if put in that situation.

"Craig. Please. Don't let him do this. What happened to you? What have you become?"

He looked over at her, then to Brent, who glanced back at him for confirmation. Craig nodded, and Brent reached down and grabbed Reyna by the hair.

She screamed in protest.

"Oh, that's not even the start of it, Professor."

"No! Please! Someone! Help!"

Craig's phone vibrated in his pocket, interrupting the proceedings.

"Hold on!" he yelled over the woman's pleas.

Brent looked back at him and waited, still gripping a fistful of her hair in his left hand.

Craig removed the phone from his pocket and looked at the screen. "It's Sean."

He hit the green button and held the device to his ear. "Look who came crawling back," he drawled.

"In your dreams, Craig," Sean answered.

"You called at a bad time. Reyna here was just about to tell us what she discovered inside the sculpture."

"If you're going to lie, Craig, you really need to work on your game. There's nothing in the bust."

Craig froze for a moment. Brent stared at him, obviously wanting to know what was going on, what was being said.

"What makes you think I'm lying, Sean? Bluffing? You shouldn't bluff a player who holds all the cards."

"That's true. But if you know me, you know I don't bluff."

"Why are you calling, Sean? You must have some reason. Are you going to try to convince me to let Dr. Oluk go? Appeal to my merciful side?"

"I wouldn't be so trite," Sean said in a grim voice. "But I will tell you this: If you hurt her, even a little, I'll make sure that pain is brought down on you tenfold."

Craig felt a chill creep across his skin like a hundred spiders. He maintained his calm, though, at least audibly. "So, you called to make idle threats. That's great, Sean. But we're wasting time. I have something you want. The question is, what do you have that I want? You wouldn't have called if there wasn't something inside the bust. And I know you're not risking working with the cops. Not after what just happened at the warehouse. I'm sure your and Tommy's faces are all over the security camera footage. In fact, I would be surprised if they weren't looking for you right now."

"That would put your faces on the recordings, too, Craig. Don't be so linear. The answer is yes, by the way. We have something you want. We know where the scroll is."

The chill that had swept over Craig disappeared, and he felt a tempered sense of hope swell in his gut. He knew whatever Sean was offering would come with a price, though—a catch of monumental proportions.

Dealing with Wyatt and Schultz again would come with great risks, but he'd come too far to surrender now.

"Really?" he asked, elongating the word with a heavy dose of skepticism. "How did you come to that solution?"

"What do you care? We know where it is. At least the general area."

There was what Craig expected to be the first of a few catches. "Let me guess. You'll tell me if I let Reyna go."

"I know that's not going to happen, Craig. You'll want to do some kind of exchange. The scroll's location for Reyna. But even then, how would you know if we were giving you the real place or not?"

"I wouldn't."

"Exactly. So, your request will be that we meet you wherever the scroll is hidden, and we find it together, mitigating all risk on your end."

Craig had to hand it to him; Sean was reading his mind, which made him even more suspicious. "And where is this meeting going to take place, Sean? Somewhere remote where the authorities can ambush us? I don't think so."

"I wouldn't think of it," Sean said. That one was a lie. The first thing he'd considered was luring Craig and Brent into some kind of ambush. While Craig might fall for something like that, a professional like Brent wouldn't. He'd have a backup plan ready, and it would not work out well for Reyna.

"What then?"

"The scroll is located in the tomb of Archimedes in Syracuse."

Craig thought for a second. The answer made sense except for one enormous flaw. "That's great, Sean. Except no one knows where Archimedes was buried. The tomb has never been found."

"I'm aware of that. It hasn't been. Not yet. But we know where it is."

"Okay, I'm listening."

"Syracuse is where Archimedes lived most of his life. He was born there, died there."

"We all know the history, Sean. Get to the point where you tell me what I want to know."

Sean ignored his impatience. "The bust didn't have a map inside it. The bust was the map. It was engraved into the hair of Cicero."

"And this... map pointed to the city of Syracuse?" Craig's skepticism remained intact.

"Yes. As well as the area where the tomb is hidden."

"What area is that?"

"You'll have to meet us in Syracuse to find that out, Craig. If we tell you now, there's no assurances that we'd get Reyna back, or that she'd even still be okay."

"She's alive and well, Sean. I'm no monster."

"Let me speak to her," Sean demanded.

Craig held out his phone and nodded to Brent, who pulled Reyna's hair harder. She yelled at the pain, then Craig returned the phone to his ear. "See? She's fine."

"She doesn't sound fine. What are you doing to her?"

"Just making sure she doesn't try to run. She hasn't been harmed, and won't be if you play your cards right."

"You'd better make sure it stays that way. Get to Syracuse by tomorrow afternoon. Five o'clock local time. I'll call you then, and tell you where to meet us."

"And then your friends from the government will swoop in and take us down? I don't think so."

"We'll be alone, Craig. Just make sure you are, too. If you're not, I'll know."

Craig considered the offer. Getting to Syracuse with a hostage would be tricky. It wasn't as if they could simply buy a commercial airline ticket to get there. Then again, perhaps Brent had a few strings he could pull. And there was always the option of a private charter.

Pricey, for sure, but that cost would be nothing compared to the immense wealth that awaited.

If Sean was telling the truth.

Craig weighed the possibilities. He knew Sean wouldn't risk Reyna's life on a lie, or a trap. This was a gamble Craig had to take. But that didn't mean he wouldn't put precautions in place.

"We'll see you in Italy," Craig said. "And you'd better be alone."

"We will be."

The line went dead, and Craig checked the screen to make sure it had ended. Then he stuffed the phone back into his pocket and looked across the room to Brent. "We're going to Sicily. They believe they know where the tomb of Archimedes is located."

"And the scroll is there?" Brent said, still holding Reyna by the hair.

"That's what they believe. At worst, it will be another clue. But it would make sense for the scroll to be there, if that is indeed where Archimedes is buried."

"What do you want to do?"

Craig considered the question before answering. "Do you have a few guys who can help us out? We need transport to the island, and it might be nice to have a few men watching our backs when we get there."

"Sure," Brent said with a nod. "But that'll cost you."

"The money is of no consequence," Craig said. "Make the call."

39

Tension as thick as Carrara marble Texas chili loomed in the warm air around them.

None of the other visitors to the quarries felt it. They were there on holiday, taking some time to visit a historic landmark before heading off to dinner, or drinks, at one of the many local restaurants.

For Sean and Tommy, however, the tension was palpable.

The sun, a molten orb hanging in the western sky, had begun its descent toward the horizon, casting a golden hue over the ancient quarries of Latomia del Paradiso. Its rays, filtered through the canopy of orange and olive trees that had taken root in this historic place, dappled the rugged limestone walls with light and shadow. The warm air carried the scent of wild herbs and the salt of the distant sea, mingling with the earthy aroma of stone and age.

Sean and Tommy stood in one of the quarry's more secluded recesses, a natural amphitheater carved from the earth by human hands millennia ago, shaded by the many trees that grew in the miniature oasis. The walls around them rose steeply, encrusted with pockets of green, where more plants had found precarious purchase.

The stone absorbed the sound of their voices, ensuring their conversation remained private, an auditory cloak of secrecy.

The place felt suspended in time, the scars of extraction now softened by nature's reclaiming hand. The "floor" beneath their feet was a mosaic of stone and grass, with patches of wildflowers adding bursts of color. Here and there, remnants of ancient columns and carved stones hinted at the quarry's storied past, a silent testament to the difficult, and often terrible, labor of those who had once toiled in this place.

"Ever feel like we're just two kids looking for pirate treasure?" Tommy quipped, breaking the silence as they ventured deeper into the quarry.

Sean forced a laugh. "Yeah, except the pirates are real, and they're not very friendly."

He checked his watch. It was nearly four o'clock.

He and Tommy found themselves in the delicate position of hoping Craig and Brent had found a way to get to Sicily with Reyna in tow. Seeing the two former partners again was the last thing either of them wanted, but for Reyna's sake they had to hope.

The two friends had arrived here at the quarry two hours ago. They spent the time reconnoitering every nook, cranny, vantage point, and tactical position they thought Brent might use to his advantage while they hunted without success for the secret entrance to Archimedes' tomb.

Sean had no misgivings about their enemy obeying the order to come alone. With no way to enforce it, he and Tommy were at their mercy. The one advantage Sean knew he had was the people still wandering about the ruins, but they would be leaving soon, which was a blessing and a curse.

Sean glanced down at the phone in his hand, again checking the time out of habit. The contrast between the ancient setting and the modern technology in his palm was stark, yet it underscored the timeless nature of human conflict and the pursuit of power. The secluded spot they had chosen, away from prying eyes, was perfect for their rendezvous.

The tranquility of the setting belied the apprehension of the moment, a calm before the storm. The quarry, with its beauty and echoes of history, an unwitting witness to the unfolding drama, a reminder of the enduring human saga of adventure and intrigue.

"We have an hour," Sean said. His voice died in the breeze as it reached the rock walls. He saw the nervousness in Tommy's eyes. "You okay, man?"

Tommy bobbed his head once. "I don't like these kinds of situations. Especially when the hostage is someone I once called a friend. Tangling innocent people into messes like this makes me question everything we do."

"I know." Sean peered off toward the western wall of the quarry and stared at the golden, orange painting in the sky.

"What keeps you coming back? If what we do puts people in danger, how do you deal with that?"

"Like, how do I sleep at night?"

"Yeah."

Sean took a deep breath of the dry, warm air and held it for a few seconds. He found doing that stimulated his brain, cleared his mind of unwanted distractions, and helped him clarify his thoughts.

He exhaled. "Bad things happen to good people. It's a sad fact of this journey we call life. And with bad people out there, guys like Brent and Craig, or any others we've encountered in our time working together, more unfortunate stuff is going to happen. They'll kill the innocent, run over them like they're squirrels jumping in front of a car. They drive on as if nothing happened, giving no thought to the animals they've murdered and discarded. Those things would happen if we were involved or not, Schultzie. Craig would have found someone else to partner with if we'd said no from the beginning. And it's possible that whoever he teamed up with would have also found the tomb in Jordan, the chamber in the Hall of Records, and eventually gotten to Reyna in Alexandria. There's no way to know one way or the other."

"Yeah. I guess you're right." Tommy thought about it for a few seconds. "And here I thought we were the only ones out there who could do what we do."

Sean chuckled at the notion. "We both know that isn't true. I can name three or four guys like us, all trying to figure out ancient riddles, solving clues, scouring the earth for treasures lost to history."

The first face to come to mind was his wife's. Adriana was somewhere in the world at that very moment investigating the possible location of a lost piece of history stolen by the Nazis during the war. Other faces danced through his mind's eye, friends who worked for other agencies or on their own in the perpetual hunt to preserve history.

"You okay?" Tommy asked, shaking Sean from his daydreaming state.

"Yeah. I'm good. We have an hour."

"You said that already."

"I was thinking maybe we should stop reminiscing and continue our search for the entrance to the tomb. That way when they arrive, we can go straight there."

A child laughed from somewhere in the quarry. It was distant and came from above. The two looked around for a second but never saw the kid, or their family, that was surely close by.

"I don't know," Tommy said. "Might be nice to split the group up to hunt for the entrance. Divide and conquer. The oldest trick in warfare."

"And in politics," Sean added. "But Craig will never go for it. He knows both you and I are too dangerous to be alone with, even if he is armed." He looked around at the rocks, trees, and shrubs surrounding them. "That reminds me, we should hide our weapons for now."

"Hide them?"

"When they get here, Brent will check us for weapons. If he takes them, we won't get them back."

"Yeah, but if we ditch them, we might not get them back, either. They'll be watching us like an owl."

Sean frowned at the expression. "You mean like a hawk?"

"I thought you hated clichés. And besides, owls can see really well, too. Especially at night. Many biologists think owls are equally deadly predators."

"You're funny." Sean turned and took a step toward a narrow path worn by time into the rocky soil.

"What?" Tommy wondered, throwing up his hands as he followed. "You didn't like the owl bit?"

Sean let the question go unanswered and peered at the wall in front of him. He stood in a corner of the quarry, carefully inspecting the rock. "We should start looking," he said. "The sooner we get Reyna out of this mess, the better. And why postpone the inevitable? If Craig intends to kill us here, we might as well get it over with."

"I love your positivity. You know that, right?"

Sean snorted at his friend's comment. "Just being real, Schultzie."

"So, what are we looking for?" Tommy sidled up next to his friend and planted his hands on his hips as he stared at the rock wall.

"Your guess is as good as mine. A symbol. Something relating to Ra or Horus maybe? The eye keeps popping up in the most unusual places. My guess is that's what we're looking for."

"The quarries are pretty big. We could hunt all day and all night here and still not find what we're looking for."

Sean knew he was right. It was a problem he'd considered. On top of that, there would likely be security personnel here watching over the grounds. They'd more likely operate in patrols, looping around the quarries every so often to make sure no one was trespassing.

"Where would Archimedes want his tomb to be?" Sean said, thinking out loud. "The quarry seems an unusual place."

"It's not far from the sea," Tommy said. "But then again, it's not close either. He did love the sea from what I remember reading about him."

"Who doesn't?" Sean scanned the wall to his left. "What was his greatest contribution to math and science? The one he is most famous for?"

"I thought you knew this stuff?"

"I do. But I'm working through it out loud. Obviously, the Principle of Buoyancy, also known as Archimedes' Principle, is probably the most famous. Wouldn't you agree?"

"Definitely. It states that any object, wholly or partially immersed in a fluid is buoyed up by a force equal to the weight of the fluid displaced by the object. It was the foundation for the science of hydrostatics."

"Thank you, Mr. Wizard," Sean said dryly. "So, what's another one?"

Tommy shrugged, ignoring the barb about Mr. Wizard. "I did like that show, by the way." He glanced off to his right at a tree. The limbs blew in the wind, causing the leaves to shimmer and dance. "I guess the Archimedes Screw would be the other big one. It was a machine used for transferring water from a low-lying body of water into irrigation ditches. It consisted of a hollow shaft, encased in a waterproof tube." He could see Sean was getting ready to yawn, so he wrapped it up. "Anyway, when the bottom end is placed in water and the screw is turned, water is drawn up the ramp and out the top of the tube. People still use that machine in Second- and Third-World countries for their farms."

Sean scratched the back of his head as he considered the information. "Okay, so maybe we look for either one of those Egyptian symbols, or something that relates to the screw or the buoyancy thing. Not sure what that would look like."

"Ugh. How could I forget," Tommy exclaimed. "Of course. It's so simple."

"What is? What are you talking about?"

"The symbol. Cicero said when he found the grave it was marked by a symbol of a sphere with a cylinder inside it. It's an emblem of the buoyancy principle he was so famous for. That must be what we're looking for."

"Great," Sean said. "So, all we have to do is wander around these quarries for a few days and maybe find a symbol that was carved a few thousand years ago."

Tommy sighed. "Yeah, that does seem to be the big drawback."

Sean crossed his arms and paced back away from the wall. He

looked up at the sky and thought. The solution had to be here. And it wasn't just using a brute force technique of scouring the grounds until they located the symbol. There had to be an easier way.

Tommy pulled a bottle of water out of the sleeve on the side of his backpack and unscrewed the top. He took a long drink, gulping several times before he let out a refreshed "Ah."

He held the bottle in his hand as he turned and looked around the quarry. "I forget how dry this part of the world can be," he said. "Even surrounded by the ocean, they don't have the humidity we have back home."

Sean hummed his agreement but said nothing.

"I always have to remind myself to drink more water than usual," Tommy went on before taking another drink.

"Water," Sean said. His eyes brightened with an idea.

"What?" Tommy lowered the bottle from his lips.

"Water. That's it."

Tommy wondered if his friend had started to go a little loopy. "Have... you been hydrating properly? Maybe you should take mine." He extended the bottle toward Sean, who dismissed it with a wave of the hand.

"I have my own. I know how to hydrate. That's not what I'm talking about." He started looking around the area more frantically. "Don't you see? Water was super important to Archimedes. It was the key component to his greatest achievement. It would make sense that his tomb would be near the water. Especially if Cicero relocated it like you said."

"I didn't say that. I suggested he might have moved the grave. We know it isn't near the Agrigentine Gate anymore as Cicero claimed before."

"Right. Like you said, he moved it." Sean ignored his friend's eye roll and continued searching. Then he stopped abruptly and paused. "There's water here in the quarry."

Tommy looked around. "Yeah. So?"

"I mean, not right here. But back over there." Sean pointed to the far corner, where a large rock jutted out from the ground next to a stand of olive trees. "There was a natural spring over there. Remember?"

Finally, Tommy's eyes lit up as well. "Oh yeah? Right. We noticed it on our way through, checking all the vantage points Craig and his men could kill us from."

Sean appreciated the dry, morbid humor of the statement. "Exactly."

"I don't remember seeing a symbol on the rock there, though."

"That's because we didn't look hard enough. Come on. Let's check it out." He looked at his watch. They still had plenty of time.

The two picked their way along the narrow path, winding between outcroppings of shrubs, an olive tree here and there, and loose stones left where they lay for thousands of years before.

They rounded the huge boulder and stopped next to a roughly hewn block of stone that looked as if it had been carved simply to provide a seat to weary travelers. Beyond it, in the corner, a clear pool of water rippled gently in the breeze.

Sean and Tommy followed an ancient set of crumbled stone steps down to the edge and stopped.

The pool was only seven feet wide at most, and from the edge to the wall maybe four feet. Moss and ferns dangled from crags on the wall around it, partially covering the back edge of the water. The oasis was a serene little place, and one easily missed by those not looking for it.

The sunlight illuminated the rock under the surface, but down toward the base of the wall, shadows took over, and neither of the men could see if it simply stopped there or if the shaft went beyond.

"That water is coming from somewhere," Sean said, staring into the liquid. "I bet it's from behind the wall."

"Sean?" Tommy said, tapping on his friend's shoulder with one finger as he pointed to the wall above the water with the other. "I think you're right."

Ten feet above the surface, Sean saw what his friend had noticed. Carved into the rock was a circle six inches in circumference, with a vertical shaft cut into the center of it.

"This is it," Sean whispered.

"Yeah." He looked over at Sean with a grim expression on his face. "You don't think Craig doesn't know how to swim, do you?"

"I think we both know neither of us are that lucky. But one can always hope."

40

Sean and Tommy waited by the pool for exactly thirty-four minutes before they saw Craig and Brent appear at the top of the quarry to the east. Reyna walked between them wearing an exhausted expression that reminded Sean of the countless kidnapping victims he'd rescued in his former career.

She was still wearing the same clothes she'd had on the day before, which didn't surprise him, though he noted that Craig and Brent had changed.

Sean also spotted hired guns accompanying the men and their hostage. The two mercenaries were doing their best to remain inconspicuous, but that was what gave them away.

Whenever someone was trying to look like they were up to no good was a huge clue that they were exactly that.

Sean had called Craig and given him the rendezvous location and exactly how to get there in the shortest amount of time possible.

The sun had vanished behind the western wall of the quarry, though it still provided plenty of daylight for their clandestine operation.

Sean and Tommy had both hidden their pistols in a patch of flowers growing near the boulder, though neither guessed how they would get to the weapons and turn them on their enemies. At the very least, they reasoned Craig and his men wouldn't get their hands on them.

It was a small victory, but at this point the two friends would take what they could get.

They watched as Craig led the way down the stairs into the depths of the quarry, and then across the open area until they stopped twenty feet away.

"So," Craig said, allowing himself a second to look around and take in the surroundings, "is this really where you think the tomb is? Cicero said that he found it at the Agrigentine Gate."

"We're aware of that, Craig," Tommy sneered.

"Why are we here, then?" Craig extended his hands out wide. "Or is this some kind of a trick?" He rounded on Brent, twirled his hand at the two friends. "Make sure they don't have any weapons."

Brent stepped over to Tommy first, motioning for him to raise his hands. Brent began a routine he looked familiar with, checking first the upper body on one side.

"No tricks," Sean said. "You said to come alone. And we did." He nodded to one of the walkways up above on the other side of the quarry. One of Craig's thugs stood there pretending to take in the sights. "I can see you didn't."

Satisfied Tommy was clean, Brent moved to check Sean. Brent was especially cautious with him, digging his pistol deep into Sean's back to reinforce that he was in control.

Craig looked back in the direction Sean indicated then shrugged as if to say, "Aw shucks."

"You got me. But I still have trouble believing you don't have some kind of backup too, Sean. That just isn't your style."

"And I have trouble believing you didn't have the common decency to get Dr. Oluk a fresh change of clothes. I hope you at least let her take a shower."

Sean looked at Reyna with pity. She looked as if she'd given up all hope, like she would never be happy again.

"She took a shower last night before we left for Italy," Craig said.

"It wasn't easy to get transportation on short notice. I hope you're not wasting my time."

"See for yourself," Sean said, turning and extending his left arm toward the wall above the water.

Craig narrowed his eyes, staring at the wall.

While he did, Sean took the opportunity to look back at Brent, who still stood with his hand concealed behind Reyna's back. He knew the killer held a gun. He could tell from the positioning of his arm; the way Brent kept it concealed behind the folds of her cardigan.

Sean and Brent locked eyes for a moment. The testosterone-fueled tension seemed to flood the entire quarry, like two alpha lions facing off to decide who would rule the pride.

"I don't believe it," Craig said. "That's the symbol for—"

"We know, Craig," Tommy cut him off. "That's why we think this is the spot."

Craig looked around, as if searching for a doorway into the tomb. "I'm sorry. What is the spot? I don't see a tomb or catacombs or even a grave."

Tommy shook his head in disappointed mockery. "In the water, man. Seriously. You have to swim through that spring to get to it."

"Have you gone down there?"

"No. We didn't want to get wet and then stand around here in soaked clothes waiting for you and your cronies to show up."

"So, you're not certain?"

Sean grew tired of the argument and broke his stare with Brent. "Look, this has to be the spot, Craig. That's the symbol Cicero mentioned that marked the grave of Archimedes. Clearly, he moved the body here and remade the mark. I imagine only a select few ever knew the reason it was here. If you don't feel like taking a swim with us to check it out, fine by me. Let Reyna go, and do whatever you want with us. But we've done our part."

Craig assessed him with keen, penetrating eyes. He looked down into the water, wondering what kind of trick Sean was trying to pull.

"Convenient," he said. "The water neutralizes our advantage."

Sean knew he was partially correct. "It neutralizes us, too, Craig.

What, am I going to fight you underwater? You're going to have to take a leap of faith here. And you're going to have to trust me. The entrance to the tomb is on the other side of that pool. We've all come this far. Might as well take that leap."

Craig breathed steadily as he considered the scant options available to him. He moved over to the water's edge, keeping a safe distance between himself and Sean, and knelt down next to it. He dipped his hand in the water and drew it up, letting the liquid drip back into the pool.

"Cold?" Brent asked.

"It's not freezing. But it's not hot, either." He faced Sean again. "I'll go first. Then you and Tommy follow." He turned to Brent. "You and Reyna come last. And in case you were thinking of escaping, Dr. Oluk, a pistol can still fire underwater with enough force for the bullet to penetrate your body."

The warning didn't change her exhausted affect, and she didn't say anything in response. She looked like a person who'd completely given up hope.

Craig swept his gaze around at the group, as if checking to make sure everyone understood how this was going to go down. Then he set his bag down on the ground a few feet from the water and removed a head lamp and a flashlight. He switched on the flashlight and then sat down on the lip of the pool, lowering his feet into the water.

It wasn't as cold as he'd thought it would be, even though he'd just tested it with his hand. It was cool but not abrasively so. His socks and shoes instantly filled with the liquid as he lowered them deeper into the pool.

Sean watched as Craig took a breath and dropped down into the water and out of sight.

"Both of you, over to the edge," Brent ordered.

Sean and Tommy exchanged an irritated glance then did as they were told and shifted over to the water's edge.

Brent forced Reyna forward but maintained a safe eight feet between her and the two men.

"What do you see?" Brent asked.

Sean leaned over the water. He saw Craig kicking his legs as he dove deeper into the spring. The waterproof flashlight danced around as he pulled himself through the liquid, until it disappeared underneath an overhang.

"I think he made it through to the other side."

"That or he's drowning," Tommy quipped.

Sean forced an uneasy laugh.

"For your sakes, I hope that isn't the case. Because you're going in next. You first, Sean. And remember. If you do anything stupid—"

"Yeah, I get the gist. You'll kill them both. This isn't my first tango, Brent. I'm sure you're well aware of that."

"Shut up, and get in the water."

"I got it. Jeez. Loosen up, man."

Sean lowered himself down, dropping his feet into the cool water, then he looked back over his shoulder at Brent. "Hey, it's pretty dark down there. Mind if I get a flashlight?"

"I guess you two will just have to risk it," Brent snarled.

"I had a feeling you'd say that," Sean grumbled.

He took a few quick breaths, then a deep one, and plunged in.

The waning sunlight still illuminated the first section of the underground spring, but after a few kicks and strokes, he reached the dark edge where the quarry wall ended about ten feet below the surface.

He made out the dark outline of a smoothly carved archway, but without a light couldn't tell if it was man-made or natural. His instincts suggested it was cut by human hands, but how anyone could have done that underwater so long ago was a baffling and useless thing to ponder at the moment.

Sean had to focus on getting through to the other side.

He'd never been great at holding his breath. A minute was the longest he'd managed, and that was back when he was training with Axis—twenty plus years younger, and in slightly better shape. He'd maintained his physique and athleticism through the years with rigorous training, usually five days per week, but this was different.

His lung capacity was still good; that much he knew. This, however, was a dangerous proposition, especially without a light.

He counted the seconds in his head. Only ten had passed as he cleared underneath the archway and into the darkness on the other side. The blackness around him would have been a claustrophobe's nightmare. Up ahead, he saw a pair of lights that shimmered. Their beams danced in the water around him.

Craig had made it to the surface.

Sean kicked harder, feeling a greater sense of urgency as his time underwater reached closer to thirty seconds.

He broke through, his head shooting up above the rippling water. He gasped, taking in big hulks of air. Craig pointed his flashlights down onto Sean's face, causing him to hold up a hand to shield his eyes from the bright light.

"Do you mind?" Sean complained as he kicked his feet to drive himself over to the landing.

"I guess you were right about this place," Craig said, looking around for a second while keeping the lights focused on the water below.

"Yeah." Sean grumbled and found a natural slope to the stone where he could touch with his feet and walk up out of the water. His clothes and hair were soaked, and he shook his head like a dog before running his hands through his hair to squeeze the water out of it.

He looked back toward the pool, knowing Tommy would be coming up any second—he hoped.

Ten seconds later, his friend emerged, blowing air out of his lungs in a wet mist. He swam over to the natural ramp and waded up out of the water, rubbing his eyes along the way.

"Well, that was uncomfortable," he said.

Craig held a pistol in one hand and a flashlight in the other, aiming the latter down toward the rippling surface.

"I guess we'll see if Reyna is a good swimmer," Craig joked.

Anxiety gripped Sean as he watched the dark pool for signs of the last two people. He saw movement, and then the colors of her cardigan flashed in the light. Another beam followed her as Brent stayed close behind the hostage.

"Come on, Reyna," Tommy urged quietly.

The tension gripped both him and Sean, but it broke the second Reyna's head burst through the water.

As they'd done before her, she gasped for air, relieved to have broken through the surface.

She dog-paddled toward the ledge until her feet found purchase on the ramp below, and then she gradually walked up out of the water.

Brent followed behind her immediately, reaching the surface and then swimming over to the landing while keeping both his pistol and flashlight above water. Once he was on dry land, he tilted the weapon down to allow the water to spill out, then leveled it at the hostage again.

Sean recognized the Glock—a fine firearm. Water, sand, didn't matter. A quick shake, and those guns would fire every time. Even though he was a Springfield man, he respected the quality of the Glock brand.

Brent herded the three prisoners farther into the room, his head lamp and flashlight merging with Craig's to cast an eerie glow onto the walls around them.

The underground chamber was a testament to ancient craftsmanship, circular in shape with walls that had been smoothed over centuries. Intricate carvings and bas-reliefs adorned these surfaces, narrating the life and works of Archimedes through stone. The room's air was cool and damp, filled with the scent of earth and rock long untouched by the sun.

In the center of the chamber stood a pedestal adorned with carefully arranged geometric shapes. These symbols of Archimedes' contributions to mathematics and science were meticulously carved from stone and metal, catching the sparse light and casting elongated shadows across the chamber.

Everyone took in the spectacle in reverent awe. Even Brent seemed to grasp the gravity of what they were seeing.

"What is that?" Reyna asked, the first to speak.

Her question surprised Sean and Tommy, who felt sure she'd be in some kind of shock from being held captive by a couple of psychopaths.

She pointed to a sealed doorway on the far side of the chamber, opposite where they had entered the pool on the other side of the walled divide. Framed by the simplicity of Doric columns, the doorway was constructed from several stone slabs that fit together with extraordinary precision. No mortar filled the gaps between the stones; rather, they were cut so finely that not even a hair could pass between them.

Tommy risked venturing over to the doorway and ran his fingers across one of the seams. "They didn't use anything to adhere these together," he said. "They just fit them all in here with laser precision."

"Sort of like Cusco," Sean added.

"Yeah."

"What is all this?" Craig asked, ripping the awe from the moment to get down to his sinister business. He ran his light beam across the wall, the doorway, and the pedestal in the center of the landing.

Tommy and Sean ignored him, still inspecting the sealed entrance to what they hoped was the tomb of Archimedes.

"Look at that," Sean muttered.

All eyes followed, looking up to the top of the doorway. Above it, the keystone was adorned with the carving of the Eye of Horus, an homage to Egyptian symbolism amid the Greek surroundings, but also to the power Craig believed Archimedes had harnessed millennia before.

Flanking this eye were inscriptions in Ancient Greek, suggesting a blending of cultures and knowledge. This symbol, paired with the Greek inscriptions, hinted at the doorway's significance and the complexity of the puzzle that protected it.

"It's like a tribute to the Library of Alexandria," Tommy said. "A coming together of cultures, knowledge, and learning."

Reyna took a step closer, her fear completely replaced by astonished wonder. "How... is this possible?" she wondered.

"What is that?" Brent asked, pointing at a series of bronze discs set into the walls around the entrance.

"It must be the mechanism to open the door," Sean answered.

"How does it work?"

"I hadn't sorted that out just yet. Would you mind shutting your yap so we can think?"

"I'm going to enjoy killing you, Sean. You know that?"

"Take a number, pal."

Sean went back to analyzing the ancient puzzle that stood as their final barrier between them and being the first to lay eyes on the tomb of Archimedes in over two thousand years.

The mechanism to open this sealed doorway was ingeniously integrated into the chamber's design. Each of the bronze discs was inscribed with Ancient Greek letters and geometric symbols. These discs were connected to a network of levers and gears concealed within the chamber's stone structure, culminating in a sophisticated puzzle that required both a deep understanding of Archimedes' mathematical principles and a familiarity with Ancient Greek language and mythology.

To solve the puzzle and gain entry through the sealed doorway, the discs needed to be aligned in a specific sequence. It was obvious to Sean and Tommy that the task was not merely about physical alignment; it involved deciphering a riddle inscribed alongside the Eye of Horus—a riddle that spoke to the balance between light and shadow, the physical and the metaphysical.

"What does that say?" Craig demanded. A sense of urgency and impatience drove his words. They were so close now, and he didn't want to wait any longer.

Tommy read the ancient inscription out loud, slowly working his way through the translation. "In the shadow where light meets the eye, balance the spheres where the secrets dwell. Through Greek wisdom and Horus' gaze, unlock the tomb of the great student."

"Any idea what that means?"

Tommy nodded, though he wasn't absolutely sure. "I think so." His eyes darted from one disc to another.

Sean also studied the layout of the mechanism. "It's a safe bet that if we get this wrong, something bad is likely to happen."

Craig narrowed his eyes, matching the menacing expression on his face. "Then don't screw up."

"The solution lies in manipulating the discs to reflect these concepts," Reyna said to the surprise of everyone else. "Achieving a harmony between the elements symbolized by the Eye of Horus and the inscribed Ancient Greek knowledge."

Tommy and Sean both looked at her, impressed with the elegant solution.

"Nice," Tommy said.

She shrugged as if it didn't matter. "It seems pretty obvious to me."

"Maybe you have a little treasure hunter in you after all."

"I wouldn't go that far," she countered but blushed at the suggestion.

"Fine," Craig said. "Open the door. But we will be watching you carefully. Don't think you can trigger some ancient booby trap like you did before to get away."

"Wouldn't dream of it, Craig," Sean answered. He looked to Tommy. "You want to do it? Or you want me?"

"I will," Reyna said, cutting in.

They both turned to her, surprised again.

"Are you sure?" Sean asked. "It could be dangerous."

"I'm sure." She affirmed the decision with a nod and warily stepped to the doorway, raising her hand to the first disc on her left.

41

In the dimly lit confines of the ancient underground chamber, Reyna stood before the sealed doorway, her intense focus on the bronze discs embedded in the walls. With the riddle echoing in her mind, she fully understood the weight of the moment. The solution to the ancient puzzle was within her grasp, a key that could unlock secrets hidden for millennia. Beyond that, her life and the lives of Sean and Tommy also hung in the balance.

Not that it mattered. She had no misgivings about getting out of this place alive. She doubted either of them did as well.

After being abducted by Craig and Brent, she'd surfed a wave of emotions—panic, fear, shock, and eventually resolution. She didn't want to die, but Reyna knew that was going to happen someday, whether she wanted it to or not. If she was going to go, then it would be on her own terms.

She wasn't some damsel in distress. She'd built a career out of nothing, coming out of a poor home with little chance of a future. Over time, she had become one of the foremost archaeologists in the world, respected by her peers, and a teacher to those who would come after.

Reyna held her hand out in front of the first disc, hesitating for a moment as she studied the inscriptions, and the messages etched in time.

The Ancient Greek letters and geometric symbols held the answer. She understood that these were not merely decorative elements, but part of a sophisticated mechanism designed by minds as brilliant as Archimedes himself. The Eye of Horus spoke to his appreciation of one of the world's earliest and most powerful civilizations, but beyond that it held esoteric wisdom, secrets that had been purged through millennia in desperate grasps for control by those whose sole focus was material power.

Reyna stretched her fingers toward the first disc, brushing them against the cool bronze. She carefully rotated it, feeling the weight of the metal and the resistance of time. Still, she was surprised that the thing actually moved after so many years had passed—another tribute to the ingenuity of the builders of this place.

The disc clicked into place with a satisfying sound, its symbols aligning with the patterns described in the riddle. Reyna moved to the next disc, repeating the process until that disc also aligned with what she believed was the correct solution.

Each click and shift of the discs echoed through the chamber, a testament to the mechanism's enduring precision, but also a harbinger of potential danger if she were to get one component wrong.

The men in the room watched in rapt silence.

Sean thought he caught Craig flinching each time one of the discs clicked. He must have been shell-shocked from his previous experience in the Hall of Records, fearful that any wrong move might bring the ceiling down on them or close some unseen door behind them and barricade them in this place forever—adding one more tomb to the quarry's bowels.

No one dared say anything for fear they might cause her to slip up and make a mistake. Sean and Tommy knew she must have surely been exceedingly nervous, but they also figured an excitement probably pulsed through her at the same time. They both felt it, and this was her first time—that they knew of—for her working with anything like this.

Her job had always been entrenched in the unglamorous side of archaeology—digging, sifting, wading through mud. This was a whole different ballgame.

As she worked, Reyna's mind raced, piecing together the fragments of knowledge gleaned from her studies and the clues they had discovered on their journey. The balance between light and shadow, the Principles of Buoyancy and Leverage, the wisdom of the Greeks intertwined with the mysticism of the Egyptians—all these elements were encapsulated in the puzzle before her.

The arrangement of the discs required not just a linear solution but a spatial understanding of how the symbols interacted with each other and the environment. Reyna realized that the reflections in the water basin beneath the niches—fed by a steady drip from the ceiling above—played a crucial role. The water, acting as a mirror, inverted the symbols, suggesting that the puzzle's solution lay in considering not just the physical arrangement of the discs but their reflections—the duality of above and below, the seen and unseen.

Certain this had to be correct, Reyna adjusted the discs again, aligning them so that their reflected images in the water's surface formed a coherent pattern. The symbols, once fragmented and obscure, now told a story of balance and harmony, echoing the principles that had guided Archimedes' work.

After nearly five minutes of working through the puzzle, the last disc clicked into place. A palpable sense of anticipation mingled with trepidation.

Reyna stepped back; her breath held in suspense. For a moment, nothing happened; the chamber remained silent, the doorway sealed. Then, almost imperceptibly at first, a low rumble vibrated through the stone floor.

The unseen, aged mechanism began to activate. The stone slabs of the doorway, immovable for thousands of years, started to shift. Dust and small pebbles tumbled from the crevices as the ancient gears, hidden within the walls, turned at long last. The movement was slow, deliberate, as if the chamber itself was awakening from a long slumber.

Everyone in the room watched, awestruck, as the slabs retracted, sliding into recesses in the walls with a grace that belied their massive weight. It was an engineering marvel and a testament to the ancients' ingenuity—a doorway and a machine that had stood the tests of millennia, guarding its secrets with a puzzle that required wisdom and insight to solve.

As the door opened, it revealed a dark corridor beyond. A cool draft whispered through the chamber, carrying with it the scent of untouched air, and the promise of discovery as well as danger.

Sean stared into the opening. The passage stretched into darkness, beckoning them forward into the heart of the tomb.

He and Tommy glanced over at Reyna. They could sense her heart racing with the realization of what they had just done. They had unlocked the door to Archimedes' tomb, overcoming a challenge that may well have repelled countless seekers over the centuries.

The opening of the door was more than a physical passage; it was a symbolic gateway between the past and the present, a link between the wisdom of the ancients and the quest for knowledge that drove humanity up through the modern people in this tomb.

In that moment, as they stared into the corridor and the depths of the tomb, the significance of their journey was clear. They were not just adventurers or historians; they were part of a continuum of discovery, walking in the footsteps of giants like Archimedes, who had shaped the course of human knowledge with their genius.

"Incredible," Reyna said. "I never believed things like this really existed."

"You mean ancient doors that open with a difficult to solve puzzle?" Tommy clarified.

She nodded, still gazing into the opening. "Is this normal for you?"

"Happens more often than you'd think."

Even Craig appreciated the moment. While he may have turned into an evil son of a gun, that didn't change the fact that he'd spent his entire life in search of historical truths, uncovering layers of the past to share with the world. As he stepped forward and pointed his light into the darkness, his eyes filled with wonder—his face a painted expression of absolute exhilaration.

The flashlight beam combined with his headlamp illuminated a short passage, cut smooth on all sides. The corridor only ran twenty feet before giving way to a larger opening beyond.

Craig, with his lights cutting through the darkness, took the lead and stepped forward. The light glowed against the chamber walls, revealing a stunning array of symbols and inscriptions that melded the rich tapestry of Greek and Egyptian cultures.

"Move," Brent ordered the three prisoners. "Slowly. And keep your distance."

The order caused Craig to pause. He turned his pistol at Sean and motioned for him and Tommy to go first.

"What's the problem, Craig?" Sean asked. "Worried about another trap?"

"Better safe than sorry."

Sean obeyed and walked by their mutinous former partner, following the passage into the next room—the tomb of Archimedes.

42

T he moment they stepped inside, they were enveloped by a cool, almost cold, air that was a stark contrast of the warmth of the Sicilian sun above, filled with the musty odors of millennia. It smelled overwhelmingly ancient—a blend of earth and stone that whispered of secrets long buried. The chamber, a vast, shadowed expanse carved directly from the heart of Sicily's unforgiving bedrock, was a marvel of architectural genius and historical convergence.

The chamber, roughly circular in shape, spanned some thirty feet in diameter, giving it a vast, almost cathedral-like sense of space. The limestone ceiling arched overhead, reaching a height of twenty feet at its apex.

The floors were covered in thousands of colorful mosaic tiles radiating out from the center like the sun casting rays across the surface. The walls of the tomb were like a tapestry of history, meticulously carved with an array of symbols that melded with mathematical precision from Greek culture and blended with the mystical elements of Egyptian iconography and religion. These carvings covered nearly every inch of the chamber's circumference, starting from a height of three feet from the ground and reaching up to the shadowy reaches of the ceiling.

Scenes from Archimedes' life, his discoveries, and mathematical principles were depicted in bas-relief, interspersed with hieroglyphs. One such symbol presided over all, positioned along the back wall, directly behind a sarcophagus—the Eye of Horus.

The sarcophagus itself was in the center of the room atop a raised dais that seemed to elevate Archimedes' final resting place of honor. Both the platform and the sarcophagus were made of white marble adorned with intricate carvings that mirrored the symbols along the chamber walls. On the lid's surface, the emblem of the sphere with a cylinder within was engraved into the white stone—a subtle declaration of the resting place of the visionary inventor.

The base of the dais was covered in a golden molding. Two interconnected grooves ran horizontal to the floor, merging with vertical ones at various points. Bronze discs adorned with geometric patterns and figures danced in the beams of light as Craig stepped near the coffin. The discs, like everything else in this place, had been designed as a long-standing tribute to Archimedes' pursuits. The symbols, interwoven with mathematical precision, seemed to pulse with a life of their own, as if imbued with the spirits of those who had crafted them.

As the group surrounded the sarcophagus, the marble seemed to radiate a solemn dignity.

"This is more amazing than I could have ever expected," Craig muttered. There was true reverence in his voice, a solemn appreciation for this most profound moment of discovery.

Reyna didn't blink for nearly a minute as she turned around in circles, taking in the splendor of it all. "How... is this possible?" she wondered.

Tommy and Sean noticed everything around them, but their focus gravitated to the sarcophagus, and a devious mechanism that awaited them.

"What do you think that is?" Tommy asked, pointing at the molding belt that wrapped around the sarcophagus.

"Another puzzle," Sean realized. "The last test left for us to solve."

Brent scowled at the statement. "Both of you, step back," he ordered, brandishing the pistol.

Sean and Tommy glanced at each other, then did as they'd been told and retreated a few steps away from the dais.

Brent moved closer to it and pressed his left hand against the lid, obviously hoping to shove it off the marble container.

At first, his effort was feeble, a lazy attempt that he believed would yield results. But the lid didn't move.

Sean arched a derisive eyebrow at him but said nothing as he watched Brent lean harder into the heavy marble. Again, the top didn't budge.

"You want to give me a hand here?" Brent said to Craig. A vein popped up on his rapidly reddening forehead.

Craig relented and stepped up to the sarcophagus. He pushed against it with both hands—using the base of his right hand that held the pistol—while Brent continued his useless toil. The men grunted with every shove, but nothing happened.

After twenty seconds, they gave up and stepped back, both gasping for air.

"What gives?" Brent asked between breaths. "Why won't that thing move?"

"Because it's locked from the inside," Tommy said.

"What?"

The only thing keeping Tommy from giggling at their cluelessness was the fact that both of them still had firearms.

Sean folded his arms across his chest, rubbing his chin with his index finger as he, too, tried to contain the humor wrapped in the looming cloak of doom.

Brent raised his pistol and pointed it straight at Tommy's head. "How do you know that?"

Tommy sighed. His exasperation might have stopped that bullet had Brent pulled the trigger and if physics worked that way. "It's written on the side of the sarcophagus," he said, indicating a line of Greek chiseled into the container's white wall.

"What does it say?"

"It's weird," Tommy confessed.

"These things usually are, though," Sean said.

"True."

"Just shut up and tell us what it says," Brent demanded.

"Well, which is it? Shut up, or tell you?"

Brent jabbed the gun toward Tommy like it was a knife. "What. Does. It. Say?"

Tommy held up his hands in mocking surrender. "Okay. Okay, take it easy. Jeez. Somebody's compensating for something. It says, 'Align the wisdom of old, let spheres and shadows merge. But be warned. Err and face the tomb's embrace, or find the narrow path.'"

Neither Craig nor Brent said anything for a few seconds as the echo of Tommy's voice faded into the rock around them.

Sean thumbed his chin as he studied the inscription on the band.

"Well?" Craig finally blurted. "What is that supposed to mean?"

"Why don't you move some of those discs along the rails there and find out?"

Craig inclined his head, peering at Sean over the tip of his nose. "Maybe I shoot Reyna in the knee to hurry you along." He aimed the pistol toward her leg.

Tommy stepped in between the weapon and Reyna. "Hey, take it easy, Craig. Come on, man."

"Open the sarcophagus, Tommy. I know you understand these kinds of things. Do it. I'm tired of your games."

"Fine. Just point that thing somewhere else. It's like you never took a firearm safety class or something."

"Is that supposed to be a joke?"

"Look at the discs," Tommy said, nodding at the dais. "The first line tells us to align the discs in a way that represents the merging of Greek and Egyptian wisdom, as displayed on the surface of the discs. The spheres-and-shadows part is a hint at placing the disc with the image of a sphere within a cylinder in a position that is central or foundational to solving the puzzle."

"Okay," Craig said, seeming to accept the solution. "And the second part? The part about the tomb's embrace?"

"It's a warning," Sean answered. "The consequences of failure—incorrectly aligning the discs would trigger a trap, potentially sealing the chamber. The humility piece refers to being brought to one's knees, probably because once the trap is sprung, it would take a miracle from the gods to escape."

Craig stared hard into Sean's eyes, searching for a lie. Sean held his gaze steadily, unwilling to flinch.

"Do you know what the alignment should be?" Craig asked after considering the answer.

"I think so," Tommy said. He turned to Reyna. "But I would love a second opinion. Just stop pointing those guns at her. You can point them at me or Sean, but not her."

"I'll aim at whoever I please," Brent said.

"Whomever," Sean corrected.

"What?"

"Nothing."

"No," Craig interrupted. "It's okay. Do as he says. Don't aim at her. Let them solve the problem. But if I think for a second you're going to double-cross us—"

"How and why would I do that, Craig?" Tommy asked. "I would rather take a bullet to the head than be stuck in this tomb with you."

"You can leave us down here if you want, Craig," Sean said. "I'll not beg for our lives. But let Reyna go. Once this is done, she goes free."

"You're in no position to make deals, Sean." Despite the response, he still seemed to consider the proposition. "Fine. Do it. And she can help. But Sean, you stay back."

"Fine."

Craig motioned to the other two. "Go ahead."

The cool air tensed as Tommy and Reyna approached the mechanism. Fear gripped them, but they also knew they were on the cusp of finding something no one had seen for thousands of years, and that had been sought by treasure hunters throughout time.

The puzzle was a direct challenge, a gatekeeper that demanded acknowledgment of Archimedes' brilliance, the ancient wisdom he embraced, and the humility to tread carefully in the presence of greatness. Failure would trigger a catastrophic response; perhaps the collapse of the ceiling, a blockage of the door, or something worse.

Sean couldn't think of what might be worse than those things. He'd seen some pretty wild concepts delivered by the film industry— poisoned arrows flung from holes in the wall were one of his favorite outlandish Hollywood booby traps. Still, he found himself glancing around the room to make sure such holes weren't concealed by shadows along the wall.

He shook off the ludicrous notion and resumed analyzing the four discs on their side of the sarcophagus.

"I need to see the other side, Craig," Tommy said after studying the discs. "There are four over there, right?"

"Yes," Craig hissed. "Fine. But just you. And move slowly."

Tommy resisted the urge to make a wisecrack and shifted carefully around to the other side.

He knelt down and studied the first disc to his left. It was the cylinder within the sphere, the iconic emblem of Archimedes' most famous discovery. Next was the pi symbol. "This represents his contribution to understanding the value of pi," Tommy said with a vague wave of the hand toward the second disc in that row.

The two discs set in the grooves below those two displayed a lever —symbolizing Archimedes' work in physics and the sun.

"You have the Eye of Horus over there, yeah?" Tommy asked, looking over at Reyna.

"Yes."

"And the next one?" He tried to recall the other three, but wanted to make sure.

"A ship."

"Okay." From the sound of his voice, it was clear Tommy wasn't quite sure about that one.

"Also commemorates the Principle of Buoyancy," Sean reasoned.

"Right. Good one, Sean. What's the next one?"

"It looks like a palimpsest," Reyna answered. "He did a great deal of writing on many subjects."

"And the last?"

"A screw."

"The water screw. One of his ingenious inventions." Tommy remained down on one knee as he weighed the options. The puzzle reminded him of things he'd seen children play with. Only theirs were on boards purchased at a toy store, and usually had way more grooves, and instead of discs there were knobs.

Tommy reached out and pressed the disc with the sphere and cylinder to the right until it hit the intersection where the vertical groove met the horizontal one. He continued pushing it to the right until it hit the end. Then he pulled back his hand and waited.

A click echoed from the sarcophagus.

Sean breathed steadily as he watched his friend work. He also kept a close eye on Brent, assessing him for a weakness, a break that might give Sean the opportunity to take advantage.

"Okay," Tommy said to Reyna, take the one with the ship, and move it over to the top left."

Reyna bent down and started sliding the disc. She was surprised how easily it moved. The object made a slight grinding sound, as if on a wheel within a stone track. She stopped at the intersection and paused. "You're sure about that?"

Tommy raised up and peeked over the sarcophagus. "No. But what's the worst that could happen?"

"Wait," Brent said. "Is he serious?"

"No," Craig answered. "Keep going. Do as he said."

Reyna choked back her anger-infused fear cocktail and continued sliding the disc until it reached the other end of the groove.

The same click they heard before sounded through the room.

"Great," Tommy said. "Now, which corners should these go to?" he muttered to himself.

He spied the sun disc set behind the one with a lever on it. His mind made up, Tommy slid the lever disc to the side, then up on the vertical groove, making way for the other. Stretching out his free hand, he moved the sun disc to the center, then all the way to the other side where it produced another click.

"Okay, Reyna," he said. "Slide the Eye of Horus underneath the one you moved first."

"But there's another disc in the way. Oh." She realized the solution before he could respond. "I got it."

She shifted the water screw out of the way, then up the vertical groove before sliding the Eye of Horus into place.

Another click signaled they were nearly there.

"Now," Tommy said. "This one should go here." He slid the disc with the lever back down and to the end near where it began. The click confirmed the correct position.

"The screw should go down on the bottom opposite of where I just moved this one."

She nodded and moved the disc to the corresponding slot. It clicked into place, and she waited for the final instruction.

Tommy peered at the disc with the symbol of pi on it. "The one with pi should correspond with the palimpsest," he said, reasoning both had to do with using writing, either for math or text.

He took a breath, then slid the disc to the end. When it clicked, he stood and nodded to Reyna. "Last one. Move it all the way to the end."

Her throat throbbed as she swallowed. Then she reached out and moved the final disc into position.

"Moment of truth," Sean breathed.

43

Everyone in the room felt an overpowering sense of dread that seemed to last minutes. In truth, it was a fraction of a second.

The final click resonated through the chamber. Then a new sound followed it. The grinding of stone on stone echoed around the room's occupants as the lid to the sarcophagus began sliding away toward the exit.

Sean stared at the head of the ancient marble coffin as it opened, revealing first a skull, then the neck, and a torso of a skeleton clad in tattered, weathered robes.

The skull's hollow eyes stared up at the ceiling, frozen in death for all time. The fabric that had once been white was stained and dingy, frayed and disintegrating, though still remarkably well preserved considering how old it was.

The lid kept sliding away, propelled by some unseen gears within, until the sarcophagus was half-open. Then it stopped with a click, leaving half of the slab overhanging the mosaic tile below.

Craig took a step closer. He hovered over the open sarcophagus, staring into it with greed-infused wonder.

The archaeologist in him couldn't deny how absolutely incredible it felt to find this, the lost tomb of Archimedes. His ego ran wild with the headlines in every major media outlet in the world, each one proclaiming his fame to the find that had been, up to that point, deemed nearly impossible.

His mind raced to the other discoveries he would claim—the fabled tomb of Cleopatra in Jordan, and the Hall of Records under the Sphinx. He would be hailed as the greatest archaeologist in all of history, and with it would come fame and glory unlike anyone would ever dream of.

Those things alone would grant him wealth beyond most people's imaginations.

But that wasn't the motive behind all of this. Those finds were child's play compared to what he beheld resting atop the ribcage of Archimedes and clutched in his bony fingers.

A scroll, bound by a single leather strap, lay clutched in the inventor's hands.

"I don't believe it," Reyna said, her voice low as if she were in a cathedral during mass.

"Never gets old," Tommy said. "Finding stuff like this."

"I hope you're not planning on picking that up, Craig," Sean cautioned. "You're still wet from the swim, and you know as well as anyone else that getting water on that thing will basically destroy it."

"Oh, Sean," Craig said, setting down the day pack he'd brought with him. Water pooled around it on the floor as he unzipped the main pouch and pulled out a glass tube and a large plastic freezer bag. "Always be prepared."

"Got any rope in there?" Tommy joked.

Sean snorted at the comment but kept his eyes on Craig as he returned to the side of the sarcophagus. He unscrewed the lid of the tube and then stuffed his right hand into the freezer bag as a sort of glove.

Then, with it cinched around his hand, he reached down and gently, carefully, tugged on the scroll.

Sean's eyes flicked away from Craig to Brent.

The hired gun's eyes watched hungrily as his partner in crime gradually pried the scroll from the skeletal grip.

The archaeologists in the room collectively knew that if Craig moved too fast, or was too rough in handling the document, it could break into unreadable fragments. Once that happened, it would take an extraordinary amount of time and effort to piece them back together.

Tommy reflected on the Dead Sea Scrolls with that line of thought, and the painstaking work that had gone into fitting all the fragments together to form a cohesive message.

Everyone in the room held their breath as Craig continued slowly sliding the scroll out of the skeleton's fingers. He barely moved it a millimeter at a time. On top of the risk of damaging the ancient document by force, he also had to make certain he didn't drip any water on it from his arms or head. Craig's solution to this issue was standing at an awkward angle, bending over the sarcophagus with his elbows spread out wide.

The task took minutes, but felt like hours.

Finally, the last bit of parchment was freed from Archimedes' deathly grasp, and Craig cradled it in his gloved hand.

He blinked rapidly as he held up the tube and slowly eased the scroll into it with enough room to spare at the top, and on all sides for it to fit comfortably.

Craig exhaled and swallowed in relief, quickly picking up the lid and screwing it on top of the tube until it was tightly sealed.

Then his breath quickened, and excitement filled his eyes.

He smiled as he held the tube aloft, illuminating it with the light of his headlamp.

Faded black ink showed through the wrapped papyrus. He looked closer, and made out the faint details of Greek lettering on the outermost shell.

Brent took a step closer to Craig, standing directly behind him as if to get a better look at the prize.

Then a muted pop echoed through the room.

Craig's eyes widened in an instant. Pain streaked across his face, followed by a look of confused shock.

He grimaced, his breath speeding up. His fingers clutched the glass tube, but he was visibly weakened.

Brent reached around him and grabbed the container as Craig slowly turned to look at his killer.

The color drained from his face as he met Brent's gaze. "Why?" Craig managed.

Tommy extended his hand out to Reyna as if to block her from the next assault and cautiously guided her a step closer to the tunnel.

"Because I'm not going to split the profits from this with anyone, Craig," Brent sneered. "And because I'm not an idiot. You would have killed me the first chance you got. Or at least you would have tried."

Craig looked down at the pistol he'd set next to his day pack. It seemed miles away now.

"Don't bother," Brent warned and raised his gun to Craig's head.

This was the moment Sean had been waiting for, and he'd only get one shot at it.

"Schultzie, down," he snapped.

In a single, swift movement, Sean ducked and kicked out his right foot at the nearest disc on the bottom row. His boot struck the bronze piece and sent it sliding to the center, where it clanged to a stop in the vertical groove.

Tommy took a step to the side and shoved Reyna back and down toward the floor.

A deafening thud sent a shock wave through the room.

Brent stepped to the side to aim his weapon at Sean but couldn't get a clear shot over the sarcophagus he hid behind.

Shifting again in the other direction, Brent readied himself to fire at a crouching, helpless Sean Wyatt.

Instead, another loud boom rocked the chamber, this time from near the exit.

Brent turned toward the source of the sound and watched in horror as a fifteen-foot section of the mosaic floor suddenly collapsed.

He saw Reyna lose her balance and fall backward, tipping over the edge of the newly made pit.

She screamed and flailed her hands. Tommy reacted in a flash and grabbed her wrists with both hands as her legs dropped out of view.

Tommy hit the floor, nearly striking it with his chin. But his thick chest took the brunt of the fall, and he squeezed with all of his strength to keep his grip on Reyna as she dangled over the dark abyss.

Brent rushed toward the edge, taking five quick steps as if he was going to make a leap for it, but skidded to a stop as dust plumed up from a dark crevasse in the floor.

Sean crept around the sarcophagus, crouching like a tiger in the reeds, and then sprang forward past Craig as he fell to his knees.

Brent only lost focus for a second, distracted by the abrupt collapse of the floor. Then he remembered the other hostages and turned to protect himself only to find Sean barreling toward him at full speed.

He leveled the pistol, but Sean dropped to the floor and slid like a baseball player, kicking up his right foot at the last second.

Brent squeezed the trigger as the tip of Sean's boot struck the bottom of the suppressor barrel. The muzzle flashed, but the round flew just beyond Sean's shoulder, shattering a section of tile.

His momentum carried him to Brent's feet, where he twisted and kicked up with his other foot, landing the top of his boot squarely in Brent's groin.

Brent doubled over, which was an unfortunate side effect of the blow. Sean would have preferred to knock him backward into the pit. The glass tube in his other hand fell from his fingers and clattered on the floor, miraculously not shattering to pieces. It rolled to a stop perilously close to the edge, mere inches from falling into the darkness.

Instead, he fell forward onto Sean as he slid to a stop at Brent's feet.

Sean reached up for the pistol, snatching it with his left hand and twisting it hard to the side just as Brent squeezed the trigger again. The barrel aimed away toward the wall to Sean's left, and the bullet shot harmlessly into the tile, ricocheting up against the wall before it fell impotently to the surface.

Sean wrenched the gun harder, pulling it down and forcing Brent's wrist into a painfully awkward position.

His grip loosened, and he had no choice but to let go, but as he did, he swung with his other fist, striking Sean across the jaw.

The hard blow hit square, and Sean's head snapped to the side, dazing him for a split second.

To his right, Tommy struggled to keep his balance, spreading out his weight along the surface of the floor, still digging the toes of his shoes into the tile.

"Hold on, Reyna!" he shouted. "I've got you!"

"I can't hold it!" she screamed in desperate fear.

"Yes, you can."

But Tommy felt his body slipping ever closer to the edge. He was heavier than her by a good amount of weight, but part of his body was also hanging over the lip of the drop.

"See if you can find a foothold," he ordered.

"There isn't one."

She looked up into Tommy's eyes, tears welling in the corners of hers. Reyna knew this was the end.

Her fingers weakened against his wrists, which only made Tommy squeeze harder. "I'm not going to let you die. Not today."

Ten feet away, Sean grappled with Brent.

He blocked another attempted punch with his right forearm while still twisting and manipulating the gun.

Brent reared back to deliver another blow, but Sean quickly grabbed him by the shirt, jerked him closer, and drove his forehead into Brent's nose.

The gun freed itself from Brent's grip as blood fell from his nostrils. He leaned back for a second, momentarily fazed by the blinding pain.

Sean twisted the gun around, looped a finger around the trigger, and aimed.

Brent swung his fist wildly at the weapon, smacking it on the side of the barrel as Sean fired.

The round missed, sailing no more than two inches past Brent's right shoulder.

He rolled over to the left, grabbing the pistol again and using his weight to rip it out of Sean's grasp.

Sean had no choice. His fingers bent at a painful angle, and it was either hold on and let them break or let go.

He released the pistol but quickly shifted his hands and pressed down on the button to release the magazine as Brent's shoulder hit the ground. The magazine clattered to the tile between them just as Brent turned the pistol and squeezed the trigger.

The only remaining round in the weapon cracked just beyond Sean's head and crashed into the ceiling.

Brent rolled away and to his feet, tossing the now-useless weapon to the floor.

Sean stood mere feet from him, taking a fighting stance that mirrored Brent's.

"You got a little blood on your face, there, Brent," Sean taunted.

He received an expletive as a first response. "Time to see what you got, Sean," he sneered through bloodstained lips.

"Tommy," Reyna said behind Sean. "You're slipping!"

"I know. Just hold on. I'll think of something."

Tommy felt his body continue inching toward the black doom of the crevasse. He pressed his toes harder into the floor, and for a second thought it was making a difference. But then he slid another inch farther. His waist had nearly reached the lip, and he knew once that happened, they were both beyond the tipping point.

He clenched his jaw and squinted his eyes, his face reddening from the effort. Summoning every ounce of strength he had left; he gave one last pull. But it was no use. His forearms and shoulders burned from the burden, and he knew it was either let go or they both would die.

"Let me go, Tommy," she said, resolution filling her words now. "It's okay. You don't have to die with me."

"I'm not going to do that, Reyna," he answered.

"Still stubborn," she said, her fingers loosening. "It's okay."

"Shut up," he said. "We're getting out of this."

"Maybe you still can."

Her eyes met his. Tears streaked down her face. "Let me go."

He shook his head, the corners of his eyes welling. "No."

Suddenly, Tommy felt a pair of hands slap against his ankles. He looked back over his shoulder at Craig gripping tight with both hands.

"Craig?" Tommy said.

The man looked like a ghost. Sweat beaded on his pale skin, and his lips had turned a light purple.

He didn't say anything. But with the last of his strength, he leaned back with all of his weight like a lever, and let gravity do the work.

Tommy felt himself sliding backward, and Reyna with him.

Once her hands were visible above the edge, he ordered her to plant one hand on the surface so he could get a better stance.

She did as he said and clawed at the lip with her right hand.

Tommy shifted his weight as Craig's grip loosened, and he grabbed Reyna's other forearm with both hands, standing up at the same time.

To his left, Sean squared off with Brent, launching the first attack with a jab that narrowly missed Brent's cheek.

Brent countered with a jab to Sean's ribcage, sending a sharp pain through his torso. Brent followed the shot with another from his opposite hand, but Sean blocked this one and delivered a round-house punch that snapped Brent's head to the side.

He stumbled backward a few steps, rubbed his jaw, and reset the menacing look of determination on his face.

He lunged forward, intent on making Sean pay for that and the broken nose, and quickly launched a flurry of kicks and punches.

Sean retreated a step, then two as he fended off most of the blows. The few that caught him were glancing and did little damage.

He countered Brent's furious attack with a sidestep and punch to the abdomen, then grabbed him by the back of the head as he doubled over and drove his knee up to finish the job with a blow to the face.

Somehow, even with the wind knocked out of him from the gut punch, Brent managed to dive to his right and clear of the knee shot —leaving Sean with a tuft of hair in his fingers in the process.

Brent rolled back to his feet, blinking rapidly from the multiple pain points Sean had delivered.

"You aren't as good as your reputation suggests, Sean," he sneered, staring at him in defiant fury.

Sean faced him with his back to the pit, acutely aware of the drop behind him, as he always was with heights.

"That broken nose would beg to differ, Brent."

Brent breathed hard through his mouth; his nostrils unable to provide the air he needed. His shirt was stained red with blood, sweat, and spring water.

"I heard you didn't know when to shut that yap of yours. I guess it's time someone did it for you."

"You won't be the first to try."

Brent growled, then charged. It was a desperate attack, one with the intention of taking the fight to the floor, which would turn it into a grappling match instead of a fistfight. Sean preferred to stay on his feet. A natural striker, and trained more heavily in that style, hand-to-hand combat was his best skill set. But he didn't fear grappling either. He could hold his own.

But he had no intention of letting it get to that point.

He braced himself for impact, balancing his weight until the last second.

Then, as Brent lunged forward, Sean ducked to the side and stuck out his right leg, catching Brent on the shin.

The henchman stumbled forward, his momentum too much to slow. He fell over just before reaching the edge of the pit, rolled, and then slid over.

Sean stepped over to where he'd disappeared, unwilling to get too close to the precipice. From a safe distance of a few feet, he angled his head out enough to look over and see Brent clinging to a crag jutting out from just below the end of the floor.

His white eyes contrasted the darkness beneath him as he desperately tried to find purchase with his feet on the wall below.

He gasped for air. His fingers slipped. "Aren't you supposed to help me?" he sneered.

"Sorry, Brent," Sean said. "I'm terrified of heights."

Brent's grip on the narrow ledge broke free, and he fell back, screaming as he disappeared into the black.

44

"Are you guys okay?" Sean asked, turning to Tommy and Reyna to his right.

Tommy nodded. Reyna trembled, but she bobbed her head, too.

"I'm... fine," Craig coughed from behind them.

Sean walked to where he lay in a growing pool of blood on the mosaic floor. His face was a ghastly pale now. Sean recognized the frigid embrace of death in the man's eyes. There was no stopping it now.

Tommy and Reyna joined Sean, hovering over the dying man.

"You saved us," Tommy said, indicating Reyna with a sideways nod.

Craig's breathing grew shallow. His chest rose and fell less dramatically. He looked up at them with what almost appeared to be pity in his eyes. "I got off easy," he said. "You three are stuck here in this tomb with no way out. For what it's worth, I'm sorry."

Sean shook his head. "There's another way out," he said.

"Yeah. That part in the riddle about the path of humility, there's another exit here somewhere. My guess is it will appear when we close the sarcophagus."

Reyna's unbelieving gaze went from Tommy to Sean and back again.

Craig forced a weak grin. "You really are a clever archaeologist, Schultzie," he said. His words were followed by a fit of coughing. Then, he laid his head back, blinked once, and exhaled for the last time.

His eyes remained fixed on the ceiling overhead.

Sean bent down and ran his fingers over Craig's eyelids, closing them permanently. He sighed as he stood upright again and looked over at the open sarcophagus.

"So, should we see if that theory is right?" he asked.

"It's that or we stay here until we starve to death," Tommy answered.

"Is there really another way out?" Reyna wondered. "I thought you said the path of humility was—"

"We couldn't let them know there was another way out of here," Sean interrupted. "Just in case they decided to leave us here and cave in the entrance. Which seems like something Brent would have done."

Tommy knelt down next to one side of the sarcophagus. "We should just need to reverse the positions of these discs to get the sarcophagus to close." Something caught the corner of his eye near the opening in the floor. "Um, Reyna, could you grab that? I would hate to have come all this way only to forget the scroll."

Her eyes flashed wide and she hurried over to the drop-off, bent down, and picked up the glass tube.

"Miracle the thing didn't break," Sean said as he took a knee on the other side of the marble dais. He shifted the discs around, placing the ones that had been on top on the bottom, and vice versa. Each time he pushed one to the end of the groove, something clicked on the inside.

"How's it looking over there?" Tommy asked.

"One more to go, and I'll be all set."

"Are you two sure this is going to work?" Reyna said.

"No," Tommy answered. "But the other option is to sit here until we die of dehydration."

"Okay, keep going," she urged.

Tommy maneuvered the last of the discs into place and stepped back to see what would happen.

Something bumped from within the floor, and for a moment, they all thought they'd triggered a second collapse that would plunge them to a gruesome death in the bowls of the quarry.

Instead, the lid on the sarcophagus began retracting, sliding forward again to cover the body of the fabled mathematician.

"Until we meet again, sir," Sean said, looking down at the skull as shadows crept over it.

When the lid stopped, sealing the sarcophagus again, a deep thud shook the ground. Then a new grinding sound vibrated from underneath the dais.

Sean and the others all stepped back. He and Tommy picked up the flashlights dropped by their captors, and shined the beams onto the floor beneath the sarcophagus.

"Wow," Reyna gasped.

The entire marble piece began to move, sliding toward the back wall. As it moved, it revealed a dark recess in the floor, and stone steps carved from the bedrock of the island.

The group moved together at the top of the shaft as the dais stopped with the head of the sarcophagus nearly flush with the wall, directly underneath the Eye of Horus.

Sean and Tommy aimed the lights down into the stairwell, then cast a sidelong glance at each other.

"You wanna go, or you want me to?" Sean asked.

"I'll go. There might be a long drop or something in there."

Sean's expression darkened. "That's not funny."

Tommy descended into the passage with Reyna close behind, followed by Sean at the rear. He lingered for a few seconds longer, staring in wonder at the chamber around him. He looked at Craig's body one last time too. It felt strange to leave him here in this sacred place. The man had betrayed him and Tommy, and would have let Reyna die in the process.

Sean didn't feel regret about his death, only that leaving him in this place seemed to desecrate it. But there was no stopping that. If the tomb was good enough for one, it could hold one more. At least for now.

Eventually, they would lead a team back through the water and create a bridge across the gap leading into the chamber. Then they could remove Craig's body and begin the process of analyzing the tomb and its intended occupant.

After one last look, he descended the stairs into the tunnel.

The walls were cut smooth, as if ground by machinery. He and Tommy had been in dozens of hidden corridors such as this, and it never ceased to marvel him at the workmanship that went into every one.

They kept walking ahead, winding their way through the passage for fifteen minutes until the scent of salty, moist air touched their nostrils.

"Is that the sea?" Reyna asked.

"Smells like it," Tommy said.

His flashlight beam sprayed across a stone surface directly ahead of them. Cracks around the edges of the blockage allowed the fading light of day to break through into the corridor.

"It's blocked," Reyna said, fear creeping into her throat again.

"I'm sure there's a way to open it," Sean said from just behind her. He pointed his light around on the wall to the left, then the right. The beam landed on a bronze disc the size of a Frisbee fixed to a bronze track not dissimilar to the gold one on the sides of the dais.

Tommy stepped close to the disc, wrapped his fingers around it, and turned it counterclockwise.

It took effort to spin the wheel, but as he did, the heavy stone began to descend into the passage floor.

"It's opening," Reyna exclaimed, relief replacing the worry in her voice.

Tommy continued spinning the wheel, faster and faster until

there was a wide enough opening at the top of the stone they could all easily fit through.

The salty air of the Mediterranean blasted into the corridor on a gust of wind.

"Ladies first," Tommy said, offering his hand as a brace to let Reyna out through the opening.

She smiled at him and took his hand, climbed up onto the stone, and crawled out into the Sicilian evening.

Tommy followed her, then Sean, until the three found themselves standing on a landing on the edge of a rocky cliff about fifteen feet off the ground.

A natural formation of stairs to the left provided an easy way down to the shore, but none of them moved.

They simply stood there, taking in the sights of the foamy sea waves crashing into the beach, framed by a fiery sky of pink, orange, and yellow.

For a few minutes, none of them said anything.

Then Reyna turned to Tommy and smiled at him. "You saved my life back there."

He shrugged. "I also got you into this mess."

"I would've been in this mess with or without your help, thank you very much. Craig came to me on his own."

"I guess."

"But I was wrong about you, Tommy. About your agency too. I guess I was too proud to admit it before. I wanted things to always be done by the book. But now I see... there's room in our field for doing things differently."

"I appreciate that, Reyna. And listen, I'm sorry I hurt you all those years ago. I really did love you as a friend. And I'd like to go back to that if we could."

She laughed. "Tommy, did you think I was still hung up on you after all these years? That was like two decades ago. I've been married for twelve years now."

"Oh. I... didn't know that."

"Awkward," Sean interjected.

"Shut up, dude."

Reyna shook her head. "Boys. Let's get out of here. And Tommy, unless I miss my guess, I think your agency is going to have quite a bit of work to do on this excavation in the coming months. Just let me know if you need any help getting permits from the Italians."

Hey eyed her sideways. "You have connections with them too?"

She crossed her arms. "Schulztie, I got connections worldwide."

THANK YOU

I just wanted to say thank you for reading this story. I am truly honored you chose to spend your time with my friends Sean and his crew.

Remember to subscribe to the Sean Wyatt VIP reader club to get a free story, character guides, exclusive concept art, and updates on the next project so you never miss out. Join here: https://readerlinks.com/l/3411801

I hope to see you in the next story.

Your friendly neighborhood author,

Ernest

ALSO BY ERNEST DEMPSEY

Adriana Villa Adventures:

War of Thieves Box Set

When Shadows Call

Shadows Rising

Shadow Hour

The Relic Runner - A Dak Harper Series:

The Relic Runner Origin Story

The Courier

Two Nights In Mumbai

Country Roads

Heavy Lies the Crown

Moscow Sky

The Adventure Guild (ALL AGES):

The Caesar Secret: Books 1-3

The Carolina Caper

Beta Force:

Operation Zulu

London Calling

Paranormal Archaeology Division:

Hell's Gate

Guardians of Earth:

Emergence: Gideon Wolf Book 1

Righteous Dawn: Gideon Wolf Book 2

Crimson Winter: Gideon Wolf Book 3

ACKNOWLEDGMENTS

As always, I would like to thank my terrific editors, Anne and Jason, for their hard work. What they do makes my stories so much better for readers all over the world. Anne Storer and Jason Whited are the best editorial team a writer could hope for and I appreciate everything they do.

I also want to thank Elena at Li Graphics for her tremendous work on my book covers and for always overdelivering. Elena definitely rocks.

A big thank you has to go out to my friend James Slater for his proofing work. James has added another layer of quality control to these stories, and I can't thank him enough.

Last but not least, I need to thank all my wonderful fans and especially the advance reader team. Their feedback and reviews are always so helpful and I can't say enough good things about all of them.

Made in United States
Orlando, FL
09 January 2025

57107977R00195